The
DEATH
of the POET

N. QUENTIN WOOLF

A complete catalogue record for this book can be
obtained from the British Library on request

The right of N. Quentin Woolf to be identified as the author
of this work has been asserted by him in accordance with
the Copyright, Designs and Patents Act 1988

First published in 2014 by Serpent's Tail,
an imprint of Profile Books Ltd
3A Exmouth House
Pine Street
London EC1R OJH
www.serpentstail.com

ISBN 978 1 84668 933 8
eISBN 978 1 84765 947 7

Designed and typeset by MacGuru Ltd
info@macguru.org.uk

Printed and bound in Italy by L.E.G.O.S.p.A., Lavis (TN)

1 3 5 7 9 10 8 6 4 2

For the hyphen and the lime

The DEATH *of the* POET

NINE

And I had thought that I was at home, gazing out upon a herb garden like my own, its colours bleached by a cold sunlight, and I fancied that I was a butterfly, able to absorb the sun's medicine from the sunbeams – a sensation that made all the little hairs on my butterfly body shiver delightfully. Somewhere, unseen, a choir lamented. Miserere! The air tasted of Sunday roast beef, and iron. And yes, I thought, yes, I shall remain here eternally, for this is my home, and it is perfectly peaceful, and I shall open and close my wings for as long as I please.

Yet all the while some persistent thing scratched away at the back of my mind, wanting to remind me… of what? A chill light rain had started to fall: icy darts pricking my face. It hurt, and I had a good idea why, but even as the earth shook under me, I determined that I should keep my eyes tight shut.

I tried so very hard to hold on to home.

The choristers had started to scream, individually and in fear of their lives.

I tried to touch the pain in my face, but my face wasn't there.

EIGHT

078

At the exact moment you entered into my life (1994, February twenty-ninth, maybe six and a half minutes before the top-hour link into the commercials and the ten o'clock news), I was raring to slap down Louis from Modesto. Louis believed we all had worms in our heads that controlled how we behaved and would one day force the human race to exterminate itself.

Louis wasn't what I'd call my typical caller to KVOC. Most of the callers were tight.

Louis was already pretty heated up by the time the producer ushered you into the studio. You didn't so much as glance my way. You had a Winona Ryder complexion and owl glasses, and a tweed jacket that probably belonged to someone else. Kinda scatty; kinda hot. Within the hour you'd sock me in the mouth.

Down the line, Louis was demanding, 'So how do you explain war?'

'How do *you* explain war, Louis?' I said. 'Oh, I'll bet it's worms again, right?'

'Yes sir.'

'No such thing as free agency out there in Modesto?'

'That's what I'm trying to tell you. Once it's inside your head, you're locked into doing what it says.'

'Louis, do you have a worm inside your head?'

'Yes sir.'

'What kind of work do you do, Louis?'

'I'm a security professional.'

'You stand in front of a store?'

'Yes sir.'

Ordinarily, new guests to the station made a performance of settling down – getting tangled up in the headphone leads, mostly, or playing with the mic arms like safari monkeys – you didn't do that. You paused to check out a framed black-and-white photo of the station owner meeting Salvador Dali – you smiled at it like someone recognising an old friend; then you pulled a book out of your bag, threw yourself on the couch, and made it clear you could give a damn what the rest of the world thought about that. An old bald-headed professor came in, and then a jock in a blazer: my interview crowd. You didn't look up once.

'OK, one thing, Louis, stop calling me sir, save that for your mom. You carry a gun, professionally, right?'

Once I'd reassured Louis I was only kidding about his mom, he admitted to the gun.

'And this worm of yours is in control?'

Louis agreed that it was.

'Be honest with me, Louis,' I said, dropping my voice low. '*Mano a mano*. You think that worm might make you do something crazy, one day?'

Louis deliberated. We were four minutes off the news. The clock was counting down. While Louis spoke, I tapped on the glass screen that separated you from me, and you started out of your reading. I pointed at my phones and you put yours on. Like the jacket, they were too big for you. You were twenty-seven and you smiled at me like you were ready for me to be very, very stupid.

'Carry on, Louis, I'm listening,' I told him, and on the internal circuit I said to you, 'Hi, I'm John Knox.'

'Sorry?'

'I'm John Knox.'

'Yes, I know that,' you said.

'So you're my historian?'

'I'm *an* historian. Art history. Postgrad.' There was seasoning in your accent I couldn't place.

'You don't look like one.'

'I beg your pardon?'

I said, 'That was meant as a compliment.'

Your smile was starting to look like it was hard work.

'Yeah,' I said. 'I mean, I meet a lot of historians in this job and most of 'em look like the 'before' for some kinda procedure, whereas...'

We stared each other down for a moment; and then we both looked at the bald-headed professor of history, who regarded us disapprovingly over his half-moons. You nearly cracked and laughed, but kept up the professional face.

Louis kept talking. He sure believed in that worm.

You asked if this was gonna take long. Not that it seemed to matter: you'd unselfconsciously brought the world's biggest book, with a butterfly on the dust jacket – *Papillon*, you told me, when prompted. I named the author, Henri Charrière, saying his name the French way. That made you take the time to look at me, through narrowed eyes.

I imagined what you'd be like to kiss.

There was one minute left on the clock. I apologised with a gesture and put my fader back up.

'OK – Louis, I tell you what I'm hearing. I'm hearing there's a dude in a uniform out there, he's been given a weapon and right now he *isn't sure* whether he might one day spray bullets into the good citizens of Modesto. The worm you describe – no, shut up, man, you've had your say – the worm you describe was identified ninety years ago as your id, Louis. Not Satan, not some worm – the part of you that, as a human being, you have a responsibility to keep in check, dude. Don't construct some belief-fantasy why it could be OK to act like a whack-job. It's never OK just to feel and do. Common sense is not a disease. Dan Quayle is not the norm. Pull your shit together, Louis, and face life like the man you are. We have news next; later we'll be remembering our guest from last year, the mighty and dearly missed Bill Hicks, but first I'll be talking to the smouldering student of history Rachel McAllistair and a couple of other folk about America at war and propaganda imagery. This is John Knox, telling it exactly like it is, on KVOC, the Voice of the Bay, 1510. We're on the airwaves because you guys buy stuff from our sponsors, so thank you for keepin' us talking. Here are some messages about the great products we're proud to endorse. Stay with.'

I looked to see what you'd made of my flattery, but you were reading your butterfly book.

In honour of Louis, I put on a Nirvana song just before you came on air – the one that starts with loading guns. The shine was gone off grunge (this was way post-*Badmotorfinger* and *Dirt* and *Nevermind*), but playing it still felt right. While I joined you and the jock and the professor from the war museum in the discussion part of the studio, a digital clock counted down to the end of the song. Unlike real life, radio is all about knowing how many minutes and seconds you have left.

The professor was old-school – he existed in a cloud of chalk dust. You, on the other hand, looked like a girl playing dress-up; beneath the outsize tweed with the *Dynasty* shoulder pads, you wore a black shirt buttoned low, the way only flat-chested girls can, and a zillion pendants, and Doc Martens. You shook my hand. You had a soft, hot hand. I wanted to hold on to it.

'So you've listened to the show, right?' You hadn't. 'Callers call in, I give them a hard time if they say something stupid, which some will; you guys get an easy ride. The idea is we just stir up the topic, get into the angles.'

'I heard this is filmed,' said the professor.

'Yes it is.'

Yes it was. It was taped on a single camera, in a resolution basically unsuitable for broadcast. We had a hook-up with a low-rent satellite outfit in Santa Monica. They used to get OK ratings off the back of our show – that was before we got the FM licence for the Bay area, before we knew what simulcasting and syndication were.

I still have the tape. It's getting old, now. Sometimes, when I want to remember you the way you were right at the beginning, I drag the old VHS machine out of the spare room and put it on. I get scared in case the thin tape might tangle or snap. One day it will. One day, without warning, you'll be gone.

In the tape, we sit around the studio table in 1994, headphones on: a pretty random quartet of human beings, set against a backdrop of my autograph written in blue neon. Your long hair is down as though you want to hide behind it, and you seldom look up, until I say the word Chomsky, at least.

Until that point, the debate has been measured and academic – the kind of brain-food I got famous for making famous. We're discussing mustard gas. It's part of your specialism. The fucked-upness of World War One has been sketched. For Americans that war was a one-year nothing, but in Europe it was four long years of every known thing getting blown away, and gas drifting across fields, and I still have enough Canada in me to recognise the names Passchendaele and Somme. We talk about the image of a butterfly sitting on the muzzle of a cannon from the Great War, and the flowers in gun barrels in Washington in '67. But whereas the older two guests are talk-circuit pros and know the hand signs that mean speed up and hand over, and know how to be inter-rogated, when I coax you to be more specific you say, 'So annoy-ing,' and when I invite you to develop the conversation in a new direction you throw a total shit-fit, claiming discrimination on the grounds of age, or because you're a woman.

'As listeners to this show will know,' I warn you, 'I love every-body, and especially women.'

'That's great, I love men.'

'I'm happy to hear that.'

'You gotta love 'em, don't you? Otherwise they're fucking *intolerable*.'

Inside the first three minutes, it's clear to me, the other guests and everyone listening in that you hate my guts.

But I catch the swear with the mute and the delay, and we labour on through that show: the show I can recite verbatim, the show I play over and over again in the dark: my only moving pictures of you. The best time, the time when you are most you, is when you riff on Woodrow Wilson's response to the sinking of the *Lusitania*. God, you're on fire. The smoke signals say *this is what I believe*. That was his moment to respond, you scoff, but all he did was send diplomatic notes. It should have been his Boston Tea Party, his Pearl Harbor – the point of no return, the first step in a ballet of revenges. You actually use that phrase: a ballet of revenges. I don't know what about you to fall in love with first. The Great War, you pronounce, sent one half of the poets looking for refuge in an imagined golden past, while the rest tried to craft a language beyond violence with which to report the apocalypse. You say that without notes, and without blinking, and you are beautiful.

We talk about how some things never change; how history doesn't just repeat, but crosses over and tangles up. Nineteen and a half minutes before you channel Mike Tyson, Iran–Iraq from the eighties comes up. The same trench warfare; the same mustard gas; the same eventual US involvement after provocation. The Ivy Leaguers reel off facts like they're teaching class. You call them cowards. Everyone sucks their teeth. We're at war. At twenty-eight minutes exactly, I try to turn the conversation, but you resist. You want the academics to grow souls. Yeah: the atmosphere is strained, OK, but the discussion carries on, because we're professionals.

After the show, everyone chills – everyone but you. We all take positions for a living; you do it because you believe. Papers are gathered up; you won't shake anyone's hand. Off-screen, the producer escorts the others out. You shovel things into your bag at the edge of the frame, in a flurry of tweed.

'Could I talk to you?' I say.

'What, so you can patronise me some more?'

'Nah, man, the opposite. Sit down, will ya? Just for a minute. Please?'

The shovelling is arrested. You look at the picture of Dali again, and then you come back to the debating table, and sit.

'Look, I know you're new to this whole thing,' I say, with great caution, 'and I can see you think that didn't go well. I just wanted you to know you were actually brilliant.'

'Don't. Just don't.'

'No, I mean it. That was some impassioned shit. Really inspiring. You don't believe me? Man, words are cheap; it's something else to hear people talk about things they *believe* in. You were great.'

This type of talk is visibly pissing you off.

Oh, Rachel.

'And that whole "ballet of revenges" thing …'

The counter in the upper left of the screen reaches 47.45.00: time for me to say the Chomsky thing. It's just a name-check, mostly to show I read Chomsky. I say, 'I totally believe in you. And Chomsky'd love you.'

That's all. For all the years I've spent trying to figure it out, I have no clue what outrage you thought those words contained. On the tape, the whole thing's over in three seconds: the flailing tweed arm, my startlement as I realised I've been hit and that I'm falling backwards off my chair. Then the moments afterward, where you sit with both hands over your mouth, begging to know if I'm OK; my eventual re-emergence from under the table, stemming blood from my nose with a bunched-up shirt. I'm remarkably well mannered about the whole episode, considering. I only swear a little bit. I remember the taste of blood in my mouth and I remember being surprised by wanting nothing more than to tear from your body your too-big jacket and your big skirt; to meet violence with violence; to feel you struggle under me and submit. I wanted to fuck you and as I fucked you, whisper in your ear that I was a pacifist.

That was some strange shit going on.

As I bat away your apologies and show you the thumbs-up, and you leave, I'm starting to sway. I gotta hold on to things for support. The last thing I do is lurch towards the camera. The timer stops, and the world goes dark.

I was, it turned out, mightily concussed. Not from the punch, but because careening backward off my chair had made me hit my head on some furniture. I didn't notice the blood in my hair until I got home later that day, by which time I couldn't see straight. I bundled myself into a cab, in mounting, stabbing pain, to a place where a doctor who'd seen worse ran me through tests I thought were reserved for drunks on the highway. Touch your nose! Count backwards from one hundred in sevens!

'No computers or TV for at least three days,' he warned me. 'Preferably seven, otherwise you're risking damage. No loud noise, either. No radio. Radio's bad for you.'

'Got that,' I said.

It was still bright enough in the city for shades, but the cotton wool up my nose needed explanation. Everyone from my barber to the kids in the neighbourhood tried to winkle out what I'd done finally to earn a punch (yeah: they all assumed I'd been hit. It wasn't whether, but who). My busted nose even got twenty-seven words on page 14 of the *Bay Chronicle*, from whose offices a dyspeptic hack called me, in the afternoon.

'You got in a fight in a bar over Noam Chomsky?' she repeated back to me, sceptically. 'You filing against them?'

I said, 'Do you know how long I've wanted to see someone throw a punch over Chomsky?'

'C'mon, John. Aren't you angry?'

And that's when I realised that no, I wasn't angry with you, not even a little bit.

Enduring cosmic migraines, yes. I genuinely felt that removing my shades was to risk the two halves of my skull dropping off, one each side, leaving my exposed brain sitting there damp and proud like an avocado stone.

At home I listened for as long as I could endure to cassette tapes of whale-song, left behind by Fi when she'd shipped out; abandoned with good reason, as it transpired. Whales are all warm-up and no set. There was a ziggurat of review copies sent in by publishers who wanted a plug on the *John Knox Show*. I picked up one called *The Celestine Prophecy*. A few pages in, I was already hoping someone had locked up the guy who wrote it. I tossed it in the trash at page 10, fearing prolonged exposure might prove fatal. Instead, I rang Barney to ask if I could come be an invalid at his place on the bay in San Diego, and he said sure and asked what was wrong, and when I told him he asked if I was angry and I said no, I wasn't angry. I really wasn't angry.

077

I think, if Hemingway's Old Man had done twenty years of acid and six for draft-dodging, he might have ended up looking like Barney. Always the muttony, over-tanned skin, the open Hawaiian shirts, the unkempt grey beard; always the bottles of something new from Napa and the clink of clean glasses. How does it go? *His eyes were undefeated, and the same colour as the sea.* Something like that.

We threw bread to the gulls from the balcony overlooking the bay, the three of us – one or other of Barney's studs was already installed – and let ourselves be mesmerised by the hushing of the waves and distant sloops cutting through the teal swell. They seemed sometimes to be stationary and yet they'd suddenly pirouette, or skate a curve, while occasional speedboats bounced around: minnows among the angel fish. We puffed on a vast hookah, which remedied my head-pain pretty much instantly.

Later, we talked about you.

'In my opinion she's James Dean,' Barney grunted, checking to see what we both thought of that. 'Eh? I think she's a rebel without a cause. No cause to get behind, but she punches you regardless.'

The plus-one, who was even younger than I'd thought, said, 'Maybe she just really doesn't like Chomsky. Maybe that's, like, the super-worst thing you could say to her. What *is* it, anyway?'

'How can you not know Chomsky?'

I said, 'Chomsky's a polymath, basically an anarchist – he was anti-Vietnam—'

'Yeah, Chomsky's a good guy,' said Barney. 'OK, so maybe she wants you to fuck her.'

'And she shows it this way?'

'Women are from Venus, my friend.'

'Barney, she's in her twenties.'

'When I was your age, that would have been a good thing. You're thirty, man, not a freakin' thousand.'

'Thirty-one,' I said.

He was resisting turning the thing into a joke, but rather pulled his basket chair up closer to mine and poured a tumbler of Cabernet, and, realising I would refuse it, settled into it. 'Be honest with me,' he said. 'Since you and Fi wiped out – what's been going on for you? You making time to see anyone?'

I glanced at the boy.

'Come on, let's take a walk,' said Barney.

Even with the bay breeze, the ozone and the soft sea spit where the waves jumble against the harbour wall, the heat of the day remained insistent toward sundown. Asphalt clung. We got off the Boulevard into Marina Park, the pair of us, and schlepped down along the trail of lime trees; keeping to the grass, skirting around the soulless grey brick plaza, still hot as a skillet. Girls on roller blades lowered their shades my way. To the left of us: the bleached boardwalks and their bobbing ranks of playboys' boats, and, beyond them, tiers of sun-blinded hotels. To the right: the majesty of the bay. Silently, a leviathan branded *US Navy* was crawling back to its nest.

Barney and I sat against a cypress. We talked about the children we didn't have and our ex-wives – far gone, now. We congratulated ourselves on how we'd noticed each other grow older, even in the few years since Mendocino. Like a fine wine, said Barney, for whom everything good was like a fine wine. He toked from a joint, and passed it. 'But let me tell ya, it's a real kick in the butt, turning fifty,' he told me. 'You think thirty's bad? Hoo-ee! Never done this, never done that…'

'You got plenty of time,' I said, but when he looked into my eyes he wore a dark expression I'd never seen before.

'Talk about something else,' he said. 'Talk about your boxer girlfriend. Huh? Or something. Talk about something.'

So we talked about Bobby Ross fixing the Chargers; about Clinton; about John Wayne Bobbitt. As the sky caught fire come sundown we were young again, and we talked about dead poets a while, the Beats and the Metaphysicals, like two schoolkids perched on the lip of their adolescence, capable only of future perspective, feeling the moment of passage from the angel's age, to the plummet, the rush: the six-days-world, transposing in an hour. Listening to the waters chopping tirelessly against the jetties, I understood the intimate connection between time and waves. I understood Shakespeare standing resolute on the pebbled shore, watching the waves of days contend towards him. I understood Otis Redding feigning defiance with a jaunty whistle, as his tide rolls away.

Fleetingly, we transcended ourselves – we really did. Barney pinched off blades of grass and preached his portmanteau spiritualism: yin and yang and the Confucian analects, all mixed up with the Rig Veda and the Tao. It was muddled as hell, but there was that low fire that burned in his eyes when he spoke.

Gulls were skirling. The air smelt of ocean salt, and diesel from the returning yachts, which gunned their engines as they eased around the breakwater; and warm earth. It smelt like my California.

'Guess we're all just packing for the journey,' said Barney, as we dawdled homeward.

'And if there's no journey?'

'You mean if this is it?' Barney looked at me saucily, and lit himself a cigarette. He said, 'This ain't it.'

076

I used to go up north to see my people. In southern Cali, when you say north people think NorCal, redwood country; I meant Canada. One day, Mom and Dad rented out their great clapboard house in Ontario to a couple of teachers and moved down to CA, to the sun.

The institution of Saturday lunch established itself the day they moved to Napa. For four years it went that if I opened the front door any given Saturday, Mom would be standing there with her arms already outstretched as though she hadn't seen me in decades, all fizzed up and sparky, best jewellery on. She'd squawk, do jazz hands, then kiss me all over my face. While that was happening, Dad would stand five feet behind, grave as hell, looking like the admiral on a ship as it goes down. When Mom was done hugging he'd step forward, and in a gruff voice say, 'How are you, son?' and he'd take me by the hand and pull me into a half-hug. And that would be the opening part of the ritual done, and we could all stop behaving like we were playing parts.

After Fi left, I thought maybe they might can the routine and let me bury myself in a hole and see no one but Jack Daniel. But no: I still had to bake a ham or whatever, and they'd come eat it and ask what the celebrities I'd interviewed were really like – they didn't see how that question impugned my interview skills. They were probably trying to do me a favour.

This time it was like that, except while she was kissing me Mom saw my black eye and her squawking turned into wailing – 'John, darling, what's happened to your *face*?'

'A crazy historian smacked me, Mom.'

'What do you mean, he smacked you?'

'He was a girl, Mom. She thought I insulted her.'

'Well—'

'It's OK – she was beautiful and smart; I'd been hitting on her.'

It worried me how easily this seemed to assuage Mom's concern. After a few clucks and tuts, she abandoned the issue.

'I don't understand why you ever broke up with Fiona,' Dad observed, opening a beer. '*She* was beautiful and smart.'

'She was an iceberg, Dad.'

'That's as maybe,' he said. 'In my book, you don't just give up on people. Not if you care about them. You stick with them and work it out.' He glanced at Mom, who returned the look. I wondered what communication had passed between them.

And after that, everything was back to normal. I put asparagus on the griddle, and Dad installed himself on the couch. Mom fluttered around. Momentarily, she said, 'Have you been gardening?'

'I have not. Is that even a verb?'

She told me not to be cheeky. She was looking out of the window at the shared scrap of grass. 'That's a buddleia. Someone's been planting new shrubs.'

I knew the other occupants of the block. They were either deadbeats, or too elderly for garden work. It must have been there before, and I told Mom so.

That got her riled up. She turned down the heat under the shitake, dragged me out into the garden and pointed. Yup, there it was: a bush. As we approached, a couple of butterflies flew off it. They were pretty: big and red like wounds. They were Monarch butterflies, Mom said. Buddleia was catnip, for them. The earth around the bottom of the bush was obviously freshly dug.

She said, 'There, that bush was not here this time last week.'

I said, 'Well, I don't know.'

'Well, I do, and it wasn't. Goodness me, you need to pay a little more attention to what's going on under your nose.'

In the absence of anything constructive we could say about this damned bush, we let it go.

Dad was dead when we got back in the house. As soon as we came through the door, Mom started scolding him because he'd dropped his bottle on the carpet, then she stopped mid-sentence when she saw his head tipped to one side, and the chiding became a panic. She went to him and he looked exactly the same as he always did, sitting there, except his head was rolled. We both shook him. I willed it to be some dumb-ass joke. But he was gone. Just like that. They say that with a big enough arrest you can go twenty seconds without your heart beating before you even know about it. Then comes a pain down your left arm. That's the blood trying to get back around, without a pump to pump it there. You can be, for twenty seconds of your life, fully alert and conscious, and have no heartbeat. That's what my dad went through, they say.

My dad was a tall, bald-headed man, with a rim of white hair around the top of his ears and the back of his head and a white stubbly beard that never looked like it could grow properly. He had the air of a military man, and all he'd ever done was work in a library. My dad was not the sort of person who dies.

Dad, the priest said, as part of the eulogy, had been Falkirk County cross-country running champion three consecutive years in the 1950s. I never knew that. It was said on a sunny fresh May day in San Francisco, a day when the doors and windows of the chapel were left open after everyone had taken their seats in front of the coffin. He'd been the only person to hold the title three times. All the other mourners murmured approval, as though they remembered it well. As the priest spoke, pictures of Dad were projected on to the wall of the chapel. Beardless, lanky and delirious in 1957 at the end of the first race, in a black and white world on a cold Canadian day. There was a picture of him holding me when I was an hour old – the sixties blues of my eyes too blue and the edges of the picture bleached. There was the ceremony when he got his Dewey qualification; there was his wedding day. They'd had me late, and his life seemed to belong to ancient history. A whole life lived so close – so close. My heart ached for me. Yes: this man had sat at my table every Saturday for years, and I never asked him who he was.

The funeral was small. The family was small. Fiona came. We didn't talk, except to tell each other that we were sorry. She was very specific about it: 'I'm sorry about your dad,' in case there was any mix-up. A couple of ancient aunts were there, and my mom stood between us, and a photographer turned up and hung about the peripheries of the graveyard until he got shooed away by the funeral director.

A photo made it onto page 12 of the *Bay Herald*: a picture of me leading Mom down the steps of the church, our heads craned in towards one another. I wore shades. The caption said *Talk Host Buries Father*. They didn't name me in the headline, to fool the reader it might refer to someone actually famous.

075

Two days after putting that old man in the earth, I went back to work. I had to go back. I needed someone to talk to.

There were a lot of white supremacists outside the station around that time, on account of some stuff I'd said supporting Rodney King. It was easy to tell the Nazis from the pro-lifers who kept up a token presence twenty-four-seven, and the occasional autograph hunter, and the generally unhinged, who sensed in me a kindred spirit and either wanted to kill me, provide me with offspring or unburden themselves about being sexually abused by their stepfathers. Me, I was wearing my hair mop-long and scruffy around the time you met me, *Point Break*-style, and generally came to work in a T-shirt and Levi's, and a big pair of aviators. Lunatics sometimes threw stuff at me: condoms or eggs or the *Communist Manifesto*, or transcripts of the ruling of Roe v. Wade. I never heard of people throwing things outside *Pozner/Donahue* or *Larry King Live*. I think they threw shit at me because they knew I'd pick it up and read it. The Nazis never threw anything, which made them seem more threatening. Anyway, it was pretty unusual to get unexpected callers. You had to really want to pay the visit.

I was in Galtieri's office eating granola when the call from reception came on the internal line. Fox was showing the Cobain vigil in Seattle Park. The two of us watched it, munching, like cows in a field.

Galtieri took it. After he'd put the receiver back and shovelled in another mouthful, he gestured at the door and said, 'For you. She's coming up.'

You want to know the truth, Rachel? I didn't think I'd ever see you again, and by the time I'd gotten through the funeral you'd reduced from the first thing on my mind to a nameless ache somewhere inside me. There was a lot of aching going on. Every sentence I said, I wanted to finish with 'my dad died'. The words weighed a lot, and I carried them around inside.

And then you came round the corner of the door frame in the station that day, and adrenalin or something like it made my whole body feel like a snap of the fingers. I could smell your perfume, again, and see your skin.

'Float like a butterfly, right?' my mouth said. I guess it was the first thing that came to mind. I meant Ali, but you looked at me like I meant something else. You had intelligent eyes.

You sighed. 'I came to say I'm sorry.' You looked sorry, too. There was a shadow on you, and I felt bad. You said, 'I feel very strongly about what I do and it's difficult to hear it ridiculed. I had no idea what sort of show it was going to be.'

'What makes you think I was ridiculing you?'

'Because that's what you do.'

'What I do is make intellectualism cool.'

'What you do,' said Galtieri, 'is get not enough sponsorship, still.' He poked a spoon at the TV screen. 'Way to go, uh? Top of your game, pull the trigger.' A sea of grunge kids had lit candles in the park. They looked like refugees from an apocalypse.

'Coward's way out, man.'

You said, 'He made a choice.'

The blinds were down against the cold April sun. You had on your owl-glasses and Seattle was reflected in them, twice.

You told Galtieri, 'Would you give us a moment?' When he'd gone, looking like a dog being kicked into the yard, I offered you a chair, which you declined.

'I don't want to take up your time,' you said. 'But I do want to say I'm so, so sorry for what I did. I don't know what got into me, I just – well, it doesn't matter. I tried saying it another way, but – well, I just wanted to apologise to you face to face, OK? I was out of line and I disgraced myself.'

Just talking about it made the throbbing come back. One side of your sweater hung down off a shoulder made for touching; for kissing. I said, 'You know I switched the tape out, right? No, how could you? I swapped in a blank, told 'em I forgot to hit "Record".

No show went out. No one knows what happened.' It all seemed so fucking trivial.

'Yeah, well… *I* know.' We both stood there, suspended in the moment. Courtney Love was on TV. Eventually you said, 'Thank you.'

'Would you please sit down?'

'No, I'm going to go.'

'Not fucking fair. Not you as well.'

'Excuse me?'

'I'm kinda done with people leaving.'

You hesitated, and then reached for the handle of the door.

'Rachel.' Your name tasted strange. 'Look, let me buy you dinner. I know this new taqueria in Mission, it's totally the bomb, I can get us in.'

Now you laughed, and it was without much humour. 'I'm sorry, do you think because I've embarrassed myself I'm now obliged to sleep with you?'

'Christ, who said anything about sleeping with anyone? You're beating yourself up about this whole thing, and I want to talk you out of that, or try to at least. And…'

'And?'

'I really want you not to go.'

'Best you can do?'

'Please?'

'Goodbye, John Knox,' you said. Before I could think how to delay you, you were gone, leaving the door open in your wake.

I caught up with you in the parking lot. You'd gotten into a small European car that looked like it might shed important parts any moment. I felt like I'd seen it somewhere before. There was what looked like a household's worth of belongings on the back seat, pillows and shovels and bookends, and you were gunning the engine hard.

Through the open window I said, 'Come on, Rachel, no one's died. Can we just start over?'

'Be so much better for you if we didn't.'

'Why?'

'Because I'm fucking complicated.'

'I know you're complicated.'

'I know you know, bless your heart, but fuckin' triple it.'

'And I'm still here.'

On top of the dash was that damned book, again. *Papillon*. I felt the tectonic plates of my head shift. 'It was you who put that bush in my garden, wasn't it? The butterfly bush?' You didn't look me in the eye. 'I know it was. Fuck, and you expect me not to be just a little bit curious about you?'

'You oughta know what they say about curiosity,' you said, and the car lurched out of its parking spot, describing a wild arc before you crunched its gears and made the tyres squeal out on the asphalt – and then your car was accelerating away, a receding block of colour that sluiced into the flow of the highway to a chorus of horns, and vanished. I looked down: around me was a black rainbow of tyre rubber.

On its crest, the station building looked, against the blue sky, like a fifties idea of the future. I thought of the kids grieving in Washington State. And then I remembered the times I'd skipped dinners with Dad, and my body shook with sobs like laughter, and the tears came, and they wouldn't stop.

'This is John Knox, telling it exactly like it is on KVOC, the Voice of the Bay, 1510.

'As you know, there's no format on this show – my producer Renzo Galtieri lets me do whatever I want, and I spend most of my time being an arrogant, pretentious, iconoclastic prick.

'Normally at about this time I'd be getting ready to spray my liberal agenda all over the Bush–Quayle legacy or soccer moms or the NRA, but I'm giving those guys the day off because things have happened that are more important, and I need to tell you.

'There's no doubt that Kurt Cobain was at least as arrogant and pretentious as the prick talking to you now. He pumped himself full of a lot of drugs, but he was a human being too and he managed to portray the futility of human existence in a way few of us could hope to do.

'This is what he said in a magazine interview. "If you die you're completely happy and your soul somewhere lives on. I'm not afraid of dying. Total peace after death, becoming someone else, is the best hope I've got." Kurt Cobain believed he'd be happier dead, and after a long time being unhappy he acted on that belief.

'Around the same time as Kurt Cobain shot himself, another man, known by almost nobody, died too. My dad was happy being himself, I believe, and he had a woman who loved him, my mother, by his side.

'I don't see any contradiction between the deaths of these two men. They practised their beliefs. I urge you to do the same. If you cherish life, and you're doing anything but living it fully, look in the mirror and ask yourself why – and then get out there and do whatever it is you think will make you happy. Quit your job, or climb a mountain or write a screenplay – whatever, man. But if you believe that there's nothing to live for, then look at Kurt Cobain and decide whether you shouldn't take his choice as an example. It's simple: put a gun in your mouth and pull the trigger, or live.

'All you have, as an individual, are your beliefs. If you don't act upon your beliefs, my friend, you don't exist.

'My dad, like his son, was an atheist. Here's Nirvana performing "Jesus Don't Want Me For A Sunbeam".

'This is John Knox on KVOC, Voice of the Bay, 1510. Goodbye, Dad.'

Galtieri had hauled me out of my chair before the song was even ten seconds in. I mean he actually lifted me by my shoulders, letting the headphones ping off on their wire. I'd had no idea he could kick ass like that. 'Go the fuck home, get drunk and drive your car into a fucking tree, John,' he was roaring, propelling me out of the studio by force. The station techs looked at me like it was none of their affair.

'Life is short! You object to my broadcasting that revelation?'

'You advised everyone listening to shoot themselves dead.'

'Henry Miller did it. And Lenny Bruce.'

'Man, oh fuck, we have our licence renewal in a *week*.' In the corridor, he spun me around and made me face him. Man, he was pissed. He said, 'I don't care how cool you are. I love you like a brother, but we only need one self-harming fuckhead to put a toaster in the bath tonight and we don't have a station, understand me?'

'Fine, I'll quit.'

'No you won't quit, I invested too much in you already; you'll go get drunk like I told you to, keep your mouth shut and let me clean this mess up. Capiche?' I remember the smell of garlic on his breath, and the luxuriance of his devil-beard. I shook him off me.

'All right.'

'All right.'

074

City Lights Bookstore on Columbus is one of those old-school places with chequered tile floors. It was started by some Beat poet in the fifties. Ferlinghetti, I think. On the walls are photographs from even farther back: portraits of long-dead writers; poetry readings from wartime, with sailors like Popeyes in the front row.

You'd arranged yourself in a nook by a vast four-pane window like a model for an Edward Hopper entitled 'Young Woman Reading', wearing a skirt and shirt, like this was your business: the only woman wearing dark clothes in a world of luminous T-shirt dresses and 90210. Your legs were crossed at the knee, bringing out the shape of your calf; you supported your head with the fingers of one hand and held the book flat with the other. You read with poise, haloed by the light from outside. The expression on your face implied utter disdain for the views of the author. I sat at the chair on the other side of the small table. It was mid-morning and quiet, except for the voice of the manager, which drifted up the wooden stairs. In spite of there being no one else around, you didn't look up.

You were reading Rupert Brooke. We sat like that for several minutes, in each other's company, even though you were miles away. You read; I watched. Once, after dark, I walked by a house with its windows lit up, and saw an old couple dancing. I couldn't hear the music, and that made it more beautiful. I couldn't see the poetry, either. Eventually, and for no particular reason, you glanced up at me. I think it took you a full five seconds to figure out where you'd seen me before, or to overcome your confusion at how I could be there. Then you stuck out your chin and smiled without humour. You said, 'Well, gosh. You don't take no for an answer, do you?'

'I can't stop thinking about you. Sorry, that needed a cliché warning. But it's true.'

'You don't know me. How did you even find me?'

'Your faculty administrator,' I said, and I realised how that sounded. 'You know, I'm sure you said Brooke was hokey.'

You looked at the cover of the book; read the poet's name on it. 'This is work, not pleasure.'

'Well, how about some pleasure, instead?' I held up my hands. 'A gallery, maybe, or a walk by the bay?' I felt nervous, like a schoolkid.

'Does it usually work, if you say it all breezy like that?'

Your scorn made me laugh. 'Wow, you really think I'm a player?'

'Oh, come *on*,' you said. 'You're a big celebrity…'

'You're kidding. I'm on radio.'

'You're famous and attractive. You can have whoever you want. You get some sort of kick out of going after the ugly ones?'

I said, '*What?* You're about as far from—'

You slammed the book shut. '*Don't*,' you hissed. Downstairs, the conversation at the checkout paused.

'Rachel, I didn't mean to make you pissed.'

'Well, don't play games, then. It's wrong to put good things in front of people and then snatch them away.' Everything about you burned: your cheeks and your glare and your presence in the nook of the bookstore. I could have warmed myself near you. In your haste to stuff your Discman back in your bag, it got dropped, and your anger made your hands shake so that you couldn't get the batteries in the slot.

I said, 'My dad died, and I'm really struggling with it. There ya go: that's really me.'

'I'm sorry.' You exhaled evenly. 'I mean that. I really am sorry.'

'Say,' I said. 'Can we start over? I'm totally sincere. I'm a little hurt that you think I'm not.'

You were ready to leave, and trying hard not to meet my eye. Then I noticed your face soften. I realised you were trying to suppress laughter.

'What?' I asked.

'Did you just start that sentence with "say"?'

'So?'

'When are you from, the fucking fifties? No one's started a sentence with "say" since they invented Technicolor.'

'What can I say? I see a lot of Jimmy Stewart.'

'You don't like Jimmy Stewart,' you informed me. '*I* like Jimmy Stewart.'

'In fact, I do,' I said. 'I got all his films on video; all except *Harvey*, for some reason. Want me to name 'em?'

'I have *Harvey*,' you said, and we stopped talking for a moment. A moment or two more, and you said, 'Well, that was disgustingly cheesy.'

'Come eat with me,' I said.

You made a grunt of frustration, like you were being strangled.

'Just say yes,' I said.

'Fine.'

'Fine? Really?'

'Yes. Fine. But you are not paying for me.' You looked at me levelly.

I wanted nothing more than to kiss you. But I didn't.

073

The place we went to on our first date – you never let me refer to it as a date afterwards, on the grounds it made it sound like a pick-up – was a fusion joint two blocks from the bookstore, in Chinatown. Eggrolls and cherry pork and dry-fried chicken wings were cooked on personal griddles, then served on to big square black plates. Eating with you, I felt like I'd never eaten before. I ordered a Napa Merlot, and before the waiter could go get it, you corrected the order for an Anderson Valley Gewürztraminer that wasn't on the list.

'Might as well do it properly,' you said; and you smiled like we were on the same team.

Once we started talking, we didn't stop. As we ate you were enthusiastic and bright-eyed. I wondered if I'd imagined that anger. You made me describe the place I was from: a little nowhere town called Clinton, in the countryside of Ontario, Canada, in amongst the rocks and the lakes and the woody hills with their wind-blasted long grasses and long, bitter winters. You looked out of the window at the blue sky, the sun in the street and the colourful canopies over the storefronts, and asked, 'So why San Fran?'

'Read too much Kerouac when I was a kid.'

'Did you grow up yet?'

I told you how coming here made me feel free, for the first time in my life. I felt more at home on desert roads and smelling sage and lavender after sunset than at my parents' old place, a great grey haunted house on a rise near some beaver swamps on the old road out of Clinton, a place called Bryde's Crossing: not really anything but a loose collection of properties spaced too far apart to ever meet your neighbours. When I was a kid, the only other people for ten miles had been two ancient brothers called Freeman, who lived in a cabin out in the forest a mile down the road, until they died of old age. Bryde's Crossing bored the pants off me, and Clinton too, I said. 'Nothing ever changes, in Clinton. Same people do the same things their whole lives and die. Just the seasons change, everything freezes, everything thaws.'

'I like the sound of that.'

'One winter'd change that. How about you? Southerner, right?'

Right away, I knew that had been the wrong question to ask. You suddenly had an itchy forehead; then a need to check everything in the room. You wore your hair down, and now let it partly fall in front of your face. In a while I said, 'Any idea where I should be taking the conversation?'

'Isn't that what you do for a living?'

'My producer would usually be making suggestions in my ear right now.'

You considered me for a moment, and then stood up and leant over the table and whispered in my ear: 'Talk about something other than me.' Our faces were so close when you did that, your neck exposed, that before I was even able to make a choice about it I found myself turning my head and kissing your lips. It caught us both off guard. You tasted great. You kissed me back. After a moment we both opened our eyes, an inch of air between us, and stared, bewildered – and then kissed again. In my heart I knocked down tables, sending black square plates crashing to the floor as I held you against me and made love, but instead I shut my eyes and stayed drunk on kisses.

'Excuse me,' said a voice.

'We're fine, thanks,' I said, out of the corner of my mouth.

'Yo, excuse me,' the voice said again. 'You're John Knox. I get your autograph?'

I looked from you to him, pointedly. 'You're fucking kidding, right?'

He wasn't kidding.

When he'd gone, we were alone again, you and I, the taste of each other still on our lips, the bubble around us starting to reform. You examined the tabletop; you drank half a glass of wine straight down. Elvis mourned his love. He hadn't loved her quite as good as he should have. There was no 'maybe' about it: you could tell from the way he knew every little act of negligence he'd committed, but still he sang maybe, maybe, maybe.

I asked you about the art history thing. I said, 'What makes you want to look into the past?'

'Is this you in interview mode?' you said.

'Yeah, probably.' I touched my temples. 'Sorry, hard-wired. Let me try again. I mean, we all go to the museum, but all day every day? Where does that come from?'

'That was absolutely no better.'

'OK: why history?'

You said, 'How much longer can he keep going?'

The waiter set our food down before us, and you didn't touch it.

'OK,' you said. 'History has all the answers. Goethe said that someone living without two thousand years of history on their shoulder is living hand to mouth. Without history, we're perpetual teenagers, thinking no one's ever experienced these things before. But look at history. It's all there: the way it repeats, the way it loops back and tangles up – all these voices. Real people. Real lives.'

'Real like this?'

'You're only potentially real, at this stage,' you said. As the conversation went on you were looking at my lips, not my eyes, when I spoke.

'OK. Thank you.'

'So, why're you working in radio? Apart from having a huge ego and so on.'

'Nah, you have to be humble, for live radio. Gotta *sound* like the man, but you live or die on calls to your switchboard. I guess maybe I like that danger.'

'You seek constant affirmation from strangers.'

'I didn't say they gotta *like* me. Just call me, is all. Takes a bigger man to stand there and take a lot of shit if you know it's good radio. Knowing when not to speak is at least as important as having something smart to say.'

'Sounds very constructed.'

'We all make choices what to say.'

You said, 'Will you go back to Canada?'

I shook my head. 'Our house is still there. I think Mom fanta-
sises I'll go back, but I'm a sunshine person.'

'A sunshine person,' you echoed, as though it made you wistful
for days when you'd been a sunshine person too. You had a habit
of holding chopsticked morsels of food somewhere over your
shoulder between bites, like Audrey Hepburn smoking with a
filter, and being quite surprised to discover them there when your
focus drifted back to the meal.

'So what about you, Rachel? How'd you get here?'

You said, 'When I was fourteen I ran away from home. One of
the times. Ended up in San Francisco.'

'Naturally.'

'Well, where else? New York was too far and I couldn't get to Paris.'

I imagined the waif teenager, fresh off the Greyhound. 'What
were you running from?' I asked. 'Or where from, anyway?'

'Alabama.'

'Yeah? You don't talk like a Southerner.'

'I worked at that,' you said. You dropped your voice and in
perfect Deep South said, 'I didn't come such a far piece to look
dumb. Anyways, I reckon it's only polite to try and fit in.'

You told me you grew up in a one-bed condo where the TV was
always on; your half-Cajun mother took in laundry and ironed in
a cigarette haze. You sat in the bedroom, listening to *Match Game*
and *The Price Is Right* coming muffled through the walls.

'It's not very interesting, anyway,' you said, and finished the
wine. 'Waiter, we get another bottle of this?'

'Fourteen's young. You had people here?'

'I took care of myself,' you said, tucking your hair behind your
ear.

'I can see that.'

'No you can't.'

I ticked items off an imaginary list on my palm: 'Childhood –
check. Reasons for living here – check.'

'What kind of art do you like?'

Maybe that was the question that sealed the deal. I remember
how you sat there, cool and tough and pre-Raphaelite, and I had
to be with you.

'Today, I'm feeling a little Caravaggio,' I said. 'Muscle and sinew and shadow. You?'

'I like British artists. Bacon, Freud… Henry Moore sometimes.'

'Bodies again. Horror.'

You said yes.

'Horror *of* bodies?' I tried.

'Let's get out of here,' you said.

We walked, and the fragrances of sourdough and crabmeat followed us around. There was a music party I was meant to be at somewhere on East 14th, but that didn't matter to me. I was with you. When we walked, too close felt contrived, too far felt dangerous.

On the Wharf, we shot zombies who'd invaded a nuclear power plant. Our plastic guns were chained to the machine.

'You kinda suck at killing the living dead,' you noted, saving my ass yet again, your colour up. 'I thought warfare was a boy thing?'

'Well, I tend to keep as far the fuck away from war as possible.' I was out of credit, so I just let you shoot.

'Maybe you're an honorary woman.'

'A non-violent man is a woman?'

'Aw, come on. All violence in the home, all violent street crime, every war – it's all men.' The zombies were coming crazy fast by now.

'You think men *choose* that shit?'

'Yeah,' you said, putting the gun back in its holster, 'I do.'

Zombies were taking bites out of you, but you didn't seem to care. I nearly grabbed the gun myself, but it was too late – the screen turned first crimson, then went dark.

'Real man would have finished them off,' you said, mock sad.

We stopped under a tall street lamp and kissed each other properly to wolf-whistles, and our tongues found each other. When we were done kissing, we hugged, and I held you and looked past the sailboat rigging and the masts over the water to the Bridge spanning the Bay and the suggestions of hills hiding in the darkness beyond, and breathed you.

There was music on the radio coming out of one of the bars. A girl, singing. She sang about missing someone, in a song called 'I Miss You'; and I miss you.

072

Sex with Fi had been all about tongueless kisses and tissues and routines; with you, I forgot all about myself. Christ, I lost my mind. We were an urgent vigorous mess on the bed and then on the floor, and objects around us were there to be pushed aside or grabbed for purchase. I swear I never felt properly satisfied until that day. I felt like a man.

I didn't at first understand why you wanted to keep the lights off. I guess I thought it was a prude's way of letting go. I noticed that your skin felt weird, textured in places like a rumpled brow, but I assumed it was the way you were lying. You could have had three extra heads and I doubt I'd have taken note.

In the morning, when you were still asleep and the light was seeping in, I saw you. Your body was tangled naked in the sheets, and it was a work of art. I looked on you and thought, this is some complex shit's been going on.

I remembered the Falkirk County Cross-Country Running Championships.

I'd never seen a real cigarette burn before in my life, but the circles on your breasts and your belly were too regular for, say, chickenpox, and were concave where the scar tissue had been. I pulled the sheet away a little, fearful of waking you. There were cigarette burns on the inside of your thigh. On the fronts were long series of gashes, mostly healed, like tallies without fives. That's a you I won't forget. Spread on the bed like a human sacrifice, moon-skinned, naked, your legs spread apart and sliced into, your body used for an ashtray. The skin I'd made love to in the dark was a fabric of marks and scars, some of them old and healed, like white worms under your skin, others burgundy and new. I remember thinking how sleep seemed to have lifted the weight out of your expression. I wondered if you dreamt. I wanted to scoop you up in my arms and tell you it was OK, but I knew you'd be horrified that I'd seen you.

Distinctly, I remember avoiding making a choice. I remember putting the options away someplace deep in me; deciding not to know they were there.

I looked at your face. Your eyes were open and looking back at me. It was like watching a painting blink.

'Damaged goods,' you said.

You turned away, your eyes glassy like a doll's. I took your head in my hands very gently and turned it to me. I kissed your lips. You curled close to me as I sat on the bed, moulding yourself to me. We stayed a long time like that, as the sun came up on San Francisco.

I was putting on coffee in the kitchen when you came downstairs. You were already dressed, or partially anyway. You told me you were leaving.

I said, 'Hey, wait a second, what's the big hurry?' but you weren't listening, and I had to race you to the door and interpose myself. 'Would you stop?' I said. 'It's really going to offend my sense of hospitality if you rush out like this.' You stood looking at the door, paralysed by I don't know what.

I said, 'I want to know what's going on, of course I do, but most of all I don't want you to go right now because I like you being around, I like your company, I like you.'

That may have been the worst thing I could have said.

'No you don't like me!' you screamed, snatching at the door handle. 'You're fixin' to leave me first chance you get.' This burst of fury made you clumsy, you couldn't open the damned thing. I tried to help you, but for you everything was an attack. In the kitchen, the coffee was spitting and hissing as it dropped on to the hotplate where the jug should have been. I arrested you with a hug and held your head into the nook of my neck. You were shaking. I said, 'It's OK, it's OK,' but you were rigid in my arms, and you didn't melt. Later, I risked letting go of you in the hope you wouldn't dart out of the door. I was sure if you did that I'd never see you again. You didn't bolt. You just stood there with your head held high.

Rachel, I'd make the same choice a hundred times over.

Later, we sat drinking coffee, feeling awkward. You did feeling awkward very well. I tried to take your hand, but you had made it stiff. So instead I took your coffee cup from your hand and made love to you there on the couch. At first you let me fuck you like you were a dead thing, and I was terrified I'd made the wrong call. But something in the sex communicated with you and you were reanimated. And you ground against me and kissed me, and when we were finished, we were connected. Fused, like burnt-out wires. And somewhere a clock was counting down.

071

I met Pastor Lang late in the summer of '94. He'd come to talk about miracles, so I'd set him up on a round table with an atheist and a magician. I regret I did that.

He was a bear of a man. He wore short-sleeved pastor garb, and his forearms were thick and tanned: great serpents of muscle lying dormant beneath the skin. Behind a beard and thick glasses, the irises of Pastor Lang's eyes were tinged with yellow.

At the time, I didn't agree with what the atheist said about credulity. I used to think we're born ready to believe – it's the path of least resistance. Believing means never having to think again – just feel and do. *Not* believing is the big act of bravery.

After we wrapped up, the magician put his trick cigarette and a pack of cards away, and the atheist left on a cloud of contempt. Pastor Lang, still seated, clamped a paw over my hand, indicating that I should stay.

'Those off?' he said. He meant the mics. He told me he wanted to speak to me as a friend. His wedding ring and his palm weighed heavy on the back of my hand. I was thirty-one years old.

The pastor told me he had a son. The declaration made him well up and he had to take his glasses off and collect himself. When he'd done that, and steeled himself for telling the story, he told me again that he had a son. The son had been a blessing: the pastor and his wife had believed they couldn't conceive.

'You got kids?'

I told him no.

'It tested our faith, but we kept praying and we kept trying for a child, and other people prayed for us, and we had a baby. I can't tell you the joy he brought us.'

The boy, his name was Mikey, sounded like a great kid. Active and positive minded, helpful, curious. In the course of recording four years of call-in shows I'd heard plenty of stories about plenty of sons, and the way this guy painted his child, there was a deep love between them. It sounded like a tragedy being constructed.

'He was always the kid, if there was a fight he'd step in and try to stop it. Never violent. I tried to encourage him to take the same path as his old man. We talked about him being an army chaplain. That would have made me proud, to see my son ordained. And one day he came to our house and said he was going to enlist as a mechanic. He wanted to do something *practical* – that's what he called it. We gave him our blessing. And he went out to Missouri to do basic.

'Then Saddam invaded Kuwait and Mikey was sent with the rest of his unit to stop him.'

I remember Galtieri poking his head around the door just then with a mouthful of complaint that we were still in the studio, and he saw Pastor Lang and crossed himself and apologised, and withdrew. I'd had no idea until that point that Galtieri had any god other than himself.

'I should get to the point,' the pastor said, straightening his tunic. 'Mikey's lying in a hospital bed in the city right now. He has symptoms they call a "terminal profile". They don't know exactly what it is but they do know he is going to die of it. And he's not the only one. Some from his company, and plenty others, with the same illness.'

'What type of illness we talking?'

'It happened in Iraq. That's all we know. That's all we know.' He was unable to continue and he sat there, his hands clamped together on the table, his whole frame trembling. I offered him a tissue, but he refused, telling me he was all right.

After some time had gone by, I asked the pastor what help he thought I could be. He told me the government didn't want to talk. He told me about the families who'd first identified that something was horribly wrong, how they'd probed for information and been blocked by army physicians. How the symptoms seemed to have something in common with chemical poisoning leading to cancer, but no one knew if it was radioactivity or asbestos or something else altogether. The symptoms got more severe: chronic fatigue, burns on the skin, organ degradation. The families had started to band together, and although their number included important men like the pastor, as well as ordinary moms and dads, they were dismissed, first as conspiracy theorists, then as liars, then as out-and-out whack-jobs.

'And what I need to know,' Pastor Lang told me, 'is what they could have done that killed my child. I don't seek retribution, I don't seek punishment – they're not mine to give. But I poured my life into my boy, and raised him twenty-four years, and now he's gonna die, and it's not enough for anyone to tell me that that's just the way it is.'

I felt numb after hearing that. No, that's not right – I felt like a kid playing a game. I said, 'What do you think I can do?'

He said, 'People listen to you. They listen to me, but more of them listen to you. I know how you get people to talk about stuff. As long as this thing is in the shadows, it can be ignored. I'm ready to be the figurehead if I have to be. Whatever it takes. But I want you, please, to make some noise.'

I told him there were way bigger fish than me. Big names, with punch.

'I know that. But I've heard you. I heard that show where you got the guy his job back.'

That evening when I left the station, the little crowd was there as usual. Some hardcore fans, plus assorted freaks. A guy in a *Pulp Fiction* gimp suit had started showing up regularly. There were some lesbians, and some messengers from God. Me, I was zoned. I stood outside the station and let the double doors close behind me. I looked across their shouting faces. I remember marvelling that I'd become a focal point for so many feelings; that this thing I did, saying words out loud, could matter.

070

Anyone who speaks for a living oughta say something worth being heard.

When I arrived in California, fresh out of college and college radio, I kind of knew I needed to keep talking. I played Cinderella and Van Halen on The Rock 91.2, unpaid, and slipped The Melvins in when I could, and there wasn't much room for words in between – just track titles; the weather. I got recognised hardly ever, because this was sound waves, but I told everyone who'd listen I was a DJ. When I got laid, I was convinced it was because I did radio, rather than because I was twenty-two.

I did my first fill-in gig on NPR the day the cops beat on Rodney King. Six days after my shift was done, I stood on Twin Peaks and watched the city burn. The next time I got behind a mic, I talked about that shit, and two people wrote to the station saying I was right, and a third wrote in and offered to kill me.

It felt like I'd been underwater a long time, and could breathe again. After that, I decided I wasn't gonna waste words. You could spin your dial twenty, thirty, forty stations and there would be the same pompous voices introducing the same mediocre tracks. I tried to be different. I put CDs on to play and said a few words about the artiste and in between times I'd remark on Reagan or Live Aid or Chernobyl or *Challenger*. And then I moved up a salary bracket – that is to say they started paying me.

KMTT was a two-bit station outside of Santa Rosa. The owner told me he was the son of a Croatian rock star. The son didn't care much for talk, or music, or radio. He was in it for the advertising revenue, which was slight. The station was housed in a temporary building overlooking an industrial park. They liked me at KMTT, so they gave me phone-in shows. Phone-ins are a fast high. First thing I learned talking to people on phone-ins was inside every house, apartment, mansion, or condo there are people whose assumptions and habits and beliefs would scare the shit out of you. I started out treating the callers with respect, whatever their point of view. That got real hard, real quick.

'AIDS is God's way of cleaning out the queers.'

I had to cut that asshole off, instead of take him apart.

'I'll just tell you the truth, I don't like white people, I don't trust them.'

I had to be cordial and restrained with that asshole.

'A woman's place is in the home.'

I couldn't tell that asshole she was an asshole.

At night I'd drive through the sprawl: Sausalito, Campbell, Santa Clara. My car was a woodie: a '74 Pontiac Grand Safari with long panels on each side, pocked with dings from road dirt. I'd stop, smoke a jay, read a book, and think about all the things I'd have liked to have said but didn't. Being given a voice and failing to use it is a crime of negligence, of deception, even. I knew that. I guess I started getting surly.

The desire to speak out gnaws at your gut.

One night I came into the station and I just lost my shit. Professional suicide, I guess. I just couldn't hold my belly any longer. That was the best fucking show I ever did. It all went by in a blur. I wasn't deliberately offensive; that is to say I wasn't profane for profanity's sake. All the same, it was carnage. I reduced callers to tears, others to cussing, I cut people off and was told by one woman I should win the Nobel Prize. For the first time in years of having a voice, I spoke.

I got called in by the Croatian rock star's son the next morning. I drove across town with my knuckles clamped tight along the top of the wheel. When we were sitting at opposite sides of his desk, he kept me in suspense with flared nostrils, making sounds like a bull.

I said, 'If you're going to fire me would you just do it?'

'No. I don't gonna fire you. I was listening to your show at home last night.' He looked straight at me. 'It was bloody funny,' he nodded, 'bloody funny. You want to be shock-jock, is it right?'

I asked him what that meant.

'You know, controversial, making controversial. Cut people off you don't like what they're saying, you know?'

I didn't know. I guessed so. It felt like I was being more real. The Croatian rock star's son pushed himself away from the desk, wiped his jowls with a fat hand. Nodded.

'Jonathan, this wrong radio station for you.'

I said, 'Shit, I thought you said you wouldn't fire me?'

'I don't fire you, I do you favour.' He put his big hands with their gold rings flat down. He said, 'This small operation, you can see for yourself. We play some music, we have easy conversation, nobody fucking listening. You make this new style, I have to hire lawyer, switchboard, advertising, I need employ extra person for answer phone, public relation for explain why I have bigmouth DJ.'

I said, 'You want me to carry on the way it was before?'

'No,' said the Croatian rock star's son. 'I'm not fucking idiot, it's hella good style. You can be successful. I don't need successful DJ, I just need wallpaper DJ. I give you good reference, go get yourself fame. Show on a bigger station.'

That's how I learned how to speak.

'So. You're a pretty boy, you're still in your twenties, and you think you've got something to say. I already don't like you.' These were the first words spoken to me by Renzo Galtieri, senior producer at the Voice of the Bay, a station as old as radio. He had a face like a paper bag, and a beard borrowed from someone younger.

I hadn't even gotten in the office door yet. Behind me, in the waiting room, was the biggest assortment of misfits in the country, looking like they needed a meal: my competition to be a talk-show host. The job hadn't even been advertised.

Galtieri closed the door behind me. 'Don't sit down,' he said. 'I'll tell you the truth, we already know who we're going to pick, so this is a formality, 'kay? We're commercially funded except for a booster from the State of California, so we have to go through the process of selection. But we already did our selection. I just say this so you don't get upset when we don't pick you.'

I was twenty-six. The only job interview I had ever done was for weekend work at Peet's. The job at the previous station had been secured merely by turning up for the first shift and continuing to turn up every night thereafter.

You didn't know Galtieri at this time. He hadn't filled out yet, he was lean, with preternaturally tanned skin and no discernible sense of humour. He never sweated and he never smelt of anything.

'So I'm going to look at your résumé. We're going to agree you are no good for the job, and I'm going to wish you a very good day,' said Galtieri.

I told him I didn't have a résumé. I said, 'If we've got a minute to fill, and I know we haven't but humour me, what did the guy who got the job have?'

'A good agent, and one of the biggest names in talk radio,' said Galtieri, challenging me with it. 'And what the fuck do you mean, you have no résumé? You came to a job interview for a peak-time slot without a résumé?'

'You don't have an interview for me, I don't have a résumé. What is this guy worth?'

'You mean his salary?' said Galtieri. 'Please don't embarrass yourself by offering to work for free.'

'I wouldn't work for a cent less than you'd pay him.'

'Yeah, you just went from overconfident to obnoxious.'

'That's right, that's what I do. And I do it in an erudite and informative fashion. Whoever you've got lined up for the gig, if they are a known quantity, they've got too much to lose to be interesting. Me: I think, and I say what I think.'

Galtieri's stare was hateful and piercing. He said, 'So when you tell me your name I better have fucking heard it.'

I told him my name, and he carried on looking at me, but now he didn't speak.

I sat in a chair in front of the desk. 'Gimme a break,' I said. 'Let's up the game. That's what you do radio for, right, what KVOC's about? Freedom of speech? That's what you believe in. If you were in it for money, you'd be in TV. I want to do smart radio. I want to be a poster boy for the First Amendment.'

'Smart doesn't sell.'

I said, 'Let's find a way.'

'You're too young, anyway. Our best talk hosts are fifty, sixty. What are you, twenty-five?'

'You need a voice for the next generation.'

'Good pitch,' he said. 'Go sell brushes.'

I said, 'C'mon, man. You got your producer job at Atlanta straight out of college, right? Someone gave you a chance.'

Galtieri licked his teeth. 'Dug up my résumé, huh? I don't have a better side if that's what you are trying to appeal to.' He got out of his chair and paced the thin carpet of the office, the sunshine cool and strong off the white walls, and him in a blue shirt and chinos like he was ready for a day on the yacht. The big incongruity there was me, dressed out of Gap, making the place look untidy. ''Kay,' he said, 'so the fairy tale goes – how does it go? I say, hey, kid, you've got some balls, I tell the nationally famous DJ to go fuck himself, I bet my career and the future of the station on some nobody talk-show host who thinks he's an intellectual. Everyone lives crappily ever after. This ain't Hollywood. Ain't gonna happen. Thank you for coming in, Jonathan,' he said, indicating I should rise, like a priest raising his congregation to their feet to sing. 'No happy ending this time around.'

As he held the door open for me I said, 'OK, promise me one thing. You see all these people? If after seeing all of these guys, I still stick in your mind, give me a chance. Maybe it'll take more time before I bring in big money, just make me a space to do what I do.'

'Goodbye Jonathan,' said Galtieri.

On the way out, I said, 'Do what you believe, that's all I ask.'

Two days later I got a call from Galtieri. 'Turns out I'm your fairy fucking godmother,' he said. 'Owner thinks we need new blood.'

'Yeah?'

'Someone with attitude, but centre-left, connect with the younger people in this fine city of ours. Get on this political correctness ride. I happen to agree with him.'

'You recommended me?'

'The guy we lined up was a big-shot. That means people heard him already. Time to hear someone new speak out.'

'Say the word.'

'I already did,' said Galtieri. 'You got your chance. And Jonathan sounds like you don't connect. From here on in, you're John.'

069

And then some years passed, and there was you. There was always you. We hung out in Sausalito, and visited fairgrounds like regular couples did and threw popcorn at kids when their mothers weren't looking – you mostly tried to maintain a cynical distance from actual enjoyment, but enjoyed yourself by accident, and there would come moments when your eyes were full of light and you smiled. Oh, that smile. Mischief and carnivorousness and ageless beauty. If I close my eyes, it's your smile I see first. Who wouldn't have fallen in love with you when you shone that way, Rachel? There was a picture of you, taken in the pink champagne sunset in the High Sierras. You wore your long hair down and a gypsy skirt, and you were golden. Somehow the light wrapped itself around you, so that it immediately looked like nostalgia, and that was right, because those moments were few, but damn, they were good.

It's hard to say when we actually started living together, in the place in Potrero; your belongings seemed to consist of your car, a carful of stuff and the clothes you stood in, so any time you came round in your car you were already basically resident.

'REM?' you'd query, with an arched eyebrow; or, 'Simply Red?'

'What? They've done some good stuff.'

'You have Patti Smith and host talks on quantum mechanics. Please throw these out.'

You used to come around and we'd cook vegetarian food and go see European movies together. You'd help me think of topics for the show, giving discourses on the achievements of potential guests like you'd researched a thesis on each one. We had a lot of food fights. You took to spending Sundays in my bed, reading Tolstoy and calling for hot chocolate. Before long we gave up pretending you didn't live there, and that felt right.

Maybe the butterfly bush was the only item you consciously brought along.

You throwing stuff at me came out of the limerick game. The game wasn't complex. We'd say a first line in the tone that meant it was Line One, and then the other person had to finish.

I started you off with 'the craziest thing about life'.

'The craziest thing about life,' you said,
'That cuts through my heart like a knife'

– I egged you on.

'Is to look at we two
Perfect me, perfect you
And remember you once had a wife.'

That hit an off-key all right. You were quite the bard.

For the sake of something to talk about, I asked if you wanted to see a picture of Fi. It was an insensitive thing to have done, but you'd already moved in, we were hooked up, and I just wanted to share that part of my life with you.

You said, 'Do I what? Do I want to see a picture of your ex-wife?' And then you were yelling: 'The woman you used to *fuck*. What, am I not *good enough*?' – and you threw a coffee cup at me. It burst on the wall. I'd always thought that kind of thing only happened in comedy movies.

Within ten seconds you were in the bedroom, seething, and appeared actually to be packing your things to leave. I don't mean all of your things, I mean just random objects around you, as if you'd been visiting and had to collect up your purse.

'What are you doing?'

'What does it look like?' you said. 'If you're so fucking hung up on her, why don't you go ask for her back? You obviously don't want me.'

Our neighbour, the old Japanese lady, was sweeping leaves off her front step when you stormed out of the house. You turned around and yelled 'Fuck you!' so loud you bent double to yell it; and then you slammed the car door behind you and gunned the engine, and were gone down the street. Yeah, that was pretty bad. Fortunately the old lady had her Walkman on: she didn't hear squat. I stood in your wake feeling I'd just screwed up the best thing in the world.

'I tried to show her a picture of Fiona,' I told Barney over beer, later that day. 'She went freakin' postal, man. Like totally out there.'

'It was a dumb move,' said Barney. 'No one wants to hear about the ex.'

'I guess.'

'You call her yet?'

I said I figured she'd want time to cool down.

'Sure, she's amped, she wants time to cool down,' said Barney. 'But you gotta make an effort, or she'll think you don't care. Got to let her know that you know you're in the wrong.'

I said, 'Am I in the wrong?'

'Hell, yeah,' Barney said.

Later on I made the call, and of course you didn't answer. I left a long message that started: 'Rachel, it's me. I screwed up.'

You didn't come back that night, and I didn't sleep. The next morning I went to work half-conscious, and cancelled recording TV voiceovers in Milpitas, and when I got back the curtains of my – our – apartment had been pulled shut.

Inside, no lights were on. You were sitting at the bare table.

You said hello as though I'd interrupted you, and you smiled a smile that was like a bad lie.

You'd gotten me flowers. They were in a vase on the kitchen counter, with a note saying sorry. No one had ever gotten me flowers. You said your car 'fell into a creek'. You said it in a way that warned me not to ask.

'I was done with it, anyway,' you said.

It was eleven in the morning, it was fall, and a creamy-grey Bay fug hung outside. Half my mind was full of Pastor Lang and the other half with you, as I pulled open more curtains to let light in.

You sat at the table.

'I picked up food,' I told you. Later, I said, 'OK, why can't I shake the feeling something's going on here?'

You looked fine. Nothing seemed out of its place and as I spread out the vegetables for the meal I found myself hating how suspicious I felt. I put the chopping board down, hunted for the knife, but then, to my shame, couldn't resist the impulse any longer and went into the bedroom to look for signs. The bed had been unmade when I'd left home earlier and it looked exactly the same kind of unmade now. I buried my face deep into the sheets. It smelt like you and it smelt like me. By the time I got back into the kitchen you were engrossed in an art book on Christian paintings. I wondered how much of an asshole I was to have doubted you. I ran water on the zucchini and romaine, took the knife out of the rack and started chopping. And then I stopped chopping. I retraced my steps in my mind: Yeah, the knife hadn't been there before.

'What's going on?' I said

'You can surely see I'm more than you planned on biting off.' Oh, man, your colour was up.

I said, 'And what? You don't just give up on people. Not if you believe in them.'

'People?'

'You.'

You scoffed, 'Yeah, right.'

You were pacing. There was a little blood on your thigh. You circled close to the kitchen counter.

'OK,' I said, 'OK. Let's do it. What are the scars?'

'Every fucking thing I ever did wrong.'

'Hell does that mean?'

'Nothing.'

'You did that to yourself?'

'Some of it.'

'Some of it. Meaning?'

'Some of it I have other people to thank for; I'm keeping up their work.'

'You did it again just now?'

'That's private!' you said. 'It's for *me*!'

'Not when someone cares about you it isn't.'

'Then why the hell don't you just leave me alone?'

And I heard my voice start a sentence, because I never knew when to shut up, and the sentence included 'I love you', and even as it was said I knew that this was not the right time to be saying that, and that there would never be a right time.

And now you were on your feet, screaming obscenities, like I'd told you the worst lie. I blocked your way to the kitchen. You grabbed the book on church art and hurled it through the window, which splashed into a thousand pieces, with the sound of a broken bell. I don't remember what I thought. I was pumped. The breaking of the glass made you angrier. You were hollering so loud that the old Japanese lady next door had started to holler back, and it was only by the time I'd gotten to the knife so you couldn't hurt yourself again that I realised that you'd taken my car keys.

From the street you were telling me, and the rest of the world, that I hated you; you demanded to know why I didn't just kill you.

'What the hell are you talking about? Would you just come back inside?' Various pairs of eyes spied on us from balconies and passing cars and people walking by. And then you were in my car and reversing out, forcing the traffic to brake hard not to hit you. I still had the knife in my hand. After you'd driven away, I stood in the pool of broken glass, feeling like I'd been slapped in the face.

Hours later, I was shooting the shit with the window contractor about the Giants and the state of baseball generally, in between passing up tools to him, when I noticed something black and white moving in my peripheral vision. An engine stopped on the road near by. They'd sent two cops, one of each gender, both packing. They put on their hats as they walked towards us. They asked if I lived there. At first I figured a neighbour must have bitched about the noise, and then I started to wonder if this was preamble, if they had news about you. I mean, Christ, how does a car 'fall in a creek', anyway? The female officer spoke into her lapel radio. The window contractor, who didn't speak great English, was trying hard not to look twitchy. If I'd been one of the cops I would have arrested him right there on body language alone.

'Mind if we come in?' said the male cop. He was the twin of Judge Reinhold.

I said, 'If you're here to admire my new window, it's right there.'

'OK, sir, I just came off an eleven-eighty,' said Judge. 'Kid with his face all over the pavement. So I'm not in the mood for wise-acres, OK? We come in or not?'

I said, 'How about tell me what you want, first?'

'We got reports of a man with a knife. Your wife home?'

You were complicated, but damaged complicated, and having these guys up in our shit would only make it worse. I told him I wasn't married; I said we'd gotten into a fight and I'd thrown the book.

'The knife was because I was cooking dinner.' I explained my day was cock-eyed, on account of my breakfast show at the radio station.

'Aw, you're John Knox!' exclaimed Judge. 'I knew I knew your voice.' The female cop looked on askance. Maybe she'd never heard the show, or maybe in another life she'd been one of the crazies waiting to pelt me with fruit outside.

I showed them in and made them coffee. Judge couldn't get over how small my apartment was. He assumed radio people all lived in mansions, I guess.

'First ten years doing radio, you do it for free,' I told him.

After that he seemed to decide there were no real grounds for pursuing matters. 'Just keep in touch, let us know when she comes back,' he said. The female officer never took her eyes off me.

The first day after you smashed the window, you didn't come back to the apartment. Your belongings lay just where they'd been. I sat around eating Dunkaroos and getting peppy on Surge. I tried to get interested in the Mikey Lang thing, but my heart wasn't there.

Day Two, I looked through your clothes, to try to guess whether you'd have to come back through having nothing to wear. Each piece of clothing was of a different style from all of the others, like a dressing-up box at kindergarten. I held your big, soft jersey up to my face and breathed you in, and for a moment you were there – a spicy musk, like nights on an island. I held your silk panties to my lips. The jacket you'd been wearing, that tweed thing, wasn't with the rest, and I wondered what had become of that. I called the station sick and watched *Saved by the Bell* and *Donahue* with the phone by my feet.

Another day went by. The university knew nothing. Your purse was where you'd left it, containing your bank cards and your Amex. From your driving licence, you looked at me: a cold version of you I didn't know, with a hick hairstyle and earrings I'd never seen you wear. The renewal date was just a year before.

Mom called. She sounded very much frailer than I ever heard before. 'The results say it's come back,' she told me. She sounded like she'd given up. She said, 'I don't think I can do it again, not without your father.'

'I don't want to hear that from you,' I told her. 'You don't have the right to quit. There are people who want you around.'

'Being sick all the time. Not being able to eat. You remember how it was.'

'You were really brave.'

'I had your father, last time.'

I said, 'Jeez, Mom, can you imagine if he heard you talking this way? What do you think he'd say about giving up?'

'He'd want me to come to him,' she said.

I held the receiver to my chest, and smeared the tears around my face with the ball of my palm. I didn't know whether she was crying too, or if the crying was past, for her. We sat listening to each other's breathing. I wanted to go to her, but I really believed you'd come and clear out your things if I left the apartment. Mom had started to force small-talk, anyway. How was the garden? How was Rachel? I had intended to keep my mouth shut, but somehow I found myself telling her everything – the anger; the cops; how you'd been gone three days.

She said, 'I'm just going to say it. You don't need someone like her in your life. You're doing such big things. She's going to drag you down.'

'She's damaged.'

'She's damaged, exactly. Be with someone who will be good for you.'

There was anger: first a flash directed towards my mother; then self-disgust for daring to feel that way.

'We're *all* damaged. I don't want to tell you you don't understand, Mom, but I care a lot for her. She's a good person.'

'Good people do bad things too,' she said.

'But—'

'I don't care that she took your car,' she said. 'That's just money. But the police in your home? That's bad, John. You don't need that.'

'She's complicated.'

'You think I don't see that?'

'I don't know how you'd know without meeting her.'

'I don't want to meet her. I don't need to,' she said.

I told her it was OK. I thought I was reassuring her.

'No it isn't OK, John,' she said, sadly. 'Sooner you see that, the better.'

068

It was after 2 a.m. on the fourth night when you came back. You smelt of beer, and you parked the car crooked on the drive. The first I knew of it, you were there in my bed – our bed – and you threw yourself on me and I realised you were naked. I tried to speak, but you put your hand over my mouth and pulled my dick out from my shorts and put it in yourself. Only when we were fucking did you take your hand off my face. On the wall was your Uncle Sam poster: Your Country Needs YOU. When we were done, you lay down, dewy, next to me, nuzzling into the nook of my arm, and fell asleep, and I was left wide awake in the dark, looking at the stripes of moonlight on the ceiling, wondering about the OK-ness of it all.

The next day, you made breakfast, and you were funny and smart: you did an impression of Charles Baudelaire cooking an egg, and I nearly died laughing. Afterwards, you went to put on make-up in the bathroom mirror, going Cleopatra on the eyeliner for the hell of it. I kissed your shoulders and got in your light.

In the bedroom, I saw you'd thrown all your clothes – the ones you'd gone away in, and the new ones – in the trash.

My first show back was on conscription. I'd slept a coupla hours, max, and everything seemed furry. Messages on the pager or PowWow came as anagrams, and I couldn't stop yawning – every bit as fatal as hiccups or dry-out.

'Look like shit,' Galtieri informed me.

One of the guests had built up his *oeuvre* on the back of Kennedy's what-your-country-can-do-for-you speech. His argument was a socialisation of death, that the right to fight and die should not be diced up on race or gender lines, and yet it was the male underclass, that is to say black boys, who were repeatedly thrown into the meat grinder.

'Oh, my heart bleeds,' the Australian academic interrupted him. 'The male societal role is all about seeking out situations that license physical aggression. War. Domestic abuse. Contact sports. Action film fantasies. Rape.' Her voice was all over the place in pitch and volume, a killer for the guy riding the mixers. 'Your first resort, when you want to establish control, is violence, threatened or actual.'

'Let's bring it back to conscription—'

'Conscription,' she said, thumping the new table. 'It must be like winning the lotto for these men. At last they can go and hurt somebody.'

I looked around at the people I could see. Mr Pro-Kennedy was in his sixties, a moon-faced man without much hair. The professor from Berkeley, whilst younger, was the type who seemed afraid of shaking hands. I tried to imagine these guys, these men, fighting in a war. The thought made me almost laugh out loud. But she wasn't talking about that. When she said violence she meant beating on their wives at home.

067

'I have Marie from the Castro Valley on the line. Go ahead, Marie.'

'Hi, John, thanks, I listen every day. Um, I just wanna say I think President Clinton's bleeding-heart appeasement of foreign countries is gonna debase the United States and turn us into a whipping boy for the oil producers of the world.'

'And that's your point of view?'

'That's my point of view, John.'

'What do you do for a living, Marie?'

'I'm a trainee realtor.'

'Trainee realtor. OK. You're not a journalist on the side? Do you write for the papers?'

'No.'

'And you're not Chinese–American?'

'Uh—'

'The reason I ask is, this morning in the *Bay Herald*, in the political editorial section on page 7, I read the following, expressed by a writer calling themselves Lee Kwang: "President Clinton's bleeding-heart appeasement of foreign countries is gonna debase the United States and turn us into a whipping boy for the oil producers of the world." Marie, you can't possibly have imagined in your wildest tiny dreams that you would successfully pass off the views of a journalist and good friend of mine, a journalist read by eighty-four thousand readers across the Bay area, as your own?'

'Um—'

'Um indeed. Let's try again, Marie. Obviously you take an interest in this area of political governance. I want you to tell me what *you* think.'

'I... I...'

'Let me help you with those difficult first few words there, let me get you started: "I think that...'"

'I...'

'Marie, let's straighten this out. One of the fundamental rights granted to us by the founding fathers is one of free speech. There is zero point having the right to express your views if you don't have the wherewithal to formulate some thought of your own. Now I know this is turning difficult for you, Marie, trainee realtor from the Castro Valley, but of course if you hang up now, we're going to know that you are all talk, not even talk in your own words. Can you, Marie, express a political thought of your very own? And I don't want to hear the rustling of newspaper, now, Marie.'

'I think you are being unnecessarily rude. I think you are being aggressive.'

'You call in to my talk-show, I've asked for your opinion, and that offends your sensibilities.'

'I've already told you what I think.'

'No, Marie, you've told me what Lee Kwang thinks. If I wanted to know what Lee Kwang thinks, and frequently I do, then I could pick up my cell to him. Know what, why don't we call Lee Kwang right now? We can do that. Yeah, we're going to get Lee Kwang on the line. These are the growing pains of democratic free speech, Marie, it is the hurt that tells you you're alive, and believe me, you're not alive if you're living through someone else's words.'

'Says the man hosting a phone-in show.'

I hesitated, just for a beat.

'You know what, John, you can act the big man and belittle me all you want, but for all your talking, what actual good do you do?'

We had fifteen seconds to the pre-news commercials. I tried to think of something smart. Instead I thought of you and of Mom; and then there were ten seconds.

I said, 'You know what? We're gonna be right back after a word from our sponsors, on KVOC, the Voice of the Bay, 1510.'

As the ads started, I threw my headphones down. 'Fucking headshot, man.'

Behind the glass wall, the producer held his brow.

066

The hospital where Michael Lang was being kept, in a curve of Route 101 near the Mission District, was built like a drum of brick and windows – the tallest structure for miles. There was a metal halo around the topmost floor. On *ER*, hospital looked like hospital; this place was just a bunch of ordinary interconnecting rooms that could equally have been let out as offices. Instead they happened to contain a few people on gurneys; sometimes a bit of medical equipment, as if for show.

Pastor Lang led the way, past a children's ward decorated with Thanksgiving balloons, into the guts of the building. His big body filled the width and height of the corridor. He had to turn sideways to let convalescents in wheelchairs get pushed by.

The room they kept his son in was about as far from the reception as it seemed possible to go. The pastor held the doorknob, knocked twice, almost silently, and without waiting to hear anything, went in. The room was not darkened. A radio was playing. I hung back, but the pastor beckoned me with a movement of his head: come.

And, then, there he was: Michael Lang, hero of the Gulf War, lying in bed with his upper half propped up on a ramp of pillows, his eyes open and vacant, surrounded by militaria, photographs, flowers and empty packets of Cheez Doodle O's.

Mikey was twenty-four, the pastor had told me. He looked more like forty-five. As the pastor closed the door, I took a closer look at Mikey's face, which was pulled taut over the cheekbones and pitted and creased like sponge. He had alopecia, making his buzz-cut seemed moth-eaten. His wasted arms lay straight by his sides. The only sign of medical treatment was a little plastic dish full of no pills.

'Hello, John,' Mikey said.

My heart pounded.

'Can you speak?' I asked. 'I mean, is it easier—'

'It's fine,' Mikey said. It sounded like he had to work for each word. There came a pause, and then, 'I listen to your show.'

'Yeah?'

'Every day.'

The pictures in the frames were of soldiers in camouflage uniform, posing with their weapons on a sandy ridge somewhere. In one there was a pretty girl kissing a young man as they toasted the camera. I remembered the picture of my dad, winning the race. The young man had the same tattoo on his arm that Mikey Lang wore, but he didn't look like him. He was someone I'd never know.

'That your girl?' I said.

'Used to be.'

We fell into silence. I knew that silence: it was the one that precedes a revelation. Mikey composed himself: he put himself back together. He said, 'She wanted to marry me, but I wouldn't let her be a— She's too—' and then he couldn't speak.

I glanced at the pastor, but he was now sitting in the corner, in a wicker chair, with his eyes closed.

After I'd pulled up a chair, Mikey told me they'd dropped chemical bombs during Iran–Iraq, when Reagan had backed Saddam against the ayatollahs. Worse than World War One, Mikey said: mustard gas everywhere. He told me he suspected they'd prepared for chemical bombs in the Gulf this time around, too, but no one would say if they'd been used.

'They gave us pills,' he told me, while outside the insulating windows the hot sun shone and songbirds sang. 'We got vaccinations before we shipped out – and I mean a lot, like twenty different needles. That was supposed to keep us safe from diseases and chemicals; and then in theatre we were given chemical pills.'

'What were they for?'

'What were what for?' Mikey looked at me as though he'd never seen me before.

I said, 'The chemical pills you took in the Gulf.'

'The pills? No clue, man, I'm an engineer. Company medic said take 'em, we took 'em.'

Mikey Lang had been a warrant officer second class in the engineers. 'Used to build cars on the weekend when I was at school,' he said. 'Drove Dad crazy.'

'He wanted you to go into the church.'

'Nah, man, he wanted me to stop leaving grease-stains on everything. Yeah. Well, I got to the end of school and I was no academic. Did well not to flunk out. They had careers day: people came to talk about what we could do, you know? A recruiting sergeant was there. Big, tough-looking guy. Had a military cross. You see one of those? He impressed me. It was like, there was another thing you could believe in, you know? Brothers-in-arms, man.

'Out of basic I did MOS at Fort Eustis, Virginia; then I joined the 11th Armoured, stationed out of Irwin.'

'You were tank crew?'

'MT Second Platoon – that's maintenance. Field repairs on wheeled vehicles – same as I was doing before – steering gears, differentials, transmissions, the whole nine yards. All kind of vehicles.'

When I said, 'That won't do. Name five vehicles you worked on,' Mikey Lang's eyes widened. 'I have to ask you,' I said. 'If I'm going the whole way with this, I'm gonna ask.'

'Army used a lot of Humvees for pretty much everything – put Avengers on, TOW, turn 'em into ambulances – you name it. LAVs – they can be amphibious, they obviously were not in Iraq. Transports – HEMTTS, mostly – sometimes unimogs. Bikes from the base. They gave us Bradleys once, but they're tracked, outside our specialisation.'

'Have you said five yet?'

'Yes, sir, with the Humvees I've said like fifty. Army vehicles are a few base designs, lots of customisations.'

'Sorry to ask you that.'

'Sorry you felt you had to.'

We paused a little while. I knew I had to ask him about his symptoms. In radio, the subject of health can be a killer. Want the switchboard to go nuts with boring calls? Ask people how they feel.

During the pause, Mikey rolled his head my way and said, 'Did you ask me something?'

'Just now? No.'

Mikey looked at the ceiling, and a tear crawled out of the corner of his eye and into his hair.

The symptoms Mikey described started out embarrassing to listen to, but within a moment or two had made me angry. Here was a kid, mostly lucid, telling me how he was losing his hair in clumps and how, without drugs, he couldn't stop shitting himself. He was chronically fatigued, and yet couldn't sleep; for Mikey Lang, the boy who used to fix cars, life was lying in a stupor in this bed, numb in the feet and hands, his limbs painful for no known reason, his head relentlessly throbbing. His blood pressure had been climbing steadily since admission, Mikey told me: it was now equivalent to that of an unfit sixty-year-old, so he was on beta blockers, which made him sweat constantly. His hands had started to shake. The nurse said the only other time she'd seen nervous decline in someone so young was a girl who'd injected herself with horse tranquilliser in search of a high, who now couldn't raise her hand. The prognosis was decline and, if nothing changed – and there was no reason to suppose it would – death from cardiac arrest or stroke, or maybe from another illness, since Mikey's immune system seemed to be shot.

'Why'd you join up?' I said. I realised I was holding his hand. 'If you want to stay alive, why join the freakin' army?'

Mikey said, 'I love my country.'

'Yeah, *I* love my country,' I said. 'It never made want to go to Iraq and shoot people.'

The pastor said, 'If there are ethical or moral reasons why you don't feel able—'

'I just need to understand, that's all.'

'Didn't you ever believe in something?' said Mikey. 'Freedom of speech. You always talk about that. You do what you can, right? I'm good at fixing vehicles. I put my skill in the service of the United States.'

'Even if it cost you your life?'

'Some things are bigger than that,' he said. His breath was really irregular, now, and he'd started to whiten.

Pastor Lang said, 'Let's break off for now.'

'Army let us down, John. We believed they were taking care of us.'

'Mikey,' I said, 'I'll do what I can. I promise you.'

'It isn't just me,' he managed. 'It isn't just me.' And then he couldn't keep his head raised.

When you spend your whole time performing feeling, it's easy to forget what feeling is. Man, I could sneeze on-air and if I didn't hit the dead-switch in time I'd get letters from housewives in freaking Queens offering traditional cold remedies and sympathy, and handwritten letters from eccentrics in Chicago telling me about cousins of theirs who'd had a cough and been dead within the week, and meanwhile Warrant Officer Second Class Mikey Lang suffered quietly, in a hospital room no one knew about: a man without a voice.

'We have to do this right,' I told the pastor, when we got down to the ward lobby. 'My main trouble is gonna be getting Mikey on to the show at all. The station won't want to take that kind of chance.'

'I understand. But we have to get started, if we're going to do it. No one's giving us a timeline on this thing.'

'I know that. Look, I'm no investigative journalist. Best way I can help you is to make some theatre, get people talking.'

I left Pastor Lang in the lobby of Male Acute, and I walked down the antiseptic-smelling corridors thinking about how easy it was to put one foot in front of the other; to breathe; to speak.

065

The year turned. The year grew. Coasting through the hills of Cali to Alice in Chains, I drummed one hand on the hot car roof. The sky was an ocean, and the sea mist spilled over the hilltops on the horizon. Below it, the hills were brown patchy scrub with rock poking through like bone from a wound.

On Wenden Hook, I pulled the car up and looked out over the land. Vineyards clothed the opposite slope. Nearer to, tyre ruts led off the road and wound their way to a broad wooden shack that looked as if someone might live there. A wheelbarrow leant against the front wall. I'd kept a jay in my glovebox. I listened to Pantera and Nine Inch Nails on Casey Miles' show on KROC, and wondered about the life of the person in that shack. When I closed my eyes, the clouds raced across the sky and the cold seasons lasted longer, and the track off the road led into the forest, to a clearing occupied by a crooked house with a blank gaze. Being there made me feel desperate. I shivered. On Wenden Hook it was sixty-five, even with the sun lost behind the thick grey gnarled skin of the cloudscape. Heat rose up off the asphalt and the red dirt, and the nodding spines of the bunchgrass and sedge were hot to the touch.

I drove the PCH with the top down. After a while I turned off, and then I was driving among low buildings. At first, they were sparse; after a while the buildings were closer together and taller and had fire escapes and sometimes big glass fronts. The trees were incorporated into sidewalks. The sky was boxed above the stop lights. Everywhere I drove, there were people living lives: loading rental trucks, or watching the world from benches, or buying fries at In-N-Out.

You were away. This was back in the early days, when you'd only just started to need to go to week-long conferences far out of the state. There was calm in the place. The first night, I'd watched

The Crow and drunk beer and slept on the couch; after that, I missed you too much and called you in Atlanta, but you didn't answer. Now when I got home the apartment was a place where you weren't. Every room: no you. Your black velveteen jacket hung on the back of the bedroom chair, and your sandals, the inners imprinted with the shape of your feet, lay by the front door. I picked up the sandals and smelt them.

There was a knock on the door. My skin turned goosey.

Mom hadn't been to the apartment since you'd moved in, and deliveries always came before lunch. Fuck, not the cops? I thought about how I'd been driving after the jay. I tried to recollect whether I'd seen the blue-and-white anywhere along my route. Maybe they'd picked up the roach off the side of the road and followed me all the way here. Maybe without knowing it I'd mown down pedestrians by the dozen, slapping the paintwork in time to 'Check My Brain' and thinking what a great place San Mateo County was all the while.

The knock came again. It was harder, this time.

I opened the door.

The guy with the beard had stood well back, and was checking the upper windows when he realised I'd opened up. He was younger than his clothes. There were dark fans of sweat in the armpits of his blue shirt.

He looked at me. For the longest moment, I had the impression we'd been separated a long, long time, and now were reunited; but I didn't recognise him. He held himself like an office clerk.

'You're John Knox.' He said it maintaining very solid eye contact. His hands were held like a gunfighter's. I wasn't sure whether I wanted to be John Knox or not.

'Who are you?'

'Are you John Knox?' he said, slowly.

I knew all about stalkers acting like this when they went after the object of their delusions – we'd done shows on the Orange County murders, and that crazy who killed the actress out of *My Sister Sam*. They watched and got very excited and then did something insane and people ended up dead. At the station they filtered my mail for that kind of stuff. Maybe this guy had been writing me for months.

I said, 'I can't really talk right now.'

He said, 'Yeah, you're him. I know your voice.' I guess I'd started backing behind the door, because he said, 'It's OK, I don't want any trouble.' A little boy, maybe four years old, was playing with a bit of grass in the driveway.

'What do you want, man?'

'You have to understand I don't bear you any malice at all, and I swear I won't ever come here again. I just had to this one time.'

'OK.' Now I was damned sure he was going to shoot me.

'You're involved with someone called Rachel McAllistair, aren't you?'

'There are laws against this, dude.'

'We're just talking.' His hair was cut into a Caesar, and his pants were plaid. 'You do know her, though, right?'

I got brave or something, and shut the door with me on the outside, and advanced up the driveway towards him.

'Wait,' he said, showing me his hands. 'Wait, I told you I don't want trouble, seriously. We've been through enough already.'

'We?'

'Me and Dylan.' He meant the kid. 'That's my boy, Dylan.'

Dylan was a cute kid, and totally unaware of what was passing between the grown-ups.

I stopped where I was. Dylan's dad breathed a little better. 'I tried to stay away, but a friend of mine saw a picture of you both in *Variety* and I thought, that's her—'

'You mean Rachel?'

'My wife,' he said.

Time stretched and elongated and twisted out of all shape. I said, 'Nah, that's just – that doesn't…' but I knew already that this was real.

He simply held my gaze.

Fuck, my darling.

I stood there with your husband that day feeling like I fucking stole you, or something, like I didn't have a right to my own life.

'I don't know what to say.'

He said, 'There's nothing to say.'

The plates on the Lincoln said 'TENN' in blue letters.

'She's never said…' The sentence stuck in my throat.

'Yeah.'

'Fuck.'

He'd brought some pictures. I didn't want to look at them, but I looked at them. It was like it had been with my dad: a whole secret life, lived by someone I thought I knew. You'd worn black on your wedding day. My legs wouldn't support me. I sank to the path and sat there. Frankly, if the guy had wanted to blow my brains out or kick me to death he could have done it with the greatest of ease right then, but there was no weapon unless you counted the photographs of you. Instead he sat down with me on the path, and Dylan came over and sat in his lap and told him about the apartment building.

I gabbled a little, and he talked over me – to save my dignity, I think. I had no right to that. He told me he wasn't proud of it, but he'd tracked you down through his job with the IRS.

'What did she do? Just walk out?' I asked him.

'Two years ago, nearly. One afternoon. We'd gotten through a lot of difficult times – she got very angry about stuff – but we were through that and I thought everything was going to be OK. Then one day I came home and she'd gone. Took the car, and just went. No Dear John, nothing.'

The afternoon was still. One of the deadbeats from the top apartment came by, acknowledging us suspiciously before entering the building.

'Does she still get angry?' your husband said.

'Yeah, she gets angry,' I said. 'Look, man, this is nuts. How do we deal with this?'

'I don't know; I didn't think beyond getting here.'

'She's in Atlanta right now, talking about Soviet poster art.'

He repeated the city name back. It was like half his bones had dissolved.

Dylan said, 'What's Atlanta?'

After a while I said, 'So is Dylan—'

'He's ours.'

I said, 'You wanna come in?'

'No.' He rubbed the back of his neck. 'My name's Maxwell, by the way.'

'John.'

We seemed nearly to shake hands. Then I said, 'I gotta ask you something. This whole anger thing – she ever, uh…' I jerked my head towards Dylan.

Maxwell shook his head. 'Nah, man. 'Part from walking out. That was big enough.'

'Right.'

'Look, I'm gonna go. Here's my number.'

'You drove all this way.'

'Yeah, I'm gonna go. I shouldn't have come here.'

We all got up, and Maxwell shepherded Dylan back to their Lincoln, hesitating a couple of times along the way.

It was all about Maxwell and Dylan, right then; I hadn't even begun to have feelings towards you. I knew if I let feelings come, they'd rip up everything. Maxwell was back in the car, and I wanted so much for him to understand that you'd never said a word about him or his kid, or about that life, whatever that life had been, but I knew that to say so could only cause him pain. What would I have wanted, in his place? Cold-blooded fact, or room for a little doubt? Something told me maybe I would have wanted to know. I'd have wanted to see the life you were living and know you were making a career for yourself. So I guess the reason I didn't tell Maxwell that stuff was because I was a coward. I wasn't protecting him: I was protecting me.

'You want me to pass her a message, or something?' I said.

Maxwell gunned the engine. 'Tell her if she ever wants to, she can come home,' he said. 'But I don't think she ever will.'

'I'll tell her.'

'Will you?' he said. 'Really? I mean, why would you?' In the kiddie seat, Dylan waved at some imaginary thing through the window. Maxwell said, 'Don't say stuff you don't mean, man. It's just false hope. That's wrong.'

'Look after your kid, there,' I said.

'Promise me you'll take care of her?'

'I'm doing my best.'

What would you have thought, if you could have seen the two of us talking, then? Your life, decompartmentalised. Oh, you'd have gone crazy. You'd have turned into a whirlwind, and you'd have smashed everything in sight.

After Maxwell and Dylan had gone, I tried to make myself understand, but couldn't. He looked like a normal guy, but maybe there were things about Maxwell I couldn't guess: reasons why you'd chosen to absent yourself from him without warning. What had the feminist professor said? Something about control.

Where were you, at that moment? In Atlanta, maybe; or maybe not. Who were you with? Thinking about it tied my mind in knots. You weren't here.

I bunched my hands to hit something, but there was nothing to hit. I thought about going to some bar and taking a girl to bed.

I went back into the house, and looked at the phone, which I knew wouldn't ring, however long I waited for it to, and I told myself, no you don't. No you don't.

064

'Kyle in the Tendernob, go ahead.'

'Yo, John, my man, you're talking about games we play? I play a game. When I see people using a crosswalk but they're walking off of the stripes, I actually speed up my car and see if I can get them because legally that's their fault.'

'What a great, socially minded pastime.'

'Yeah.'

'You're from the Darwinist school of thinking?'

'Yeah, man. I hit 'em up if they're, you know, from the dark side.'

'Are you a Jedi, Kyle? What are you talking about?'

'If they're nizzles.'

'OK, fantastic, so we're moving away from natural selection towards social engineering. Am I detecting a little pleasure in the important function you're performing, Kyle?'

'Yeah, it's cool, just like bucking 'em. I drive a four-by-four, so they gotta recognise.'

'That's right, there's nothing quite like trying to run your car over a Negro.'

'That's it, my man.'

'You are putting me out of a job, my friend. You are self-satirising. Let me give it a shot, though: Good news to all non-white listeners – race-hate now delivers! You can save yourself and your loved ones the hassle of going into town and being abducted by a braying supremacist mob: instead why not let Kyle in the Tendernob run you down right outside your own front door? And don't you worry, K-K-Kyle says it's all completely legal. That's because our friend Kyle is a homicidal, racist bama! Has Kyle gone? What a shame. Dear listener, I can't use most of the words I'd like to use to describe Kyle because I'd be taken off air. You might want to call in with some of those words, but you know what: there are times when the most elegant response is silence. I say we let the SFPD do their work on Kyle's telephone number, which my producer will be faxing to them during the next call. Dwayne in Santa Barbara, you're up after these short audio documentaries about capitalism.'

The FCC were so delighted by the phrase 'there's nothing quite like trying to run your car over a Negro' they gave me a five-thousand-dollar fine and a day's suspension.

So the production meetings got tougher and the number of suits increased, and the ratings climbed. We were going out to six US cities on FM by summer of '95. South of the station, in San Jose, the tech industry was multiplying like bacteria in a dish, and the Rolling Stones gig had shown us we could go global if we could figure out streaming. There was now a lot of money tied up in what I said.

I wasn't really a shock-jock. I didn't try to outrage decency. I wanted to make things better. I tried once a fortnight to get the Langs' story on to the schedule, but Panagakos, who owned the station, thought it would make him the wrong sort of enemies. My ratings were getting difficult for him to argue with. The morning I came in with a nosebleed and a split lip, I started the show with, 'Life is like a box of chocolates: bad for you. I'm John Knox, and this is my show.' We got a warning shot from Paramount's lawyers by bike *that afternoon*, and then I knew it was getting big.

We'd moved out of the little apartment and were renting the big house in Pacific Heights by then. There was supposed to be a heat-wave on, but the city has its own cooling system that works just fine: the fogs that rise up around mid-morning and wash across the Bay area, keeping the temp in the mid-twenties. Sunset and Richmond, you're permanently socked in with fog. The place in Pacific Heights had a pretty view down the hill to the waterfront, and, beyond the wide bay, flecked with yachts, and Alcatraz, receding hill ranges becoming bluer as they vanished into the far distance. On an afternoon, I could go out on our rented balcony with a copy of the *Chronicle* in my lap and a whisky sour and watch the container ships inch by. Christ, that place bored the shit out of me.

The best thing about the house in the Heights was that there were a few yards of thick air between us and the houses around us. I could put 'Heart Shaped Box' retching out of the stereo and no one would come banging on the walls; also you couldn't be heard the times you started screaming.

There was a grandfather clock in the hallway. It came as part of the deal, and it ticked like a lifetime.

063

You refused to help me with Mikey Lang outright, or even hear about it. You said, 'My whole work is on imagery around war. If I take sides, that's all my military contacts gone in a second. It's your show. You figure it out.'

It took me a long while to come around to the idea that you were right. Trouble was, I was a talk-show presenter, not a journalist. No one ever understood the distinction, and it sounded lame as an excuse, even to me. I didn't know how to do much except talk.

And now you were pregnant, and I wanted you so much. You were powerful. You could do real damage, now. You were the most orderly, sullen, happy, beautiful, eccentric pregnant woman there ever was; you didn't get morning sickness and you did go through a phase that involved eating a lot of lobster, although I kind of suspected that that was just because you wanted more lobster. You already ate more lobster than any other historian in the world. You watched British romantic comedies and tried to hide that you were crying. And there were a lot of times when we fucked out of frustration, or in anger, or in love, or in desperation. Eyes shut, I can still trace the outline of your body.

You were a bomb, ticking. Except bombs don't tick, right? – that's just in cartoons. Really bombs just go off when you least expect them to, and rip down everything around them. You asked me why we didn't see my friends, and it was because of all the apologising I had to do whenever we had seen them. I couldn't tell you that. The bomb would've gone off, again. How's Rachel? they'd ask. You guys have been together – how long, now? I'd tell them six months or a year, or one and a half, and I'd always be amazed that so much time had flown by. They'd tentatively ask whether things were better between us – they'd be thinking of the time when I'd had to stay overnight with them, or enlist their help in checking hospitals, or ask them to apologise to women at awards ceremonies while I smuggled you out into the car. Things were OK, I'd say. Things were getting better. But they didn't suggest meeting up any more.

I couldn't ever trust I'd see you again, from one hour to the next. I'd learned not to have trust in anything, including that I'd ever see our baby born. It was a hand-to-mouth love.

'You want me to be a friend to you?' said Barney.

It was a hot day. We were on a boardwalk in the harbour. Barney was dressed for Hawaii, in doggers and huarache sandals and a Pendleton; I could've passed for Cobain. The air was alive with the shrieking of seabirds.

'This going to involve you saying something I don't want to hear?'

Barney was attaching a coloured float to a hook. 'So you know what I'm talking about.'

I leant over and looked down the lazy lines into the water. The spume and the shade cast by the pier made it impossible to see if there were fish down there; but there were plenty of guys of all ages up and down the boardwalk, casting and tending their rods, or slumped into folding chairs, or standing looking out to sea.

'You ever catch anything like this?' I asked Barney.

'Few sharks,' he said.

'Right. Orcas, maybe? What about the great white whale?'

'Them too.'

'And all with this little net?' I marvelled. 'You are a talented angler, my friend.'

'She's gonna kill ya, John.'

'Yeah, I don't want to have this conversation so much.'

Barney heaved his ass out of his little chair, and held the rod high, attaching the bait like someone hanging a bell on a Christmas tree. Then he did a thing like cracking a whip, and I felt the weight buzz my face as it flew out over the water. We heard the plop as it dropped in, and then Barney adjusted the reel and leant the rod against the rail.

'You should try this, some time,' he said, collapsing back into the chair. 'Hodad like you.'

'Are you actually trying to catch anything? These other guys are – I don't know… Doing stuff.'

'You want me to look busier?' Barney slipped a sip out of his flask, and offered me some.

I'd been expecting Irish whiskey, and it tasted far wrong. It tasted like tomato juice.

'It's tomato juice,' Barney said. We traded long glances. 'Which conversation you want to have first?'

I sat on the rail.

'I know you don't like Rachel,' I said.

Barney said, 'Doesn't matter what I think. You've gotten old since you knew her. When's the last time you felt good?'

'That's bullshit, right off. We have good things between us.'

'OK.'

Big groups of Japanese flocked by, photographing everything.

'You're loyal,' said Barney.

'Loyal is good.'

'Meh.' He shrugged, like some Jewish comedian.

'Meh what?'

'Meh-be you should think about fucking someone else instead.'

I said, 'Is that supposed to be funny?'

'Yeah,' said Barney. 'No. Not really. Who's gonna tell you if I don't? Obviously you're attracted to her. She can count up to three, which I know you like, she's got the vamp thing going on, and she's a challenge. And God knows you love a challenge. She sucks you off three times a day, I don't know. But listen to me, there are people who've got all of that *and* who have positive energies and by whom you'll be supported and nurtured in what you do, and made to feel good, and you know, it's not her. You can't just ignore that.'

'We have a good life.'

'Sure, in that big house. When do I get an invite there, anyway? Doesn't matter. But that's you, not her. You've set sail and she's back there drilling holes in the boat.'

I said, 'So just quit on people? Trade up, now I'm doing well?' The sun was uncomfortably hot, even in the late afternoon.

He looked genuinely hurt. 'I'm pointing out you have options.'

'I might actually be able to help her.'

'That what you're doing with Rachel? Helping her?'

'Is she my charity case? No. She's the person I fell in love with.'

'Well, what I'm saying is that there are better people.'

I told him, 'That's about the edge, right there.'

'There's a kid I was seeing, told me about his ex-boyfriend – used to knock him all around. I mean, put him in traction twice. You never met someone who was more protective over the good name of their partner than this kid.'

Playing a drumbeat on the rail, I said, 'Great human interest; I'd go for the queers-have-feelings-too angle if it were on the show, stir up the right. Nothing to do with my situation.' The nearest fisherman was staring at us. I stared back, better.

Barney chuckled. 'You're choosing not to see.'

'I'm wondering what the fuck you think Rachel is going to do. She's seeing a therapist, we're working through our problems.'

'You're working through *her* problems. She's married, and she still thinks you don't know…'

'OK, whatever.' I was on my feet. 'You know what, we're done, all right? I love the woman you're talking about. If you can't respect that—'

'John, I'm trying to look out for you.'

'I know what the fuck you're doing. You know what? She *told* me you'd try something like this.'

I was talking too loud, now. Every atom in me was splitting. I walked backwards down the boardwalk, leaving Barney and his pointless fishing, shouting, 'I am not quitting on her. Maybe if your life wasn't such a pathetic mess you'd stop shitting on mine. Long overdue you fucking dried out.'

Everyone was watching me, and I didn't care. Everyone, that is, but Barney, who stood with his head bowed and his gut hanging out, in amongst the other fishermen. He didn't look up. I wanted to shout other things, but I had nothing. When it got too much to look at him, I turned and nearly crashed into a bunch of kids on rollerblades, and I shoved one of them, and I slammed into the car and cut a path on to the streets of the city.

062

The argument with Barney burned inside me for days, and the days turned into weeks. Our new house in the Heights reverberated with the sound of cracked ice and no phones ringing.

You were away a lot more than you had been. You were asked to attend a conference, even though you hated talking to people; then you were asked to attend another. You were vague about whether they wanted you to give an address, or whether you were there to make up the numbers, and of course I didn't push it, partly because anything having to do with status was pretty much guaranteed to tip us into disaster, but mostly because you'd wear that crocodile non-smile that told me we were on real thin ice. When you came back – the first time from New York, the next time from Cambridge, England – you were more industrious and angrier. Everyone else was way ahead of you, you'd say, especially on the Middle East. Not having Arabic was a handicap, and they were laughing at you. You tried to convince me it was OK to drink just a little wine.

After the third conference, in London, you came home with your legs in ribbons.

Every morning John Knox spoke in my voice to seven states of the union, and we made radio. Letters and calls of complaint were up; so were plaudits. John Knox was unnecessarily aggressive. John Knox was hilarious. When I pulled the mic arm down to my mouth and said the words, 'I'm John Knox, telling it like it is,' I was John Knox, and I was ready for war.

The higher you rise, the greater the number of people who want to knock you down, and the bigger the bad guys get. The battles got nastier. A seventeen-stone ex-con attempted to murder Dennis Schwartz of the *New Yorker* by strangulation in the studio. Callers routinely threatened to cut my throat. Smarter callers made their threats longer, to try to work around the ten-second delay. Or they took time to paste it in little letters on to paper and post it to the station.

And there were voices. It was all voices: the voices of producers – Galtieri, Jenna, Dick Guppy; voices of sponsors offering dental insurance and senior care, until the show got big and the voices got younger and blacker and talked about jeans and job boards and PlayStations. There was the macho voice, belonging to a grey-haired voiceover artist who said, 'John Knox,' making the long vowels growl and my name sound like the definitive answer. The studio was sterile. The voices were clamorous and dirty: teeming, inexhaustible humanity.

The days were long, like I couldn't shut my eyes. Porsche gave me a '57 Spyder for recording a TV commercial, on condition I drive it. It was a better car than Galtieri drove. I used to take it out on Seventeen Mile Drive, past that single tree on the clifftop they got there, and on Highway 1 down the coast road, over the high bridge at Big Sur, down past San Simeon, in among the lush hillsides with their burnt earth and sometimes eagles high up in the blue.

I drove alone in the Mohave and watched storms coming from hours away.

Someone smart once said that the big danger is you might end up where you're headed. Truth is, I feared you, and I don't think you ever realised how much. I can't tell you – I never did tell you – how many times there were when I was ready to leave you. But you were either talking about drinking bathroom cleaner or about running your car into the sea, or else you were cool and amazing, and those moments were too precious. You were the perfect pair of handcuffs. Once I kept my foot on the floor on the Five and then the Ten, and I played *Dookie* and *Mother's Milk* and I drove all night, and by the time my show was due to start I'd gotten to Tucson, Arizona.

'You're fucking where?' was what Galtieri said, an hour before we were due to go out.

I was hanging off a Bell Pacific booth outside a roadside shack that sold gas and snacks. A truck full of pigs was filling up. A guy in overalls was sweeping dust out front.

'Nowhere near the studio,' I told him.

'Have you quit?'

'No.'

'Sounds like you quit. Sounds like you walked out on your own show.'

'Oh, fuck you, G, it's not like that.'

'Don't call me fucking G,' said Galtieri – he'd gone falsetto through rage. The phone blipped, so I fed it more quarters. He said, 'I'll tell you what it's like. It's like you not being at the microphone in fifty-two minutes from now. It's like my job, your job, and the jobs of the nine people who work on your show.'

'Stop shouting, man,' I told him.

'Stop *shouting*?'

'G, you don't understand, OK. I got stuff going on. My mom's sick—'

'So you talk to me. You don't disappear.'

'It's talking that's the problem. I need not to talk.'

That made him shut up. Freightliners bowled by on the Interstate. 'All right,' he said, eventually. 'All right. This is one time only. We're gonna have serious technical problems here. They'll be my fault.'

'Thank you, G.'

'I told you don't call me fucking G. I hate that. Understand this: it happens again, I hang you out to dry. Got that?'

'I got it.'

'See you tomorrow morning at six-thirty, John,' said Galtieri.

061

'They're just old war wounds,' I breezed, to the air-conditioned group of men around the boardroom table at KVOC.

The owner's main avatar was an upright type, trained in law. He said, 'This is the second time in a month you've come into this room with facial injuries. We need to discuss your lifestyle.'

'Yeah,' I agreed. 'You could shove my lifestyle up your ass as well if you want. How about that? Can we get back to planning my show?'

'*Our* show,' said one of the other avatars, an older one. 'You are a station employee. You think you're the only person capable of hosting a radio show, John?'

'Lemme handle this,' said Galtieri. Galtieri had never had much of a sense of humour, and since the show had gotten big he had even less of one. I tried to interrupt and he said, 'John, shut your fucking mouth for once. Gentlemen, as senior producer here, let me talk this over with the talent – that's you, John. OK with everyone?'

'We'll need to hear back on this issue.'

'And so you will,' Galtieri said. 'OK if we move on for now?'

After the meeting, Galtieri told me we were going for something to eat. In his Alfa, he didn't say a word; just shoved the gearshift up through the scale as we ran the red lights all the way down to a pool hall on Fourth Street. It was a wide-open sports bar smelling of beer and salsa. I saw Galtieri hadn't chosen it for the ambience – there were TVs everywhere you looked – but because of the total lack of media eavesdroppers. We ordered burgers we didn't want.

'So I'm good cop,' he said. 'Try me.'

I'd spent the whole damned trip holding on to the dash for dear life, trying to work out how I was going to explain having a black eye yet again. Facial cuts, too. Anything to do with drink or drugs, and I'd be out on my ass. On the East Coast I could have come into work with needles hanging out of my arms – it was probably mandatory – but there was just no way here. The station owner had a granola business. I preached non-violence. There were no easy outs.

I mentally flipped through a catalogue of improbable domestic accidents and contact sports. But mostly I thought of you, beautiful you, pregnant you (you'd started to show, and it suited you), hurling my clothes out of the bedroom window, picture-glass exploding against the walls. The sound of you breaking everything in the kitchen while Billy Corgan of Smashing Pumpkins screamed about his rage. That was a year of my life, that ballet of revenges. A year of yours. Oh, Rachel. It doesn't get easier to think about those things, my darling.

One time Kimberly, the producer who often took sick days, whose husband never came to station parties, told me if I ever needed to talk, I could talk to her. 'It isn't your fault,' she said. 'You don't have to feel like it is, you know?'

You were getting counselling and I thought I could take whatever you threw at me – in both senses. I could be strong for both of us. I told her I didn't know what she was talking about.

There were times I sat in the car outside the house in Pacific Heights, just like I used to do outside the apartment in Potrero, cloaked in the shade of the trees, with a gulf of traffic between you and me – sometimes for hours. I'd listen to the aria 'When I Am Laid In Earth' from *Dido and Aeneas*, a plangent mezzo-soprano mourning the brevity of existence; and Ella singing 'Gloomy Sunday'; and, when I'd gotten drunk enough, Van Halen or whatever bull got me up and ballsy. That feeling as I got out of the car and realised how far the whisky had gone, as I crossed the peaceful street braced for war – that was how life felt, in the months towards the end.

The one thing I couldn't tell Galtieri was the truth. I did free weights twice a week, and you were half my size. So I said the black eye – and the one a couple of weeks before – had come from problems I had with my eldest brother, Mark. Oh, I invented a whole backstory of schizophrenia for my made-up brother. I'm really proud I had to do that. First I claimed he was mentally sick, and then I made up a story about how we – you and me – were trying to do the best for him, but he turned nasty sometimes.

After I'd finished my story, Galtieri considered me. The silence went on while the server took away our plates, and came back to take away the glasses, and then came back to wipe the table down. The compulsion to fill the silence with more details was hard to fight. Finally, Galtieri said to me, 'My son is schizophrenic.'

Someone scored in some sports game somewhere in the world, and about half the patrons around us sent up a cheer. Some guy whooped.

'You have a son?'

Galtieri said yeah, he had a son. Twelve years old. The kid was kept awake by voices telling him to do stuff he knew he shouldn't do – taking stuff, hurting other kids, sometimes worse. It was, like, unheard of. They were having to medicate, and they'd increased the dose four times, but it wasn't working. Any more, and he wouldn't be able to learn. Still the school wanted to throw him out. Galtieri and his wife were at their wits' end.

'So I understand where you're coming from, OK?' he told me. 'But these suits, for them, you're product. Me too. Gotta keep the personal stuff personal.'

While he went to the restroom, I closed my eyes and you were somewhere near by and I was sitting on a chair at home, with a horizontal plane of flashing metal moving towards me. I tilted my head, curious. It was a candlestick, coming at me in slo-mo. I wasn't gonna have time to get out of its path.

A hand on my shoulder made me spasm, and I was back in the restaurant. The pain remained. Galtieri was putting his jacket on.

'I appreciate you being on the level with me,' he said. 'Takes a man to do that.'

'Tell it like it is, right?'

He didn't reply.

On the way home, I stopped at a public phone.

I said, 'I've got to be sure – did she ever hurt him?'

'Never laid a hand on him, if that's what you mean,' said Maxwell.

060

The fourth time I saw Mikey Lang, his state had deteriorated some. His skin had gotten that fishlike transparency human beings get when they're really going under.

When he opened his eyes, he said, 'Fuck happened to you, man?'

The thought of making up more lies made me feel sick. 'Fight,' I told him. Which was sort of true.

'Thought you said you were a pacifist.'

'Yeah. Apparently that doesn't stop you getting in fights.'

Mikey raised a weak smile. 'Man, he did a number on you.'

Having a black eye in the hospital made me feel validated. I'm ashamed to admit it, but it's true. My black eye could have happened in a car wreck which I had miraculously survived, or maybe rescuing a kid out of a burning building. One thing is for sure: we all have stories. The stories that happened, the stories we tell and the stories other people tell about us. Maybe I was the guy who'd gotten into a bar brawl. I probably wasn't the guy whose girlfriend had done this to him. No, that story probably wasn't getting told.

I took the stairs – *Speed* had put me off elevators. When I came out on to the ground floor, a security guard took the time to look me up and down. I guess no one uses stairs. I passed around a phalanx of what looked like trainee doctors, and then I was face to face with someone coming the other way down the passage. We both stopped dead.

'Hi,' I said.

You looked at me like you'd slice me up with your eyes if you could; and you could. Before either of us had spoken, I fell in love with you all over again.

'What are you doing here?' you said, looking behind me for clues.

'Visiting a…' The security guard was still close. 'Actually this isn't the place to talk about it, I'll tell you outside. What about you?'

'Oh my God, that's John Knox,' someone informed their friend, as they passed.

'No it isn't.'

'Sure it is.' They'd stopped now.

'Are you coming or going?' I asked you.

You said, 'Going. I'm parked catawampus from Twenty-third and—'

'Parked what?'

'On the other corner. I want to know why you're here.' You were speaking pretty loud. The fans were pushing each other and saying, *No, you ask him.*

We were in the way of a gurney and even when the nurses asked you to move off your spot, you resisted.

'I came to visit a friend.'

'Who?'

'What does it matter who?' This whole Mikey Lang thing was too important to blow it through eavesdroppers. 'Look, I'm going for coffee, come with me.' And I headed out towards coffee.

I hadn't expected you to fall into step with me, and you didn't. But when I'd gotten served a latte in a coffee shop in Potrero and had drunk most of it, and read the sports pages of the *Chronicle* too, and thought what Barney would have said if I knew him any more, you showed up outside the window. I'd never been to that coffee shop before. I don't know how you figured I was there.

You didn't want coffee, so we hunched over the dregs of mine, like kids in a bar. 'I'm sorry,' you said, holding my hands in yours.

'It's OK. I just couldn't talk there. I was meeting a guy for a future show… That's the soldier I've been trying to tell you about. He's sick. I've been trying to get the army to talk to us about what made him that way. Him and a lot of others. No one's listening to the exposés, so I'm tryin'a create something dramatic.'

Your eyes were wide. You kissed me on the lips, and the kiss was long, and you meant it.

'What was that for?'

'Because you're wonderful.'

Rachel, do you remember you said that about me, once?

You said, 'I've been at a rally for the troops supporting the Kurds.'

You sat there shining at me, holding my hands – looking at me like I was your hero. It filled the world with honey, it made me want you. My show was done for the day; the next day was the weekend. I suggested we should maybe go to a hotel someplace upstate.

'So you can use me for your sexual gratification?' you said. 'OK.'

I said, 'So what about you?'

'What about me?'

'Why were you at the hospital?'

Your expression clouded. You fished about in your satchel for something you couldn't find, quite probably on account of the amount of shit also in there, and it became the most important quest any woman had ever been on. Mascara; chopsticks; an Indian scarf; an anthology of war poetry – everything from Balaclava to Mogadishu. While you excavated further, I read some lines out of the book.

The summing-up: false histories
Of duty done that never was
A trade in limbs for liberty,
The ambulance, the boat across
No more to issue 'charge' and 'fire'
To friendless pals, who passed alone
Regathered in the Flanders' mire
The lowest hell: the coming home

'That's kinda good,' I said. The poet was James Lyons. 'I think Mikey Lang might like this. The guy I was visiting.' The pile of bag-crap on the table was now enormous. It seemed way bigger than the capacity of the bag. 'So what is it you're looking for in there, exactly?'

'It doesn't matter.'

'I see that.'

A rectangle of paper dropped clear of the bag. It said 'prescription'.

You went white when you saw it, and tried to get it into the bag before I could see what it said. The speed with which you were dumping the stuff back into your bag told me what was going to happen next.

'Aw, don't do this,' I said.

'Do what?'

'Run away again. It's getting a little boring.'

'No one's asking you to follow.'

'I'm actually begging you. Stay and talk with me, will you, this one time? We live in the same place. What use is running away?'

'I ain't ever in my life run away,' you hissed, getting up. I grabbed on to your wrist, and immediately felt the eyes of other people in the café on me. Done by a man, grabbing's thuggery. I hadn't grabbed someone since kiss-chase when I was five.

I apologised to you. 'Please will you sit down?'

Where you stood, the afternoon light from the door gave you an aura. You looked down on me like a sad angel. 'I warned you I was damaged goods,' you said, ruefully. 'Physically and mentally: *I am fucked*.'

The waitress came back. It seemed to cow you into sitting down. You fished out the prescription and laid it in front of me, and in your eyes was triumph.

I looked from you to the script, and back.

You said, 'So I've started with a new so-called therapist.'

'Hence the hospital.'

'It's where he works.'

A few months earlier, I might have challenged how you could pay for that, but I knew better than to ask. Maybe I didn't want to know.

'Anyway, it's a lot of bullshit,' you were telling me. 'He doesn't know what he's talking about. None of them do. There was a cushion on a chair when I went in and I was like, no, please God don't tell me to talk to that like it's my brother or my mother or whatever, and he was like, you're familiar with that form of therapy, and I was like, yes thank you, it's a Gestalt method, they tried that already, it doesn't work on me; then it was a half-hour of word association – *what do I associate with the word darkness* – the cunt – and checking whether maybe I was just feeling a little sad or on the fucking rag or something. I was like, have you actually bothered to read my records? So at last he reads them, and he's like, oh, I see you've had a diagnosis of clinical depression, so I'm like, no, it's not post-partum depression, I don't have any drug or drink addiction, I wasn't abused as a child, I'm just fucking *nuts*. Your next move is to write me a note for a bunch of tricyclics that will make me fall asleep all the time and won't work or maybe, if I'm really lucky, some SSRIs that won't make me fall asleep but also won't work.'

I felt proud of you – grudgingly. You were the client out of hell.

'So… what did he say to that?'

'What they always say. We've got this new drug, it's been getting very good results.'

'This one?'

'That one.'

I looked at the piece of paper.

'So there you go,' you said, with venom.

'Don't say damaged goods.'

You smiled – a smile like you'd just come. 'Ah, you're starting to know me.'

'Maybe.'

'You should really get away.'

We held hands across the table. I said, 'It's tough sometimes, you know that. But people have gotten through worse. I promised you, and I meant it: I won't give up on you.'

The way you met my eye was more intense than I ever remembered. 'Please, John,' you said, 'please be sure of that.'

059

Most of the journalists who came to interview me knew the ropes, but sometimes they'd send a kid. One got so embarrassed I basically had to interview myself into her tape recorder; another one, whose gender I spent the whole interview trying to figure out, insisted I was hypocritical to talk about equal rights when I was a white male with a privileged upbringing. When the interview was printed, I had been described as 'overbearing, cocksure and intransigent'. He or she described how I'd been leering at his or her body, and implied that I'd thought my celebrity status would gain me a conquest. I prayed you wouldn't come across this bullshit. It would have been all you needed to go postal.

After the sexism interview, a short bald man in a buttoned-up shirt and pebble specs materialised at my elbow, bitching about the traffic. He was a publicist, he said. He felt I might want to talk to him. He tried to show me something out of his briefcase, but he couldn't get the combination to work. 'My mother's birthdate,' he told me, as it failed to open the third time.

I followed him to the B studio. He told me his name was Lud, in his thick German accent. 'It's a German name,' he added.

'Really?' I asked, to which he said yes.

'OK. And you read that Maxim interview, huh?' I said.

'It was a disaster.'

'Thank you, Lud.'

Lud looked at me through his spectacles, made a noise of recognition. 'The owner of the station feels that your image would benefit from better media relations.'

I pointed at a mic. 'There's my media relations, right there.'

Lud smiled. His face muscles didn't look like they were used to being made to do that. He said, 'You have need of image control.'

'I just told you I'm good.'

Lud ignored me and began to unpack his case on to the studio table. He took care in making sure the pen and the jotter pad were all lined up straight. My presence seemed to be a given.

'Mr Lud, I have a show in here in twenty-three minutes.'

'Just Lud. It's short,' he confided, 'for Ludwig.'

'That's good to know, Lud. OK, this isn't talky-talky time, this is get-the-studio-set-for-the-show time.'

Lud gestured me towards a chair on the opposite side of the table. 'Actually,' he said, 'it is entirely talky-talky time. Whenever a journalist picks up the phone to you it is talky-talky time. Everything you say on air is talky-talky time. Your life—'

'Talky-talky time, I'm feeling the riff, man.'

'You are not a law unto yourself. You represent the radio station...' He scrutinised a piece of paper. 'Voice of the Bay.'

'And who do you represent?'

'You,' he said. 'My job is to try to stop you from bringing the station into disrepute, making remarks that will cost money, and so on. I protect you from yourself.'

That made me laugh out loud. I put my feet up on the desk. 'You think I need someone to wipe my ass for me in case I forget?'

'I don't hold an opinion about your ass.'

'Funny man.'

Lud looked at me through his specs. 'The radio station – your employer – notices that you have a dirty hiney. I have read your recent interview, in which you are depicted as a sexist pig, and I could be persuaded that your hiney is unclean. So from time to time, we will pull your trousers down and have a little look.'

I've had a lot of surreal conversations in my time. I told Lud, 'You're fucking hilarious,' and I really meant it.

'Whereas you are primitive.'

'I think I was nicer to you just then.'

The false smile again. 'You have a show starting in...' He checked his watch, which he wore on the inside of his wrist. '...Nineteen minutes. From now on, every interview you wish to give, every statement, will happen through me and with my prior approval.'

'How about if I don't feel like doing that?'

Lud had gotten a contract out of his case. He told me there was some stipulation in my contract with the station that obliged me to sign it.

'For a radio station that champions free thinking and, ergo, free speech, to want to gag its presenters? That's whack.'

'It's very far from whack,' Lud informed me.

I said, 'Man, you are the most German German I have ever met.'

'It's exactly that type of comment that prompted the station to engage my services,' said Lud. 'Sixteen minutes.'

I licked my lips. A producer was in the control room, pretending not to be listening to this on the internal circuit.

'And this won't affect what I say on air?' I hissed, and signed the damned agreement. I used my real signature. Without speaking, Lud slipped the contract into his briefcase, which he clicked shut. He placed his business card in front of me, making it snap on the table, like a croupier dealing blackjack.

'Golden rule?' he asked, standing.

'Talk to you first.'

'Talk to me first. One day it will save your ass,' he said.

'Man, you sure are all about the asses.'

Lud paused, then fished in his pants pocket for a sparse bunch of keys, which he showed me. One of them had a coloured fob, painted like a rainbow. 'You know what that means?' he said. I felt myself turning scarlet. He said, 'Upwards of five thousand dollars, plus dismissal, on the grounds of discriminatory behaviour.' He smiled, using a lot of teeth and no humour. 'We'll see us soon,' he said. 'Ten minutes to go. You had better get a wiggle on.'

058

There was a favour I wanted Pastor Lang to do. After I'd been putting out the *John Knox Show* every day for five years, I could have picked up the phone to fifty men of religion. But Pastor Russell Lang was *simpatico*. He saw people.

In my car, I told him, 'All the free time I get, I go at this. The station doesn't want to touch it, army won't talk to me, the White House press office stonewalls, the doctors won't say anything about a syndrome, just the specific symptoms. If Mikey can't come on the show and talk directly, I don't know where to go.'

'Army pays his health insurance. If he lost that…'

I understood. I was all out.

'You a believer?' He asked me just as I was running a red. I'd left it late: we came within two inches of a truck's fender. Lang held tight on to the door until we were over the junction. Damn, that Spyder kicked ass.

'I believed when I was a kid,' I said.

'Something in particular change that?'

I checked the mirror, and pulled wide into the next lane.

I'd stopped believing when I was in my teens, I told him, as we drove up into the hills in Napa. Mom and Dad had both been church worshippers. I told him what I could remember: no confession, no gospel, no hands in the air – old-school church, with hymns that sounded like hymns. The kind of stone church with people sitting in pews, trying not to fall asleep. No offence, I added.

None was taken. Lang told me people really did fall asleep in the church, however good a speaker you were. The old men and the hoboes, fine, but sometimes they had the temperature up just a little too warm on a winter day, and he'd be playing gopher-whack with the congregation, using big loud declaratives if he spotted someone had gone under, or banging on the side of the pulpit wearing his heavy ring.

'I lost the entire front pew one time,' he told me. 'Eight of 'em, mouths open. I swear to you, one of them even snored.'

'I once did a four-hour drivetime phone-in without a single caller.'

'What did you do?'

'Same as you. Kept talking.'

The cypresses that lined the short roadway up to the whitewashed Golden Haven Hospice looked parched.

Mom's room led off from a sort of communal area that was full of armchairs with no one sitting in them. Her door was open when I arrived. The architecture of her face seemed to be collapsing under her skin. Her hands had given themselves over to arthritis – they were no good for picking stuff up any more – and her legs were in thick bandages.

'Water,' she explained. 'My feet fill with water if I don't keep them elevated. How are you, John?' She kissed my forehead and it hurt her.

There wasn't much space in that room – just enough for her rocking chair and the single bed, and a table full of photographs. Dad was there, contemplating a mountain. There were pictures of people I didn't recognise: people from way back before me.

On a shelf under the pictures were magazines on knitting. I knew she couldn't hold the needles any more.

I sat on the bed. 'Are they treating you right?'

'It's not too bad. I won't be here long, anyhow,' she said.

'Mom.'

'Well… What's the use? I miss your father.'

'We all miss him.'

'Fifty-one years.'

A withered old man on a walking frame crept by the open door. As he passed he turned and stuck his tongue out at us.

'I don't know who he is,' Mom told me. 'He always does that.'

Old age could be a pretty good disguise, I thought. Maybe he'd been doing that his whole life.

'So I brought someone to see you,' I told her.

'Not that girl.' She turned, with difficulty. 'You're not still seeing her?'

My job was shooting from the hip – I took a breath before I could tell her yes, I was still seeing you. 'You gotta understand, Mom, she's not a bad person.'

'There are a million and one girls out there who would look after you.'

'I don't need looking after.'

'One day you will.'

There was a knock at the open door. I said, 'This is the pastor I was telling you about…' but Mom was already trying to clamber up on her feet to meet him. He persuaded her to stay in her chair, and they held hands, all their hands together. It was like two old friends, separated by time. She loved him, or something like it. He was used to taking the love too, to channelling it where it was meant to go. It was a side of Mom I'd never seen. She made me get off the bed so he could sit there instead, and squeezed my hand too before I left them alone, but not in the same way she'd held his.

I'd expected to come back to Mom's room and find her and the pastor as I'd left them, chewing over the meaning of life, but they weren't there. I found them out on the Golden Haven grounds, way ahead on the path, Mom in a wheelchair. The grass was green, not brown or golden, and lawn sprinklers whizzed in the far distance. Mom and Pastor Lang had stopped before a bed dense with orange poppies. They didn't see me approach.

'…can't accept it,' Mom was saying, as I drew close. Her voice was in a high register I'd never heard. I realised again my mom was an old woman. 'She's a real Delilah. Oh, a proper bitch. I don't swear, but that's the only word for it. A proper bitch. And then he comes here sometimes, and he has – oh – such scratches and cuts.' Mom held her hand up, and the pastor took it. 'She wrecks the house, you know. At the start he used to call me, and you could hear her carrying on, and I had to try to calm him down. Well, I'm an old woman. What can I do? If his father were alive, God rest his soul, he'd go around and talk to him; put him straight.'

Standing behind the chair, the pastor kept his own counsel.

I should have spoken, but I didn't. It burned to hear her talk that way. She didn't see the good part of you, and a part of me knew she never would. But I wasn't rooted to the spot in the sunlight because of her, but because of the pastor. I wanted to hear what he would say about you.

For the longest time we stayed like that, the trinity of us: the mother, the son and the holy man. Butterflies inundated a clump of bushes farther up the grounds, their folding wings making it twinkle. I searched for the bush's right name – what had Mom told me? I couldn't remember. It was just the butterfly bush.

There are moments when everything else around me is still, and I can step between them, like time travel. There is getting accidentally locked in the dark of the cold woodshed when I was seven years old – the first time I'd ever known isolation, surrounded by the sounds of empty Ontario forests. There is the first time I looked across the water from the Marin headlands and saw the sun rise over San Francisco, and knew that if I just stretched out my arms I could glide off the rise and surf the air over the soft-edged gold light of the city.

'You've been happier since you moved here, haven't you?' she called, without turning in her chair. 'You were always rooting around for something to do, when you lived back home.'

A breath of breeze rippled the poppies, bringing with it a hint of mist from the water sprinklers. I saw Mom close her eyes when it touched her face. The poppies were bright colours: oranges; whites; butter yellow. That type didn't grow well in Canada, Mom said. She'd tried. She grew little red-and-black ones instead, the ones from World War One. They worked out better.

'You think you'll go back home, John?' she said.

'I am home.'

She clucked, 'You know what I mean. Back to Canada. We kept the house in case one day you wanted to.'

I told her I didn't think so.

'So what will you do? Stay? With her?'

'Rachel.'

'They've put me on a new course of tablets,' she said, brightly. 'They—'

Lang said he'd maybe go stretch his legs.

'Stay,' said Mom, 'stay and talk some sense into this boy.'

The pastor took his glasses off to rub his eyes. When he'd put them back on again, and after smiling at me, he said, 'You know what? No one was never able to talk any sense into me. I like to think I turned out OK.'

After he'd meandered away up the long path and gone, Mom fussed with the blanket on her legs, pretending not to remember we'd been talking.

I said, 'C'mon. How long we gonna do this?'

She made a dismissive noise. 'Oh, I don't have very long left in this world, and do you know what? – that's just fine with me.'

'Don't say that.'

'That's just the point: I'll say what I like. Someone's got to say something. That girl's not a part of my family; never will be. She won't stick around. I don't know why you've decided that she's the only person in the world, but I want to know you're safe when I go.'

'She has good in her.'

'What good?'

'She's not a bad person. She's mentally ill,' I said. 'You remember the butterfly bush? That was her way of trying to be friends. The same as you got physically ill, she is mentally ill.'

I'd never thought that before. Now that I did, or had said it at least, our relationship seemed to crystallise and make sense. What had seemed difficult to bear now became a duty of love.

And you know something, I'd never realised before that that made me a saint. I'd passed the trials that got me close, tests I knew all but one person in a trillion would fail. The worse you got, the better I was. Tolerance and silence made me good, right?

'That doesn't mean you should stay with her,' Mom said. 'I loved your father from the moment I met him, May third, 1948, but if he'd treated me the way she does you—'

'Mom.'

'I'd have left him quicker than you can say Jack Flash. That's your father I'm talking about. You think I don't care about him?'

From somewhere near my mouth, I heard my voice say, 'I didn't know how to tell you. She's carrying our baby.'

Something happened to Mom in that instant. There was a single spasm, gone as quickly as it came, and then she was still, and frail, and silent, watching the last of the fall poppies.

'That's how they do it,' she pronounced, eventually.

'All right, that's enough.' There were people around, who weren't so far away that they didn't notice when I raised my voice. I repeated, softer, quieter; harder, 'That's enough.'

'Well, she's got you, hasn't she? Now it doesn't matter what she does, you're stuck with her. Unless she walks out again, for good this time.'

'I want to be with her.'

'Do you?' said Mom. 'Do you really? Apart from because you're a good, soft-hearted idiot? Listen to your parents. It says that in 1 Peter.'

'You know I don't believe in that.'

'What *do* you believe?'

I felt like we were having the type of hysterical argument you get in war movies, where big-name Hollywood stars in uniform yell and thump desks with their fists – me and my little old mom. It felt pretty stupid. I wanted to chuck Mom on the arm and for both of us to laugh about what goofs we were being, but that wasn't going to work. We weren't being goofs. We were making a stand for the things we believed in, except I wasn't so sure how good a believer I was, any more.

I wish I'd climbed down, but I couldn't. Instead, I stayed away.

Mom passed away a month later.

'Sometimes we find that when someone has lost a spouse, the surviving partner loses the motivation to carry on,' the voice of the care home manager told me, while I sat in the dark in my jockeys, cradling the receiver on the stairs of the house in Pacific Heights, 1.04 a.m. that October. The days had gotten a lot shorter; the nights a lot darker.

Mom had laid out her clothes for the next day on the chair by her bed every day she'd been in the home, the manager said. When the attendant came to open the curtains at eight o'clock, she found Mom apparently still asleep, with her Bible by her side, and pictures of Dad, in their frames, scattered on the comforter. The attendant called her – Mrs Knox? Time to wake up, Mrs Knox. Then she touched her hand, which was cold. There had been no clothes laid out on the chair, the manager said.

057

I could have cut and run, Rachel. I could've stumped up the maintenance, and seen the kid on weekends, same as half the men in the USA; but if I did I knew I'd never see either of you again. If I'd taken Josh it would have destroyed you, and there was no way I was abandoning him – or you. I could take it. I was a saint, or a rock, or something.

At the Met they stopped *La traviata* midway through the fourth act because someone was yelling in the front row: you. You were convinced I wanted to bone the singer playing Speranza. You'd caught me 'looking at her'. (Yeah – I was *in the audience*.) Attendants swung their torchbeams on me, and four thousand people craned to look. Disdainful upper-west-side voices belonging to people I couldn't see said, Isn't that the radio guy? And they were right. It was the radio guy, whose girlfriend had just thrown all her shit at him in the front row of the opera.

Jesus, even the *New Yorker* took a pop. By way of an apology you tried to be sexy, though I was far from in the mood, and cooked a lamb roast. I went and splurged at Nordstrom. Lud called a bunch of times and I had to talk him down. I wondered how he'd handle the Mikey Lang thing. Maybe not well. In any case, I couldn't get any traction. More and more doors kept closing.

056

'I'm John Knox, and I have with me Senator Archie Newton. It is customary, of course, to show deference to the senator's exalted position, but Senator Newton has been making a lot of comments suggesting that this show and specifically your presenter are somehow morally degenerate. Is that a fair representation of your views, Senator?'

Archie Newton had a Jesus complex. He'd survived Pearl Harbor, for one thing, and he wore the experience heavily, physically as well as in his demeanour. You don't get to return from the dead without it giving you big ideas. But this Jesus was old now, and he couldn't sit on a chair straight, and one side of his face was a scramble of smooth white scar tissue. In spite of all of that, and the angry look he wore habitually, the senator seemed to have reserved a special grade of contempt just for me. I'd asked him to count to ten, for level; instead he'd recited 'Mary Had a Little Lamb', all the while giving me the deadeye.

'Good morning, Mr Knox, good morning, listeners,' he began, saying 'Mister' as though the matter was in doubt. This was a point to me, straight off. Broadcasting 101: never pluralise the listener. (*American Life*'s Bob Grainger told me the golden rules my first week at KVOC: treat the listeners like they're one person, never put your water near the faders, never mention where you live.) The senator said, 'I'd like to say it's a pleasure to be here, but it is not.'

My head was full of cotton and dust, that morning. It was the morning after – it was *a* morning after – a fight about nothing at all, a fight that had resulted, as they inevitably seemed to do, in you trying to take the car out, drunk and seven months pregnant, followed by hours of reasoning and pleading while birds started singing and the sun came up on California. Eventually, here I was, on no sleep at all and a ton of caffeine. My depth perception and short-term memory were toast. I couldn't read the scrolling text messages from the producer that flashed on the computer screen. 'Say something,' said Galtieri, in my cans, and I realised I'd been drifting. These mornings were getting to be like pile-ups on the freeway: the first morning jack-knifing and then morning after morning ploughing in behind, smash after smash.

'Senator, you hate me. Why is that? What'd I do to you?'

'A typically juvenile start to the conversation,' sneered Senator Jesus.

'In the *Washington Post* you say, quote, "Knox, Springer, Stern and other cheap sensationalists like them must be stopped from poisoning our country, and exploiting the vulnerable." Let me ask you a question, Senator. You ever actually listen to this show before?'

'I don't expect,' he said, 'to get a fair hearing, here of all places. But I came on the air this morning to make a stand. Someone has to draw a line and say, enough is enough.'

'Enough of what, though?'

He smirked. 'You're not going to trip me up that easily,' he said.

'I'm asking what offends you.'

'No you don't, fella. I wasn't born yesterday.'

I guess old Archie was trying to avoid naming any negative practices in case we turned them into soundbites: Archie Newton listing vices, Archie Newton talking dirty. I guess he was watching his ass. When Tom Foley had lost his speakership in the House of Representatives the year before, they'd said our remix of his speeches had been a major part. Senator Newton wasn't about to fall into the same trap.

I said, 'How are we meant to debate an issue if we can't say what it is?'

'It's your radio show. You figure it out.' The senator was pretty pleased with himself about that one. He shot a twinkle to the Secret Service type by the door.

'You seem to consider that some form of amoral depravity is being broadcast from this station. You think I am a pollutant of the airwaves of America.'

'Now you're getting there.'

'And that's based on what, Senator?'

'Understand this. I fought two wars to make this world a better place. I saw men, good buddies of mine, die—'

'Your record—'

'You think I'm going to let some abusive loudmouth come and wreck what I fought for?'

Galtieri said, 'Get back in the saddle, John.'

'Listen, Sen—'

'No, you listen to me. The American people are not stupid. They're not fooled by you any more than I am. I love my country, and you are not fit to be a mouthpiece for it. I have lodged complaints about you with the Federal Communications Commission and the radio stations that carry this show.'

'I know. That's why we invited you on this morning: so we could have a debate. You're just ranting. What issue is it that has you so riled up, Senator?'

The senator's expression was deeply satisfied. He felt inside the pocket of his jacket.

'The senator is taking a piece of paper from inside his jacket and putting it on the table. Now he's unfolding it...'

It was a little wad of newspaper. Under Senator Newton's swollen old fingers, it became a single page, torn out of a recent edition. He rotated it so I could see. On it, there was a picture of you. My heart thumped. Yeah, it was you. You were outside our house, getting into the car. This thing had been published in a newspaper. I recognised the perspective: whoever took it must've been parked exactly where I often sat, across the street from the house. I was in the shot also. I was coming out of the front door. Even blown up, the range made it unclear what emotion I was displaying – I had my mouth open, and it was me, but that was about all. Your state of mind was clear. Your body language said keep the fuck away. Your pregnant belly was unmissable. And then there was an insert, part of the picture they'd enlarged: your face, with a black eye and blood on your face. It was a colour picture. The blood was red.

The rule was to think of the whole audience as one person.

But right then the whole audience was there in the room, all 6.2 million people, all waiting to hear what I said next.

'What's on the paper?' Galtieri said.

The caption to the picture read 'Woman leaves Knox house with facial injuries (see inset).' In the text, I caught the quotation: 'She was screaming about him trying to kill her and her baby.'

I looked at the senator, and back at the page.

The dimensions of time had transfigured. The seconds were falling off the studio clock like leaves in a fall gust. I heard myself say um several times to stop the dead-air sequence from triggering.

'Speak now or I'll pull this,' said Galtieri.

I thought about describing what had been put in front of me, but there was no way. What could I have said? That it wasn't true, when it looked like that? Even talking about it would have made everyone tuned in go out and buy the thing.

I signalled cut-throat to Galtieri through the glass, and even before the commercials had started I'd thrown my cans on to the table and was pacing the room. I wanted to put myself everywhere and nowhere at once. Newton was smiling like an alligator. I wanted to grab that smug bastard by the lapels. The Secret Service guy, his hands clasped in front of him, shifted his weight. So *that* was what he was here for.

I squared up to Newton from across the room. 'You've got this wrong,' I told him, as Galtieri stormed in.

'Call yourself a man?' said Newton, taking the page up. 'You disgust me.'

'You got this all wrong.'

Galtieri demanded to see the paper. He digested it matter-of-factly, and did not look at me. He was done inside of fifteen seconds. He said to the senator, who was lapping it up, 'We've had no calls on this. Every phone in a mile would be ringing. This isn't on the news-stands, Senator, so what is this?'

It was from that day's *Examiner*, the senator explained. As we spoke, that paper was being delivered to homes up and down San Francisco and Marin counties. He couldn't have been prouder of himself if he'd just fucked someone's kid sister.

'Did you do this?' I said.

'No,' he told me. 'You did.'

Galtieri stood in front of me, and the thug stood at the senator's arm. 'You bastard,' I told him. 'You set me up – why? Because I don't like your party's line on something? Abortion? Gun control?'

The senator cast a leisurely eye across the sound-recording equipment. 'Naturally I don't know what you're referring to. You beat on your pregnant girlfriend, you son of a bitch, and you dare to sit in here preaching to the nation about morals?'

After Senator Newton had gone, and Galtieri had barked into the production suite that they should run with a stand-by package called, ironically enough, *The Golden Age of Radio*, we came to a dead stop.

I said, 'That picture makes it look like—'

'Yeah.'

'You know I didn't—'

A call came through on the air-phone. 'You got journalists in the lobby,' Galtieri said.

When you work on any kind of live performance, whether it's stage or radio or TV, the one binding principle is that at the right time, and for the right duration, you perform, come whatever may. That the *Golden Age* pre-record was going out and we were standing around in the studio felt contrary to every instinct we had – Galtieri kept glancing at output level meters and the clock as though they might jump up and bite him.

'Get Lud on the phone, tell him to call my cell,' I told Galtieri.

'No – tell him meet me upstairs.'

'Before you move, understand this: I'm going to have a lot of people up my ass on this. Anything you want to share?'

I looked Galtieri in the eye. 'I didn't hurt her,' I said.

'Picture says you did.'

I went to the windows in the back of the station building, and looked down on to the yard there. A TV cameraman was loitering by the back door, the camera up on his shoulder and the lens cap off. Another figure had a mic with a wind baffle. They bristled, like they were waiting for someone. I put my face on the cold glass and watched them for as long as I dared.

Even now, I don't think I can tell you how that morning felt. Phones were starting to ring all through the station; fax machines were retching up notes from journalists wanting exclusives. I tore one off the fax in the accountant's office. It was handwritten, and promised me an opportunity to give my side of the story. The accountant wasn't in. I sat there in the unlit booth with the note in my hand.

When I closed my eyes I was in complete darkness, feeling wind breathing on me between the slats of a shed. It was colder; it was Canada. I was seven years old.

Outside the shed, ravens cawed in the forest. Wind bustled among the trees. In the quiet, all around me in the woodshed I began to hear organisms scratching around unseen.

And then, after the light had started to falter, the heavy footsteps came. I listened to them crunching through the undergrowth around the back of the woodshed. They hadn't come from the direction of the house, but from the forest. They stopped outside the woodshed door. I stood sniffling in the little shed in my shorts, and listened.

'John?'

I opened my eyes.

'John?' It was Lud. I have never been so happy to see a man. He was wearing zip-up sports clothes.

'Who have you spoken to?' he said, closing the window and turning the blinds. I said no one. As he pulled the phone cable out of the wall socket, he said, 'Keep it that way. Not one word to anybody unless I explicitly tell you to.'

'I should just talk to them. Hiding makes me look like I've something to hide.'

'As soon as you agree to an interview, they will print whatever they wish and claim you said it. No interview, no validation. We'll make a release, in writing.'

'Dude, I can call on some friends. Lee Kwang at the *Chronicle*, for example.'

Lud pulled up a chair opposite me, which was about all there was space to do in that office. He still had sweatbands on.

'Let us be completely clear about your position,' said Lud. 'At this moment, after OJ, you are the highest-profile wife-beater in California.' He checked his watch, which wasn't there. 'You don't have any friends. You have me.'

I guess I stood up and acted like a prima donna for a minute – hands on hips. I even said, 'She isn't my wife.' I didn't say you were someone else's wife. It would have made things worse.

Lud told me to sit down again. For want of a better option, I sat. I tried to figure out where you'd be – what you knew.

A pen and paper had appeared in his hands. 'Who are the other figures directly involved in the situation?'

We sat eyeballing each other for the longest time.

'Rachel McAllistair,' I said, 'and me.'

'What is your relationship – official and actual?'

Acid was rising in my throat as I thought of you at home. 'Shit, Lud, they're going to…' I scrabbled my cell out from a pocket. There were missed calls and messages by the dozen.

Lud took it out of my hand, and put it on a desk out of reach.

'What is your relationship with Rachel – official and actual?'

'We've lived together for like a year and a half. She's carrying our child.'

'Have you ever injured Rachel?'

For a few seconds I couldn't respond to that question. Not because I didn't know the answer – the answer was no – but because the question was necessary. Lud watched me.

'No,' I said, eventually.

'You're quite certain?'

This isn't happening.

He said, 'The article quotes Rachel making accusations of threats of violence against her and your child. Why has she said this?'

In my head was the swirl of your skirts and the crocodile smile and the breaking of plates. I buried my face in my hands.

'Does your partner have a history of mental illness?' he said. 'A depression, for example? Does she take some medication?'

'You're looking for a way to make this her fault.'

Lud sniffed, and pushed his spectacles up the bridge of his nose.

'She is pregnant. It would be normal to experience mood swings during pregnancy.'

We sat in the quiet of the room for what seemed like an hour – it may have been a minute or it may have been less. Neither Lud nor I spoke. The silence was complicity.

In our silence, a spooked intern came looking for me, with messages from Galtieri. He said there were four TV crews out front and that neither Lud nor Rachel was picking up. There were probably only a half-dozen years between our two ages, but I felt unspeakably old. 'You're doing good, kid,' I said. It didn't look like it reassured him any.

Lud informed him, 'If you speak to anybody I'll see to it you never work in this state again.' When the kid had gone, Lud said, 'Now the facial injuries.' He had a copy of the *Examiner*. 'They say you hit her. You must therefore sue them.'

I knew that meant proving what kind of person you were.

'No way.'

'Yes,' he said.

'I can't do this.'

'You are already doing this. What is the true explanation for this blood?'

055

On the day before, I'd seen the strange glow at the windows of the house immediately I'd woken up in the car. The street was dark. My cell display said 10.30. It didn't look like the lights were fully on – more like they were low power or something – but the blinds were open, and there seemed to be something else making light, something that flickered and danced and gave an orange glow. Wakefulness rushed through me.

The wall of heat hit me as I opened the front door. A lake of flames. The draught from the door made the flames of all the tea lights in their silver dishes gutter and rally. The candlelight from the sideboards danced. There must have been two hundred candles lit. It felt like an altar.

You were upstairs, lying on the floorboards, naked, with just a pillow; you'd pulled a sheet over you when I called out your name. Underneath the sheet was the swollen part of you that contained our child.

'Back pains?' I asked; but you said nothing.

I sat by you. Your eyes were open, but the only movement was the shallow rise and fall of your chest.

'Who's Kimberly?' you said.

'What's the context?'

'In the context of someone who's left a message on the answer machine. She seemed very friendly.'

'There's a Kimberly who works as a producer. Did she sound like she's smoked too much pot?'

'She sounded young and attractive.'

I said, 'What's with all the candles?'

'How come you've never mentioned her before?'

Oh, man. This was the pattern. This was the mechanical crunch as the brakes of the rollercoaster got taken off, and the whine as the thing started to move forward from a dead stop, doubling its speed every second. Kimberly was no one. Everyone was no one, but you never got that.

I said, 'I really can't do this again. Whoever Kimberly is, she's not a secret, she's just a colleague.'

'And yet she has your home number. *Our* home number. I'll bet you didn't tell her about me, did you?'

And so it started: reliably; inevitably; again. You called it a conniption fit, like it was something funny. I noted the objects around you that could be broken or thrown.

The question was no longer whether we could avoid a conniption fit, because we couldn't; nor was it about avoiding pain. For me, it was usually about finding novel ways to handle the violence, ways that I thought might work and didn't. I'd tried kissing you unexpectedly or holding your hand; I'd reason with you; empathise with you; argue against you; I'd tried getting angry back and sometimes I'd gotten angry without meaning to, just out of frustration; I'd tried walking out. I'd tried sidetracking the conversation in the early stages; I'd tried making jokes; I'd tried threatening you; I'd tried asking what your therapist would feel about the situation. Sometimes when you got mad I performed oral sex in the hope of damping down the flames. Sometimes it worked – sometimes. Mostly there was no stopping short and there was no circumvention. Like an aircraft passing through a storm cloud, we had no option but to keep flying and pray.

I pleaded with you not to let that argument go full term. I had Senator Archie Newton on the show the next morning. I said no one should have to face a neocon on less than eight hours' sleep – yes, I actually tried to appeal to the Democrat in you – but you were past the point of no return.

There was screaming, and there was you slamming the bathroom door. You were incensed when you found I'd taken the key out of the lock, so that you couldn't shut yourself away with a blade; you started stamping out the candles downstairs with your bare feet. By the time I realised that's what you were doing, your feet were caked in candle wax. I got to the main room just in time to see you fall on the wax, and land on the coffee table.

I said Oh God.

'Rachel, you gotta stop this, that's our baby you have inside you,' I said, as I tried to help you on to a chair.

You batted my hand away. 'Like you give a shit.'

A curtain was smouldering, and needed to be put out.

Could you see yourself, in those days? I think all that therapy just made you focus even more on the galaxy inside your head, inward to a black hole, not outward, to the future. For all the diabolic anger you felt towards the bitch you saw when you looked in the mirror, I don't think you ever really knew her.

That night, the night you burned the soles of your feet on the candles, you were prepared to destroy everything to prove that Kimberly represented some clear and present threat. When the daylight came – and it was an insipid, mealy day, stillborn – you got the idea to punish me really bad. We were spent; I'd sat in a chair and fallen asleep, and when you saw that, from somewhere you found the energy.

I woke up some time around five, with a headache and a feeling of dread. How long had I been out for? Few minutes maybe. The French door was ajar, letting in a cold trickle of morning air. I cracked my neck and went to shut it. You were in the garden, bare assed, and you looked like you were getting ready to stamp on a bug – a big bug, a bug you really wanted dead: your knee was raised up as high as you could get it. Neighbours' windows stared over blindly at the yard.

'Rachel?' I said.

When you looked over your shoulder, I thought you were dead. Your face wasn't your own. I mean, your face was a fucking mess: there was blood all down the left side, from your hairline to your chin, and blood from your nose had dripped off your mouth and chin and on to your chest. One eye was swollen closed.

'Fuck you,' you said. You turned away again. At your feet was a rake with its metal end resting on a brick. You got in one last shot before I could reach you, stamping on the metal so the handle sprang up and hit you in the face. This time it hit you in the stomach instead, because I'd gotten to you and was pulling you away.

You called me every name under the sun. We lay struggling in a flower bed, as your voice brought neighbours to their windows to look.

'This is insane,' I remember saying. 'This is insane.'

'If you didn't want insane,' you said, 'then *why did you say you loved me?*'

'Because I do love you.'

'You don't,' you said. 'You just don't.' And you started crying, and tore yourself out of my arms, and clambered to your feet with the difficulty of a cow standing on its hind legs, and then you were in the house again, sliding the door shut behind you.

I remember thinking: I'm lying in a flower bed, having just wrestled a naked pregnant woman to the ground in view of my neighbours. This should be fucking hilarious. I tried the idea that there was something intrinsically comic about the situation: but there wasn't. It had already been some time, I realised, since I'd stopped feeling like we were equals. I guess I was closer to being your carer, a really crappy one. I was making a bad job of keeping you safe.

Inside the house, you were dressed already, and by the time I got in the back door, you were out the front, car keys and shoes in your hand. I never saw anyone parked up on the other side of the street. All I'd seen was all I've ever seen since the first day we met: a big universe converging on a central point that was you.

'We have very little time, so I will ask you again,' said Lud, 'What is the true explanation for the blood on your partner's face?'

I took a deep breath.

'I hit her,' I said.

Lud's expression did not change. I think his physiology did: I think his face got harder.

'You are sure of what you are saying?'

'Yeah. I beat on her.'

'You said earlier that you did not.'

'You asked me for the truth. This is it.'

At last, Lud quit staring at me. 'You are not a very good liar,' he said. 'You understand this will be the career-end for both of us, yes?'

I couldn't meet his eye.
'Why don't you tell the truth?' he said.
And I said nothing.

054

Unless they've been through it themselves, people don't understand the way a media shitstorm works. Oh yeah, I thought I knew what to expect – there's a media mob scene in every legal drama. I had no fucking clue. The TV vans and the radio reporters and the press people and the magazine features hacks and the ambulance chasers – all rolling around the corner within minutes, like they were hiding around there all this time, waiting for the call to come.

They had me pinned down in the station and you in the house, putting microphones through the open windows and rushing the reception desk. Hell, you got it as bad as I did. When I dialled our home, it gave the busy tone. I didn't know if that meant you were talking to someone already or had pulled it out of the wall. Please don't talk to anyone, I whispered to the bleep. Please don't talk to them.

I don't know where they got my cell number from, but they got it all right. I was getting about a call a minute.

Fiona called. She sounded breathless. I said, 'Hi, Fi.'

She didn't bother with pleasantries. 'I have just been offered,' she said, 'an enormous sum of money to talk about our sex life.'

I said, 'OK, what are we talking, print media?'

'The *Star*, and it really was a lot of money.'

I asked her how much and she told me. I said, 'Shit, that really is a lot of money. Personally, I'd have taken it.'

'Oh, I took it.'

I felt my gut turn to ice. 'What exactly did you tell them, Fi?'

In truth our sex life had been pedestrian. We'd gotten together too young, grown bored fast, and sex was mechanical. But one of the first things I learnt when I started to work in controversy is that anything looks eccentric when it's without a context. What was only a facet of you *becomes* you. Remember Bush senior looking at his watch in the presidential debates?

'They wanted to know if you were abusive,' she said.

'You told them the truth, right?'

'Obviously. They weren't interested in that, then. They were like, did he make you do anything kinky in bed?'

I tried to think what would look like perversion on the cover of a supermarket tabloid. We'd had a little more sex, towards the end, when our careers had started to preclude affairs, even. It had been what kept us together when we realised we didn't like each other very much.

'Basically,' she said, 'it got to the point where they were, like, reading off a list. Did you do this? Check. What about that? Oh my God, he made you do that?'

'I made you do what?'

Sex acts, they're called, when they're decontextualised and filtered back to a prurient readership who want to be scandalised. They couldn't say I'd hit her, so instead I'd made her 'perform disgusting sex acts' – one of them on the night before our wedding. We both did, and it was great. I don't know what human being that particular sex act would disgust, but by refusing to name it, it played into the dirtiest imaginings of any reader.

I guess it all happened inside an hour: my life, filleted. Fi told me she was sorry, in the sense of being sorry for the inconvenience it would cause me, rather than sorry for selling me out. Meanwhile G was on the phone to a journalist on the *Boston Globe*, explaining how a lot of people had it in for me, particularly the pro-lifers who lived in the parking lot, and that I wasn't getting a fair deal.

While she was occupied keeping journalists out of the building until a security guard could be arranged, the station receptionist happened to agree that I did sometimes look pissy when I came into work mornings. Hell, she was only being honest. That got turned into: 'Radio insiders have blown the lid on John Knox's dangerous temper tantrums. Knox, whose pregnant partner was photographed leaving his house with fresh facial injuries.' The report carried the byline of my good buddy Lee Kwang.

'We need to get out there and make a statement,' Lud told me.

Galtieri said, 'Much better keeping outta sight.'

'No, no,' said Lud, 'Never do nothing. Construct an alternative.'

'Silence implies assent,' I said. 'Got it. I need to go out and say I did it.'

'Fuck are you talking about?' said Galtieri.

Lud said, 'He wants to admit that the allegations are true.'

'Since when are they true?' demanded Galtieri – and I had to love him for it. He didn't even look at me. 'What do they fucking employ you for, Lud? Huh? Get in here.' He threw open the door of his office, and threw Lud in there. When the door was shut behind us, he went off like a bomb. You never saw anger until you saw a pissed Italiano with chest hair let rip. His anger reminded me of yours.

'You don't just fucking regurgitate what he says,' he roared. He meant me. 'You're the publicity guy. You protect him.'

'He chose—'

'Fuck what he chose.'

Lud had been making a show of straightening his sleeve where Galtieri had grabbed him. Now he tutted.

That was the last straw. When Galtieri shoved Lud against the wall, I thought he was gonna kill him. He called him a faggot. He called him a lot of stuff, and the spit from his shouting speckled Lud's spectacles. He pressed his arm against Lud's throat, fist raised, and dared him to say something smart.

Lud could barely speak. 'Take your hands off me now,' was what he managed. Then, when he'd been released, 'You are an animal.'

'Useless fucking asshole.'

Lud's head was a dangerous shade of pink. He gasped for breath. 'You deserve each other.'

'Why don't you shut your mouth?'

'What are you going to do, strangle me again? Go ahead.'

Galtieri shoved some furniture around in the act of sitting down. He told Lud and me to sit down too, so we did. He pointed at me. 'He isn't admitting to anything. She fell down the stairs.'

'Very plausible,' sneered Lud.

'I just took on a second mortgage,' said Galtieri.

That was when you phoned.

You'd been under siege since the story broke. There had been reporters making live broadcasts in the street outside the house, you said, and cajoling voices calling though the screen door, and a persistent pizza delivery you hadn't ordered. 'I'm pregnant,' you said, quietly.

I tried to reassure you, while Lud and Galtieri argued about the right strategy for our lives. I tried telling you that we'd work through this, although I didn't believe we would. We'd passed a point, but I didn't know what it was called.

'Are you coming home?' you wanted to know.

'Home's difficult, right now. I'm kind of surrounded.'

You said, 'What have I got to do to make this better?'

'I don't know if that's possible.'

Our conversation fell into a gap in the argument between the two men. Lud was trying to raise the station owner on his cell. 'That her?' Galtieri said. 'John? Is that Rachel? Lemme talk to her.'

I remember how the last thing you wanted in the world was to talk to anyone involved in the crisis. Maybe you thought that if you just ignored it hard enough, it would all go away. It wasn't going anywhere.

'I have Panagakos on the line,' said Lud. 'He's seen the TV.'

'Will you let me talk to her?' said Galtieri.

If there was a moment when my life stopped being merely shared with other people, people who hated me, and started being rented from them, that was it. When I surrendered the phone to Galtieri, I knew I was passing control of my future with it: the future of my career, the future of my life with you. Those things were going to become accidents of convenience. It seemed like that was the best deal I could cut for you.

I went to the bathroom. On the way there, every room I passed through, everyone stared at me. When I got there, my mouth was already full of puke, and I dropped it out of my mouth into the toilet pan, and then allowed my gut to heave properly, again and again, until all I had were the acid and the dry gag and the tears running down my face.

053

Joshua was born on 19 February 1996, a day when the sun never came out and the rains never came either: just grey sky, and a grey ocean, the day Tupac brought out *All Eyez On Me*. You were stoic, and during childbirth you looked like you were in denial, as though the whole thing were happening to someone else, somewhere else, and whatever it was that had pissed you off was a different matter altogether. You held my hand, and until the pain got too bad I kissed your fingers, making you smile. Then we did the breathing thing, and you said 'why me why me why me'.

At the very last moment you remembered I was there and said, 'John, I'm about to have our baby,' and I said yes, yes you were, and you looked between your legs in disbelief.

When Josh was cleaned and swaddled, a nurse passed you the bundle, and I watched you make decisions about the armful of life you'd been given. You examined it sceptically, with your cheeks sucked in. Then you smiled. Josh lay there with his eyes shut and lips no bigger than a fingernail puckered for air, unaware, I guess, of everything but the comfort of your touch. You told him how wonderful he was, how beautiful, and he started to cry. The nurse showed you how to support his head; and then we were crooning and cooing over him in exactly the way we'd mocked when it had been other people, and other people's babies. I held him, and holding him was awkward because I had two newly broken fingers on my right hand, the little one and the fourth, strapped together with white tape like a catcher's mitt to mend, but I didn't notice they hurt until afterwards.

You were carrying that guy around for nine months. That blew my mind. He'd been the kind of baby that didn't jump around in the womb, and each scan had been a necessary reassurance that he was doing OK in there. That baby, swimming about in the picture like a submersible on a sonar screen, had survived the pregnancy. I felt a massive weight off my heart. I started sobbing uncontrollably there at your bedside, looking on him.

'I know, he's beautiful, isn't he?' you said, softly, never taking your eyes off Joshua.

I drove you home, later that day: you and Josh. In the parking lot I got spat at, and at the stop junction the car waiting alongside mine sounded its horn, and when I looked, the driver, a family guy, leant over his wife to give me the bird. I don't know what he was yelling.

I gave interviews, of course. Lud set 'em up, and I said what he'd told me to say. He said I had to do it for the sake of keeping our biggest commercial sponsor from cancelling, so I had to talk about the baby like he was a product, and when the inevitable questions came about the 'domestic abuse', I had to make up stuff that made it sound like not my fault and not your fault either. I don't remember a lot about it. I just focused on keeping you alive, and on keeping the show alive for Mikey Lang.

At one point, I remember thinking that I was glad Mom was dead.

That day, the day our boy was born, was the first day I knew I wasn't going to make it. I can't explain it, but it was as clear a feeling as any I ever had. Since you took to hitting me, something had moved around in my head. I couldn't shave, because of where your ring had caught my jaw. I couldn't take the hair out of my face because they'd want to know what trouble I was in now. Jesus, Rachel, the broken fingers made it hurt to take a slash. I thought of the last pictures of Cobain, when his eyes had gotten red rims and he looked right out of and beyond every image they made of him.

There was whisky under the sink in the kitchen, behind the detergents, where only the cleaning woman looked. I fucking hated whisky. It was an expensive malt too, so I should probably have appreciated it better than to swig it down. I wanted it to make me puke, but it didn't. It just made my eyes water – like tears, but not tears.

The phone was in the lounge room, prim and pristine. I circled it a couple of times, the way a bullfighter approaches a bull when it's already injured. *You fucking asshole. You total asshole.* I licked my lips. They'd say, 'Hello, this is…' – or would I have to say something first? The whisky made my heart hot. *You piece of shit, that you'd do this to her the day she bore your child.* I was burning up. 'Hello, I'm John Knox.' I couldn't say that. That was my fucking catchphrase. I gave the whole thing up as an awful, awful idea. I went into the kitchen. I came back from the kitchen, wiping whisky off my mouth with the back of my hand. The number was scrawled on the back of a report on sicknesses in Gulf War veterans.

I picked up the phone and dialled.

'Hello,' I said, 'I need help, please.'

'May I know your name, sir?'

'Can we do this without names?'

'I will need your name to progress this case beyond a general enquiry.'

I said, 'OK. My name is John Smith.'

There was a pause before the voice said, 'OK, Mr Smith, how can I help you today?'

'I've got a – my partner…'

'Will you speak up, please, sir?'

'Sorry. Sorry. She's upstairs.' The liquor had made the world soft-focus. 'I need help.'

'Are you in danger, sir?'

'How do I get someone looked after professionally? I can't do it. I don't know what I'm doing. How do I get a person committed?'

'What you're talking about in the first instance is called a five-one-fifty hold, which is a temporary holding order for psychological evaluation.'

I wrote that down: *Five-One-Fifty Hold.* 'To evaluate what?'

'That's in the case of someone posing a direct threat to themselves or others. Does the person in question have a history of mental illness?'

I realised I didn't fucking know.

'She sees a therapist. I mean—'

'Has she been clinically diagnosed with any mental health issue?'

'I don't know,' I said. 'She said she used to get depression – does that count? Can you get drugs without a diagnosis? Look, she poses a threat, okay? And I need to be sure you won't just evaluate her and throw her back out again, 'cause she's gonna be real pissed. We have a baby…'

Something had been striking me as wrong with the conversation already; now I realised it wasn't the conversation but a background noise. It was noises in the next room. A spasm of adrenalin shot made me slam down the phone. I tripped on the cable.

You were in the living room already, wearing my robe. Josh was in a carrycot.

'Who were you talking to?' you said.

'Work.'

Outside the window, the day had gotten dark once more. It had been nine hours since you'd given birth. You looked at me in a way that made me feel like I ought to remind you of my name. But all I had in my head was John Smith. Yeah: I was John Smith.

052

'This is John Knox telling it exactly like it is on KVOC, the Voice of the Bay, 1510. We're all talk here at KVOC.'

I checked the studio clocks: the normal clock that told the time, and the other one, the one I used most, the one that counted down to the next scheduled event. The travel bulletin was due at five past the hour, giving me one minute.

In radio, the number of words per minute is reckoned at around a hundred and sixty; a typical person intro would be forty to eighty words. Forty to eighty words to summarise a life. I had a hundred and fifty to talk about mine.

'A lot of people calling in to the show want to talk about the stories circulating in the papers about my partner, the mother of my child. Some people call in offering abuse and some offer support because they think it's all a crock. Thank you to everyone who's called in on the subject. It is important that you care. Thing is, neither viewpoint is based on anything more than your prejudices: about me, about men in general, or about how the world works. In spite of that photograph they're running, which some folk are ready to interpret in one way only, the biggest part of my life gets lived out in public behind this microphone every morning. I share it all with you. But what happens behind the front door of the house where I live: that's for me alone. Now, I know what you're thinking: wanting privacy implies I've got something to hide.

'The fact is, I've learnt that some experiences go beyond words. Maybe that sounds lame to you; it sure would sound lame to me.'

Dick Guppy's voice in my cans said, 'Nothing on the board.'

'Apparently that sounds lame to you.'

I had two guests in the studio. There was meant to have been a third, but their agent had gotten downwind of the shitstorm and had pulled them out. They'd gone the same way as our two biggest advertisers, who made family products, and didn't want a wife-beater plugging them. If Panagakos and Galtieri hadn't both taken so public a gamble when they first gave me the job, I'd have been toast by now.

The two remaining guests either didn't know, or knew and wanted their fifteen minutes just the same. I said, 'I've got Tyler McGovern in the studio with me: she's the author of *Where There's a Will*, a book about putting your ideas into action; I've also got Jerome C. Waller, Emeritus Professor of Sociology at Penn State: he's written *The Sixth Killer*, a study of assassin Gavrilo Princip, looking at what happens when you put people under pressure.'

The guests looked like all the other guests, every guest who'd come before and every guest there would ever be on that show; on any show. Man, people pushing books are whores – bitchy ones, at that, with sharp elbows. No wonder they need the stupid elbow patches on their jackets.

One of the false impressions of the world that discussion-show hosts have: that every single person in the world just finished writing a book.

I remembered how you'd sat at that table: how you'd talked about the sinking of the *Lusitania*. It seemed so far away, now. The syndicated traffic report was being piped in; then it would be weather, then us. In the control room, Dick Guppy was talking to the two kids who handled incoming calls. They'd been briefed to screen out stuff about me and you. Consequently, we had nothing we could use. The picture of Princip on the cover showed a haunted youth with a weak-ass moustache. I looked from Guppy to the reflection of me in the pane of glass. I was like a ghost in there.

'Ten seconds to weather, forty to studio.'

I looked at the girl with her fucking book, self-satisfied as if she'd laid an egg, and the professor with his fucking book, all pumped because they thought they knew who I was.

I looked again at my ghost.

Some Nirvana bassline started in my head.

I thought about my child.

'Twenty,' said Dick Guppy.

I checked the clock. We were nearly out of time.

051

In the first days of Joshua being at home, we were too damned tired to do anything but wonder at this strange and perfect little creature who now existed, and recalibrate the gravity of our universes. After the third day, we were out of the energy required to go running to him every time he burbled or squeaked, but we went all the same. Two weeks, and he had to really holler to get heard. I'd taken to sleeping in my clothes on the couch.

After a fortnight, you'd gotten your vim back, I guess. After a fortnight, you got drunk and got angry about something you thought I'd said – I don't know what it was. I had to go fetch my Speech Broadcaster of the Year award from the street. It was dented, and had made a dink in the car. It made you feel bad to see me trying to smooth out the dent with spittle and a thumb, so you got angrier still. You knocked it out of my hands and started shoving me, to make me react, but I didn't react.

After three weeks, it was like Joshua had never been born. You went to work on your arms. You cut across them, cutting deep enough to draw blood, but you didn't slice the veins lengthways, the way you'd told me serious self-harmers do. I suppose that made you an amateur, or a faker, or something. You broke my nose again, that week.

'How bad does it have to get before you'll take this seriously?' I asked the woman at the SFPD. She was just another in a string of voices on the phone who didn't understand me. It was like I was talking in a whole other language. They'd start out sceptical, as though I was calling in for kicks, then they'd get suspicious, and want my particulars, and they'd ask the sort of questions that meant they thought this was a cover-up, and that I was hurting you. I told them I didn't want you to get arrested, or prosecuted. I wanted them to keep you somewhere safe and talk to you or give you medication or whatever it was that needed to happen for you to be OK.

'If this is handled wrong, and she comes back seventy-two hours later having been held in a jail cell, it's going to get really ugly around here.'

'Is that a threat, sir?'

'No, it's not a threat. Why in God's name would you say that?'

'Do not use profanity, sir, I'm warning you.'

They said that if you were doing what I said you were doing – physically injuring both of us – I should press charges. It was clear from their tone that what they meant was, 'If this were real, you'd report it'. Oh yeah, I know what their tone meant. I'd made a career out of listening to people talk.

050

Two weeks before the end, I met with Pastor Lang. We met in a bar downtown, but we had to move to a different one on account of a massive Latino with a business suit and tattoos on his neck. He asked me how I liked my chances fighting him instead of a pregnant girl. He asked me if I thought I was a man. His buddies didn't intervene. In the mirrors behind the bar, I saw what he saw: a dirty white jerk in a T-shirt and a beard, with sticking plaster across his nose and his hand all busted up. I reckon I looked like the kind of tomcat that gets in fights, and loses.

In the second bar, the pastor nursed his Bud and I drank mine down, and ordered another. The place was dark and felt like a speakeasy.

He said, 'It's none of my business—'

'That's right.'

He said, 'Go easy on that beer, will you, John? It's none of my business, but I know there's more to your domestic situation than they're saying on the TV.'

I finished the second bottle.

The pastor had aged twenty years since I'd met him first. That impression he used to give of being as big as an ox wasn't there any more. His clothes hung a little too loose on his body, and when he sat he sat as though he were prepared to wait a long time.

'So we've got to move on this now,' I said. 'DoD won't come to California, let alone come on the show. Army's banned from talking to us. The UN already did a review of what chemical weapons were used, but it's classified. We keep getting the same refusal, word for word.'

'Then…?'

'So we've finally got put in touch with an army officer: Lieutenant General O'Donnell. He was a big gun, served under

Schwarzkopf in Desert Shield and Desert Storm; now he's up for statutory retirement. This guy used to advise Rumsfeld, he hangs out with Colin Powell...'

Lang's watery eyes were watching me very intently through the thick specs.

'It *sounds*,' I said, 'like this guy O'Donnell is willing to meet with Mikey if...'

Lang exhaled a breath he'd been holding for six years.

'...*if*,' I went on, 'it's a pre-record, and *if* he gets full censorship on the material, and *if* it's handled by me. He's heard the show enough to know it's the real deal.'

'My God,' said Lang, closing his eyes. 'Lord God, I want to thank you for this man John Knox.'

'Whoa – this ain't cashed. OK? This is not a done deal,' I told him. 'You know the dirt I'm getting thrown at me right now? This general could still be scared off.'

Pastor Lang came to. 'There's more the papers haven't published?'

'There's always more, when you want there to be. Doesn't matter if it's true or not: throw enough, eventually some sticks. The station's losing sponsorship big-time because of it. I'm fucking fantastic publicity right now, but I'm killing their revenue.'

I saw him decide not to dig any deeper. He said, 'They can't fire you, can they?'

'I was them, I'd fire me.'

'So what about this thing?' said the pastor, necking Bud out of a bottle.

'It's the right thing to do.'

'The right thing isn't always easy.'

I laughed. 'How many times you had to say that to someone?'

'Too many, I guess. It's a truth, though. Doing what you believe often means putting yourself outside the understanding of other people.'

We sat in silence a while. Posters on the wall advertised a Tribute to Morrissey.

'How's Mikey?' I said.

The pastor opened his hands. 'He's dying.'

We sat there longer.

'I'm sorry I couldn't do this faster, or better,' I said.

'He wanted me to thank you for the book of poems.'

I told him, 'He's welcome. Look, this army guy will be here in two weeks, if he comes at all. I'll try to hold on to my job that long. That's all I can do.'

'You know what this will mean to Mikey. And to the other families.'

'No promises, OK?'

I guess I believed I could pull it off. I'd spoken myself to the broker, a soldier assigned to public relations who seemed like he'd been around the block. The lieutenant general was willing to meet. He had a book to plug.

049

One and a half weeks before the end, a store security guard in Modesto shot four customers and then himself. His name was Delgado – Louis Delgado. He left a note about what the worm in his head had made him believe, and how he'd tried to reach out for help.

I don't know who remembered he'd ever called my show, but they remembered all right. *Wifebeater Knox Spoke to Killer* read the headline. When I got home from the station, the TV news vans were outside again. When they saw me, the reporters and the camera ops and the stills photographers ran at me. I had to plough through. The reporters asked questions like, What did you say to the killer that tipped him over the edge?

When I'd put the front door between me and the news reporters, my head hurt. I could hear doors slamming upstairs. You yelled, 'I'm trying to raise a fucking baby!' The heap of rags at the foot of the stairs seemed to be my clothes.

They had your name, meaning your co-academics would be well aware of your private life. They didn't yet know about Maxwell and Dylan – *Secret Family of Knox Victim*. But they would.

I went into the kitchen and dug the glass bottle out from amongst the Mr Clean and the drain unblocker and drank a long, long draught of whisky. It burned beautifully, until I felt like I could breathe fire out of my nostrils.

I imagined how it would be for me to go upstairs: how you'd push past me if I was in your way, how you might hit me. When you hit me or shoved me, the impulse was to shove back. I'd always been a shover-back until I met you. There would be the twin dangers: your relentless offensive, and the danger of retaliating instinctively.

Or maybe I'd sit in a chair and wait for your storm to come to me, and then you'd hit me until I got out of the chair and did what you wanted me to do.

There was knocking on the door. I closed my eyes and saw an eye looking back at me. It made my heart thump so hard I thought I was going to suffer cardiac arrest. Twenty seconds without a heartbeat. Maybe that wasn't so bad.

You were coming down the stairs when I opened my eyes and you were wearing clothes I'd never seen before: skirts that billowed and a blouse, and you had rings on all your fingers and murder in your face. You stood on the second step so you stayed taller than me.

'There are reporters everywhere,' you spat. 'Everywhere.' You were so angry you could hardly form the words. 'Take your stuff and *get out*.'

'Rachel, we gotta get help for this.'

Even before I'd finished speaking, you were snatching up handfuls of my shirts and heading for the front door.

'God, please don't do that.' I was quick enough to get hold of your arm to pull you back, but not before you'd gotten the door open and hurled my things at the feet of the news crews waiting there. Cameras flashed. I slammed the door.

You tried to wrest yourself free from my grip. 'No more,' I shouted. 'No more.' I had your other wrist now. I realised what a long time it had been since we'd touched. 'I love you, Rachel, but this has to stop, you hear me?' You were screaming at the top of your voice that I didn't love you, screaming for me to let you go, but I couldn't. I wouldn't. I shoved you down behind the couch, out of view of the windows. Oh, there would have been a camera crew looking through there any moment, the volume you were howling at. I sat on you and pinned your arms, and you snapped at me with your teeth.

'Listen to me,' I said. 'We're dying, here. Everything's getting fucked up, Rachel.'

You'd started barking like a dog. Your face was red.

'Darling, we have to get you help.'

'What help?' you yelled. 'Look at me! Who's gonna help a piece of shit like this?'

'I would if I knew how.'

'You fucking liar!'

I itched to put a fist through your head and out the other side. I wanted you to be out of pain and I wanted the noise to stop. Can you forgive me that I felt like that? I don't know if I can. Yeah: I wanted you to be dead, my darling. You hadn't stopped struggling, not for a moment, and this was as good as it got: a hiatus in the destruction, bought with brute force.

'You can't keep pushing like this,' I said.

'Who's being violent? Look at you,' you said, 'the big, big man. Poor little John. Is he going to have a temper tantrum?' You spat into my face. 'Come on, then, what have you got?'

'Stop talking.'

'Make me!'

I resisted what every fibre told me to do. I did not move my hands to your throat and I did not crush your throat with my hands. The moment came that I would've done those things, if I'd been another man, and the moment passed, and you lay there, looking up at me. There was no anger, now. There was the fact of you lying on the floor, and the fact of our eyes.

You said, as if to console me, 'It's OK. It's OK. I do know I'm crazy.'

'Do you?' I said. 'I'm in way out of my depth. We have a child. We can't be getting it this wrong.' The strength was draining out of me.

'I would never hurt our child,' you said.

I wanted to say that I wished you would never hurt me, too. I couldn't say that, or anything like that. I wanted to say that I believed you, because you hadn't touched the kid who'd once been in your life, Dylan, but I couldn't say anything about him. I couldn't tell you I'd called the mental health services, and I couldn't tell you that I was convinced that one day you were going to kill me, and that you'd regret it before my body hit the floor, but I'd be dead. I wanted to tell you I loved you, but I couldn't tell you that right then.

'You threw my boxer shorts at the reporter from *Channel Nine News*,' I said, and when you realised there was nothing to do but laugh at that, you laughed, and you really thought that when I laughed too we were sharing a joke, and that we both found it funny. I lay on top of you, in convulsions of something that wasn't laughter, and held your head to mine, and laughed.

048

I went to the bayside, and looked out at the ocean. Shakespeare got it right. Death by a thousand cuts: suicide by waves.

Even at the bayside, people recognised me. They recognised something evil. They recognised all the bullies and all the bad guys they'd ever known; they recognised the ex-boyfriend who used to beat on them, or the drunk who once hit their kid sister. They recognised their asshole father with the belt in his hand. So do our days hasten to their end.

One week before the end, after the picture through our front door of me grabbing you as you threw my clothes out of our home, the Voice of the Bay's Montreal affiliate station dropped the show on moral grounds. We found out about it in a pious editorial from a French–Canadian pundit I'd never met, who made big points about the changing role of the man in society, and used me to characterise a dying breed. I was thirty-two years old. Every fact he gave about me was wrong. One thing I learned fast in those final weeks was that when the media decide you're a bad guy, you lose all your rights to fair reporting. This Montreal journalist mentioned abuse he imagined I'd dished out to Fiona, and alluded to my sordid sexual peccadilloes. He revealed that I'd told callers to my show that there was 'nothing quite like trying to run your car over a Negro', and demanded to know how long filth like me could be tolerated.

Five days before the end, reporters had gotten to old school friends who were happy to declare, looking at it in retrospect, that I had been a domestic abuser in formation right from the very start. As a child, I'd stamped my foot or pulled someone's hair – proof positive that I was evil, even then. The positive impressions people held of me were the result of my 'chameleon nature' – domestic abusers are charming and persuasive, you see. A realtor called Marie, in the Castro Valley, gave an interview about how I'd yelled at her on the show and belittled her views because she was a woman. She knew that if I'd been physically close to her, I would have abused her. The trauma had made it difficult for her to be around men.

The siege around our house had gotten unbearable. We hadn't been able to open the curtains because of the camera crews. I sat with you indoors, in darkness. I drank whisky. I drank a lot of whisky, and when Lud called to tell me what else was being said around the country, I don't remember what I said. Leaving the house meant running the gauntlet, so we didn't do it, and a moped guy from the Yellow Pages fetched in groceries.

The California Department of Social Services called up, and arranged to come around. They sounded like the type of doctor who plays everything down, right until the end.

Four days before the end, you said you were sorry. We were a million miles beyond sorry.

'I think we should go away,' you said, brightly. 'We should take a long holiday somewhere, just the three of us, and start all over again.'

I looked at you from far down the drunk's tunnel, and thought what a stupid, thoughtless thing that was for you to say. Were we even living in the same reality? And that drinking, you went on, that's not helping. Don't you have to meet that army officer in a couple of days? He wasn't going to want to talk to a presenter who stank of liquor. *Damn it*, I thought. How was it possible you could be suddenly so right?

Will you promise me you'll get proper help was what I wanted to say, but right then you didn't need proper help. You were rational and reasoning. I thought about saying it anyway, but all it could have done was provoke you to anger, and you know something? I missed you. Every time that look came across your face and you started to fill up with thunder, I lost my friend, just at the moment I needed her most. So I pretended to believe in the fantasy of going away and starting over.

Three days before the end, in the middle of the night, I woke up covered in sweat, having dreamt of being trapped in a room with no windows, and no light.

I had been relegated to weekends, mostly, just until the shit had passed, and I went in for Saturday. Dick Guppy wasn't my producer on the show that morning. A woman with a Jennifer Aniston cut had been shipped in from someplace. She didn't make eye contact with me once.

047

The worst type of shame is a shame whose name cannot be spoken. To talk about it, even to talk about how no one's talking about it, is to break the unwritten contract of silence. We will not mention your shame: that is how we condemn you.

Panagakos, the station's small, Greek owner, wore a black suit that belonged in the sixties. Flanked by the senior station managers, he bounced a pencil up and down on the glass table and watched me come in and sit down.

Lud took a seat on Panagakos' side of the table, and exchanged nods with the managers.

We sat in silence.

I said, 'If you'll allow—'

'What I'm struggling to understand,' said Panagakos, 'is how we got to this point. I've been in broadcasting a long time. I've seen controversies, you understand me? What I don't understand is your role in this. I see accusations here, there and everywhere, yes? Do I hear you making a statement? No. Do you offer to quit? No. Do I hear so much as a little bird from our favourite presenter?'

'I don't like to be patronised,' I said.

'Oh, don't you? I'll try to correct my tone for you.' He looked at the pencil, and then he looked at Lud, who was surprised to find himself involved. 'What about you?' said Panagakos. 'You were hired to handle the public image of this cunt.'

'I have tried—'

'Do I sound as though I'm done talking?'

'No, sir.'

'No, sir. His public image is so bad, I got the CEOs of companies refusing to do business with me while he's on the air. Big companies. Boston wants to drop the simulcast by the end of the week. That's half our advertising revenue. He's on the TV news. People are asking me why it is that my company employs an animal like this.' He said, 'My wife runs a charity for raped women, did you know that?'

One of the managers said, 'He could resign, form an independent production company and then we hire...' but the idea trailed off.

'Let's get this exactly straight,' said Panagakos. 'This situation is excellent publicity for this radio station, the first time someone hears about it. The second time they hear our name, it's bad for us. The third, worse still. Right now, everyone's heard our name one hundred times.'

Lud started to say, 'John may have something he wishes—'

'*Malaka*, I told you don't interrupt me,' said Panagakos. 'Didn't everyone hear me say that? That's it, you're done here. Get out.'

Lud corrected the position of his spectacles on the bridge of his nose. He cast his gaze around the faces in the room. Mine was the last one he looked at.

'This is how you want it?' he said.

I closed my eyes.

And then he was gone.

Silence remained in Lud's wake.

When I started making radio, I didn't do it to climb a ladder. I didn't want a lawn to mow.

The owner of the Voice of the Bay was OK. He was looking out for himself, same as anyone else, calling everybody *mounopano*, but I didn't intend sitting in that fear soup any longer than I had to. Me, I could walk on eggshells any time I wanted.

I pushed my chair back, and I would have stood up, but for a line of poetry that drifted into my head:

The lowest hell: the coming home

– and I knew I was going nowhere. Not for three days, at least. When three days were up, and I'd done my duty to Mikey Lang, I could do all the walking out I pleased. And maybe I would. I thought about taking my money and my son and going back to Canada, where you couldn't fuck things up.

The whole millennium was coming to an end. My life was just a little part of the grand finale.

046

A day before the end, I found you in the living room. There was paper on every inch of floor. Pages from a book. I couldn't get to the kitchen without walking on them. You stood in among the pages, marshalling them, it seemed, naked except for a bra and bleeding from the stomach. 'It's fine,' you told me; and you meant it. 'Just superficial.' The blood had run over your genitals and down the inside of your thighs.

I asked you what was going on.

'I thought I might brush up my French,' you said. They were pages from a French/English dictionary. They didn't seem to be laid in any particular order.

'And this is how it's done?' Where you were standing, the pages were crumpled and marked with bits of footprint in blood.

There was music on – some classical piece.

'How's Josh?'

You looked at me like I was a dope for asking. 'He's fine,' you said. 'I haven't put him in the washing machine or something.'

'Where is he?'

'Upstairs, I think.'

In his crib, Josh looked like a little Bob Hope, or like the lieutenant general, judging from the photographs. I listened to the soft animal breathing. I wanted very much to touch that soft head.

Can a person grow up right if the papers and the whole world says their dad beat on their mom? I still believed you might get better, and that he wouldn't remember, but around me a legacy was building. Words on paper are immortal, and omnipotent – even the wrong ones. Yeah, the bullshit they wrote about me and put on videotape was gonna live longer than I would, longer by generations. It'd be what my kid looked at when he was old and wrinkled and unable to remember my face any more.

'I promise I'm gonna fix this,' I whispered. 'I'm gonna put this back together for you.'

On the last day, I didn't know it was the end. I heard someone say that the best end is a beginning, and I swear: I thought we were gonna make a new start. Me and our child, and maybe you.

I cleaned, and Galtieri stopped by the house in the afternoon. His skin was deep ochre from Sicilian sun. We hugged each other.

'So, a daddy now,' he said, as we leaned over Josh's crib. 'Congratulations. I shoulda bought something. Got yourself a cute kid, there.'

'Don't I know it.'

He cast his dog-eyes around the place. 'Who's sick, with all these curtains shut?'

I said, 'Prying eyes.'

'Yeah, these fuckin' journos? I saw a few of those outside.'

Galtieri sucked his teeth and took a lot of interest in whatever was lying around. A stack of browned British newspapers talking about war; the Gavrilo Princip biography on the mantelpiece. He lifted the covers open and dropped them shut. 'I heard about our friends at the station the morning we got back.'

'Guppy.'

'Yeah, I heard he went. And the German prick.'

I didn't want to badmouth Lud. 'He was OK,' I said. 'He went out with his head held high.'

'Fuck that shit.'

'Jesus, G.' I made a gesture towards Joshua.

Galtieri growled, but he made himself comfortable in an easy chair, looking like the dog that stole the steak. 'So, we gonna do this thing?' he said.

We were gonna do this thing. Lieutenant General O'Donnell's adjutant had called me around midday. There were vehicle sounds in the background. O'Donnell had landed at LAX and was on the 101 right now, for a night's stopover in Berkeley. I'd suggested meeting beforehand.

'I don't think so,' said the adjutant. 'Confirm an oh-six-hundred RV tomorrow at the Voice of the Bay station HQ?'

'If you just said we meet at six, then yeah.'

'I need to confirm that this will be a pre-recorded show only. Nothing live. No cameras.'

'Yeah, he's got full say what comes out. Just tell him to give me clean outs when he's talking, make the edit easier.'

'I picked up a paper at the airport. Quite the controversial character, aren't you, Mr Knox?'

We'd ended the call cordially, but cordial was about all.

Galtieri listened while I told him about the arrival of the general, with his head propped by one hand on the arm of the couch and his eyes closed. I told him it had taken a year and a half to get it to this. When I'd finished, he didn't open his eyes. 'All right,' he said, eventually. 'And what about the kid? Mikey?'

'He's good. I left a message for him at the hospital.'

'He healthy enough to make the recording?'

I said, 'All he's got to do is talk on the phone.'

'And he can do that?'

I didn't answer.

Galtieri said, 'The suits start coming in at nine, so I need these military people out of there eight-thirty, latest. Any one of our people picks up a phone to Panagakos, that recording won't be going out.'

'I hear ya. Listen, G?'

He looked at me.

'Thank you for doing this.'

'This ain't a favour,' he said. 'Understand that. This is business. I went out on a limb, bringing you in. Big noise comes from the right, always has – Rush, Savage, Glenn Beck. You go, I'm gone. So, all due respect, I ain't doin' it for you.'

'Me either. Ain't about me.'

'Yeah, well, this army thing's the only thing you got to stay in the game. You gotta come out of this looking righteous.'

'Main challenge is gonna be when Mikey comes on the line. I gotta have the general on board by then, else he'll just pull it.'

'You can do that.'

'You better believe it.'

'And you're gonna sue the news channels, too. You don't sue them, it's good as putting your hands up.'

'I don't want to do that,' I said.

'No one asked what you wanted.'

That was when you came in through the front door, threatening someone outside with prosecution if they didn't leave you the fuck alone. You didn't notice us sitting there in the easy chairs, at first. When you did, it gave you a visible shock.

'Rachel,' said Galtieri. 'Tough times.'

You narrowed your eyes, trying to figure out what we were up to.

'I'm just leaving,' he added, pulling himself to his feet. He took your shoulders in both his hands and air-kissed you. 'You doing OK, with all this? Must be tough. First his brother and his ma, now this. You don't need this. See you, Rachel. Look after this guy.'

You hadn't moved since you'd first come in. 'His brother?' you said to Galtieri. 'What about his brother?'

I said, 'OK, G, I guess I'll see you tomorrow morning...' but you were already looking from Galtieri to me and back like you'd been the butt of some funny.

'What about your brother?' you said.

Galtieri said, 'The one with the schizophrenia. I told John: my kid has that.'

'Is this some sort of joke?'

I said, 'Maybe we should let G go—'

'My son has a disease; you think I'd joke about that?'

I tried to shepherd Galtieri out. He wasn't going.

You said, 'Oh, y'all must think I'm some stupid fucking tramp.' Then you dropped your voice to a whisper. 'Tell everybody about the stupid bitch and her mental health condition.'

Galtieri told me, 'I'm outta here. John, would you speak to her? I'm talking about his brother. His *brother.*'

'Of course you are. You don't think I'd know if he had a brother?'

'Fuck are you saying?'

'That he's an only child.'

Galtieri made a strangled noise, and looked from you to me. 'I don't know,' he said, 'what the hell is going on here, but it fuckin' stinks, you hear me? It stinks. I mean, what?' He said, 'John, did you lie to me?'

I hesitated.

'I don't believe it,' said Galtieri, shaking his head.

'It was basically true—'

'Save it,' he said. He was out of the screen door, now, heading down the drive to where the reporters were. I wanted to shout out after him that I'd been trying to save your dignity, that the facts were true but the names had been changed, but already camera shutters were clacking, and I had to watch through the spyhole to see his back disappear up the street.

'Great,' I said, once we were back inside. 'That's great.'

'You shouldn't have lied,' you said.

My heart was pounding like a bass pedal as I threw myself into a chair. Implications that you might be in the wrong were exactly how fingers and noses got broken. No: the whole fantasy had to be that I'd lied to Galtieri for no reason at all, and that I was a bad person for having done so. I was getting weary of being that person.

You were pouring wine into a glass in the kitchen. I thought: shit, it's going to be that kind of night.

I closed my eyes.

The air tasted different, in the cool of the woodshed. It tasted… fresher. Air filtered through the needles of trees. On the other side of the door, which stood in feeble outline in the dusk, there was a whole other world. Ontario, Canada, 1970. Inside the woodshed, I was cold, and my belly ached. Visions of poutine swam before my eyes, and for a moment I swore I could smell the beef gravy.

If I could have reached out in the dark and pushed open that door, I would have seen the house, in washed-out colours, far up the dirt track, and heard the individual cries of forest birds in the still. Once every so often, a branch might break, somewhere deep out of sight in the woods – broken by a deer, maybe; or by rot: a dead branch dropping off a dead tree.

But I couldn't push the door open, because like an idiot I'd gotten myself locked in.

045

On the final day, the one person prospering from the fucked-upness of our relationship and my job and my life was the delivery guy we'd hired to fetch in groceries. On the final day, I told him to get me cheese curds, potatoes and gravy powder.

'Cheese what?' he said.

'It's a Canadian thing.'

'Uh, what is it?'

'It's like little bits of cheese. Kinda rubbery.'

'You wanna eat that?'

I told him which farmer's market he needed to go visit. He told me I was the boss.

After his voice was gone, I lay in the chair a long time, a rented life in this rented house, thinking about how I'd gotten here. The whisky was down to the dregs. I thought about Kurt Cobain, lying in his sneakers on the garage floor. You'd been shopping and bought a lot, which meant you'd had a good day. Clothes were being emptied out of big square bags in the bedroom. On bad days, when your body was too despicable to clothe, they'd go out of the window or become a pyre in the yard. I thought of Galtieri. I wondered what he thought right then. I thought of every caller to every station I'd ever worked for who'd ever told me I was an asshole, and it seemed to me that a person is only ever the last word said about them. I wondered about myself, and why I was gonna wake up the next day and record that interview between Lieutenant General O'Connell and Mikey Lang. What insane thing was it, for one man to start a war?

I thought that maybe that's what Mikey Lang did, what every soldier does, when they sign on the line or get in the truck or whatever and go to war. Theoretically it's one army against another, but really it's just one little person made out of person-stuff – bones and teeth and bits of meat – with their photograph of someone they care about in their pocket, heading off to fight a whole army.

I thought about that crazy bastard store guard with the head full of worms and I understood that whatever fight you pick, belief makes it possible, and right. Belief is a seduction, like whispers from a radio late at night.

Upstairs, you were yelling along with Patti Smith, and I tipped the bottle back. A single drop dripped out on to my tongue.

When a man forgets his size and belief lets him think he's equal to the world, it isn't heroic, it's a fucking tragedy, and everyone ought to mourn that man they lost.

Mikey Lang phoned. His voice scraped out of his throat. 'Can't stop coughing, man. They got me on the strongest palliatives they can.'

'You gonna be OK to talk tomorrow?'

'You bet. I been waiting too long for this.'

I told Mikey I was proud of him. 'I did some research on the general's son.'

Mikey was done being able to talk.

I said, 'Here's what you need to say. His boy's a serving officer in the Eighth Army in Seoul, South Korea. "General, what would you do if your son, Captain Patrick Francis O'Connell, was sick, and the South Korean government knew why and wouldn't tell you? Would you abandon your son, or would you want answers?" That'll make the needle jump. They don't expect you to know anything. You got that?'

'Got it.'

'Tomorrow at six, then,' I said.

'John?' said Mikey Lang. 'Thanks, brother.'

'How do I look?' you asked. You were draped around the door frame wearing a sparkly yellow tube of a dress, with long white gloves and a white scarf. The dress showed off your body as faithfully as if it were painted on. You looked stupendous, like you were from another world. Your hair hung on your bare shoulders like an invitation.

'Like heaven,' I said. 'I must be dead.'

You did a little twirl, and looked over your shoulder at me in that way that made my balls tingle. Christ, Rachel, I never understood how you were able to turn from one person into another like that.

I told you you were the most beautiful woman I ever knew. You flared a nostril in disdain, like Elvis.

'I splashed out,' you said, conspiratorially.

'I can see that.'

'Well…'

'Something special happening?'

'Just conferences.'

'History conferences?'

You said, 'Yes, the conferences I go to.'

What I wasn't to do was allow any trace of disapproval or surprise or confusion to cross my face, because you were pumped. The times I especially couldn't say the wrong things were when you were up, when you were down, or when you were somewhere between and therefore easy to tip. What were you doing, standing at the lectern wearing a fur-trimmed ball gown and one of those hats with an entire pineapple on it?

In the final hour of the final day, the delivery guy dropped off the cheese curds. I heard him outside the front door, telling a reporter what he was delivering: cheese curds.

'Search me, man,' I heard him say. 'He says they're like rubber. He's Canadian.'

The notes for the interview the next day were thickish, and held together with a bull clip. I set them on the kitchen counter. The uppermost page had a list of symptoms of the sicknesses the soldiers had been experiencing. Numb limbs. Hair loss. Migraines. I cut the potatoes with the serrated knife, the one I thought you didn't know about, the one I kept on top of a cupboard. Bloating, vomiting, nausea. The potatoes fizzed as they sank into the hot oil. I wound the timer to five minutes, and it buzzed like a hornet as it counted down. I set a pan of water on the stove. Not all the soldiers had suffered all the symptoms, but the families had pooled their knowledge and recognised commonalities. Tumours. Deformed babies. Turning through page after page of soldiers' testimonies was like being beaten with sticks. It was a catalogue of senseless loss. Young men, and a few young women, forgotten in hospitals across the USA. New cases coming to light every day. Sicknesses of types that had nothing to do with soldiering, but with growing old, like each soldier had gotten a whole lifetime's illness visited upon them in a year or two: everything they could ever expect to happen to them, catching up with them all at once and without parades and guns and honour, but in the most ordinary way possible, once and for all.

After the last page had been turned, I felt weak. It tasted so good to be able to breathe.

The buzzer went off.

When I looked up, feeling sick, you were in the doorway again, in a new dress, a black one, with your hair pinned up. You looked like a movie star. I barely saw you. I said, 'That's cute, Rachel. It's like that dress you wore when you…' And then I stopped talking.

I knew I'd done wrong, but for a long time I didn't know what it was I'd done. Your eyes were locked on mine. The timer kept buzzing. You looked at me, and you looked at the pages spread out on the counter. I followed your gaze to my handwriting.

Five-One-Fifty Hold, it said.

Oh, I estimated it all wrong, that span of years I thought I had; that infinite duration I based my ideas on, even against all the evidence and all the surprises and the iron fact of the randomness of everything. Yeah, I overestimated it, infinitely. I thought it was never gonna crack, that little eggshell I put all my hopes and desires into, my grand plans.

The world has no time for us, and the days aren't ours. We're at the mercy of moments of inattention or biological chance that light our flames and the happenstance that snuffs it out. *America's Funniest Home Videos* is a carnival of pratfalls; it's also a catalogue of miracles. People escaping paralysis. Human beings not dying. Every edition of *America's Funniest Home Videos* has a ghost: a show that will never go to broadcast, in which the home video cameras are left running as the family rushes to aid the kid who's just broken his neck, or to scrape the funny little pet dog from the road while the kids cry. That's the world we live in, too.

I sometimes wonder what I looked like in the last moments while I was still me. Pretty ordinary, I'd guess. I looked like someone to whom something awful was not just about to happen. Which is about all the warning you get. I remember you screaming the sort of things you liked to scream. Anything that would find a target. And I remember using all the tricks I knew to disengage and soak it up like a sponge, without provoking you any further. You had to feel like you were hurting me. You wouldn't stop until then. I had to look injured, which wasn't hard, but without making you feel bad, and therefore angrier, which was. The relentlessness of your anger made me sometimes want to laugh. You called me names. You insisted I didn't love Joshua. You said I used you like a whore. You told me what a real man would have done in this situation or that. You told me I'd be happier if you were dead. I'd learnt by that time in our relationship not to offer counter-arguments. You got nasty if you thought there was fight in me. So maybe it was my saying nothing that provoked you to go that one step farther. I took the timer, and first of all you slapped it out of my hand and it smashed against the wall and broke, and you shoved me. You weren't mad yet. Not yet. I sucked it up and resisted every adrenal impulse in me to react. While you kept on screaming, I kept my cool. And perhaps that's what did it. Perhaps it was my fault.

I can see the hot oil now, rearing up like an ice sculpture. An opalescent beast of great beauty, big as a bear. Towering over me; moving towards me through the air. By the time I recognised what was happening, by the time I realised that Fate had chosen this moment to ambush me, it was too late to react. The moment was on me. I thought of Otis Redding, watching the tide. I thought of Shakespeare as his waves broke upon the pebbled shore, and Cobain, godless and gunless. Mostly I thought of you, a few yards behind the beast, looking like I'd deserved this all along. You were swinging now with the empty pan, using your whole body like a batter taking the swing of his career, the one that gets replayed when he dies, twenty, forty years later, and you were beautiful.

At the last moment, just before the beast attacked, I turned my head to the side. The oil enveloped me. A riot of pain: my skin seared, and lifted from my body.

The heavy edge of the pan swung towards me.

The world went dark.

SEVEN

'Chin up – you're going home,' the voice kept telling me, from the pitch darkness.

The pain was so great that at first it was impossible to grasp the meaning of the words. Instead, I concentrated on the voice. The voice was a young woman's, nasal and well bred. I did not know where I was, nor what 'home' meant, except as an idea. I knew only that I must on no account let them take me there.

ἄνδρες: the life lived in darkness.

There was a lot of shaking. Whatever I was lying on – and I was sure I was lying down, although I couldn't see a thing – was being jolted this way and that by some brute force, and me with it. I could hear the ch-ch-ch-ch of a motor engine and, sometimes, the clopping of hooves, and my world was thrown this way and that, rattling all the while, like a barrow full of roof slates being dragged across cobbles.

At first, I suppose, I must have struggled rather, because the woman's voice became stern. She said something I didn't understand, having to do with shells. Shells? Quite distinctly, I remember thinking it queer to be talking about something as trivial as seashells when everything about me was on its beam ends. I thought of Nanny. The young woman was quite firm. 'Your dressing will come apart if you don't keep still,' she said. I tried to think of something amusing to say, but where thoughts should have been, there were only shadows.

I was quite sure my eyes were open, and yet the blackness persisted. When I tried to touch my face, I discovered that my hands and arms were no good either. A sort of panic took hold. That made me pant like billy-o, and shake, and all the while the girl's voice kept telling me that I should come to no harm, and that I would be right as rain and back on British soil before I knew it. She repeated it over and over, like a liturgy.

The pain had reached an exquisite pitch. It was now audible: at first a kettle, singing from the kitchen, then higher, until it was transcendent, like a bad rendition of 'Espirits de l'air' from Esclarmonde. *I remembered then that I was injured.* I tried to confirm this with the young woman, but of course no words came, and in any case a new species of darkness, thinner and more spectral than the first, seemed to be moving in on me. One had the sensation of being outflanked.

The poem! I tried to say. The poem!

No: I would not succumb to the pain, though it grew greater. Vincit qui se vincit! *I remembered some words: 'Think only this of me', and wondered whose words they were. Decidedly, they were not my own. I could hear the rumble and screech of heavy iron wheels on stone, and men's shouts, and the whistling, vibrating pain was now a slice of sunlight, bisecting my skull by force of its concentrated heat, cleaving me from myself; and I thought, 'Oh Christ, not like this.'*

And I dreamt, and in my dreams I was a boy locked in a room in which there was no light, and no sound, and no time.

Possibly 18 September

I awoke, and I knew the place straight away. One does not readily forget the smell of flesh going bad. I was amongst corpses, and near-corpses, and it was fearfully quiet. I should have liked to have been able either to see, in order to reassure myself that I was not the sole living patient, that I had not been abandoned here to rot; or else to have had the ability to call out – I don't know what. The helmet of bandages put paid to any of that, of course. I was locked in the kindest of prisons.

The date mentioned at the head of this entry is given as 18 September, but the truth is that my recollections of what happened cannot be ascribed to particular days. For one thing, try as I might, I could not seem to stay conscious for five minutes together before the pain became so unendurable that sleep swallowed me up against my will. The left side of my head and my left arm jangled at the slightest movement, as though broken glass had been wrapped in underneath the bandages and now lacerated my skin with every muscle spasm. Twice in as many days, I bit through the India-rubber tube that stayed between my front teeth; twice, it was replaced. My head felt as if it had expanded to three times its natural size, and seemed ready to burst, killing me outright.

The clearing stations are for sorting men into three categories: those who are to be patched up and sent back for another go; those with bits hanging off or absent, who will be evacuated for convalescence back over La Manche; and those who need to be operated on immediately – which is to say, those who will die without urgent attention. It happened that I had visited a similar encampment a year previously, in hopes of paying a visit to a fellow Old Walsinghamer, Hinchley – too late, as it turned out. I remembered the station as a conurbation of marquees of the sort one sees at garden parties, now filled with the agonies of soldiers still wearing the mud and gore of the line. Somehow, I persuaded myself that I was not one of them.

One could hear the guns, of course: ours. The battery at Amiens was five miles behind the lines. Apart from the guns, and sometimes the rain, which clattered down on to the canvas, the place was silent. It was easy to imagine that I was the only man left in the world, that the machine of war had consumed everything, but that the guns, crewed by the ghosts of men, continued to fire.

Time passed. My bedclothes had been pulled back. I woke from my morphine sleep to realise that the bandages were being undone. I feared that when they were removed completely, my skull would fall away from my brain in two halves, like a peach from its stone. They would be able to see my thoughts, to hold them in their hands! Delirium had set in, for I really believed these things, and struggled at first against the orderly, who was doing his best to help me. I was weak, however, as though a great weight were pressing down on me. Rien ne pèse tant qu'un secret.

'Stop struggling now, sir, there's a good gentleman,' the man said, as he peeled the layers of bandage back. He was a Scouser. 'You're a big fella, and I'm only little meself, and I'm on me bill, so it's not fair. I want to look at your eye, see if we can't get you back playing for England.'

In spite of the morphia, the removal of the dressing was the greatest physical pain I had experienced so far, for the gauze was thoroughly stuck to my face with congealed blood. The last pass of the ball of bandage was the most agonising: I gripped the side of the stretcher with my right hand (the left, whose lack of sensation I had begun to notice, clutched at nothing); and the world revealed itself to me.

Only until one is deprived of all sight, and made to make pale mental images to supply the want, is it possible to imagine that an ordinary soul can look about and 'see nothing'. I shall never again take colour and light for granted.

The first sight I saw when the orderly began to change my bandages was a pitched marquee roof, stained in blotches, a riot of seaweed greens and slate greys, and every colour between, with the *light of day behind it, luminous and ethereal. There was the medic, with hair of fire-orange, his freckles sharp and tan on a pale, prematurely aged face. There were the old bandages, a textured grey, and my blood upon them, looking more like the remains of some ghastly meal than the vital part of me.*

Blood or bruising had puffed my left eye shut. 'How do I look?' I asked – or tried to. The words were said through the tube, and had more in common with a sigh than with speech; all the same, the man took my meaning.

'Very pretty,' he said. 'Surgeon got the shrapnel out, and we've gor' away without infection so far. I shouldn't try to talk if I were you. We want your face to mend nicely.'

Something didn't make sense. It was after he had started to redress me that I realised what it was.

'Surgeon?'

'You don't want him. He's done twenty ops a day since he got here. He's gor' a right cob on, and who can blame him, eh? I'll see you right. Good news is you're probably as right for evac as you'll ever be. Get you back home, see your wife or your bird, eh?'

I tried to remember whether I had a wife or a 'bird'. The memory seemed painful. I only knew that I mustn't go home.

'Now let's not struggle, eh, sir? We don't want to make a scene.' The new bandage did not cover my right eye, so I was able to watch the man's deft ministrations, able to see his lips move as he said, 'I read your poem, sir. I'm no poet meself, like, not properly, but I thought it was very smart.'

Frowning didn't communicate – quite the reverse. By the time I'd recovered from the firework display of pain that danced through the dark, and I'd opened my eye again, the orderly had gone.

In the periphery of my vision there was slight movement. It was nothing – a mote of dust, perhaps – but my body gave a great spasm, as if receiving a dose of adrenalin, and my impulse was to hurl myself under the stretcher.

Sniper, I thought; and then: no – not a sniper. A trick of the light. But isn't that the clue that a sniper is taking shots? For the first time, I think, I remembered something of who I was, and where I was. Almost, at any rate. There was a man on the next stretcher, his face barely two feet from mine, and when I turned my head ever so slightly I found without alarm that we were staring at one another. He was a very young man with a delicate neck and high cheekbones, and a dreadful pallor. We gazed at one another a long time before the orderly came to touch the young man's neck and then pull the smeared sheet over his face.

The preceding days – or were they weeks? – seemed to have been shut away from my mind, and now they drifted back into partial view, surrounding an invisible presence that grew ever closer. I was afraid of the memory even before I knew what it was.

From much farther back in time came the words from the play: Weak mortals, chained to the earth, creatures of clay as frail as the foliage of the woods, you unfortunate race, whose life is but darkness, as unreal as a shadow.

I knew by then, I suppose, that I had lost my eye. I thought that if there were any such thing as justice, I deserved to have them cut out the good one, too.

Late in September 1916 – perhaps the 25th

Twice our boat had set out from Le Havre, and twice the hydrophone heard U-boats in the Channel, and we had been obliged to turn back. The boat was a converted cattle-ship. The walking wounded were kept separate from the bed-bound, and in the cavernous iron belly of the boat we lay listening to a lot of singing from the soldiers on the upper deck. It was not the drunken Saturday night songs of mess halls, but rather a positive hymn to one's hearth and family, every word sung proudly. Around me, some of those on the bunks in the cattle stalls murmured along. Voices from the East End of London and the Highlands and the Black Country and the ridings of York-shire mixed together, in song: men from every corner of Britain, half of them illiterate and most of them with bullets or shrapnel in them, or with arms or legs sawn off, and they made that song beautiful, because they meant it, every word. When those massed voices belted out Though your lads are far away, they dream of home, *they sang those three long last words – dream – of – home – at the top of their voices, as though words alone could bring them faster to their babies and their women and their old parents; and those words stood for all the dreams that had kept them alive through it all; all the dreams they had denied themselves in order to stay alive; all the dreams that were soon to be realised: a confirmation of survival, words that by being sung showed against all hope they'd come through.*

I lay with my head wrapped and my good eye closed, and listened. Since they'd patched me back together, oh God, I had not dreamt of home. I had dreamt of staying in a crater in the mud of France and waiting to die.

We reached Southampton at dusk – about twenty-thirty, in the new mode. The tower of the Royal Pier was a spectre in the gloam-ing. There, they unloaded us from the steamer like so much baggage.

A blast of frigid air greeted me as two stretcher-bearers carted me out on to the port-side rails, and left me there while the gangplank was made ready, with the grim silhouettes of the dockyard cranes for company, seeming tangled up in themselves, and the maniac shrieks of seagulls.

A platoon of conscripts was huddled on the dockside, awaiting the return crossing. At the start of the war, rugger players and burly village policemen and miners had stood there, watching the ships roll in, awaiting embarkation and adventure, and conversation had been easy because they knew one another, and they shared cigarettes and jokes and sang songs. The menagerie of creatures whose dish-plate eyes now watched my pathetic return to England was of an altogether different stripe. Irregular in shape and gait; this one with a stoop; that one knock-kneed. Their clean uniforms did not fit. The seamen set me down and I tried to thank them from the corner of my mouth, but the wind and the cries of seagulls snatched my words away. I clutched at the arm of one of the men as he passed, but he looked at me, aghast, and drew away.

8 December 1917

The previous entries were not written at the dates stated, for obvious reasons, but, rather, later in the following year – today. It is one of those bright early winter days, when the December sunlight brings a very great clarity to every detail. The gardens are bathed in glorious apricot, the frost has burnt off, and a snail has been working his way up the pane of the window that looks on to what we call the herb garden, really just a little patch, now bare except for rosemary and blasted mint, leaving his mark in a vertical trail of slime that dries and turns to nothing. A little fir, freshly felled and brought up from a wood in Surrey, leans against the exterior of the scullery wall, ready to do service as a Christmas tree, blocking half the sunlight from entering my study.

It is the first time I have come back into this room. Somehow I could not face the possibility of finding myself in here, so for two months I have passed its blind door a dozen times a day, on the way to the sitting room or hobbling back up to the bedroom, stick in hand. What ghost did I imagine lived here?

I watch this scene as though my mind and my body have nothing to do with one another. I am scarcely myself: rather, I am lodged in the body of Captain John Rutherford and am seeing through his eye, and yet am not him; am not the spirit associated with his name or experience. He is physically broken. I am spiritually broken. They are two separate traumas, *as one might say. Each must heal by itself, without the support of the other.*

I sit with my feet up on the windowsill and my old herringbone greatcoat draped over myself in a futile effort to keep the draught out. A volume of Plutarch lies unopened in my lap. Once in a while, Mary-Louisa will come in to stoke the fire, in a reverent silence that is punctuated by the popping of new coals; just now I can hear her taking down the dining-room curtains and singing 'Mademoiselle from Armentières' to herself. The men used to sing that in the trenches. She would not like the lyrics they sang. Outside, a robin watches me from its perch on the coal bunker.

The letter came through in this morning's post. The writer's name, delightfully, was Ellery Sedgwick: the editor of the Atlantic Literary Review. *It was handwritten on soft, cream-coloured paper. His manner of phrasing the letter implied an acquaintance, although I struggled to recall it. He had been impressed by the quality of the poem 'Arma Virumque Cano', seen published in* The Times, *he said. He had tracked me down through Despatches and Walsingham Boys and believed he was addressing the poet. He did not know whether poetry was something that I had taken up seriously or whether the trials of war (which he ventured to say he knew something about, his own youngest son having been lost at Gallipoli) had allowed me temporary access to an elevated poetic consciousness to whose altitude I had no intention of returning. If that were so, he said, so be it. He understood very well, he said, that unlike the American, who wears his heart on his sleeve, it is the nature of the Englishman to disdain outpourings of emotion, unguarded feeling being well left to Continentals and indiscreet lady poets and the hysterical. He said that if, however, I were interested in contributing something to the magazine, on whatever subject, with a view to publication on both sides of the ocean, he would read it with great interest.*

Five pounds, he said.

When one runs the side of Mr Ellery Sedgwick's letter quickly across one's fingertip, it is possible to make one's finger bleed. Oh, Ellery, Ellery, there is everything to say.

Tears pour from my right eye down my hot right cheek and drip on to the page, but I do not stop writing, even though the nib passes through them and the ink and the tears commingle and are shaped into letters, words, sentences: my confession. I am intent on my own destruction. Before me is the photograph of the farmhouse. Each time I blink, I see my hand reach up to knock at that white-painted door.

I must look possessed, for when Mary-Louisa enters she creeps about with such an effective regard for quiet that I do not notice her at all. When eventually I throw myself back in my chair, having brought my journal closer to the present date, she screams in alarm, and I make a sort of abbreviated cry – without thinking, I turn to face her, and she starts a second time, violently, and covers her mouth with a handful of pinafore, despite herself.

'Sorry, Captain,' she says. 'It's just—'

'Mister,' I say, from the right side of my mouth – the side that still has lips. 'Or sir. Not Captain. Not any more.'

'Beg pardon, sir.'

I tuck the photograph under the blotter, and again turn to her, although she will not meet my eye. 'Mary-Louisa,' I say – not without difficulty. 'Look at me.'

She raises her eyes with an effort. She has eyes of the clearest azure, eyes that seem now so cold, in their fear. They regard the good side of my face with an expression I have seen only in the faces of dear women at Irish wakes as they whisper loving words to the cold body in the casket. There is no line of division between life and death. It is a spectrum, and I am somewhere on it.

I pronounce, 'You said I was beautiful, once.'

She blushes thoroughly.

I tell her, 'I am still in here, Mary-Louisa. I am still me.'

But that is a lie.

10 November 1916

Iris did not come to the First London. However, the War Office, in its wisdom, sent down some damned fool covered in decorations to hobnob with the men – just the sort of chap we sent on lots of courses, back in France. He arrived at the hospital at the same time as an influx of soldiers, mostly Canadians, who were threatening to overrun the place by weight of their numbers. One could hear from their pitiable cries that some were in a ghastly condition, and yet these were the troops who had been adjudged fit enough to ship back from the front: packed on to trains and packet steamers filled with cries and the smell of carbolic, and manhandled on to British soil, and then into the wards of the First London General Hospital, where they lay minus fingers or limbs or eyes and in varying degrees of stoicism. Sometimes one of them would start to stink, and you knew he had had it.

The senior fellow was accompanied by a photographer, who kept ducking under his little cloth to take pictures of us lying there. No doubt there is a picture of me in one of the ha'penny rags even now, being used to illustrate our nation's resolve. It is a good job photography cannot capture thought.

'It's packed in tight,' I was told by one soldier, a captain in the 4th Canadian Mounted Rifles and a native of Cobb Creek, Ontario, who, having exhausted the achievements of his limitless family, the severity of Canadian winters and the solitary beauty of the Great Lakes, the pleasures of hunting and fishing and the pioneer spirit, had taken it upon himself to act as my eyes. 'You can't move for iron bed-ends. Everything's polished up real good. Most of the guys here look like they're getting along OK, sitting in their beds and joking with the nurses. There's maybe fifty men, but some of 'em are kinda quiet. You gotta look out for the quiet ones, eh? You got injured, you go to the ones who don't make any sound, right off. Hell, you know

that, I'm sure.' I wanted to be able to ask him to describe what he saw out of the window, however prosaic the scene may have appeared to him, but there was no hope. 'I forgot to tell you about my cousin Reggie, a real big-hear; he's on the Feldman side...'

The arrival of the Canadians served only to compound a crisis of staffing that had already been severe enough. It was obvious that the nurses were unable or unwilling to take more than a few hours' sleep at a time; the same voices could be heard all through the day and night, discussing medication or private arrangements or one another in low voices, or making conversation with patients – 'is that a picture of her? She's very pretty' – and, on occasion, breaking down completely. I lay entombed in the darkness, my bandages my shroud, listening to goings-on around me without a word, like the spirits in that poem by De La Mare.

'How come your missus never comes to see you?' said the fellow in the next bed, late on in my convalescence – a few days before I was discharged. He was a regular – an 'Old Contemptible'. Contemptible was right. I thought it was a pretty crude sort of question, and I told him so.

'No offence intended, old boy,' he said, and his nose was clearly out of joint. His bed was on my right side – had it been on the left, I think he might not have asked.

My wedding band was there all right – there was no denying it. A picture exists, too, to prove we've done it. The two of us, against a mottled backdrop: me, standing, in a white tie, and Iris seated, slightly farther than arms' reach away, holding a spray of roses in her lap. She looks queerly triumphant. I wear the expression of a condemned man. We weren't awfully pleased with the picture, but we had to have one. When visitors come, up it goes, on the mantelpiece. Would all that change, now?

'Well, what about your mates, then?' he wanted to know.

Six months previously, I should probably have been put out that a fellow had presumed to poke his nose about in my affairs. War, however, teaches one forbearance. The alternative is not to be borne.

'I had one good friend, but I do not suppose I shall ever speak to him again,' I breathed. It is the longest sentence I had constructed since my injury. 'And my brother died at Mons.'

'Sorry to hear it,' said the soldier. 'Where did you get yours?'

He meant my injury, of course. I did not tell him, for fear that he might recognise my name.

13 November 1916

The doctor in charge of assessing the walking wounded was in a blazing hurry. Without looking up from his notes, he told me to walk along a line on the office floor. Then he said, 'Oh – Balliol man. Sit down, old fellow, there's no need for that,' and I sat down once more.

He wore side-whiskers. He took a long look at me, his gaze settling on the side of my face, and raised his eyebrows. 'Well, well, well. Someone's been rather lucky, haven't they?'

'Lucky?' I said.

'Oh, I'm sure it doesn't feel very lucky,' he said, getting closer and squinting at what was left of my jaw through his pince-nez. 'Infection, that's the biggest problem. You fellows roll around in the mud after you've been wounded, mud gets into the wound, and bingo – gangrene.'

I tried to remember men rolling in the mud, but it wouldn't come to me. I remembered the mud itself, all right – chalk-mud, two feet deep in the six-foot trenches. I remembered the mud, and I remembered men's feet going bad.

He said, 'Now, you'll have to keep this clean, old chap. Naturally, it is somewhat difficult for you to keep food and saliva in your mouth – you'll just have to do the best you can. What you don't want is for this area here, around the eye...' He snatched up a square mirror, and set it before me '...to get dirty...'

His voice went on, but I'm afraid I didn't hear it.

One gets used to the face one will see when one looks at one's reflection. The mere shaving off of a moustache makes one reconsider oneself.

On the right side of my face, I appear to be around thirty years old, although in fact I am much younger. My hair is thick and dark, and has receded at the temple. I wore it oiled, before the war. My eye is coloured a very light blue, and looks as though it is made out of porcelain. The cheekbone is high and defined – handsome, I believe – my cheek sallow, my jaw strong. I look like a man. My effort at growing a military moustache remains above my upper lip, on the right side.

On the left side of my face, the lips, cheek and nose have been torn off my face, and most of the teeth blown out. One can see my tongue, cradled pinkly in the mouth. Sometimes it lolls too far and, were it not for one lower molar that has stayed in position, would flop out entirely. At the front of my face, both lips are drawn back from the teeth – burned off.

I will not be back to munching bulls'-eyes very soon.

My left eye is gone. My left ear is gone. My left eyebrow is gone. All of the skin on that side of my head, and on my neck and left shoulder, is scrambled and burnt, the colour of a side of bacon, over-done. The texture of my skin is like nothing so much as road-tar in summer.

'Could have been far worse, you know,' said the doctor, without any suggestion of humour. 'The burns sealed you up. That's why you're here to tell the tale.'

It is impossible to write when I think about these sorts of things. The twitching muscles of my arms won't allow it.

26 November 1916 – evening

The taxi driver had taken a look at me and said I could have the fare for nothing, but I had insisted on paying. 'Gammy leg,' he said, over his shoulder, as we drove. 'I tried to walk straight but the army doctor, he weren't having it. Said I'd march in circles.' I looked out of the window. As we passed each street light, the good side of my face was reflected in the window, and for a fleeting moment I was whole once more. 'My lads are both over there,' he went on. 'Both in the infantry. They won't tell me where they are – not allowed to. We send 'em food parcels and that. Socks. Army passes them on.'

I didn't want to know more. It was the wrong time to have sons – the wrong time to be a man. Everything was duty and expectation, and the best-respected men were those who, like lambs, gambolled off merrily to their extermination. Death was glorified, in poem and blithe song, while a desire to keep out of trouble got you a white feather, or got you shot. Oh yes, it was a very good time indeed to be dead.

I stood on my doorstep for a long time. The air was frigid, in Mavering Gardens. I felt any change in temperature acutely on the damaged side of my head – the sensation was not unlike a hangover, but only on the one side – as though half of me had been having a jolly good time, of which the other half thoroughly disapproved.

I thought about a little stone cottage on a hill, and then the cold got too much for me.

I pulled the bell.

'Is there anybody there?' said the Traveller, knocking on the moonlight door.

I dropped my kitbag on the step, and waited. Three journals, one revolver, one holster, one officer's tie, one officer's cap, one pair of non-regulation leather gloves, one notepad filled with poetry, a hospital envelope decorated with the names and addresses of fellows who imagine I will look them up after the war, one handkerchief with the name Jo. Rutherford embroidered on it, one tin mug with the enamel gone and the rust setting in, and the photograph of the cottage.

I rang the bell again, and called out, too. It was the first time I'd attempted to raise my voice since... since then. At first it did not work: the sound I made was like a goose. I tried again, and rapped on the door.

But only a host of phantom listeners
That dwelt in the lone house then
Stood listening in the quiet of the moonlight
To that voice from the world of men

'Hello?' I called, feeling rather conspicuous. 'Iris? Mary-Louisa? Anyone?'

And then came a sound of bolts being drawn, and the electric light went on, and then the door cracked open and a dam-burst of light gushed forth. It was Mary-Louisa, in her black-and-whites, and her smile turned to horror as she looked at me, her face whitened, and she collapsed on to the floor.

As I stooped to help her, the sound of running feet made me look up. Iris was coming from the back sitting room. Behind her was Millicent Davenport. Davenport pushed past Iris (who had stopped dead upon seeing me) and came to Mary-Louisa's aid, ignoring my presence entirely, but for a curt 'Hello, Rutherford. Do shut the door.'

Iris did not move – she had become rooted to the ground. 'My God,' she managed, eventually. She seemed to grasp for other words, but none came. I was at a loss for words myself. I told Millicent Davenport to let Mary-Louisa alone so that I could carry her to a chair, but Davenport hadn't changed much in two years, evidently: she was having none of it, insisting that my offer was interference and that if there was carrying to be done, she was perfectly capable of doing it. My God, in two years on the Western Front I never wanted to punch anyone in the face as much as I wanted to punch Millicent Davenport.

Ignoring Davenport's clucking, I hoisted Mary-Louisa up and deposited her on one of the chairs in the front reception room, keeping the bad side of my face turned away. My heart was beating terrifically. Davenport had fetched some salts and Cook and her boy were up as well, adding to the general bedlam. As Mary-Louisa started to come round, I saw Iris was still standing in the hallway, watching me, as though I were the walking dead.

'We were told…' *she said.*

'What do you mean? Who told you that?'

'There was a letter, from a man in your regiment. He said he'd seen a shell drop on you.' *Iris was not wearing her wedding ring, I noticed. Nor was she dressed in black. Neither my wife nor my widow, apparently.*

'He said he'd seen you killed.'

'Well,' *I said,* 'he might well have done.'

'What happened to you?'

I might have told her that I couldn't remember what happened to me, and that for all I knew I might well be *dead, but Davenport was in no mood to hear anything I had to say. With Mary-Louisa righted, Davenport – the very name feels like someone spitting in my eye – fetched off to the back room, trying to drag Iris off with her, and, when Iris would not be led, flouncing off in high dudgeon.*

We faced each other from opposite ends of the hallway.

'Oh, John,' *she said.*

'Nothing need change,' *I said.*

We went and sat in the drawing room, she on the two-seater and me on a chair that was new and rather over-sprung. When set against the privations of the past years, being here should have felt comforting, and seeing Iris' face brought back so much. She reminded me of a girl I'd met in an estaminet *in Rouen.*

Iris asked me to show her my wounds, and so I closed the door and stripped down to my waist, and showed her. I even took the dressing off my shoulder, revealing the badly healed flesh. Her eyes, however, scarcely left my face.

'Does it hurt?'

'It is a great deal less painful than before.'

She said, 'Your voice sounds different.'

I put the dressing back on, and then the shirt. It was far too small.

'And how is…?'

'Quite well. We both are.'

'This must be quite a shock for you, then. My coming back like Lazarus.'

Iris looked at me, and then took a breath and considered the hands in her lap. 'Julian Piggot-Smyth was mentioned in Despatches. They're awarding him the VC.'

'Well, good for Julian Piggot-Smyth.'

'There was a service for him.'

Presently I said to her, 'You stopped writing.'

'Well, what was I to say? Would you have wanted a letter full of lies?'

I laughed. The noise startled both of us – it came out from the place where my cheek had been, and sounded nothing like laughter.

'Yes,' I said, 'yes, lies would have done. Every word out there is a lie – everyone insisting it will all turn out all right – news reports saying how well we are doing – the talks they give the men. They said the bombardment would have cleared the wire and flushed out the German front lines, and we got halfway across' – my arms had gone into spasm – 'and it was all still there ...' I tried to talk, but I was sobbing too hard to form words, and the sobs were of such force that I could hardly breathe. I collapsed on the floor and put my head on my wife's lap, and wept properly for the first time. I knew she could not understand, and I knew it was scaring her, to see this raving madman, his head like that of a rotting cadaver. I felt as though a current were being passed through me – the jerking was so violent that it was all I could do to remain in physical contact with her.

Someone tried to come into the room, and Iris told them to leave, twice. 'I shall come up soon,' she said, and the door closed once more.

Presently – when enough time had passed that my body was once again under my control, after Iris had soothed me with gentle words and the softest of stroking on my good arm – I flopped back on the hearth, exhausted. The fire was at once in the grate and in my skull.

'I'm sorry,' I said. 'I'm so sorry.'

Iris shushed me. There was a species of determination in her expression as she looked at me.

'I didn't want something awful to happen to you.'

'Oh, let's not pretend.'

'I'm not pretending. Are you quite well? Your nerves, I mean?'

'It isn't shell shock, if that's what you're suggesting. Nor neurasthenia. I know what that looks like.'

'Well, do you know what you're saying?' She looked at me evenly. Oddly enough, her question made me feel more at home than anything up to that point had done. 'Oh, dear, dear Iris,' I said. 'Yes, I'm fully in command of my faculties. Don't worry, I'm not about to start blabbing.'

The conversation fell away.

'It's more bloody than you can imagine, out there,' I said, at length.

'We've been reading about it in the papers,' Iris replied. 'Did you have to... Did you kill anybody?'

I experienced a sudden tightening of my throat. The walls of the room seemed to glow like phosphorus, and shudder.

'I think I should prefer not to talk about that,' I said.

I do not remember falling asleep, but for three whole days I slept in the front room of the house in Belgravia, with some blankets placed over me and some cushions under my head. From the outside, the house would have seemed completely normal – no one could have guessed at the presence of the corpse in the front room. But then, every house has its secrets.

10 January 1918

I think that I shall never sleep again, not really. I had rather hoped that, after a few months, I should pass a night without seeing his face looking at me, that last time.

They're still taking the shilling in droves, poor imbeciles, like so many crusaders, off to smite Saladin. The photographs in the newspapers show His Majesty inspecting them, 'near' the front line (of course, it doesn't say where), whilst the men toss their caps into the air as one. That is not the war. Wondering whether one shall ever cease to smell rotting flesh in the air: that is war. Being obliged to confine one's excursions to the time after dark, when ladies and children are not abroad to be frighted: that is war.

The practicalities of managing a badly injured face provide one with about half an hour's grim entertainment each day. The morning of my first poetry reading proved no exception.

Firstly, there is the insertion of the eye. What a grisly ceremony this is. Of course, one might leave the eye in all the time, but I find it becomes rather uncomfortable overnight, owing perhaps to the drop in temperature; consequently, the eyeball resides in a glass of diluted spirit vinegar in the bathroom – quite the ghastliest object. I never fail to find myself amazed that so large an item can fit snugly into the socket. Placing it behind the eyelids (one real, one grafted) was at first an absurd affair; even a few weeks after the healing of the stitches, it was the work of a moment to pop the globe in and be done with it. Fishing it out again remains an ordeal; one has to scoop behind it with a sterile spoon, and one might well imagine how joyous a lark that is.

There is no concealing the fact of my cheekbone having collapsed. Often, a sort of white secretion from the tear duct gives the impression that I have been weeping milk. Worst of all is the sheer idiocy of the expression these mutilations seem to create – as though one half of my face is always wincing on hearing something obscure.

Without the flesh or skin of the cheek to protect my mouth on the left side, it is inevitable that one awakens with saliva all over one's face – one's head is no more effective for containing fluids than a bucket with a rust-hole. On the left side of my head, I look like a Jolly Roger – the skin has been burnt away from what remain of the grinning teeth, leaving a display of gum and tooth stumps and facial tendon. The raw edges of the skin, which often develop sores and splits, are supposed to be dabbed at every day with a clear solution that reeks to high heaven and stings like billy-o. The nuisance of it is that, whilst most of the burned side of my face has no need for shaving, the hair follicles having been razed from my jaw, the several places from where bristles still grow are precisely those spots most apt to tear – the awkward corners that need to be cleaned up. Shave first and dab second, or the other way around, it makes no odds – one spends one's first hours of the day in agonies, and quite often bleeding visibly from several places. Indeed, my howls have become such that for some months Millicent Davenport waged a serious campaign for my exclusion from the bathroom, insisting that I should go and make a noise below stairs where no one but the staff would have to listen to me. Ah yes: Mr Ellery Sedgwick was feting me as a hero for having saved the poems of Private James Lyons for posterity, and arranged first one reading before an audience, then several, then, when the popularity of the poems soared, began to talk of a memoir; meanwhile at home I was a pariah.

One morning, I snapped. She had taken to rapping smartly on the bathroom door every morning even before I'd so much as applied the shaving soap to my face. She was thoroughly startled when I threw open the door, not least because she was dressed only in one of my nightshirts. From it poked two legs like hams.

'Look here,' I hissed. 'Why don't you eff off?'

'How dare you?'

'I've had quite enough of you,' I told her. 'What you are remains your own affair, but I remain the man of this house, whether I sleep in the master bedroom, the boxroom or under the stairs. It bally hurts to do this every day. If you don't like what you hear, put something in your ears.'

'You'll—'

'In fact, put something in your mouth while you're about it.'

Davenport eyed me contemptuously. 'I suppose you think you've a right to speak to me like that,' she positively seethed.

'I do, as a matter of fact. I've paid quite a price for this house.'

'No,' she spat. 'That's the point – you know perfectly well where the money came from. Who do you think paid for an indoor bathroom, precisely? Do you suppose you'd be able to support your "wife" now, if she hadn't her own money?'

That was hardly the sort of price I had had in mind. 'I see you're quite happy to dish out those feathers of yours,' I said, showing her my missing cheek. 'Well, this is the result. As is my crying out in my sleep, which spoils your beauty sleep. I rather think you're getting the better end of the bargain, wouldn't you say?'

Enunciating this tirade had been quite wearying – words depending for their meaning on the letters p, b or m require contortions of the mouth that risk reopening wounds, and in truth I had resorted to shouting. Iris had appeared on the landing.

'What is it? What's going on?'

'Rutherford, making a scene, as usual,' muttered Davenport.

'Milly,' scolded Iris. 'Try to be understanding, please do. You must see he's awfully lucky not to have died.'

I thought this a rather poor argument to attempt to put to Millicent Davenport.

After old Ham-legs had gone off to bed like a dog caught snaffling the Sunday joint, Iris came to me, where I stood in my pyjamas, and she hugged me. The gesture caught me quite off guard.

'Dear John,' she said.

'Are you quite sure you wouldn't rather I had died?' I asked her. 'I'm unsure myself.'

'Don't ever say that,' she said.

'What, even when I get in the way of you and her?'

'Who else but you would understand?' my wife replied.

10 March 1918

Under different circumstances, one might have called the reading of Lyons' poetry a success. Indeed, the assortment of ancient ladies who gathered to hum and haw at it at Hatchards seemed thoroughly to approve of what they were hearing; that is, until I read out the later stuff, that composed after he had had his first taste of the trenches. To read aloud that *sort of thing should have been considered most unpatriotic.*

I have to confess no little enjoyment at seeing their faces whiten, their collective demeanour 'dusk and shiver', as they understood the prescience of the poet in his piece on soldiers' homecomings. Nobody wants us back, even when we sing for our supper.

He attended in person, of course. Throughout the reading, he stood at the back of the shop, leaning nonchalantly against a case full of Gibbons, never once meeting my eye.

4 April 1918

More than one year and seven months, now, and still, every night: his face.

18 April 1918

And still it rumbles on, this 'War to End All War'. For all the balls talked by the bright people running things, there is little doubt that we shall all be dead long before any solution to this intractable mess is discovered. Progress is measured by the inch – a tiny gain here or there. According to The Times, *the Bosch has been putting mustard gas in artillery shells, and now we're at it too. When I got my Blighty our men scraped by without clean water or food in swamps of rotting corpses – a seeming acme of human debasement. If this does not drive one to despair, then what should?*

Following a third reading of Lyons' poems, word has reached me that publication is intended of a slim volume. According to Mr Sedgwick, who writes almost daily, in feverish (and unseemly) excitement, the collection will be a fillip for serving men. It will consist of the poet's early works – in other words, those poems that say nothing to tarnish the image of the war as a confrontation between a ragtag of cowardly, deceitful Bosch suffering bloodlust, and the honest British Tommy, full of high ideals.

It is tripe, of course. I should laugh, but I do not think I can. The Germans are just the same as us – we used to shout to one another, across the wasteland, when the lines were close enough. It was the strangest thing, to risk looking over the top of the trench and see nothing, not a single living soul, and to yet know that there were, within shouting distance, hidden in trenches, hundreds of men.

Spring has come, although with the rationing and the shortages and the strikes, it is a pretty rum sort of summer. Cook is managing admirably, on so little.

Out of sight though he unquestionably is, he can hear every word I say. The impulse to jump up and tell him to let me alone, to tell him that I am already doing everything that I can do to keep him alive, requires a restraint of which I am scarcely capable.

Tues. 19 March 1919

Tea at the Murrys'. Murry himself has a certain something about him, which one would hesitate to call good looks – rather, he seems troubled and somewhat self-absorbed, and therefore utterly magnetic. But it is Katherine who is the dynamo of the pair. She is a New Zealander who wears her black hair in sharp bangs and never stops talking.

We discussed Smuts' League of Nations, this evening – a very positive proposal, we all agreed. There need never be another occasion when it is in the interest of one nation to attack another.

Iris spoke with particular warmth. Her campaigns to influence the minds of young women seem to have turned to the topic of universal peace; I often overhear her talking about it with dear old Millicent Davenport, with whom I have not exchanged a civil word in three months.

'Why not simply do away with countries altogether?' Katherine asked, at one point. 'I don't see what good they do.'

'Darling, don't be foolish,' Murry told her, for the benefit of all present. 'Where would one holiday, if there were no other countries?'

The assembled company fell about at that. I found myself exchanging weary looks with one of the women present – a writer of perhaps forty, with limpid, tired eyes. 'Will you take a turn with me?' she asked. 'A little fresh air would be very welcome.'

Her husband, a Jew, seemed perfectly at ease with the notion.

The grounds were very simple: a largish chunk of Somerset, enclosed within a slatted fence. She took my arm as we wandered down the slope towards the stream that ran there. The weather was thick; rain long overdue.

'I knew Rupert Brooke,' she said. 'I cared for him. Have you read anything of his?'

I said I had.

'I thought young Lyons' poetry resembled his in some respects,' she remarked. 'Perhaps there is something of Wilfred Owen, too, but when I read it in the paper I thought of Rupert. Of course, I am bullying you fearfully into professing a love for his work, but naturally it wasn't to everyone's taste and it does seem so very naive, now. Is your facial injury from the war, or from some other thing?'

'I got what I deserved. I paid a price.'

'The price of bravery?'

'I wasn't brave.'

'I don't suppose that can be true.'

I said, 'Young Miss Mansfield is certainly the life and soul of the party.'

'Yes, quite. Yes, she's very good at being herself. It's something I myself have never managed.'

'Still, she does flatter herself that she's a strong writer.'

'She is a very good writer. There are very few writers whose work I might wish I had written, but she is one.'

We sat on a bench, and looked out at the world. The birds seemed to be singing in Greek. I remarked upon it.

'Don't they?' she agreed. 'What a suggestive notion. According to rumour, of course, you really did notice Lyons' poetry in the thick of war at the Western Front. Tell me, can that be true?'

'To the strains of that mawkish Tipperary song.'

She permitted herself to laugh. 'Well, you have a good ear.'

'Just one, alas,' I said – I believe with some feeling.

She replied, 'I understand that quality is to be preferred over quantity.' Her remark proved indigestible until the exact moment that I realised that I was being baited. We exchanged coughs by way of confirmation.

The night air caressed us; made siblings of us.

Presently, the sounds of dinner having diminished, I suggested that we should retire to the house.

'May I ask you one question before we do?' she said, placing a long-fingered hand on my forearm. 'Please feel free to say no. I intend to be rather blunt.'

'I rather fancy that to be your style.'

'Were you right?' she said. 'What you did, I mean – the injuries, the experiences – all of it? Of course you believed something, as we all did. Protecting one's country and one's neighbours – all that. Were you right to have believed?'

The birdsong was discordant, and my voice, although it had not yet spoken, was high in my throat. I looked up at the stars: they were blurred. I said, 'I can assure you, I no longer believe in anything. The believers are the ones who die first, and those believers who are left make it their business to see to it that the rest of us perish.'

'No God?'

'No religion of any sort. No state, no nations. There I agree with Miss Mansfield entirely.'

'Then it was for nothing?' said the writer.

'It was a lesson in mortality.' I said. 'Bought at massive cost, and not yet paid for. It was a sermon against belief.'

'Thank you,' she said, nodding slowly – examining the shingle path; the chrysanthemum beds. 'You are very silly to have indulged me.'

I felt myself blush – a pain that seemed to cleave the muscle from the remainder of my cheekbone and my jawbone, and burn me. I meditated on how it might have been, had this woman been a man. She knew something, I thought. It was a queer feeling, that she was able to see into my soul.

'Shall we go indoors?' she offered.

'Yes, rather. Leonard will be wanting you back.'

As we made our way towards the house (Raff's Cavatina was playing on a phonograph), I cast my eyes around the gloaming, to see where Private James Lyons had got to. He was standing near a knot of trees, silhouetted against the navy blue of the night-time.

He was pointing at me.

11 June 1925

I can breathe again only when bloody London starts to break up, as splits and cracks appear in the conurbation; as one glimpses, not lichen-like urban parks, but rather sprawls of grass, verdant plains. I ride the train's thunder: this Juggernaut. Windows rattle in their tight casings. Beyond them, wisps of the great beast's plume lick about the carriages, fill tunnels with their grey mousse or billow voluptuously.

I must be crying. It has the usual effect on the man sitting across the carriage from me (an Englishman's social barometer: the rustle of newspaper, the nice adjustment of Harold Lloyd spectacles). He wears a bowler, and a wedding band. His nice routine would be compromised by engaging with the greatcoated figure hunched against the window, lapel up, brim down over the missing cheek. I am bigger than he is, less well dressed than he is, and I am crying.

I am grateful that Libris decided against publishing a photograph of me on the cover of the Lyons book. It would by now be in fifty thousand homes in Great Britain, and I should not be able to go abroad like this without some literary spark noting that there sits the officer with the injured face who commanded the poet in the Great War.

At the pretty town of Watford an old painted spinster is helped on board. She is helped off again, with great commotion, at Buxton Junction. She carries a hatbox and a peke and is herself a delicate sort of luggage. The iron-grey sky has not lifted. It will hang low like this all day, revealing nothing of the time of day, of the season, forcing Man back upon his station clocks, his pocket watches. 'It's thirteen minutes past eleven, sir,' the conductor tells my unwilling fellow passenger, as he clips our tickets. Then the station guard blows his whistle, and my body goes into fits. My fellow passenger is good enough to disregard me altogether.

The train presses on, ever north. His pose as he peruses the Daily
Herald *is no less starched than his collar. I shake a cigarette half
from its packet and proffer it across the compartment, noticing the
man start as I reach towards him. The gesture with which he declines
is oddly ambivalent. Something in it makes me understand that I
have been an egoist. I have seen men fearful of me, women too. This
man fears, not me, but – what? Discovery?*

*'Your collar button's undone,' I observe, through a mouthful of
acrid cigarette smoke. I fully expect the man to fold up his news-
print, hang his thin city umbrella and his coat over his arm and
resituate himself elsewhere in the train; and so he does.*

*I throw down the window, letting brisk English air turn the com-
partment into a refrigerator. Yes, this is it: my country. The bounded
fields taking the undulations of the land; flocks and herds speckling
hillsides; farmers driving paired beasts. (I once saw a horse in a tree.
People would find that funny, now.) Companies of birds scavenge in
the plough's wake.*

*There is great stability in the ages-old architecture of the land. The
ancient strips; the paddocks and meadows; the sowing of crops in
lines. A land tamed, not pulped into submission; furrows for crops,
not men.*

*It is nearly dark when I alight at Penbury station. The teashop is, as
ever, grandly closed. No official waits to check the fares of the dozen
who descend the three steps from the ticket gate on to the unmade
road. The hanging baskets are naked soil; the gaslamps unlit. I pull
my scarf up against the chill. Past cottages, the graveyard, the butcher's shop, I meander, revelling in the heady fragrance of the fields
and the air that is full-term heavy with rain. Men in caps, drifting
homewards from I know not what labours, grunt greetings as they
pass darkly by.*

*Both pubs are lit up within. The sparkle of glass is visible between
the cracks in the curtains. I cannot go in, although I would like to,
for I would have to remove my hat, and then I would be asked to
leave.*

*I go instead to the guesthouse on a nameless lane, where the front
door is opened by a matron who starts on seeing my vast shape filling*

the door; and then pats down her apron and says: 'I wondered when you'd be back. You'd better come in.'

In the night I hear him howling. It is like the hospitals, all over again. How I should recognise the scream of a stranger, I don't know, but I know him, from the moment I wake gasping. I had been dreaming of thousands of pairs of eyes.

Were anyone else lodging, they too would find themselves unable to avoid listening, in the dark, to the tortured cries of the man from the 9.15 from Paddington.

From the breakfast room of the guesthouse, through the net curtains whose unfailing whiteness is a touchstone of decorum, one is treated to a vista of Penbury, beautiful, thatched Penbury, and the moors beyond. Here, before one, is proof of the town's exact moral equilibrium: two pubs and two churches, women scrubbing doorsteps in the freezing cold, while horses clop along the main thoroughfare, pulling the brewer's dray, the milk cart, the pipe-smoking rag-and-bone men.

Of course, all this is gone from London; it has been stamped out with mechanistic ruthlessness. Everything in London is American-style department stores and motor cars, and casual murders inspired by moving pictures. That was never what I fought for. When the English Post *came down to the front, in the pockets of shivering new recruits, we used to lap it up like a tonic, savouring the photographs and line drawings of hamlet, dale, spire. We were town rats, but we pulled ourselves together and looked lively for rustic villages on pretty wolds. I lost half my face, my brother and all my mates for the pictures in the* English Post.

I am early to the breakfast room, on my first morning in Penbury. A newspaper and a plate of food are waiting, just as they always are. I place my hat within reach and sit at the window in profile.

My fellow traveller comes in due course, lured, no doubt, by the fragrance of frying bacon. To be English is to breakfast. In his case, it is to stumble quailing into the electric light and kipper smells of the breakfast room wearing one half of yesterday's clothes, not the public half. He is much reduced, and there is blood on his cuffs, the poor bastard.

He seats himself at the corner table, quaking.

'You look unwell,' I say.

He looks up, startled, and then sees me.

'You,' he realises, 'from the train.'

I sit munching on fat sausages, while he stares wildly at the wallpaper, as if trying to find answers among the fleurs-de-lis. Our hostess has fed us well, in spite of the shortages: she's scrambled the eggs with breadcrumbs to thicken them out. The blood pudding is succulent. From the corner of my eye, I cannot help see his expression betraying frantic calculation. As he eats, he tries to keep his bloodied cuffs hidden.

I tell him, 'I imagine it comes as a surprise to you to be eating breakfast at all.'

I remember the raising of the dull revolver; its flat snap, nine years ago; how the mud swallowed any reverberation.

'Not, mind you,' I continue, 'as much of a surprise as Mrs Castle might have had, finding you.'

'Leave me alone.'

'Or your wife. You have a wife, don't you? I wonder where she thinks you are.'

'Look, who are you?' he says.

'Someone else who never sleeps.' I turn towards him, and his face grows pale. 'Perhaps I understand you a little. The nightmares. I've always thought a gun would be simplest, but I can't seem to summon the nerve.'

Realisation isn't long in coming. Then, at last, he cracks. 'There's so much pain,' he says, pushing his scrambled eggs out of harm's way, burying his face in his hands. 'I don't know how to make it go away. I know it's not manly to admit that.'

'I'm only half a man. You can admit it to me.'

He takes a breath. 'Both of our boys. Both of them. They weren't even twenty, yet. Both of them within a week. And you get a letter, and...' He seems lost in himself. 'I don't know what I am any more. I mean to say, I am a good husband, stoical for my wife...'

Outside the windowpanes, a light rain is falling. A biplane cuts the air over Penbury.

I offer him my handkerchief, and he sobs silently into it. 'It's as

though the world has decided I don't feel anything,' he says, in a low
voice. 'When all I do is feel. And I go to work each day, I come home
– and what for? It was all for my boys.'

'The world would say it is your duty to carry on.'

'Duty?' he says. 'What is duty, if this is the result?'

'A fairy story, I'm afraid,' I tell him. 'Duty is merely doing the
wrong things for the right reasons.'

'Then to hell with all of it.'

'To hell indeed.'

'I'd be called a shirker every day if it got me my children back.'

'Now you're talking like a man,' I tell him. And I light a cigarette,
and feel its cool smoke filling my lungs. 'It seems to me we humans
will be better off when we stop inventing reasons to live, and reasons
to die – as though such things require reasons. We never do anything
but destroy ourselves.'

At length, he says, 'I'm sorry, I haven't asked you anything about
yourself.'

'Me? Oh, just another soul consigned to hell for doing what I
thought was right. One of God's lesser monsters.'

The landlady, Mrs Castle, has come into the breakfast room. 'I
won't have blaspheming, Captain, thank you very much,' she tells
me, clearing our plates: my Goddess of the North, with the pinny
and the bangs. She wears black. I turn half away so that she doesn't
have to see. Her little daughter, Lil, hides behind her mother's skirts,
until I reach my hand to her and she comes to me. Her girlish hair is
soft, her head so fragile. Mrs Castle says, 'Will you be wanting your
rooms made up?'

The man has been staring at me, hard; now he breaks his gaze,
and examines instead the wedding band. Then he looks up at me.
'Thank you, no,' he tells her, at length. 'No, I must return to London
today. This gentleman needs some sleep.'

'Very well,' she says. 'And you?'

I smile as best I can, conscious that I am crying again. These
damned tears! I have nothing to cry about – I got to come back.
And I look out on Penbury, where merry chimneypots evidence the
morning fires having been lit, and a pair of widows stand in earnest
conversation waiting for the butcher's shop to open.

'I have a visit to pay, and then I shall come back this evening.'

'I'll make sure your bed's turned down by then,' she says.

And I happen to glance at the mirror on the wall, in which he stands, gazing out at me, as though he's never seen me before. Not the man from the London train, of course. I don't mean him.

11 June 1925 – afternoon

They have bought new gates, I see. Solid things, with the badge of a local manufacturer screwed on. No doubt the extra money has also afforded the farm truck that can be seen from up on the road, half hidden behind the building. In her letters, his mother implores me to come and inspect the vehicle myself, as if to stamp it with my approval. I feel quite inadequate offering my apologies, but 'I regret I am unable to come so far north owing to the cooler northern temperatures and the delicacy of my health'.

Since I have been here, a butterfly has been busying itself in the bramble. It is a drab brown creature. When I first saw it fluttering about like a mad thing I wondered about the natural predators of the butterfly, and tried to imagine how it might avoid being eaten when it flaps about so. And then it settled on a bar of the gate, and it seemed to become invisible.

I wonder whether they remember anything about him but the money. Do any of us? Oh, they're very fond of Lyons in the right circles in London – looking back at previous entries in this book (and why have I not the discipline to keep up a diary properly?) it is difficult to imagine a time when those early Lyons poems inspired new recruits to the army – in 1917, 1918 – even as the war itself died.

How many men were killed by that poetry? What sort of murderer am I for having brought it to the public?

My feet are no longer used to long marches (I am far from certain they ever were) and transformed themselves into a mass of blisters very soon after starting the walk from Penbury. They now squelch in the boots. I am reluctant to let them breathe, for fear that I should not want to put the boots back on.

The house itself does not look very different from the way it appeared last year at the same time; its greyness seems revealed, rather than constructed: the turf stripped away to reveal Cheshire rock in the shape of a bungalow, the smoke curling from the fat chimney seeming to come from the very core of the Earth.

This gatepost is as far as I can make myself go. As last year, as the year before. It matters not at all whether I cab over here or endure the long walk, whether I take myself by surprise or obligate myself by means of discomfort, my quest fails, always, at this final moment: at the top of the track leading to James Lyons' home. I know that today will be no different. Next time, perhaps – qui sait? Or perhaps there will be no next time. Perhaps the shame will kill me.

I have been here an hour, so far. I will go, soon. Oh, it would be simple enough to say the words – it is, after all, in keeping with the spirit of the decade. In the twenties, one does not have to behave well: one merely has to be honest about one's bad behaviour. But no: to bare my conscience would be to set off a bomb in their quiet household. This is a burden I deserve to shoulder. I do not deserve to sleep.

Hodder and Stoughton have offered me an editing job. When I left England to fight the war, I was the junior editorial assistant at The Proposal magazine; now, merely for my promotion of a dead poet, they wish to elevate me to a position of real power – the power to grant publication to writers, to decree that this one shall speak and be heard, while this one shall have his voice taken away from him, his name erased, his beautiful ideas and objectives lost to eternity. One might only have one life to live, but that life affects every one of those it touches, however fleetingly. Selfish indeed is the fatalist, for he condemns those around him to whatever end he has decided must be.

The public must not be allowed to forget James Lyons.

He described to me, once, the image of a butterfly perched on the muzzle of a cannon.

That reduced family in the house down there; the toughest of men; me: we are all butterflies. Yes, we are all butterflies.

SIX

044

You sure as shit don't pick your kids' friends. I always thought Cody Bell was a little loudmouth, but he and Josh got on, so Thursdays Cody Bell came by to play with Josh. I'd make food and you'd open packets for me, and then we'd all four of us sit up at the table like eating there made it special. The ritual was important to you, and I couldn't see the point in disagreeing, so I just sat there trying to chew. When Cody called you Ms McAllistair, you said, '*Doctor* McAllistair,' and drank more wine.

It used to be that I didn't say anything: I was pretty happy with eating in silence. You thought I was trying to make some kind of point. After the first argument where you brought that up, I made small-talk every time Cody Bell came around, and you said, 'Can't you do better than that? You used to do it for a living, Chrissakes.'

I guess Cody knew I wasn't interested in talking, and that it was hard for me to make my mouth form the words. He let me talk, in my slurred way, and he answered and made small-talk back, like Bell senior had brought him up to do, and we played out our little piece of theatre for you.

I didn't care that it was artificial. I had no opinion on the matter.

After you got the lecturing job in Europe and had to go away, you said it was all gonna be all right. I'd cope, you said. You said it the way people say things they want to be true.

'Just stay taking your meds,' you said.

They were tiny and white, that's all I remember thinking about them. They kept me going. Kept *us* going. They kept us straight.

The first Thursday after you'd taken the plane out from Ottawa and gone five thousand miles away, Josh and Cody and I sat at the dinner table in silence, basically trying to figure out whether we had to keep up the charade without you there. You'd be coming home between semesters. If we weren't careful, we'd be out of practice when you got back. On the other hand, I liked not having to talk.

I guess it took about ten minutes of you not being there before Cody said, 'Mr Knox? What happened to your face?'

'He was in an accident,' said Josh.

'What kind of accident?'

I said, 'Aw, we can talk about that when we're done eating.'

Talking's a pain in the ass when you have food in your mouth and your mouth doesn't work right. There's mostly numbness in the places where the skin was grafted on to replace the parts that got destroyed, along the ridge of the lower jaw and around the eye socket. When Josh was there, he and I used our own sign language to talk about what crap was around my mouth and whereabouts: his hand represented my mashed face and he'd touch it in the place that needed attention, and catch my eye. I thought perhaps when you went away he'd just say it out loud.

Josh used to proudly tell people his dad had an artificial eye until, one day, some girls said 'Eew!' and mimed puking. After that he didn't tell people about the eye.

After we'd finished dinner that first time you were away – the meal we never ate because you couldn't stand zucchini – and we'd stacked the dishes in the washer and crashed in the den to watch *Stargate SG-1* while we waited for the sound of Bell senior's Volvo turning into the drive, Cody said, 'Mr Knox, can we talk about it now?'

'I was cooking,' I said.

'What were you cooking?'

'Fries for poutine,' I said. 'Then a very bad man came in and threw the oil at my face and it got burnt.'

Cody was wide-eyed. I could tell he wasn't buying it, either.

'But it doesn't look burnt,' he said. 'It looks like big bubbles.'

'That's because that's not the skin that was damaged. That skin got taken from other places on my body, and they put it on my face.'

'Why'd they make you look like a monster?'

I said, 'Thanks, Cody.'

I should have felt hurt, I guess, or angry. Instead, I got up and found the pills, and put two down with a swig of water. I was on two hundred mil, and on top of that I was double-dosing. They kept stuff even. Some of the water came out of the corner of my mouth and spilled on my shirt. There was a stash of clean shirts in the kitchen closet, all the same colour, ready for substitution. I'd changed my shirt a lot, in the seven years since the very bad man attacked me.

043

Later, after the Bells had gone and Josh was asleep, I called you. It was after midnight in the UK, but you were awake and wanted to talk.

'They've put me up in the student halls,' you said, 'and there's this condo the history faculty gives the visiting tutors – I'm supposed to be getting that soon.'

'So what's up with London?'

'I didn't see much of it yet. It's really big. Like LA, you know? When you come in to land you just see it stretching away for miles. But I've basically been preparing for the first big lecture, on Roman propaganda, so... Maybe I'll go be a cheesy tourist on the weekend. It's a Roman city after all. There's a professor from the anthropology department who wants to show me around. He's written a book on Durkheim. He seems OK.'

'Durkheim, huh?'

In a normal relationship, with the insecurities of separation and distance, the man would have made some comment to the woman at that point in the conversation – maybe something hostile, maybe some flippant aside, but all meaning the same thing – don't fuck the professor. I knew better than to do that. I knew if I did, there'd be a bombardment about trust and love and a whole lot of other stuff, and you'd slam down the phone and I'd call back and you wouldn't answer, and then I'd lie awake worrying about whether now you'd go and fuck the professor just to get back at me; and maybe just after I'd finally gotten to sleep you'd call and we'd have to work through a coupla hours of emotional ups and downs, with you getting angry because I seemed not to care.

I took the phone to an easy chair by the back porch, and turned the lamp out so I could see on to the land. The house sat like a vulture in a cage: the clearing was surrounded on all sides by tall, thick forest, and in winter, when the deciduous foliage closer to the ground died away, the view went farther, between the trunks to where the land sloped away to reach the beaver swamp far out by the sheds. When it snowed, and the forest was white, I thought of *The Lion, the Witch and the Wardrobe*. But this was September, and still hot, this late. The French doors were open. Dad built that house to keep the heat in, and now, aged thirty-seven, his son's body had also been modified so that it couldn't lose much heat – the sweat glands on half of me were gone.

I told you how I hadn't been able to sleep. You told me all about the faculty and about some of the personalities you'd already encountered – the professor of comparative literature who never did her hair; the fat old professor famous for fucking the students; the anthropology professor who'd taken you under his wing.

Yeah: under his wing. That was how you described it.

There was a deer in the forest. I caught a sight of the white fur on its throat, in the dark. I said, 'That's good.'

'Meaning what?'

'What meaning what? I just mean it sounds like you're settling in.' I didn't know what I'd said wrong. 'Do you have everything you need? Want me to send anything on?'

You did not.

In the early days, when I still wore bandages on my face and had regular visits with the doctor, you got pissed routinely because you thought my passivity was a strategy to shut you down. You couldn't stand that there was nothing you could do to make me mad. You never understood that I wasn't choosing to be that way. Now, your anger was because you felt I was trying to make you feel bad about yourself. I tried telling you, too reasonably, I was calm because I was tranked out on SSRIs and had no feelings about anything, any more. The SSRIs were why I was still alive and the SSRIs were why we were still together, but the SSRIs were also why we'd barely had sex in however many years, and why I couldn't keep my dick hard when we did. (It was the SSRIs that made me balanced enough to reflect that if you did fuck the anthropology professor, it was probably for the best, and it was the SSRIs that prevented me from saying anything about his offer to show you around. I guess you could say those pills had their moments.)

I told you what Josh and I had done in the few days since you'd gone, and for the sake of peace I didn't say that he missed his mommy. Yeah, somewhere in me, I knew that was rough on Josh. I don't just mean rough, I mean that it was wrong, totally wrong, but I couldn't access that kind of emotion, back then. Those things just killed emotion stone dead. No spark; no nothing.

We talked about the research work you'd done – mostly at the British Imperial War Museum and at the Bodleian Library at Oxford University, outside of London. You had to make appointments to look at the documents, there. There was reverence in your voice when you spoke the names of those places, and I don't know how we got there but you ended up riffing on feminism and Virginia Woolf and the temperance movement, and listening to you was like listening to a beautiful piece of music. You were you again, the you from City Lights bookstore, the you who made up limericks. The moonlight fell on my face and reflected me on the inside of the window. If I looked through my reflection, I could look at the land and the forest, and in the foreground the butterfly bush, transplanted the whole way across a continent. The sight of that mash of man in the pale light made me want to spew. You were getting ready to give your first war poetry lecture, you said.

'I'm proud of you,' I told you, and whilst I meant it, I didn't feel it. I didn't feel anything, and that was a very satisfactory way for things to be.

After you'd hung up, I sat a long time looking out at the world, seeing the little kid me running around in the yard or climbing up trees. Dad used to sit right here in the den, watching TV. That old furniture was all gone now – you'd bought a white leather couch that was sticky to the touch – the sensation was too much like when my skin melted. Josh and his friends weren't allowed to sit on the white couch, in case they left marks. There was another couch used by me and Josh and Josh's friends: a beat-up second-hand one a neighbour in the valley had been tossing out, which sat facing your couch across a divide of Native rug and the shifting stacks of books that popped up in our home like molehills. Even so soon, I missed that those heaps didn't move any more.

042

For seven years you were the one who went into the world, and then you left us. I had to remember how to talk to other people; how to drive a car.

The nearest town to my parents' house in Bryde's Crossing – it was always their house, never ours – is good old Clinton, famous for having the oldest fire station in the province.

I drove, remembering the route my dad used to take. From the house, take the turn-off after the river, and keep on down to the first set of stop lights, maybe thirty minutes' drive, past the veterinary clinic for horses, past the Canadian Tire and the Tim Horton's; then turn again at the farm that sells eggs, dill pickles, turkey meat and eggplant. Keep on another five minutes. A coupla strip malls tell you you're on the outskirts of something; then the LCBO, and then you see the old watchtower poking up over the trees, and after another corner you're in Clinton, a town with two bars and two churches, and five shops selling second-hand books, all flying the maple leaf. In Clinton, men wear lumberjack shirts with the sleeves rolled up and they drive flatbed Chrysler trucks, or pick-ups, or four-by-fours with bull-bars in summer and a plough in winter. The youth of the town are the ones who couldn't get out, and they bag customers' goods at the checkout or reprice the cheeses as they go out of date.

Now it was late fall, and there were pumpkins on sale. When Josh and I got out of the car in the parking lot by the canal, the temperature was kind and cool and there were still little bits of flowers floating in the air. That was OK. We went into the grocery store.

'This embarrassing for you?' I said.

'Not really. Everyone knows you had an accident.'

'How do they know that?'

He looked over at me like I was stupid. 'You never come to Meet the Creatures, or the end-of-year play. All the other dads do.'

'Really? Your mom said no dads ever came to those.'

It didn't feel good to be around people, but it didn't feel bad. I guess I'd have preferred that they weren't all moving around like that, in my peripheral vision, but it was the place itself that was real difficult. It wasn't the hospital and it wasn't home. The objects and the distances between them were unfamiliar. On the way in, I put my hand out and missed the door, which is a dumb-ass thing to miss. Josh got it. He said, '*Dad.*'

'What? It's easy for you. You got two eyes, so you got *perspective.*'

'Whatever.'

'Serious, dude.' We were sailing into the fresh produce hall, and most of the shoppers near us were talking confidentially to each other. A lot of secrets going on in that place. 'No one taught you this?' I picked out two apples, and set them apart from each other on the rim of a refrigerated chest. I put a Kraft dinner sideways on the opposite rim. 'OK: the apples are your eyes. Are they seeing the same thing?'

'Yeah.' My son's expression was like I smelt bad.

'Nah, not the exact same.' I showed him how one apple could see one side of the box; how the other apple could see the other. 'See? So because you can get an idea of how big the thing you're looking at is, you can say how far away it is.'

Talking of looking at stuff had made me aware of eyes, and there were a lot of those pointing our way. When one eye is out you gotta turn your head a lot to look around you, so there was no hiding that I'd noticed the staff at the deli counter and the shoppers in ones and twos and the guy restocking the bread barrow all gawking at me. That didn't stop 'em staring. Harvey freakin' Two-Face, right there in the store. I pulled up the collar of my jacket anyway.

'Let's get our shit and get out of here,' I said. 'Get our things, I mean.'

'You said shit.'

'You *heard* shit. Different thing altogether.'

At the checkout, I tried to make conversation, the way I figured an ordinary person would. Over the head of the checkout clerk, who wouldn't look at me, I could see three other checkout clerks, racked like toast, all staring. I purposely unloaded the basket with my bad hand. It was no good for precision jobs like typing or holding a pen, and even though I could still use it to manhandle bags of pasta or bottles of Clamato juice, it hurt. Not the same as it had years before – the feeling of being raw and itching and cramped all at the same time and not being able to touch it because of the dressings. No, now it was just the stuff inside it that hurt, the bones that had set badly, and the tissue and muscle that hadn't knitted up right. When I used it to put the groceries on the conveyor belt, the checkout woman tried not to touch the items herself. She pushed them past the scanner with a pencil.

The bagger was helping someone else, pointedly. Josh did his best, but he was seven years old.

'Where's your mommy today?' an old lady in a quilted jacket asked Josh, pretending she hadn't seen me.

'In Europe.'

'Is she coming back soon to look after you?'

'She's away for a year,' Josh said.

I said, 'Hey, Josh, who's your friend?' out of the working part of my mouth, and Grandma worked out I meant her and remembered something she had to do, quick-smart. At the time, it just felt a little unfortunate, that's all, but now, thinking back on the conversation, I wish I'd bludgeoned the old moose.

I wish you'd been there. Your presence might have vouched for me some.

041

Being famous is good preparation for being scarred. You get used to people thinking you can't hear their gossip about you and trying to work out who you are. The few people I'd known as a kid had left town, or died. The strip mall was new and the record store was gone.

In the bakery, the old-timer who once ran the place now spent his days in a chair in the warm by the counter, while his son, himself getting on for sixty, cooked the loaves and served. I walked in, and the old man started out of his chair and began gibbering incoherently to the world in general. He didn't have his teeth in.

'Don't mind Dad,' said the son. 'He forgets stuff. What can I get you?' That bread smelt great.

But the old man was excited, and he found his dentures and came up to me, his eyes wide, and pumped my hand.

'You came back,' he marvelled.

That was some memory on that guy. Maybe Mom had taken me in there once when I was three years old, or something; I couldn't remember him at all – I only vaguely recalled the shop – but the old man behaved like we'd been best of pals, and he clapped me on the back and talked about a bunch of stuff that meant nothing to me: people whose names I didn't recognise; events that meant zero. The more of this stuff came out, the more embarrassed I felt.

'It's been a long time,' I said. 'I look a little different now.'

'You look just how I remember you,' he assured me.

I looked in the mirror behind the counter, at the me with the half-face made out of melted pink plastic.

'Dad, leave him alone, he doesn't know you.'

'Sure he does,' said the old man. 'He lives down on Bryde Road – don'tcha, pal?'

'Yeah, but—'

'There ya go,' he said, wheeling around to his son; pointing triumphantly at his own temple – 'Ya see? I'm fine. A *residence*, he says,' he confided. 'Couldn't afford it if he tried. I built up this business. Now look at it.' The old man was bristly and gripped me with a hand that was holding on for dear life. I never saw that man before.

It was hot in that shop. I told them I'd come back for the bread, and I got out of there, to where the world was made of trees and earth instead of people, where no one acted weird around me.

Clinton had changed. I guess I stopped going there, after that: I ordered stuff in by phone, got dark windows for the car, and read more.

You didn't call.

040

The house in the valley came with ninety-nine acres of Ontario included, most of it forest. Dad had got it at a time when that kind of land could still be bought cheap.

Until I went and lived in a city, I never understood what it was that I had, as a kid: all that space. Acre on acre of forest and swamp and track, owned by my mother and father, mostly untouched by them, unseen, even. As a kid, I used to explore and camp out on the land, and play at being an Algonquin hunter before the settlers came.

For thirty years after it was built that house had my parents in it, and then my parents and their little baby boy, who grew, and then just my parents again. After a few years it housed tenants, people I only knew through anecdotes – the family that never paid rent on time; the lone writer who had a heart attack and had to move away; the hippy couple, both teachers, from out of town. Then the house stood empty a while. After a few months of the grass growing and the wind blowing in gusts, one rainy day a U-Haul truck arrived, driven by a mother with a little baby: a woman with long dark hair and piercing eyes, who supervised the offloading. Finally, coupla days later, an ambulance drove up the track. Two strong nurses brought out a gurney with a mummified figure on it, and they hauled that burden up the three steps to the front door, and took it up the wooden staircase to the big room at the top of the house. It was the boy, come home. The noises he made were pretty bad, but there weren't many ears to listen to him: just the dark-haired woman, and the new baby, and the forest.

It comes back in flashes.

The feeling of being on fire, and the pan, thumping into my face. For years, I woke up yelling and trying to fend off that pan.

The first year we lived in Bryde's Crossing, I couldn't wear clothes. Sweating the whole time because of the burns and needing electric fans pointed at me. My face was badly, badly bruised, from the injury and surgery. It was more than a month before I understood where I was. I was in my parents' bed! If they'd been alive to see me there, they wouldn't have known who the fuck I was.

You were my life support: beautiful you, who liquidised my food so that I could drink it from the side of my face that wasn't burnt off, you who changed the dressings on the burns to my right shoulder and arm and hip and leg, the places where the oil had soaked into my clothes and sizzled on me while I lay unconscious in the kitchen back in San Francisco. Twelve of my bones had been fractured or broken where you'd beaten me with the pan. It hurt my ribs too much to sit up; my right arm was in plaster and my fingers were all busted up, besides the three skull fractures which just had to be left to fix themselves. I couldn't do very much for myself at all, there wasn't another soul around for miles, and you were there to take care of me. I couldn't risk saying what I thought, so I didn't risk thinking it. I had nightmares, and wet myself sometimes, and you changed the sheets.

Oh, I was scared. I mean it: I was really fucking frightened of you. You went around like Florence Nightingale, and you looked after me, you really did. I think you stayed and nursed me as a way of hurting yourself, a sort of masochistic duty, rather than guilt – guilt would have made you vicious – but I couldn't trust the serenity that had come over you. That wasn't you, not at all. How long would it be before I did something that made you flip out? With my speech so slurred, I was shit-scared that you'd mishear me and take offence, and if you did, I was helpless. One good hit to the head, and the skin grafts from my ass holding my face together would be ripped off. So I lay there in great gratitude and total fear, and I never took my eye off you the whole time, and I tried to work out how to get away.

The doc was there, this old Jew who'd known my father. I didn't recognise him the first time he came, but he called me Johnny and after a while I realised it was old Steinwitz. He used to say,

'Look what the bastard did to you.' The bastard in question was supposed to be a burglar. I remember how you looked on me like a guardian angel. When you left the room, I asked him to help me escape. That was what did it. It was at the point when I still couldn't manage actual speech, and he must have thought I wanted him to help me kill myself, because he wrote me a script for happy pills.

After I started taking those, the years fell away like dead petals.

I started popping those pills, and suddenly being trapped in a broken body wasn't such a big deal, and I was able to gaze at the ceiling and think about nothing at all for hours at a time. So we never got to the part where I got angry with you for having done what you did. The fear dissolved, and I resigned myself to the fact of needing to get well again, and to staying home, and to father-hood. You taught art history in Ottawa and sometimes Kingston. And you were calm – so calm. I didn't worry you'd run away, but was always surprised that you didn't. I guess you were getting what you needed, somehow.

I used to think Canadian weather sucked. My childhood was all about the summer being short and hot and full of bugs that come at sunset and get in your hair, followed by endless winters, winters that extend past the excitements of Christmas and skating on the Rideau canal, past the snowmen and then the black snow and the multiple pile-ups on the 401, and past the running out of firewood well before you're done setting fires, winters that keep going through until April, getting bleaker and greyer and more dead until you wonder if the other seasons just forgot about that part of the world and went someplace else. Ontario went on for ever, beautiful and severe.

There were stars at night. There was a universe.

I went out alone, and wasn't lonely. One day, you were out of town, visiting with someone, I don't remember who; Josh had been picked up for kindergarten and I went out on the land and was preparing to take down an old rotten pine before it fell on the shed, and the breakfast show on CBC1 was getting reports about the World Trade Center being hit. Then it was both towers. North America was in lockdown, and Bush was declaring war. I knew I should have had a visceral response to it, but 9/11 stayed on the other side of a thick glass wall. I went about my business, felling the tree badly. I felt nothing about that, either.

A few days later, after bathtime, then storytime, then bed, when the TV was showing film of people jumping a hundred storeys, over and over again, Josh came downstairs, clutching his blanket. Some older kids had said the Muslims had knocked down the Trade Center towers, and he was scared and couldn't sleep. He thought the Muslims would come and kill us. We cuddled, and I told him no one was coming to kill anybody.

'We have seen the images of fire and ashes and bent steel,' Bush orated. 'The people who knocked these buildings down will hear all of us, soon.'

I wondered what you'd be thinking about that, wherever you were.

I told Josh that everything was gonna be all right.

Around the front of the house, far along the track that leads to the gap in the overgrown hedgerow and out on to the lumpy track through the valley, there's the woodshed. All the time since I came back, I never went into that shed.

The musty, sappy smell of chopped pine is what I remember. I went and stood by the shed, and I thought about loosening that treacherous latch, and opening the door, and letting the demons fly out. But it felt safer keeping them in there. I looked in through the keyhole, but out of habit I looked with the wrong eye, the one that was gone. It made no actual difference. There was no light in the shed. I should have remembered that from thirty years ago, when I had been trapped in the dark, and someone else had stood outside the door, looking in.

039

In 2003 you came back for Christmas. I'd been sitting in the dark, and then the room seemed to swing in the headlights of a car turning on the drive, and someone was dropped off. I didn't get to my feet until I heard your key in the lock.

You were standing in the vestibule without any suitcases, and your hair was all shaved off. Your face seemed sharper. It took me a moment to realise it was you. You looked around the place like a tomb raider breaking into a pyramid – I half expected you to turn on a flashlight. You put on the main light and stood under it, looking at me.

'Welcome home,' I said.

You smiled a tight smile.

I said, 'I like what you've done with your hair,' but that seemed to have been the wrong thing to say. 'I missed you,' I said.

You came over and pecked a kiss on my good side. Then Josh came downstairs and you lavished affection on him.

Later, you skipped dinner, and went instead to the room that had once been my father's study but was now yours, and you wrote letters longhand on special writing paper, your bald head bent close over, putting down words at a furious pace, like your life depended on it.

038

It was Christmas. It had snowed, and we went out on the land to pick out a tree.

We'd have missed the good trees if we stayed on the Bryde Road, along the side of the land. In the forest, the going was slower: it was untamed – fallen branches, sudden drops. It was beautiful. The space between the trees was wide, especially in winter, offering a hundred directions to walk, all carpeted with virgin snow. You wore your skirts and your boots and didn't mind that your legs got cold, but you wore a snow jacket with a hood lined with fake fur, out of which poked your shaven head. With you: me, dressed for the snow and wearing a balaclava too, to stop the aching. I looked like a terrorist, of course. You looked like a fascist. We made quite the Christmas pair.

You talked about all the different kinds of adventures you'd had in the three months you'd been an Englander; getting lost on the London Tube, getting freaked out by how close together everything was out there; being treated like shit because of Dubya. You were cynical and disparaging about your colleagues in education.

'They like to label interests,' you said, as we paused in a clearing to watch rooks high up in a tree that looked like a burned hand reaching towards the sky. 'They like art to be in one box and history in another, you know? They don't want the kids to see "historical documents", whatever they are, as having a value as imaginative or aesthetic creations, and if you're there to learn about pictures and articles, you better not go polluting them with historical context.'

'Short sighted,' I said.

'You know, I wanna be giving these kids something truthful. History doesn't exist in some cloud of bullshit dreamt up by Jacques Derrida. Am I ranting?'

You'd gotten some colour, owing to your indignation. It made me smile. I said, 'Give 'em Herodotus. That'll fry their brains.'

'Yeah.'

After a while I said, 'So how're you doing, these days?'

You concentrated on the path ahead.

Way back on the land – half an hour if you're walking through snow, half that if you're on skis – there comes a little rocky rise, and then the land dips to the lagoon. That lagoon is impassable when it's thawed. When we came to it that time, though, icicles hung from the branches of the trees and we'd been slipping and sliding plenty where puddles and streams had frozen under the snow. You could tell where the lagoon started because the snow was perfectly flat, there, and bulrushes poked out of the edges of the white plain.

'What do you think?' you said.

'Definitely risky,' I said – but you were already on your way down the bank. I heard my own voice calling out after you in the quiet.

Walking on the ice should have been a frightening experience, but I didn't get frightened since I started taking the pills, all those years ago. The expanse of sheet ice was the one place on the land that offered a clear view of the creamy grey sky. As we walked, the ice creaked beneath our feet.

'We should spread out more,' I said, and we walked farther apart, listening for the first suggestion of a cracking sound. At the mid-point, halfway to the mesh of reeds on the farthest side, I looked around me and thought that if this ice gave out now maybe no one would ever know we were here. Then I got to wondering how many people in the history of the world had simply been swallowed up by the earth, their existences never recorded, their lives never missed. It made me dizzy. They would have been people with ambitions and concerns and no idea that they were about to vanish. That's the thing about the things that change your life – they seem so fucking ordinary.

Getting to the opposite bank was done cautiously, but it was done. Even when I was a kid, I'd seldom come out much beyond this point. 'No farther than the lagoon,' Dad would say, in that tone of voice that said he meant it. Me and Jimmy Hicks used to go farther than the lagoon, of course. We had a tub we used as a coracle, and we went to the opposite bank and scouted around. There was an old shack —

'Hey, Rachel,' I said. 'This is where — yeah, right there.' Between the trees, we could see the board walls of the shack, in a cramped clearing, farther up the rise. It looked pretty miserable. The walls were badly messed up with damp, and the door, which wasn't locked, had deer-marks on it.

Inside, there was nothing much. The carcass of a stove, and a stovepipe that was probably filled with birds' nests; a fragment of mirror balanced on a crossbeam; some rectangular light patches by the windows where pictures had once been.

'Dad used to come down here once in a while,' I said.

You said, 'It's great.'

'You think?'

'Yeah, it's like a little world.'

There was a second room, as empty as the first but for a table and an armchair whose upholstery stank of damp. I couldn't see a world there, even with the snow outside the window, which can make almost anywhere seem cosy. It just looked like a shack to me.

Once upon a time there had been a footpath cut out of the bush, but it had long gotten overrun with brambles. We clambered and sang 'White Christmas' in bad Bing impersonations, mine slurred, and after a while we came to a beat-down fence that looked the same as the one at the side of the Bryde Road; and it was. We'd driven past the place where that footpath emerged on to the road a thousand times and never guessed it was there.

The sunlight was starting to fade. It was four. We weren't gonna get our tree that day. I remember how you looked in the last light: like a woman. I thought about how much you'd grown since the day you came into my studio. A doctorate; a real insight into your subject; a family of your own, now. Road grit crunched underfoot. You didn't see that I was watching you. You'd done all the hard yards, and I'd soaked up some of the slaps, and look at you now. Your eyes were alive, and as the air got sharp you panted in the shape of a smile. I thought, *It's gonna be all right.*

We kept on the road, taking care not to stray too close to the sheer embankments at the sides, which in the twilight became a lucent white mass. There were no stars. The cloud was hanging low.

Finally, it got dark.

You disappeared, that Christmas. I don't mean permanently; I mean you weren't home, and instead of hanging out with Josh and me you were someplace else, always. Even Christmas Day, you were around for only half the time – long enough for us to trade presents. You'd bought toys and books for Josh – he looked at me when he unwrapped the toys, and I willed him telepathically not to say that he'd got those ones already.

'That's Freud,' you told him, when he opened up the first book. 'He was the co-inventor of psychoanalysis.' The book was big enough to seriously injure someone. I thought about challenging whether it was OK to teach our kid to read sexual issues into everything, but I hadn't disagreed with a word you'd said in seven years, and I wasn't about to start now. I took the mince pies out of the oven and popped my pills while I was doing it.

'What on earth is this?' you asked, when you'd unwrapped the DVD I'd gotten you. '*Love Actually*?'

'It's a Christmas film,' I said. 'It's British. I thought you might recognise some of the places in it. I got you the soundtrack, too.'

You cocked your head at me like I was talking Chinese, and put Tom Waits on instead.

And then we ate turkey; or rather, you got pissed off at me for how long the turkey was taking to cook and I said I'd put it on early like the recipe said, and after about two hours, during which you slammed around the house and played Alice in Chains loud until you got bored with it and put on Stuart MacClean's story on CBC instead and some friends of yours from England phoned to wish you a merry Christmas and you took the phone to your study and stayed there an hour, *then* we ate turkey, which you said was really good, and I forked the food into the corner of my mouth and I said sorry it was late and Josh said what's penis envy?

Afterwards we watched the Hugh Grant film, all three of us together on the couch, you reading the *Cambridge Anthology of World Literature* I'd gotten you, Josh demonstrating his gag reflex every time some people kissed. After a while the tryptophan in the turkey kicked in and we passed out, me and my son. I dreamed about California. When we woke up the *Judy Garland Christmas Show* was halfway over, and the place where you'd been sitting on the couch was cold. Your car was gone. I called your cell but it rang on the kitchen counter.

037

You were in our lives for Christmas '03, and then you vanished away again, back to England, with two suitcases full of stuff. About a week after that, you called and you sounded out of breath. 'I need you to mail me something,' you said. 'Have you seen a brown book around?'

'What's the title?'

'Like a notebook. Pocket sized.'

I cast around a bit, following instructions. 'Under the couch – try the hall table. What about in my study?'

The book in question was a battered-looking thing, and it was half hidden under a pile of papers on the floor by your desk. It was full of spidery handwriting on pages that looked ready to crumble.

'Chin up – you're going home,' I read aloud to you. '…something about a life lived in darkness. Jolted around…'

'That's it.'

'OK.' I snapped the book shut. The leather cover made the sound wet. 'So I can mail that to you, no problem.'

'Use the insured service.' You sounded relieved. There was a cough in the background.

'Oh – you're out?' I said.

'I'm in the lounge of the shared house.'

'I thought you said you were in bed.'

'I was. Now I'm out of bed, and I'm in the lounge.'

'Sorry, sorry.'

'What, you want to turn this into a trust thing?' you said.

036

'Josh's picked up a lot of unusual vocabulary recently,' the teacher
told me. He wore a beard and his sleeves were rolled up. 'I mean
the kind of stuff he wouldn't learn from other kids. Anal reten-
tiveness; Eros complex; the Nirvana Principle, to name but a few.
He obviously doesn't know what they *mean*, but he's been asking
other children to discuss sexual fantasies, some parents have
become concerned...'

We were on half-size chairs at a half-sized table. Me, him and
the school principal. It felt like the John Malkovich film. You'd
have laughed your ass off. I'd never attended one of these meetings before – even after you went to England, you still did them,
by phone. Face-to-face meant it was serious. They'd shepherded
me in by a side door into an office, away from the other parents.

'You seem to be finding this funny, Mr Knox. Josh has been
spelling out the Oedipus complex to children and causing considerable distress.'

'That's bad,' I said.

'If that were my child, I'd be concerned.'

'I am concerned.'

The principal sat forward. She was in her fifties, and wore a
woollen roll-neck. 'Mr Knox, Josh says his mother is away the year
round, is that right?'

'She's an academic. She's with a university in London, England.'

'You are the primary care-giver?' she said, in a voice that told
me plenty. 'Do you have other support structures, other people at
home?'

'No, not really.'

'Josh mentioned you have experienced ill health yourself —'

'I'm over that now.'

She placed both hands on the table. 'You will understand, as teaching staff there is an element of pastoral care within our roles. When a child approaches us, we are duty bound to respond as best we can.' We'd gotten this far without her ever having looked up.

I licked my lips. ''Kay, I'll tell you the situation,' I said. 'I got in an accident seven years ago. That's just about when I moved back here. After the accident I was suffering from acute depression. I mean, I was suicidal the whole time. So the doctor put me on anti-depressants.'

'I don't understand the point you're making,' said the teacher.

'You don't feel anything about anything, you don't get upset about anything. You don't have sex, either, but that's beside the point. If it seems like I don't care, it's because those pills make me a very contented man.'

After a lengthy pause, the principal thanked me for my frankness.

'No, thank *you*,' I said. 'I wouldn't have known about this stuff otherwise.'

'He talks about you a lot,' said the teacher. 'His mother too, of course, but mostly you. He's devoted to you, as I'm sure you know.'

'Can you imagine being told that, and not feeling anything about it?' I said. 'I don't feel anything. That's the pills. Look, I'll fix this, OK?'

Both the teacher with the beard and the principal with the plucked eyebrows became absorbed by items on the desk.

'There something else, here? How about some eye contact?'

All around the room were painted pictures of square houses with triangle roofs and stick families. The man became absorbed by the reverse of a prospectus for the school.

I said, 'Aw, what? You gonna do something I won't like, here?'

'We have a duty of care —'

'Why are you shutting me out? Man, at least fucking look at me.'

But she didn't. She just took a form out of a file. On it, she wrote *fucking look at me.*

I thought about Josh using all those psychosexual terms, and I thought about the monster and the beautiful absentee with whom he shared his life.

'Do me a favour and hold off on that, will you,' I said, pointing at the form. 'Whatever that is, put it away somewhere. Let me make this right.'

'There are procedures,' said the teacher.

I said, 'I know. I get it. Social services, best interests of the child... You think I'm gonna get judged fairly, looking like this? You think you're being fair right now?'

'We're not here to judge you, Mr Knox,' said the principal. But she never looked at my face.

035

The new therapist was green, you said. It wasn't a nationality thing – at least, you didn't say it was, and besides we'd been through the same hoops with therapists in Canada.

'He was surprised when he realised I used the term CBT,' you said, in the cynical voice that told me you were at the end of your day and that you had a glass of wine in your hand. 'I ruled out all the usual stuff before he opened his mouth. I was like, yup, you've really picked one here, haven't you? I'm just a fucking basket case, plain and simple.' You laughed again. It sounded like a conspiracy of one.

I wanted to ask you why you went, if you didn't believe in the process. But I thought maybe I knew why you went. That unfixable status seemed important to you. Your status had been 'in therapy' the whole time I'd known you, and long before. So long as you could prove you were on the treadmill, you had a pass to act however you pleased.

I'd never much minded that stuff, in the past. I looked at our son, who was out on the land, sitting quietly, staring into space.

'I didn't get the book, yet,' you said.

Truth is, it was still on the kitchen table. I muttered something about Canada Post.

'I'm thinking maybe it's time I stop taking the anti-depressants,' I said.

'OK,' you said – the sort of 'OK' that meant let's deal with this. 'Why would you want to do that?'

'I haven't felt happy or sad or anything in ten years, and I guess that's no good.'

We listened to each other breathe in a five-thousand-mile silence.

'I think,' you said, at length, 'you're being incredibly selfish.'

I didn't know what you meant.

You said, 'What our son needs – we have a son, remember? – is stability. I don't think that Daddy getting all poor-little-me is going to help him, do you? I've been getting therapy for ten years. I'm not gonna stop that just because I can't be bothered.'

'I was in the bookstore. There was this book on emotional intelligence. Where's our kid gonna learn that stuff if my emotions are switched off?'

'I don't believe I'm hearing this,' you said. 'Why are you doing this to me?'

'It's not about you,' I said.

You'd already hung up.

034

I don't know what made me read the notebook – I was meant to mail it, but I sat down and I read it, cover to cover.

John Rutherford was a British guy who lived a hundred years before I did. He was the archetypal pip-pip tally-ho Englishman from the upper classes, according to his diary. That's what I got from the first line of his journal. Stiff upper lip, and all that. Except the guy has no lips.

I never had much time for the British. They seemed to me like a bunch of stuck-up assholes who still thought they ruled the world; and besides, I was half convinced you might be fucking one of them. And then there was this guy Rutherford, whose journal started in France, I think, in the aftermath of a battle in World War One, and it was like looking in a mirror. Half of his face had been damaged somehow – the left half, as opposed to the right of mine – Jesus. It was like reading my own experience, but with *feelings* in it. He cries into his wife's lap. He gets angry when people won't talk to him in the street. He wants to kill himself when a kid pukes just from looking at him. I read this thing and it was like breathing. He was more than ten years younger than me when he wrote that stuff, and he sounded like he'd lived a lifetime already.

Right at the start, on the first page, in October 1916, he's on his way to hospital. The book ends back in 'Blighty', with the words *we are butterflies*.

I tried looking Rutherford up on Wikipedia, but that thing sucks ass. There's nothing on it you don't already know. The only online reference to my man that looked right came on an anonymous page about literary figures that looked like it had been written on the internet with crayon. In amongst a list of others – T.S. Eliot, Cyril Connolly, Maxwell Perkins – it listed *John Rutherford, literary editor, 1894–1940*.

So you got through one war only for the next one to get you, eh, Rutherford? Oh yeah, we're butterflies all right.

Josh was home with the phantom stomach pains that had been keeping him out of school since term started. 'What are you looking for?' he said.

'Just tryin' to find this guy. This is his journal.' I showed the book.

'Why have you got his journal?'

'Good question. Your mom has it for some reason. The guy's dead, so he won't be needing it. How you feeling, pal?'

'Sick.'

'Still getting the nightmares?'

Josh looked doleful. I sat down with him and tried to give him a hug, but eight was too old for that stuff, apparently. He pushed me away, and sat on a chair by himself. I lay on the couch. I said, 'What do you wanna do with your life, Josho?'

'Be a psychoanalyst.'

'For real?'

'Yeah.'

'Why'd you wanna do that? Your mom put you up to this?'

'Rutger's parents are psychoanalysts.'

'Oh, Rutger's parents, right.'

'You don't know who Rutger is, do you?'

I flicked through the mental index cards of all the eight-year-olds I'd seen at the school gate. I gave up. Nope, I didn't know who Rutger was.

'Rutger,' said Josh, 'is me when I'm not here.'

'What do you mean? When you're playing?'

'No, when I go out of myself.'

I licked my lips. He seemed pretty poised.

'For real?'

'Yeah,' he said.

'And Rutger's parents – that's me and your mom, right?'

'I'm hungry.'

''Kay, I'll get you some food.'

I opened the fridge. There was a lot of juice and open jars of pickled vegetables in the top part. Neither of us liked those, and the damned things lived for ever. Whenever you were away, we ate one pickled thing per meal, and left most of that, so that at least our consciences were clear. If we were lucky, by that method we might manage to clear out all the pickles before pickling season came around again.

The packet of SSRI pills was on the top of the refrigerator. Two per day, every day at lunchtime. I looked at them a while, and they looked down on me. Josh was sitting on the floor in the den, studying under your paintings of grotesque reclining nudes in pig pinks and blues.

Selfish indeed is the fatalist, for he condemns those around him to whatever end he has decided must be.

When I served up the food, bringing one plate at a time to the table in my left hand, Josh said, 'It's OK, Dad.'

'What's OK?'

'Everything.'

'Yeah? Good to hear it, buddy-boy.' I mussed his hair, and we started to eat.

'No pickle,' said Josh.

'That's right,' I said.

033

Whichever way you look at it, it's a joke. A man getting hit by a woman is nothing serious – a little pathetic, even. A man getting hit with a frying pan: that's comedy. It's OK for Chaplin and Keaton and Tom the cat to get beaten to shit – it's hilarious. Make those characters female, and it isn't funny any more.

My name is John Knox. I am in my forties and my life is all behind me. Check my name on Wikipedia and you learn John Knox was a liberal West Coast shock-jock in the 1990s who at the height of his success had one of the most widely syndicated shows in US broadcasting history and whose spectacular fall from grace was connected with domestic abuse. There's a picture of John Knox on the page, and he looks like a punk burdened by his own ego.

Follow the links and you get to find out what became of John Knox. There are articles written by journalists who call him a wife-beater. There are editorials publicly urging boycotts of the *John Knox Show*; columns calling for John Knox's arrest; articles that dance on his grave. This is my shadow. This is the echo of my voice.

I stopped taking the anti-depressants and now there I was, locked away from the eyes of man in a backwater, haunting the house in which I grew up. When it rained, it rained in the present tense. Our son was fucked up like you and me. It happened gradually, but it happened, like a wound going bad.

The colours were bright: the gunmetal trees and the battle-group green of the grass. Wearing clothes felt like wearing clothes full of lice.

Try a while in my shoes, Rachel. Let me spell it out for you.

You hide in your home as a public service. It's easy when you order stuff on the phone, you order food or call a technical help-line: the assistant treats you like a normal individual and you feel like you are tricking them. On the TV people smile a lot and run in family groups. On the TV there isn't a single human being who is representative of your state. The cops in the crime show couldn't do what they're doing if they looked like you. The news anchors, dental insurance models, the sitcom actors: they're all perfect and they don't know how perfect they all are. You are the focal point of every place you go, because you are disgusting. Express your individuality, say the commercials. But they really mean be pretty.

Oh yeah: 2004 was a riot.

032

By June, the drugs were out of my system completely. Doc Steinwitz had told me SSRIs are like rewiring, one that happens while you're too blissed out to notice. You come off the drugs, and you're fixed. That's how it's meant to be, anyway.

The first sign something was up was I had a wet dream. I woke up at 4 a.m. feeling too good to be true, and I'd come all over everything, and it felt great. It had been three years since you and I had had sex, and in between times I hadn't felt so much as an inclination to jerk off. That morning, my dick was like a rod of iron. For a week, I had to kneel down in front of the toilet pan and pee tilted sideways.

The pills had protected me from the day-to-day business of disfigurement. Some people talk to you very slowly, like your injury means you're stupid. Some assume you represent some kind of threat: in Wendy's or Second Cup, customers see your face is messed up and their unconscious reaction will be to gather to themselves their cell phone, purse, kids, whatever. Men square up to you. People won't shake your hand, or hold a door open. Then there are the many, many more people who turn to their friends and say 'oh my God', or point at you from across the street, or make the sound of a person heaving. Occasionally, a person actually goes pale green and barfs. I used to be hot enough that girls in bars would discuss me in little groups, openly, giggling over their drinks. Now, I'm a monster. I went into one of the bars in Clinton, and the girl there checked with the manager before she'd even serve me. All the time I was on the SSRIs, I saw all of that, but I never felt hurt. I knew I didn't look good, and I didn't go out hardly ever, but I never once felt isolated by anything other than choice.

After I stopped with the pills, it stung like hell.

The first time it happened, I was in Glovers' Family Store with my erection. There was this woman there, in the coffee aisle, and she turned to me without looking properly and said, 'Excuse me, do you know where I might find—' and she saw my face and quaked. Actually shook – turned white, the whole piece. Then, after her shock had worn off, she looked violated, and went off cussing me under her breath, like I'd disfigured myself just to make her feel bad.

Long after the woman had gone, I was still standing there in the aisle wanting to tear my own face off, just like you had. It wasn't a hurt thing, at all: it was rage, pure rage. I was apoplectic, and to start off with my apoplexy was directed at her. After a while, the fury turned in on itself, and I got angry with me. I hated myself. I ground my teeth together. I resisted, barely, the compulsion to fling everything off the shelves. And you weren't in any of my thoughts, because somehow I managed to avoid remembering that you existed. I don't think that was a conscious thing, but I do think I forgot about you on purpose.

Spring was done, and with it the academic year.

Soon, you were coming home.

031

'So tell me about John Rutherford,' I said.

'John Rutherford.' You paused midway through lacing your boot. 'How do you know about him?'

'I mailed you his journal, remember?'

Animation returned to you. Or was it relief?

'I'm going out now. We can talk later.'

'I'll walk with you.'

'You never want to walk,' you said, with finality.

'It's a beautiful day. Be great to walk with you.'

'I said *no*,' you said. 'No! OK?' And you kept on tying, violently.

I felt that, too. It was a chill that went through me: one of those brain-drugs that gets released when you're fearful. Whatever it was, it hadn't been in my blood in a long, long time.

You'd been back a week, and something had been wrong from the get-go. I thought it was just that I was feeling you, again. Maybe this shit had been simmering away a decade. This was old-style Rachel. This was toss things around the room Rachel and break shit Rachel and say whatever needs to be said to bring out the pain Rachel. This was pull down panties and demand to be fucked Rachel, and throw John out of the bedroom when he didn't get wood Rachel. I didn't know the complications you had in your life; the decisions you were trying to make.

You came back for meals, was all.

I said, 'You know I love you, right?' and it made you laugh.

You put on your curious face, the one it was dangerous to fuck with. You said, 'What's going on? You're not the same as at Christmas.'

'All I did was ask about John Rutherford.'

'John Rutherford. OK, John Rutherford. A not-very-important literary type from early last century. He brought the poetry of James Lyons to public attention.'

'He got killed in World War Two, right?'

You said, 'I don't know why the sudden interest.'

I thought about what old Captain Rutherford had already been through. Seemed like he deserved a better end than that. 'So it was all for nothing, in the end.'

You said, 'No one lives for ever. He delivered us one of the most sensitive poets of World War One, didn't he?'

'So how come you have his journal?'

Apparently that was the worst thing I could have said. I didn't know what button it was I'd pressed. You were on your feet, yelling. A boot thudded into the wall by my head, making a dink in the plaster. You demanded, hot-faced, to know whether *that* was what this had all been about – but you stopped just as fast, with your eyes wide. You were looking at my hand. I looked at my hand too. In it was the golf club from the umbrella rack. I didn't remember picking it up. I looked at you, and back at the golf club. It seemed not to want to leave my hand.

'What,' you said, in a voice like poison, 'the *fuck* are you doing?'

I was pretty sure you'd go for me if I put the thing down.

I said, 'I'm scared.'

'You're the one with the weapon.'

'I know,' I said. 'I can't go through all that again. You hurt me.'

'I made one mistake. One mistake! I've been in therapy every week for eight years, and now you're ready to smash my head in with a golf club because I speak too fucking sharply?'

'I didn't— I need you to be calm.'

'Yeah, that's right. This is somehow my fault.' Your eyes could have burned the house down. 'I don't know what's got into you, but this is not how we do things. I'm going out. Don't come anywhere the fuck near me.' With that, you threw the front door open so hard it knocked everything off the nearest wall. You slammed it behind you.

Hearing your car start up meant I could risk breathing again. When I heard it drive away, I put the club back in the rack, and locked the front door from the inside. Even with this done, I couldn't shake the impression of being watched.

He was sitting at the top of the stairs, in his PJs.
For a moment there were no words.
Then my little boy got up, and went back to bed.

030

2004 was a dark year. Without the pills to fall back on, my life was raw. I woke up mornings (alone in the main bedroom, when you were still away, or in the spare room, when you were back, the room I'd had when I was a kid) well before the birds had properly gotten to singing. I'd walk out by myself on the land. I don't know whether the comfort I felt was from the isolation or from the feeling that the time of day was in sympathy with me: the cool and the not-knowing of dawn. No matter what kind of day followed it, first light always felt like it had been shaved off a frigid mountain-top. The trees stood frozen in sick procession, in the winter; in spring they burst forth in rich profusion, life budding out of every bit of organic matter in the landscape. Come summer, those dawn walks were walks through a trembling, respiring world where nothing ever really slept and all the forces of nature were ready to rise up. I'd stand out on the narrow track that went up past the beaver swamp and into the hillside, and there listen for telltale splashes in the water, which was fertile with lily pads and dam-selflies and reeds that formed thickets in the water. Amphibians croaked. Birds gossiped and bartered: jays and longspurs, warblers and orioles, and in my peripheral vision I knew I was witness-ing billions of webs being spun, leaves being stripped, great alders being throttled by ivy, poison dogwood brewing toxins in the wetlands. Some days the sun never came out. There was rain late into the year, and on those days I kept my plastic hood up, and I watched the water dance like it was frying, and inhaled the warm, wet earth smell. I felt like a human being.

My car was a '79 Crown Vic, with a long-ass wheelbase – a dumb car, in a place where the back roads pitch and screw like rollercoasters. When Josh was at school I took that thing out on the 401 and just drove up and down it, poking my nose in at places that had been newly built in the years since Dad had driven us on that road to Toronto or on special days to Detroit. I let the radio drift and auto-retune between the regional stations. I remember one DJ had his cans up too loud, so the mosquito voice of the producer could be heard over the airwaves, and he was using a computer mouse that clicked. Amateur, man, amateur. He played 'Smells Like Teen Spirit', and I slammed the brakes on when I heard that bass line behind his voice, and the car slewed bad – I felt the back end come out wide. I put it on the gravel shoulder, in the brush, and got out for air. I hit the car. Only when I realised vehicles were slowing down to take a look at me did I throw myself back behind the wheel again. By now it was Madonna, which was safe. Madonna never made me feel a damned thing.

There was an LCBO at Fairfield, and another one off the highway at Freemont. They didn't put the bottles in the window, but the L was for Liquor, and both of 'em had a Beer Store right next door, where jocks with handcarts wheeled Keiths or Creemore into station wagons by the two-four. I circled back, and drove past slower. This time, an old guy in a red checked jacket was just going in. His face was vicious pink. Before he went in through the automatic door, I saw him glance over his shoulder.

History crosses over, you once told me.

I put my foot to the gas.

029

You were taking summer and the fall semester to write about Nazi propaganda, so we started getting used to having you around all the time again – mainly working in your study, we expected, but present in our lives once more. But you weren't hardly ever home.

Josh and me practised catching on the land – he wore his mitt and I pitched low ones. Sometimes it seemed like maybe I was getting better at using my right hand, but then the ball would just fall out on the drawback of the pitch, and Josh would sigh and tell me to use my left hand.

'I can't pitch with my left,' I said.

'You also can't pitch with your right.'

'You think the Bluejays'll keep me on the team?'

'You're a freak.'

Sometimes Cody Bell would come around too, and we'd improvise a game. The first time I tried batting using my bad right hand, and bat and ball actually connected, it felt like I'd been shot – the pain was so full-on that I was rolling around holding my wrist before I knew what I was doing. It was the sort of pain that doesn't make you cry out – it's too much of a surprise. Cody stood there, dumbfounded, I guess, that an adult should carry on this way, but Josh came up to me and held me by the shoulders. 'Get on your feet now,' he told me, 'or the Jays will throw you out for sure.'

I don't know where my son learned to be such a goddamned smartass.

You got quieter and quieter, as the summer went on. When you were home, there was a frost on you, and the kids instinctively stopped having fun when you walked in the room.

The make-up you wore had gotten darker, and the foundation lighter. Somewhere along the way all your coloured clothes had gone, and now you wore black dresses with low necklines, and strings of black beads, and your hair grew back.

One mealtime, Josh asked, 'Mommy, are you a vampire?' You looked at him like he wasn't there, and you said, 'Is that Josh asking me, or Rutger?' I didn't know you knew about Rutger. Josh didn't say anything – just kept on eating, and you dabbed your mouth with a paper tissue, dropped it on your plate, and left the house.

Nightmares came. They were gentle, at first, as harmless as feeling like something was out of place, but as Thanksgiving came closer I found myself waking up in terror of violence, sure that someone was about to do something to me. What it was was never clear. I'd wake up with my arms crossed to protect my face; by October, I was waking up because the lights had been thrown on and Josh, and sometimes you, would be standing over me, trying to find out why I was screaming. Sometimes, when I woke up and saw you there, I didn't know if I was dreaming or not.

Couple of times afterwards, I came to your bed and tried to make love to you, but you moved away from me to the edge of the bed. When I put my arm around you, you went and slept on the couch.

'This is no good for Josh, seeing us like this,' I said to you, the last time it happened. 'This is fucking him up.'

'You never seemed to give a shit before. Everything was fine.'

'I was different before. Anyway, we weren't like this before,' I said. 'We got along.'

'We *never* got along.' Your volume was already rising. 'You fucking pretended to give a shit —'

'Don't wake Josh.'

'Why not? Are you going to try get me locked up if I raise my voice?'

'I don't know what you're going through, and I'm right there for you if you want me. But we will not be doing again what we did before.'

'You did it, didn't you? You stopped taking your meds.' It was obvious this was the first time you'd thought of it.

I said, 'What kind of a father —'

'You stopped taking your meds, and you didn't even fucking ask me.'

'Yes.'

'You bastard,' you said. 'You fucking bastard. Everything was perfect, but you couldn't let it be like that, could you? You can't just get on with life.'

I said, 'Just do the right thing. Be a mother to your son.'

'You piece of shit!' you screamed. 'You piece of fucking shit!'

'He needs you to be his mother, Rachel. You owe him that. Be around, once in a while. Take an interest in him. He's a good kid. Quit skulking around out of the house all the time. Where'd you go, anyway?'

The creaking of the landing told us Josh was nearing. He came into the bedroom, and in an instant you were sweetness itself. 'Hi, hon. We're fine,' you told him. 'Your dad and I were just having a conversation.'

Josh came to me, and nuzzled into my side, the way I thought he was too grown up to do. You looked from me to our son, watching you from the safety of my arm.

'OK,' you said. 'Your dad wants me to be the best mother I can be. You hear that, Josh?'

You said OK, but it didn't feel OK. You were looking around yourself a whole lot: at the lights; at the walls. I said to Josh, 'Come on, Mister. You got a game tomorrow. Need to get some rest. We all do. Say goodnight to your mom.'

He kissed you on the cheek, and you just sat there.

After he'd gone back to bed, I said, 'You know, you could come, if you want. It's a big game in their season. They're playing Thunder Bay.'

You said nothing.

'Buy you a root beer?'

But you didn't hear me. You said, 'Oh God.'

'You OK?'

'No. No, I'm down a blind alley. I've fucked everything up, like I always fuck everything up.'

'So unfuck it.'

You said, 'How do I *do* that?'

'You try, is what you do. You do the best you can. Otherwise all the therapy and the arguments – none of that was real.'

'No, I can't get away from the past. It'll just come back and destroy everything.' You looked very tired, just then. You were in focus, while the rest of the world was a blur.

'I'm sorry,' you said, after a while.

'Don't be sorry.'

'I am. I'm sorry I haven't been here. I'm sorry I've been such a shit mom to Josh —'

'If you believe that, let's fix it. We can't put things back the way they were, but we can make it work.'

'You really believe that?'

'Yeah,' I said. 'Yeah, I do.' And I did. 'You're one of the strongest-willed people I ever knew. I believe if you set your mind to it, you can take control.'

You sat back in the chair and pulled your knees up, and hugged your legs.

'Don't you want that?' I said.

'I don't want to feel like this,' you agreed.

'You're holding all the cards.'

You nodded slowly. Seemed to me like you were letting that sink in: the realisation that it was in your hands.

After we'd sat in silence for a little time, you smiled a weak smile at me, and said thank you.

I told you I loved you.

'It'll be all right,' you said.

028

The last time I spoke to you, you sounded fine. We had one of those status report calls: I told you I'd picked up the pickles and gotten to the arena in plenty of time for the game; my cell kept cutting out till eventually we gave up, and you asked me what time I thought Josh and I'd be home. We didn't talk about you and your day-so-far, and every day goes by I wish I'd asked. But there was no rumble of the distant storm; none of that usual stuff. You sounded fine.

So the Thunder Bay kids gave Josh's team a pounding, they really came down hard. Coupla their kids looked like hockey pros already, for sure. I hung with Larry and Martha Bell. We parents cheered everything our team did, loudly, just like always, meanwhile catching up out of the corners of our mouths and supping root beer that tasted like medicine. They asked after you, of course, and I covered, turning your handful of history papers into a mountain, and Larry said tough life, academia. I spent the game sharing dogs with him and his wife, and yelling at the referee whenever he gave against our kids.

And then the kids came crunching off the ice, trailing their sticks and cussing to one another and Josh and Cody and the Doc Steinwitz's grandkid Brady crashed the adults' party, and we all commiserated and figured out revenges on Thunder Bay, and I said anyway the ref was a jerk.

That was about a quarter after five. The fall light had just started to falter; the fall chill and the fragrance of decaying leaves put me in mind of Thanksgiving. About 5.30, I guess, we went our different ways: Larry and his family towards the interstate, and the five hours to family in Niagara; Josh and I home via the Steinwitz place in Mill Falls to drop off Brady Steinwitz. At 5.30, life was normal. The coroner said you were still alive then.

I miss your teeth. Is that weird? They are still the first thing I think of whenever I think of you. You had such a sexy smile, Rachel. In spite of everything, that's how I remember you – smiling.

We listened to Duke Ellington and Miles Davis on CBC 2 in the Crown Vic on the way home. Jazz can be dangerous on a long, straight drive, and I caught myself drifting, so we stopped after the first hour at the Tim Horton's near Stamford for a caffeine boost and a ton of fruit-burst muffins. It was dark, now. Ontario dark. An immense, aching blackness yawned open behind the objects illuminated fraily by the highway's lights: pale trees, blind houses covered in clapboard. A fog descended. The kids dozed. They missed seeing the mighty mythic-seeming freight train which kept pace a while before its path no longer ran parallel to ours, and its endless bulk spirited away out of sight.

Through their front windows the extended Steinwitz family could be seen around a dining table with the log fire hot and hearty. This was Mill Falls, close on seven. My half-face was reflected monochrome in the glass of the front door.

Brady's grandfather, the doctor, invited us in. We declined reluctantly – it sounded like they were having a ball.

'How's Rachel?' he asked. 'I haven't seen her in a while, now.'

'She's good. We're good.'

He nodded, standing on the crooked Steinwitz stoop with one hand on his grandson's shoulder and the other on Josh's. 'And you? Eating well?'

I grinned. 'A little too well, as you can see.'

He told me keep off the salt, and then his twinkling look changed. 'And what about the other thing?'

And I let him know things were fine there too, but this time the fine was a lie. Steinwitz was old enough to be my own father, almost, and with all the seniority and goodness of a provincial family doctor, and there I stood, feeding him a line. Lying always felt like shit; I was never any good at it. It was clear we couldn't speak frankly in front of the boys, anyway. I just told him I was OK, meaning that I'd straightened myself out, and I poked some wet leaves about on the porch with the toe of my boot.

He told me to stay with that.

So I could blame it on Brady Steinwitz having ridden with us to the game, or on the fruit-burst muffins, on Steinwitz senior being such a good egg, or on my keeping under a sacred eighty on the highway when everyone else keeps their foot hard down; but it wasn't any one of those things, it was the day, it was life, and one way or another we took our time coming home. You died some time between 7.25 and 7.45 on Sunday, 9 November 2004, the coroner said.

For the longest time, that twenty-minute window was what stopped my mind from getting around what had happened to you. I know it's stupid, but you know me, I always had to have everything spelt out for me: I needed a precise time with which to beat myself about the head. I needed to know whether, if I'd called you to say we were just turning off the highway on to the Old Bryde Road, you might have stayed alive. We saw a red Monarch butterfly, fluttering across the horror-film set of branches lit up by headlights, and when I explained to Josh that this was far out, to see a Monarch so late in the year when all the rest had migrated already, he wanted to tell you about it.

You can tell her when we get back, I told him. We're almost home.

At home, alone in that big old house, you were filling the air with promises, and songbirds, and the voice of Eva Cassidy, singing 'Songbird' for you: her voice tentative, then soaring, like a whole life in one song. When Eva promised there'd be no more crying, I know you believed the promises – you, the eternal cynic. You'd have smiled your smile, like you were in on the joke – but you'd have believed her, in spite of yourself. She promised that for you there'd be a sun, making sunshine. The house was immaculate, when you died, a real home: oak beams and pools of light, and musky incense smouldering. With your partner and your son somewhere out there in the night, you put the track on repeat-play and sat on the sticky white couch under the Lucian Freud reproductions you chose for your thirty-third birthday; you sat exactly in the middle, halfway between the two uplighters behind you, and listened to the frail beauty of Eva's harmonies, the warmth of the calming guitar. Were I able to work miracles, I'd have myself appear quietly at that moment in your life, and sit by you; we'd kiss and make love to the music, and we'd lay there a long while afterwards, still spooned together, naked and serene.

Instead, you took some fat copper-coloured bullets out of a cloth wrapping, and fed them one by one into the chambers of a revolver. You pushed the cylinder back into the body of the gun, tucked your bob of black hair behind your ear, turned the gun around, bit your perfect teeth down on the end of the barrel, and blew about a third of your scalp, a third of your skull and one half of your brains out of the back of your head. And 'Songbird' keeps singing; and the air is full of songbirds, and for the longest time it's full of you.

Because of the twenty-minute window, in my imagination that's how you stay. While the car containing Josh and I trundles homeward along the pitted track, globules of your blood and cerebrospinal fluid, moving through the air with the sluggishness of lava in a lamp, begin a twenty-minute arc toward the wall. Those parts of your brain that knew about Freud and European novelists and the French Revolution separate and turn like the birth of the universe; some chunks of you trail hair behind them like comets' tails. Your lashes flutter in climax. Over the following quarter-hour your gaze slowly fills with peace, serene like the Madonna, while behind you a red and grey fan radiates through the air; and I love you, I *love* you, like I never loved anyone or anything, and Freud's lovers kiss, and the song slows, and the singer comes to the end of her song, again, and again, and again, every time lingering on the exquisite last note with great tenderness, full of hope and wonder, every time, like she'd never sung the last line before.

Then the magic is broken. The key scrapes in the lock of the front door.

"We're home!" I holler, as Josh and I come tumbling through, in a confusion of boots and coats and sports bags. You're not in the kitchen, but all the lights are on, and the music's playing – you must be down in the den. "Rachel?" I call, sitting down to change into slippers.

"We saw a Monarch," Josh has begun telling you, as he swings into the lounge. "Dad?"

"Just a second," I tell him.

"Dad," he whimpers.

And I figure whatever's wrong – something broken, something spilt – we'll be able to fix it soon enough, the three of us. But your body is on the couch slumped to one side, with a crimson fan of spatter like a peacock's tail dripping off the wall; I have to hold Josh back by force, and Eva Cassidy is singing how it's gonna be all right; it's gonna be all right.

FIVE

027

Brightness; lightness. A biblical, awful beauty! Away under me stretches a perfect white landscape of mountains made from vapours; valleys which shape-shift ever so slowly, tumbling, reforming into more mountains and more valleys, under a sky of noblest blue. I can't see for the violence of the sunshine. So this must be Heaven. The sunlight is frigid.

'John Knox?'

Who'd have thought Heaven was cold like that?

'John Knox?'

First time I hear the name, it sparks a memory. 'I'm John Knox,' I tell myself. So I tell that to the face looking through the hatch in the door, too. 'That's my name. I'm John Knox.' It's an ugly door, with an ugly hatch, and the room stinks of disinfectant and vagrants and piss. In the corner there's a tin bucket. Where the hell is this?

'You got a visitor,' the face tells me.

I say, 'I don't want to be here.'

'No shit,' says the face, vanishing.

Nothing about the room is familiar. I even miss that ugly-ass face. 'Yo, dude, get back here, man.'

The door cracks and rolls aside, into the wall. An old Jew wearing a trenchcoat and a grave expression stands in the proscenium, eyeing me lovelessly. He greets me by name.

He comes in walking softly without taking his hooded eyes off me, never blinking. Was he in something I saw on TV? Behind him, a strong-looking and surly cop, the face from the hatch, loiters awkwardly in the corner of the cell. The old man takes his time taking a perch on the squeaky fold-down bed. He indicates I should do the same. It's difficult to keep both men in sight.

Heaven is a cold place.

'John,' he begins, sighing. 'Look at me, John.'

I look at him.

'Oh boy, Johnny. Tell me what to think, willya, because I don't know.'

He has a fascinating face, grained with a life lived fully. And his gaze stays on me, waiting for some slight indication, some all-important datum to make him love me or hate me. It feels obscene that someone so matured should care what I have to say.

'I'm so sorry,' I tell him. 'But I don't know who you are.'

The cop loses his shit. 'Cut the bullshit, Knox. You see anyone fucking laughing?'

'I *don't* know him.'

'So how come you asked for him by name, smartass?'

The old man hisses, 'John, don't do that.'

'Do what? I don't know who you are, OK? What is it you want me to do?'

With a strong hand, he grips my arm hard. It hurts. 'You look at me,' he demands. 'Look at me! Look me in the eye and tell me you don't know me.'

So I do.

Afterward, the old man looks deep within me, through and beyond my eyes, into some special part of me that confirms what I was saying. Then he releases his grip, as though defeated. 'I believe he's telling the truth,' he says.

'Is that a fact, Doctor? Maybe he just doesn't feel like talking.'

'Has he received medical attention?'

'He had a coupla lacerations; they patched him up.'

'Has he seen a doctor?'

That makes the surly cop shut up, but he doesn't move.

In the difficult silence that follows, I try standing up.

'You do not move!' the cop bellows, so I sit.

I say, 'What is it I'm supposed to have done?' Of course, this makes the cop madder, but I've known him two minutes and I know to expect that. My question is directed toward the grey-bearded man with the medical bag: clearly a stand-up guy, even though he sits like I might lash out. Incongruous images flash through my mind while we talk. A log fire. A freight train. Something insistent, calling to me from the darkness.

'OPP picked you up on the 401; you told them you were coming to see me,' says the old man.

'That's why you're here, right?'

'That's why I'm here. We've known each other thirty-five years, John.'

I can't help laughing. But my old buddy isn't laughing, and I've started to figure out the implications of what he's told me.

Jazz music, a jar of pickles.

'Why was I on the highway?'

My old buddy tells me the story. Two officers in a patrol car (one of them off-duty, hitching a ride) are making a routine run on the 401 outside Mill Falls at midnight. They notice stationary lights farther on: a Crown Vic. The car looks wild, even from a mile away. It's straddling two deserted lanes with the door hanging open, and there's some guy all fours next to it at the kerb, puking up at the side of the road. The patrolmen naturally think he's a two-five-three – a drunk. They unclip their holsters, but do not draw their guns.

So they're out of the car, now, and moving towards it, and the guy must have realised someone is approaching, because he turns around on his knees to face the officers. Although the car is in one piece and he doesn't look injured, he is covered head to toe in blood.

At this point in my old buddy's story, I glance at my own clothing – and my gut turns to ice with fear. It's me. I'm wearing a lot of someone's blood. It's browned, now, and it's crusted dry, but it's everywhere – on my stomach, my lap; there's blood on my sleeves and under my fingernails. I can't breathe.

It's all there. Oh God, the butterfly, the peacock's tail.

You.

And they draw their guns and advance defensively while I kneel there, moonlit, at the side of the 401. Dr Steinwitz can fix her, I tell them. They shout fix who. They're telling me lie down on the ground. I remember it: it seems like a fucking crazy thing to ask, in November, so I get up, instead. They haven't looked in the Crown Vic yet, and I know they mustn't because that's gonna slow us down from getting to Dr Steinwitz, so I get up, telling them everything is OK. But they aren't buying. They start shouting they do not want to hurt me, but will. And then one of them gets to an angle where he can see inside the car; and suddenly I'm not a person to them any more.

Josh watches from behind a pane of glass as his father is felled by the officers. They buckle his daddy's knees with a nightstick, and Daddy goes down like a penitent, still trying to plead his way out. It's a Chaplin movie, playing out on the car window. By the time they're done lashing his daddy's hands behind his back, as he lies face down on the road, while Mommy sits in front with her busted skull, Josh's shaking has gotten so bad they need to call in special psychotherapeutic care from Ottawa; and they separate us and can't get either one of us to speak.

026

Locked up, I couldn't hear anything for a long time and there was so much I couldn't see. The door was held shut from the outside. You couldn't have helped me because you were still at kindergarten and I was seven.

The musty, sappy smell of chopped pine is what I remember most about being locked away; that, and anger towards my father – we'd fought, and I somehow blamed him for me being stuck in the woodshed, like he'd *made* me storm out of the house in my short pants, and head down the long track and into the shed; like he'd *made* the latch fall down as I slammed the door.

I went with it, for a while. The darkness was OK so long as I could orient myself via the knots and the cracks between the wall-slats and the big fissure of sunlight at the foot of the woodshed door.

That door sure fitted well. With my flawless, unscarred cheek pressed hard into the floorboards I could still see only an inch into the brightness outside. Turned out nothing much was happening in that inch. Pretty quickly I gave up on seeing things and got up and finger-combed woodchips from my hair. My wooden jail measured two little armspans by three: there was no place to go.

I started out indignant, I guess, like any little boy. Adults were such freakin' jerks. Plus they could shove you around if you got out of line – my arm was still sore. We'd argued over nothing, but I'd wanted to make it a big deal. So long as I thought he was around, close enough to hear me, I sat there in sniffy silence, but after a while I got to wondering whether there was anyone to hear me anyway. Growing up in the country you get used to the idea of help being many miles away, deaf to little boys' shouts. My jail stood toward the far edge of the forest clearing I knew as home, near where the track from the Bryde Road had been bush-hogged through the trees. The track passed the chicken coop, the woodpile, and the coal dump, drawing up in an extravagant dusty circle at the foot of the steps up to our house, that blank-eyed, teetering thing. Around it, a moat of cultivation: clumsy lawns and a vegetable patch under canopies of nets. Swings and washing lines strung up. Butterflies on the cabbage heads. And the whole clearing was caged by the looming forest, whose leaves rattled as though threatening to surge back and reclaim their stolen land. I knew all this without having to see it. In a way, I knew it better with my eyes shut. My loudest shouts wouldn't have gotten past the first rank of pines, and even if they had and they'd somehow also slipped through mile on mile of forest and rock, past the derelict outbuildings on the far reaches of our land, over the beaver swamp and the old creek that fed the lagoon and on to the gorsey uplands beyond, they'd still have been far from anyone who could've heard them. Mom was visiting with relatives in Toronto; only my father was close, and he was in the house with the TV on. I wasn't even sure he knew I'd left the house. After a while my indignation had blown itself out.

In the quiet, all around me in the woodshed I began to hear organisms scratching around, unseen. Ravens cawed in the forest. Wind bustled among the trees. Sometimes I imagined he was outside, watching, and I called tentatively; other times I was completely alone. After what felt like hours had passed, I grew contemplative. I wondered what I'd do if he never came. What if he forgot me, the way he forgot birthdays and appointments; where he'd put his glasses?

I tried to imagine being dead. It seemed easier, the more the light waned. Was dead like sleeping? No, it was more like a pitch-black woodshed, but without the chink of light, which anyway had now almost gone. At first I imagined lying face up in a coffin, like corpses on TV, and thought how boring it must be to be dead. Then there came a long gap in the birdsong and suddenly I glimpsed the senseless horror of death: I understood that death is not being dead, but instead is not being anything at all. That was gonna happen to me, one day – I'd cease to be. The realisation hit me like a punch in the gut. I sat on a log in the dark with my arms hugging my bare knees and started to cry.

The wind got up, as the light faded – it washed through the forest, and the pines and the timbers of the outbuildings creaked like an old ship's. In the far distance, beyond the woodshed walls and the tangled woody uplands, somewhere close to the lake, a loon was crying out, its sound distinct among the rich prolixity of dusk birdsong. They're easy birds to recognise: their call is a plaintive appeal, matching the woebegone mood there in the darkness. It started to get cold. In short pants, my legs got goosefleshy. I yelled, and I yelled, and I yelled, but there was no way my voice was reaching the house.

I don't know what time it was.

Once I thought I heard something big moving through the undergrowth. A deer, perhaps? Not a bear? Then the thing started humming a tune, and I called out in relief, 'Dad, I'm in here!' Shouting out made the humming stop, and I realised it hadn't sounded much like my dad. Whoever it was, they were on our land, and they were standing out there, in the Ontario night.

For a minute or two, there was silence, but for the wind in the trees and the night animals; and then the same dragging footsteps came towards the shed. Man, I was shaking as it came right up to the door and stood there, breathing. I thought I was gonna pee myself.

And then there was a metal noise – the sound of the latch being lifted. The very thing I'd wanted the whole time – but not now. My skin was like gooseflesh and I felt my leg get warm. But the door didn't open. I stood in total silence, thinking this was the end. After a while that same shuffling noise told me the thing was moving back into the forest, and I was left alone.

Then I allowed myself to cry again, weakly and incontinently, from misery and fear and sorrow and hunger, but mostly from relief, because I had been spared, alone in the dark, and I would live.

I ran through the night as soon as I dared, up the path and into the house. The place was a flood of light and the overwhelming fragrances of the home: wood polish, paddock flowers, tobacco. There he was, in the oblong of light into the living room, on the phone to the police: he wore boots, coarse pants kept up by thick suspenders, and the fly-fishing hat which seemed always to conceal his eyes. An awkward, slightly ridiculous figure. My dad.

He dropped the phone as soon as he saw me. His eyes were red. 'Thank God you're home,' he whispered. He offered me his pale hand to take, and I gladly took it. He pulled me to him, and crushed me to his chest, and shook with tears.

I was a little boy then, and one and a half thousand miles away you were an even littler girl. While you were being shepherded with other three-year-olds to daycare in Montgomery, Alabama, colouring in with crayons and trying to stay inside the lines, my father sat making peace with his little boy in the house the little boy and the little girl would one day inherit, the house our own son would one day know as home, whose front door would close on you that one last November day when you couldn't stay inside the lines any more.

025

I open my eyes.

This room is a featureless cube containing three men: two others and me.

The eye watching me has a deep, chocolate-brown iris and luxuriant lashes; the upper lid is alert, raised to allow the organism of the eye to see all it can. The eye is clear; clean. Three major creases originate from the eye's corner, flowing out over the ridge of cheekbone, each on a different course, eventually splitting into minor tributaries. These perhaps correspond to the three distinct smile-parentheses around the full-lipped mouth. Maybe this person has three kinds of smile.

There's no smile now.

In the silence, the whine of the fluorescent light sounds insectoid. Hung up behind the men's heads there's a wall clock that doesn't tick.

The hand with the gold wedding band makes minute adjustments to the position of a pencil on the tabletop, never satisfied with the minor changes made.

The eye continues to consider me.

That full mouth says, 'I got all day, my friend. You will answer my question.'

Whatever he's talking about, it does not relate to me. He missed a little when he shaved the corner of his jaw. Beyond where the crow's feet vanish unexpectedly and the shoreline of head-hair meets the peppering of one day's stubble, just beneath the lobe, there are a few longer hairs, almost concealed by the jawline. I think—

'Hey, John?' the mouth says, talking softly. 'I'm talking to you. You hearing me?'

The voice which answers him – my voice – seems too far from

me to belong to me. It's the same when I look at that pair of hands I know are mine: they are more than just an arm's length away. Something like looking at your legs through the bottom of a Sleeman's bottle, seeing them tiny and yards distant. By imagining myself turning my head, I can swing the viewpoint up to look at the two men. They are physical types, packed into weekend clothing.

Every time I blink, the airy cool of the woodshed is there for me; when my eyelids stay closed I can stay aged seven, on my log, watching the light dwindle. It would be easy to take refuge in that shed, to hide; to offer my younger self the companionship of a second soul.

The cops are still there, miles away across the tabletop. 'I'm having trouble being here. The past seems realer than the present,' my voice explains to them. 'Everything's disjointed.'

'Disjointed, huh?' says one of the cops, like he's made a point.

'Like an acid trip,' I tell him, willing the distant hands to turn over, and seeing them do so.

'An acid trip, is that right?' says the kind mouth. 'You take a lot of narcotics, John?' His tone is not conversational.

'Still here, pal,' says the cop, when I open my eyes. He's changed his clothes, I see. 'So we've been to your house now. You want to tell us about your house?'

I don't remember any house, and tell him so.

'Don't remember it, eh?' he says, rubbing his chin. 'That's too bad. Why don't you try a little harder for me? There's plenty to remember.'

I flounder for any purchase in the present. A jar of pickles floats into view, but makes no sense. I recall a red-winged butterfly that shouldn't have been where it was – wrong time, wrong place, lit up in a car's headlights. My left eye has developed an annoying twitch. I look at my forearm, welted and sore where I've scratched the name Josh.

'My son,' I say. The thought fills me with alarm, and more nervous spasms, this time in my arm. 'Where is he?'

'You can do better than that. Talk us through when you last saw your son's mother alive.'

'Where's—'

'He's being looked after, we went through this a dozen times already. I'm asking about your girlfriend. When was the last time you saw your girlfriend, alive?'

'She's probably at home,' I venture.

'No she probably is not. Try again.'

I feel stupid. Sick of this jerk, and stupid. Who forgets his own girlfriend? My mind is one big breezy empty outbuilding, housing a single child who sits in the dark. Ten seconds of silence, the dead-air sequence will kick in. But I don't know what that means.

'You ever beat on your girlfriend?' says the other cop – they seem to have switched places and gotten coffees out of thin air. 'Ever show her who's boss?'

I'm John Knox: 1510 – no, five-one-fifty—

My hand twitches. 'Look, I'm sorry. I'm really trying,' I tell them.

'Let's see if this helps your memory along,' says the cop, and he puts a large photograph on to the table. It's our car, containing you, with all the doors open, on a section of road taped off with blue-and-white ribbons and road repair lights. The woman I met in City Lights bookstore sits awkwardly in the front passenger seat, dead.

For one brief, lucid instant, it's as though clouds have parted and I can see everything: the whole horror mapped. The chronology is as simple as a circuit diagram, but the diagram shows a short. You're dead. You're dead, and I drove you halfway to town. There was ringing in my ears as I carried you across the driveway, I remember, and your open head gave off heat-vapour in the cold night. You were warm and smelt of your perfume. I remember Josh, unnaturally silent, shivering like a ghost in the back seat. I remember wiping your gore off my hands to drive.

My son.

And now it's hurtling back toward me: the black fog of amnesia. What have I done?

I try to speak your name, Rachel. But the word emerges as a guttural bray, making both cops flinch. I try asking for help, but produce the same weird noise. Simultaneously, my arms spasm into the air, my head rolls, and suddenly I'm possessed, thrown around by convulsions I can't contain. It's fucking terrifying – like an electric mains shock. I'm blurting out non-words. As shouts go up for medical help, my frightened last thoughts are that I don't know what kind of seizure is happening to me, that I might die right here; and that I want you with me so very, very much, even though, try as I might, I can't remember who you are.

024

I wonder if you hear me, sometimes.

I never stop being the father of a child. They tell me Josh is in the best place he can be. They say seeing me isn't what he needs right now. I get it. It's for the best. Only on day two do I begin to figure out that it isn't just about health.

'Tell us again what happened,' they demand, every time they haul me into the room with the table in it. They're big, red-faced jocks who made boxing references to each other. 'Go back to the part where – yeah, before that. Tell us that part.'

But I won't. I remember the drive back, and the butterfly, but I don't want to walk through that door, not for them, not at all.

On the second day I admit, 'She's dead.'

Saying so makes me spasm like someone dying in the chair. I can't help it.

'I lost my mind,' I tell them, time and time again. 'How the hell could I have expected to find her dead?'

'You told us she talked about suicide all the time,' breezes the cop.

'And I've told you—'

'Never mind what you've told us. Tell us again. Go from when you come in the room.'

'I can't,' I say, twitching violently, and stammering.

'You will.'

A lot more time passes. 'She was dead. There was blood on the wall, there was a gun—'

'Which you never saw before.'

'I've never owned a gun.'

'Maybe you forgot you had one.'

'I never saw the gun.'

'So where'd it come from?'

At every interview I tell them I don't know. I tell them the truth – I don't know.

023

They put a shrink on my case: this older West Coast guy. He wears the kind of suit that suggests intellect rather than business.

'Of course I understand you want to see your son,' the shrink says. 'And I have no doubt you will. Right now, you and I will work together on completing the legal and medical processes which will get us there.'

'Yeah, well, I'm having trouble talking. I freak out. My body just —'

'With the cops, sure,' he understands. 'I'm not them. I'm a psychologist specialised in trauma. You're traumatised. I can help with that.'

'You get me my son, we can t-t-t-talk all you w-w-w-want.'

'John.' The psychologist snaps his fingers twice, real sharp. 'Listen to my voice, John. Who's your team? You a Sens fan?'

I don't answer.

'Let's talk like friends,' he says. 'C'mon. Are you being coy because you're a Leafs fan? Man, forty years in the wilderness.'

I say, 'It was my dad's team.'

'Yeah? What about Josh? Ever take him to see the Stanley Cup?'

'Yeah,' I tell him, uneasily. 'Look, quit fucking around.'

'There's no fucking around. Priority one for you is cooperate. That's how you get to see Josh.'

'She...' I try to say what I know. The words turn to puke in my mouth.

''Kay, take it easy.'

'She —'

'John, go slow. It's OK. I know how hard this must be for you. Talk me through what happened, nice and calm.'

What happens at home stays at home, that's the rule.

No one gets to hurt you.

'No,' I say. 'No.'

'Let me tell you,' he pronounces, after a while, 'to whom I spoke yesterday afternoon.' He meets my eye, willing me to know.

'Fuck you,' I tell him.

'Yeah, fuck me.' Like this is his cue to catch a nap, the shrink settles back in his plastic chair and closes his eyes.

For the first time since this thing began, I feel anger. He knows the manacles are there, so he knows I can't touch him, and he knows I know it too.

I say, 'Tell me what he said.'

But the asshole gives no sign of having heard: he just goes on napping.

I shout, 'What did he say?'

And later, much later, I tell him in that total silence that I want to talk, but I don't know how. That's all it takes. He opens his eyes and they are crystal clear and sleepless.

He says, 'He asked if you were dead.' He lets that sink in. 'Josh is with a cognitive behavioural therapist and a specialist in child psychology. I know them personally, they're taking good care of him.'

I said, 'What have you told him? About me?'

'There's not much he needs to be told. He was there too.'

Unexpectedly, my arm jerks into the air.

'Hey, take it easy,' the mouth's saying. 'Just relax.'

I hold up my shaking hand and say, 'How fucking long am I gonna be like this?'

'You have PTSD. It can take a long time to undo. It'll be gradual, and you'll need to work at it.'

'How do I do that?'

He allows time enough for the twitching to subside.

He says, 'Talking helps. Some people talk to the people they've lost.'

022

Guns, I've learned, are like people: they have signatures and histories, certificates of birth and records of who they got together with. Stories of their own to tell. But the revolver you bit down on has no biography. The revolver you used, you never owned. Me neither.

'I been in this job twenty-three years,' Lincoln tells me. 'Never saw a woman use a gun to kill herself. So I checked the stats. Turns out women don't use guns. Hangings, sure, plenty of them. Poisonings using prescription drugs, yes, jumping under trains, sure. I attended some of those. Never guns. That means this incident is counter-intuitive.'

The other cop, McCord, makes a fuss over adjusting his tie.

Most rural suicides are done, he says, with shotguns or hunting rifles. The gun you used was a Webley Mark 6 revolver. A four-five-five, he says, firing two hundred and sixty-grain hollow-point bullets. Old, but powerful all the same. The gun was designed to make the bullets tumble as they came out of the barrel, so that they rip up whatever they hit.

'You kept it around for personal protection, maybe?' says the cop, checking the tape is recording.

'I never saw it before,' I say. 'I'm anti-guns.'

Detective Lincoln wants to know why I refused legal representation. I wonder why I would have done that.

'The scarring on your body and face,' he says, looking through a folder on the table. 'They're old wounds. Nothing to do with the death of your girlfriend. A "very bad man" did it to you, you told the arresting officer.'

I let the silence say yes for me.

'Yeah. Pretty bad. Good face for radio,' Lincoln says. 'You were a radio host, right? Voice of the Bay, San Francisco, early nineties.

And you were in that job, say, six years; before that you DJ'd graveyard slots on two different stations, and before that you're the station gofer.' He closes the folder. 'Bryde's Crossing boy.' It is impossible to look at him but oh God he is looking at me: my skin prickles with a rash.

'We've pulled a bunch of news reports saying you beat the shit out of your girlfriend on more than one occasion. You got motive, you were the last to see her alive, you moved the body away from the crime scene, you've given vague answers to everyone who's asked you a question…'

'I didn't kill her.'

'I know you didn't fire the gun,' he says. 'With your history, I got to understand how this fits together. She's a mother with a family. She just wakes up one morning and decides to do this?'

It's the third day and I must have used up all my self-deception because suddenly the womblike interview room has become claustrophobic and terrifying and blind. I feel like those kids who die stuck in refrigerators on wasteland. You are dead, and no one is coming for me. Gasping for breath, I find myself collapsed in the dirt on the floor, close to passing out, quivering and sure I'm going to die.

On the third day, I begin to feel something else creeping into the numbness.

'She really set you up, eh?' observes Detective McCord. Something has changed in their treatment of me. They are provocative, still, and vigorous about their work, but their insinuations are growing weaker, as though they can't be bothered any more. Me, I can't keep my body still.

'Whaddya say, Knox? Rachel goes and kills herself and lets you and the kid find her, leaves you good for murder… How do you feel about your woman doing that to you? Huh?'

'I love my partner,' I manage.

'You're protecting her, aren't you? What do you think you're protecting her from? It's over.'

'It's not over.'

'You're the one in the shit, not her.'

'I was just trying to get her to the doctor,' I say. 'Please don't take my boy away. I got back from the game, and she was dead.'

'We got her psychiatric records coming in,' says the cop.

021

The fourth day is the final day, and it feels different, even though I can't say why. They still put a tray of bad food in the room like they're feeding a dog, and there's no discernible relaxing of hostility from any of the officers I see, nor from the shrink, who urges me again to get a lawyer, but I can feel something vital is going to happen. I sit on the bunk in my cast-off clothes with my body parts dancing and I pray that Josh is in better shape than me. There's no clock in this fucking cell, so you've no way of knowing even the simplest thing about your day; you just have to sit there, shaking, and wait.

Outside the station house this morning, the sunlight is steel-bright and the air vital; I see the sky and realise how long it's been since I looked up. It's cloud, all over: acres of unfallen rain.

In the lot, it smells like rain and tarmac. An old man's voice quietly says, 'Get in the car, John.'

He is there, waiting for me, the reassuring presence I remember as a kid, hands thrust deep into the pockets of his greatcoat. The Steinwitz family's Cherokee is parked up like it's ready for a getaway.

I don't get in the car; not right away: I ask the doctor about Josh. Josh is OK. He's been staying with a professional foster family in Ottawa. He's been seeing therapists three times a day. We get in the car, and I talk about seeing him.

'Let's see how that goes,' Steinwitz says.

I've been away from the house half a week, but it's altered. A blue-and-white plastic ribbon, tied at one end to a gatepost, lies twitching in the wet breeze. Police Line, it says, Do Not Cross. The Jeep crunches cautiously over it, loose stones pinging off the undercarriage like pellets from a BB gun. A fisher slips into the undergrowth. Our vehicle turns on to the entry road to the house.

Before us, now, is the house in all its vacancy.

'OK?' says Steinwitz, glancing at me.

It looks like someone else's place – someone else's life. The rain has washed the colours out of everything. From the insulating bubble of Steinwitz's Jeep I stare down the twin tracks of the long dirt driveway to where the house and its outbuildings look patched together out of driftwood, like those walls won't keep the rain out. I feel a sinking pity for whoever called that place home.

'I'm good,' I reassure the old man, sighing through my teeth. 'Yeah. I'm fucking phenomenal.'

He says, 'What do you want to do?'

'I don't know. Walk away.'

It seems like if I push it, he might let me. Old Steinwitz wears driving gloves; he stretches his fingers and flexes his grip on the wheel: it makes the leather creak softly. We sit pensively a while, during which time nothing much happens inside the vehicle or out. Every now and again, the wipers flap officiously across the windshield, distracting me from half-formed thoughts which are as transient as dreams, and from which I am instantly distracted. Steinwitz has cut the engine, deepening the emptiness; now it's just the wipers. I don't know how long we've been sitting like this. Seems we've found a place overlooking the edge of time.

I'm starting to feel dizzy, faint – I need air. Air-con never did agree with me. I guess I wasn't made to be cooped up. In trying to open the window I somehow open the door instead. 'Take it easy, willya?' Steinwitz says.

I tell Steinwitz I haven't slept in a week and he tells me the spare bed is made up at his place.

I stammer. 'I want to go home.'

He checks to see whether I am serious. 'Back in there? You don't want to go back in there, John. It's a mess.'

'It's my family home.'

'No!' he says. 'You're not thinking straight. It's not fit for anything.'

'Are the police through with it?'

'It isn't habitable. It'll be there tomorrow; leave it now.'

'I need to sleep.'

He's exasperated.

'I'm getting nightmares,' I tell him. 'Real bad ones.'

'And going in there will help how?'

'Fine,' I tell him. 'Fine.' I take the driving blanket off the back seat, and step out, into the cold of Canada.

He growls at me. Maybe he thinks I'll go to the house. As I unlatch the door of the woodshed, I half expect him to drive away.

So this is how I get to sleep my first nightmare-free night since you died: Steinwitz sleeping in his Jeep, parked at the end of our driveway right outside the old woodshed, and in the woodshed, me, curled up like a foetus, sleeping without dreaming a single dream.

020

On the morning of the night I sleep in the woodshed, I wake up in the woodshed. At first, the darkness and the cold are comforting, because they are numbing, but then the chink of light under the door begins to illuminate the shed until I can make out basic features: the dark stripes of tools and the light-coloured panels that are sacking. There is no wood in the woodshed. All the wood is in a lean-to in back of the house, where it's easier to get at. I hear footsteps crunching outside the shed.

Doc Steinwitz looks like he hasn't slept, but he looked like that before. He's been pacing the driveway, rubbing his gloved hands together. He tells me good morning. His breath hangs as crystals in the air. There's a vacuum flask of soup, which he shares, using the hood of his Jeep as a table.

'Yvetta,' he explains, filling the lid with rich tomato soup. 'We'd be happy if you want to stay with us, you know.'

I feel intense hunger, coupled with profound guilt. You are somewhere else, and here I am, tearing bread from a loaf that has also appeared, gobbling it down like I've never seen food before. Enjoying the taste of it. Who am I, to be allowed that? There is a naked canvas where the sky should be.

The house watches over us, and its eyes are empty. When I walked around the house six months ago, I thought that it was the end of the story, and now I do again. It's easy to kid yourself you're at the end of history. But history keeps coming, and maybe the story never ends. Your car might at any moment appear from the Bryde Road, pulling into the driveway, passing me and Steinwitz where we share food in the chill of the morning; pulling up by the steps to the front door. You might get out and ascend, and pass through the front door that never opens to admit you.

In the forest around us, the birds are busy, this morning, like news channels. The front of my thigh feels unnaturally warm. The soup has spilled on me. I watch the red spread down my leg. What would you think of me, unable to hold a cup of soup any more? I know what you'd say. You'd suggest I get my pants off, and we'd end up in bed together, or on the floor maybe, or on the couch—

I'm never going to have sex again.

The realisation is a body-blow. For a minute I figure there must be some way out of that one, but the more I think about it the more I understand that, no, it's true: I'm never again going to hold your body against mine, taste you, fill you up. I know it's wrong to be thinking this stuff, Rachel, but surely you would understand, of all people: you who once upon a time flew into a rage whenever we didn't fuck in a day.

No, this is my right: to want you back, to want you in every way I always wanted you.

I'm never going to have sex again. Even if I could surmount the shame of paying, even a sex worker wouldn't touch me. I have a face like a carcass, and no friends.

I got no one to talk to.

You gotta come back.

'Can we go in the warm, inside?' Steinwitz asks me. 'Not in there, necessarily, but somewhere warm.'

'Go home,' I tell him. I correct my tone: 'Thank you for what you've done. For getting me and… you know.'

'I'd prefer it if you didn't stay by yourself.'

'I know what you're thinking,' I say. 'I have a son. I ain't gonna do that.'

Steinwitz looks at me properly. I don't know how I look, but I spent a week in jail and a night in a woodshed, and my pants are drowned in tomato soup.

'What are you going to do?' he says.

What do you do when everything you had gets taken away? No routine, no purpose. I say, 'I need to take a bath, and take a look around. You know, just try to figure stuff out. Figure out what's right for Josh. I don't know what I'm doing, here.'

'There must be somebody you could call.'

'Nope, they're all gone. Do you even know what happened when I was in the States?'

His face stays blank. He doesn't know. Since I moved to Bryde's Crossing, I never spoke about my career as a wife-beater, and no one ever asked. No one in Clinton, either. Maybe they were just too Canadian to bring it up. It's untrue saying nothing is easier than speaking out. Sometimes doing nothing is the hardest thing in the world.

'Doesn't matter,' I say. What am I gonna do, anyway, Rachel? – serve up the dirt on you? I do that, there's no chance you'll ever come back. 'Let's say I screwed up and so my people don't talk to me any more.' I sigh. 'Know what? I'mma go in there and see what they've done to our house, put on some TV – just try and switch my fucking brain off.'

'You should be with people.'

'I got the worm in my head. I'm fine.'

'You'll be getting calls from me.'

'Thanks. But don't, OK?'

Going back in the house is like entering a memory. Josh's hockey pads are still in the vestibule. There are big dirty bootprints on the carpets, and bits of trash that belonged to someone else – tiny sealable plastic bags; wire twists; a soft pack of cigarettes with one left inside. When I first go inside the house, I linger around near the front door. The central heating has come on. It feels warm enough that someone could be living here. My legs are shaking like a dog's. I thought this was a kind of fear that only existed in cartoons.

I sit down on the stairs, expecting your voice to call me at any moment. You're making no sound, but the potential of you is in every room. Until I've looked in all of them, I won't know which one you're in, but I don't want to look in any room: I want to stay here sitting on the stairs, because as long as I stay here you could be anywhere.

Through the windows, I watch the forest. It's silent, and its skeletal fingers strum the clouds. This was always a big house. It keeps on getting bigger. The hardwood floors are harder. When the winds get up, the house lets itself breathe, like some old ship, like a lung, heaving and creaking and contracting.

After a long time has passed, and nothing has disturbed the silence, I get up and go to the den.

The white couch has gone; the rug, too. The rest of the furniture is stacked in the corner, and the walls have been painted – the paint smell has already gone. I figured I'd need to steel myself to deal with this, and I couldn't muster up enough feelings to make myself brave, but it's OK, as it turns out, because there's nothing to feel. The place where you were is right there before me and I don't feel anything at all. I pull out a chair and sit down opposite where I found you. My arms spasm, and it doesn't scare me. I ride it. After a while, I go get that cigarette and smoke it, but it tastes shitty and I end up drowning it in the sink and spitting to lose the taste, and then going back to the chair. They did a good job painting the wall. By the stereo there's a stack of newspapers spattered with white paint.

I think of Kurt Cobain's feet, in sneakers.

I wonder where you got the gun.

I guess some time has passed. Seems to be how it goes.

There's no point thinking in hours or days, or thinking at all, even. This isn't about thinking. There's some process working its way through my body; I don't know how it works or what it does, but I know it's necessary and I know it's fragile.

If I can sit tight and have no emotions, I might get through this unhurt.

Every little while, I wake up on the couch and fry myself some eggs or drink a little whisky – not too much, because I don't want to get drunk. Drunk would be dangerous. I mostly stay downstairs, except when I need to fetch clean clothes. When I take a bath, I leave the bathroom door open so that I don't miss anything. I feel like I'm made of glass.

The stereo and the TV and the computer don't interest me. Books interest me. Not the words in them, but the books themselves. The act of taking 'em off the shelves, holding them in my hands, flipping through the pages, seems like something that someone who was coping OK would do.

Yeah: they'd be very orderly, like I've been. They'd have it all pinned down.

I wash the dishes by hand, and stack them in the plastic rack, putting the knives point down so that no one will hurt themselves. Most of the time, I sit in the chair, and when the phone rings I let it go to answering machine, and I listen to the voices of the people who want to speak to us.

'Dr McAllistair,' they say, 'this is the Lyons family. We've been trying to reach you.'

There's a call I have to make, but I don't make it.

Time passes.

When I started out in radio, it was all about pretending to know people – celebrities, guests. The audience, especially. I sat there night after night, alone in the studio, and faked a relationship with every listener out there.

With time, that changed. I knew some listeners personally, but mostly I knew them as a personality type – the John Knox type. I could pick out people in real life and know they could be one of my listeners, the way you can tell girls who would notionally screw you, if they weren't already married or whatever. Losing the radio show was like losing the biggest friend a person could ever have. The invisible, magnificent, many-headed mess that was my listenership: all gone.

I never understood I missed them until now. Now I find myself sitting in the house in Bryde's Crossing, with you and Josh and my parents and California and my face and my youth and my listeners all gone. And now it is them, the John Knox listeners, I miss more than anyone. It feels like concrete in my gut. You were always disparaging about my listeners, like they were a lower form of life. When the DJ says 'don't touch that dial', he means 'don't leave me'. He means 'I need you'. Oftentimes I'd put personal stuff out there, and they'd give advice back, like a friend would. Sometimes it was bad advice. That was like a friend, too. And one day I'd disappeared, and they'd been left believing I was an asshole.

That's losing someone for ever. Having the mic turned off.

019

The phone keeps ringing.

Then it stops ringing – it's been lifted. He says, 'Hello?' and he sounds older than I remember. Of course he's older. It's been nine years.

'It's me,' I say.

There's a silence along the line. Why'd I think he'd know me? But he doesn't ask me who I am; instead he listens. We listen to each other, saying nothing.

Eventually he says, 'She's dead, right? That's the only thing.'

'Yeah.' The word catches in my throat.

Another aching gap. Then: 'How?'

I say, 'Gunshot. Gun.'

'She had a gun?'

'No. No, man, we never had a gun, I swear.'

From where I am, at the dining table, I can see the den, and the blank white wall. The light is the type that never turns into daylight, ailing from birth, and then atrophying back into dusk.

The voice that says my words says, 'There's going to be a funeral, here in Canada.'

'When?'

'Monday.'

I know the sound of someone struggling to speak. Sometimes not speaking makes a lot of noise. He says, 'She never even called us, not even when it was his birthday, nothing. Like we never existed. Like we was just nobody.'

It makes me wonder what your life was, for all that time when you were five thousand miles distant.

I say, 'I got something to ask of you. There's no one else I can ask.'

He listens.

I say, 'I'm keeping it together, but it's false, you know? I can feel it in me. Some time, this is gonna break down, and I don't want my kid around me when that happens.'

'What are you asking me?'

'A vacation. I'll pay – I mean, money isn't a thing. I just… I broke down, so they took him into protective care, and he shouldn't be there but he shouldn't be with me either. They're gonna assess me, and I'm gonna look fine, but I'm not fine.'

'And your family can't help you out?'

I breathe.

'What are you asking?' he says. 'Y'all want me to bring your kid back to Tennessee?'

'I can fake normal, but I'm a fucking timebomb.'

'Need some time to straighten out, is that it?'

'Something like that. I know it's a big ask. I want him away from this place. Farther the better. And he's grieving. He needs to be with someone who can tell him who his mom was.'

'How long?'

'I have no idea. I have no idea.'

The answer doesn't come right away. He sucks air through his teeth; I imagine him pacing. He says, 'Wait a minute. I'mma ask Dylan. Wait right there.'

The inside of Maxwell's house in Lebanon, Tennessee, sounds different from the inside of ours in Bryde's Crossing, near Clinton, Ontario. From inside his house I can hear traffic passing by – big vehicles, by the sound of them. There's a dog barking, somewhere close to. I don't know if it's his. Maybe a neighbour's. It seems like a long time before he comes back to the phone and says,

'I reckon y'all would have done the same for my boy.'

'You're saying yes.'

'We'll do our best for him.'

'Thank you.'

'Now you tell me the truth,' he says. 'She always talked about it, but she never did it. What happened this time?'

'Fuck, Maxwell, I'm asking myself that every minute of every day. She shaved her head and shit, but I thought we were through that.'

'Shaved her head?'

'She was in England most of the last couple of years – I barely knew who she was.'

'Always movin' on,' says Maxwell.

018

Burying you is so far outside my imagination that it doesn't seem it could actually be happening – burying you in the cemetery outside Clinton, the one I passed every time I rode with my folks into town, burying you accompanied by your husband and your two kids and a child protection officer. Dylan's grown up to be a lanky pre-teen with a rockabilly haircut. He seems OK. Maxwell looks stronger than the last time I saw him.

I don't cry, nor does Josh. We just stand there and watch the four men lower your casket into the hole. The vicar speaks, but I don't hear him. Then I pick up dirt and rub it into my hands before letting it fall on to the smooth wood lid. Josh drops flowers on you.

'Your mom was perfect, kiddo,' I tell him. He doesn't let me call him Josh any more; only Rutger, whom he speaks about like Rutger's someone else.

'You gonna be OK with these guys?' I said to Josh, meaning Maxwell and Dylan, while the officer scrutinises everything we do.

'Yeah, Rutger likes going on vacation,' says Josh.

'What about Josho? What does he think?'

'You can talk to Rutger,' he says.

There's next to nothing holding us together. All our grand schemes and jealousies and whatever else, it's all packed into this existence that could be over in the blink of an eye, without warning. Life's a piece-of-shit deal. What the hell's the point of doing anything, under these conditions?

017

Everything, everything has become you. I flick on a TV programme: it'll be some drama about your death and all the actors
will be you and will all be dead. The newspapers carry stories
about you, and the crossword clues all answer Rachel.

I've stopped reading. I've stopped taking in information.

One afternoon I hear a rumbling, the compression of brake
pads. I'm sitting in an easy chair, in my underpants, smoking a
cigarette.

'Hey, John,' says a man's voice. It's Steinwitz. There's no mistak-
ing the silhouette. He says, 'How about I put some lights on?'

Steinwitz looks older every time I see him. He says the same
about me, but not until after he's pulled up a chair opposite, looked
me over and touched my arm, a thing he never would have done
before you died. 'How you doing?' he says.

I laugh. We look at each other a while. Then he goes and does
the washing-up. When he's done he comes back and takes a cigarette from the pack; lights it; coughs. 'When did you take up
smoking?' he says. I shrug. He says, and I hope I quote him precisely here, 'Rachel Rachel Rachel Rachel Rachel Rachel Rachel.'
He says Rachel for about an hour. Then he goes to put on some
music and I yell, 'Don't fucking touch that!', making him jump.
'I'm sorry,' I say, 'I'm sorry, just don't fucking touch that.'

I ask him if he wants a drink.

'Do you want one?' he says.

I say, 'Yeah, I'm drinking too.' I notice I want to well up and cry,
but they are phoney tears. They are tears for me, they are senti-
mental, and one thing I am not going to be is inauthentic. 'Cause
if I do that, then what is all this for?

No, this is OK, so long as it is because I miss you. And oh God,
I miss you.

There was a man, once – I read his notebook. He came back from a war without half his face, and he sat in the room of the house where he'd once lived, and everything was different. He never said exactly what had happened in that war. I guess he didn't need to.

I don't want it to become a thought, but the idea keeps coming to me that I should have done something different. It's a poisonous thought, but that doesn't stop it starting to grow.

016

It gets lonely, in the country, with only yourself for company, when you have nothing to say.

I play the videotape of you over and over again. It gets scratchier with every repeat.

Josh is somewhere else, somewhere safe. I often think he might be in the next room, until I remember.

'Are you looking for your home?' is the first thing I hear, after I've logged on to the right website and the media player has started. 'Beautiful one-, two- or three-bed dream homes in the Bay area, many fully financed.'

I let that run on a while, and then the DJ comes back.

'Hey, I'm Nico Lupus and you're listening to Drive, on KVOC, Voice of the Bay: 98.8 FM, on iTunes and online,' says the voice. 'Good to have you! So Dubya's back for four more... almost like he never went away. Hey, was I the only one wondering whether Bill Renquist was gonna make it through the inauguration? I was getting scared, people! You know he's the only Chief Justice to have served under all forty-three presidents?'

Yeah, hilarious, Nico. Having the means to communicate isn't a toy. The opportunity to talk to thousands of people confers a responsibility to say words upon which the speaker would be prepared to stake their life. Or why the hell bother? Speech is a physical action; why keep repeating a movement if it doesn't mean anything? That's a sure sign of being crazy. The dangerous part about microphones is they amplify everything that is said, sense and dross alike, so that the world becomes a sea of voices. The Nicos talk as loud as the preachers.

How does anybody make themselves heard, in that?

I leave the radio on, and let the voices pour in through the Ethernet cable. There are no neighbours. I play it loud.

'Hi, Nico, I love your show. I want to say that I think... well, actually I don't know for sure, but I...'

'Hey, Nico, how's it going? Listen to your show every day. So you were talking about...'

'Thanks for taking my call. I'm outraged. I mean, are they kidding? Why...'

'Nico, man, uh, what's up? All this stuff you talking 'bout, I got to tell you, I'm listening to you talking, and I'm like, man...'

Christmas comes; Christmas goes.

You've been dead two months, and then three, and I've been waiting to feel like I knew what to do, but there's been nothing. Could it be that I never felt anything about you? Was I projecting something on to you that wasn't real? No, I loved you. I *love* you; but I can't get too close to that feeling.

The house is full of you. I didn't move much, since you went away. Josh's things; your things. I didn't open your wardrobe, yet, and the only times I've been in your study have been to sit and soak up the air, like an early morning visitor in a museum.

The books on your shelves have gotten dust on them, so that I don't know which ones you like to read and which ones you don't.

Your desk is as you left it. Your best pen remains on a writing pad where you put it down.

Someday I'm going to want to do something with all this stuff of yours. That's what happens when someone dies, right? – People reach a particular point, and then they go through the pain of throwing their loved one's possessions in the trash. I don't know, I guess I saw that in a movie somewhere. I'm not feeling it. There's nothing in me that wants to throw you away. If I move your stuff, then you won't ever have a reason to come back to me.

'Condoleezza's a role model for African–American women, and anyone hacking her's a racist and a woman-hater and oughta get their ass served, Nico. That's all there is.'

'If the British won't toe the line, then we ain't gon' help them. We already saved their lily-white asses out of two world wars. If they ain't with us, they're against us, and we should treat 'em the same as the Iraqis.'

'There's no point talking to terrorists. They don't want to talk, they just want to murder innocent citizens. You have to come down on them. Saddam is just a terrorist. People got to remember that.'

I run my finger along the dust on your desk, collecting it in a grey half-moon on my fingertip.

The desk has four drawers. The first one I try is locked.

I sit down in the easy chair in the corner by the bookcase, and think about that closed drawer. My hand spasms.

Yeah, it's locked – it doesn't respond when I shake it around a little. The others are locked, too. It's remarkable that someone who worked as hard as you could have a workspace that is so uncluttered. The desktop has a computer, and some expenses receipts impaled on a spike. All the tickets are Canadian. There's nothing about your real life there.

Finding the key takes a little while. It's on the bunch that is where you left it, in the pot in the kitchen. Going back to your study, I feel a tingle in the soles of my feet. The voices on the radio keep talking, because that's what voices do.

I wonder what deeds my voice provided the backdrop for, back in the day; what events. For example, I wonder: how many people died while I did nothing but talk?

The drawers don't have much in them – two, you didn't use at all. A third is all stationery. In the last one, the deep bottom drawer, with a tin of chump change, there are three hardcover books with dull-looking covers, and a journal bound in leather.

A shiver passes through me.

'If I was the boss of television or whatever, I would keep Martha Stewart locked up for good, throw away the key.'

Something isn't fitting into my head right.

'So they made the arm wave? Dude's dead, already, he don't care. These soldiers have been through hell at the hands of the Iraqis, man, let 'em blow some off. Iraqis are lucky we don't nuke 'em.'

That's it – didn't I already mail this book to you? *Chin up – you're going home* – that's right. But when I flip it open to the start, it doesn't say that. The handwriting's the same long, slanting script, but it starts, *On occasion, one's objective is simple and right.*

It's dated July 1914.

It's him again: John Rutherford. The only other man I know with half a face.

I feel my heart speed up.

I didn't know I gave a damn about this guy, but I do. From the date, this book must have been written right before the thing happened that screwed him up so bad. On the tape of the day we met, you talk about July 1914 – when Europe started to dance its ballet of revenges.

What was it you said? – *One half of the poets looking for refuge in an imagined golden past. A language beyond violence.*

My whole body feels like the power's been switched back on.

The other books, I nearly don't look at, I'm so excited about the journal, and scared, too, instinctually, standing here brazenly going through your things, but I do check the covers, and they make my hands and feet freeze.

The first, a big red book, is called *The Empowerment of Suicide.* The pages are yellowed at the edges.

The next is smaller, and newer, and has a melancholy black-and-white photo on the cover, and it is called *The Act of Dying: A commentary on Durkheim's spectrum of suicide.*

The last book is called *Suicide and Culture.* The cover is a composite of photographs of famous people: Ernest Hemingway, Kurt Cobain, Virginia Woolf.

'Nico,' say the voices in the house, 'people questioning America's involvement need to remember they sent terrorists to our shores and flew planes into the towers. What kind of message does it send to the rest of the world if we do not retaliate? What are we as a nation if we sit on our hands and do nothing?'

The three books are by the same author: Professor Michael D. Butler.

There is a picture of Professor Michael D. Butler inside the dust jackets. Professor Michael D. Butler is a middle-aged black man, with a confident smile. He has all of his face.

He wants to show me around. He seems OK.

I look at him and wonder why there is water dripping on to his picture.

And then it comes to me, rising like a revolution, and I try to stop it, but I can't. I just can't.

My skin's on fire, all over again, and the blood in my veins. I am incendiary.

I hold his picture in my burning hand, and he smiles at me. He *smiles* at me.

And I feel.

015

Ping.

It sounds like sonar. It's the seat-belt sign, announcing we're gonna get shook up a little. It would be useful to have that feature in life generally.

The stewardess apparently cares that I be strapped to my chair, overlooking that we're moving at 550 mph in a missile a bird can bring down. I find it hard to see people's faces any more. When the stewardess leans over to ask if I need medication, she's a silhouette against the strips of tiny spotlights above the other passengers. I tell her it's OK, I got it. The flying drugs make me grit my teeth. We exchange blank faces until she gives up on account of my not actually doing any prohibited thing, bar being ugly, and goes away. We're too far gone for them to throw me off. No turning home, not now.

The sky looks like a big bowl of nothing, but it's full of invisible jeopardy: pressure mountains, sheer drops, but with no edge to fall off, no end to hit. It thins and turns into the weak particle soup of space, isn't that right? A place where you could travel light years without running into a particle of anything at all. I'll take a piece of that. Currently I'm bombarded by air molecules at the rate of ten million per second, and every one of them feels like a punch in the gut or a kick in the head. Getting shook up is nothing.

Time has passed, Rachel, months and months. And the light is serene, where the air's so thin.

No birds warm their feathers in the sunshine: there are no birds and there is no oxygen and there is nothing but violent light. A thin piece of glass separates me from temperatures that would freeze the blood in my veins; a tin machine keeps me from falling out of the sky. I know, now, why God made Heaven so inhospitable to life. Because life is filthy. Because life is dying, decaying, every day.

I'm going away, Rachel. It's 5 a.m. on a morning in 2005. The day up here is clear: blue and beautiful like Windows. On the big screen they loop big numbers: the distance between my feet and the Earth, the killer outer temp, the phenomenal speed. In my mind, you're still smiling, but I can't smile, I can only grit my teeth.

In the airport there was a string quartet playing grunge songs. Incredible, how everything hurts.

I'm tucked into the safe, snug world of my iPod, where Ella Fitzgerald sings about dying on a Sunday, and gaze out at acre upon acre of emptiness, beautiful because there's nothing living there.

I hope I get to come back home to you, my darling. Leaving Josh was hard, and leaving you is harder, but the battlefield's for people like me, not for people like you. I've balled up my strength and I'm going to fight the war. It's what the good men *do*.

The clouds below us have thinned out and gone.

I'm gonna put things right. I'm gonna be a man for you.

FOUR

22 May 1914

On occasion, one's objective is simple and pure. There are no distractions, no moral doubts. That is when you know that what you are doing is right.

I have walked from Oxford to Kingham, a quaint little village about three miles outside of the town. There is wonderfully little to see – just a few houses scattered about, and children playing with stones, and a dairyman's dray, sans dairyman, the mare nosing about in the verge at the side of the track. It is a fine place to lose oneself. I slip the ring from my finger into a breast pocket, and whistle a jaunty tune.

'Don't you know it's Sunday?' says a fellow, and I pipe down.

The sun has been tardy in coming, but is, I think, here at last, more than the usual number of rays struggling and succeeding in penetrating the dappled clouds.

Ah, the vacuum of uncertainty. It's quite clear of course that one cannot exist in a vacuum for ever. Twenty-five shillings a week is not to be sniffed at, but if one is to establish a profession, rather than merely work at a job, one must eventually act.

The job with the magazine is something, at least; however, Mother remains utterly fixated on law. I've never seen myself in a wig, I must say. One only has to look at the long hours that Uncle Humphrey puts in, & the deep entrenched lines on his colourless face, to know that law, or Uncle Humphrey's branch of it anyway, seems to be a machine for sucking the life out of all who come into contact with it. Moreover, how can I stand before a judge without giving myself away? Nerves alone might do it. Providence is not to be provoked.

And then, of course, there is the life academic – how tiresome. One rather suspects that Father doesn't imagine his younger son to be remotely capable of performing half the mathematical thought of either Rutherford senior or Rutherford major; nevertheless, I think he should be disappointed were I not to make some effort to follow in his footsteps. That is the purpose of parenthood, is it not – to recreate oneself in miniature? Alas, I am somewhat likely to break that particular cycle.

The first time I slept with a boy, I knew it was wrong – we both did. I dare say there was plenty of buggery going on amongst the upper forms. You could tell perfectly well that some of the boys weren't boys at all, but you'd never have known it of me. I was a six-footer by the age of fourteen, and I played rugger in the First XI and rowed.

The boy's name was Phelps. He was quite an enigma among the rest of us – always keeping his own counsel. Especially good at languages, I remember. He had straw-blond hair and almond-shaped eyes, and when he laughed at something I found myself wanting to kiss him. I knew that was wrong. In the upper fourth we had had an odd sort of talk from the biology teacher, full of euphemisms and generalisations, which seemed to focus upon certain 'impulses' we were all bound to feel, and the completeness with which we had to keep these feelings in check.

'Sometimes you will find yourselves imagining that you want to commit a particular act that you know is wrong,' he said. 'This always stems from other, healthier desires that you will develop as you grow and become men. Do not confuse the base urge with the noble desire. The physical world is full of illusory sensations; do only what you know is allowed by God. One day you will be forced to give an account of your actions.'

I thought that a lot of rot. I did not believe in God, but of course in those days one did not discuss such things until much later in one's education, when debating and reasoning became more highly valued than crude 'facts'. I introduced myself to Phelps. He had a marvellous way of standing rather too close and looking around when speaking to one that made one feel part of some conspiracy, and he always smelt of Pears soap.

Phelps and I developed an interest in entomology. I cannot say that we were the most successful collectors of caterpillars and roaches and beetles, but we spent many fruitful expeditions together in the copse that backed on to the school's grounds. To this day, I cannot *help tingling when I remember Phelps kneeling before me, smiling prettily, wiping my semen from his chin with the back of his hand. I remember kissing the nape of his neck and the nook of his shoulder as I entered him between those smooth buttocks, as they consumed me and reconsumed me; I remember the delirium and the urgency of the sexual climax and the moments when a breaking branch scared us both witless and sent us scrambling to dress; and the passionate kissing on the forest floor. We were in love. It was a love made all the more passionate because it was our first love, and it was clandestine – extremely so. We would have received the whip had we been discovered, to say nothing of the involvement of our parents, who would have finished whatever corporal punishment the school had started. The requirement to conceal our intimacy made great actors of us both – we could have rivalled any Benoît-Constant Coquelin. Whereas in the woods we knew every inch of one another, body and soul, in classes we were as perfect strangers. If someone were to refer to Phelps by name, I queried which boy was Phelps. There was nothing but goodness and love and fucking in our relationship, and yet we were obliged to creep about like criminals.*

'Unfortunately, no one thought to write a story called Romeo and Romeo,' *he said, one day, as we sat together in our clearing, the one embowered by holly bushes and ivy-addled birches.*

I had my arms around him. I said, 'No, but men played all the parts. Dear old Juliet was just a chap in a wig.'

'We should have been born in Ancient Greece. We should have been born anywhere but here, with people breathing down our necks.'

I said, 'Well, who cares? We'll be adults soon enough. We'll be able to do exactly as we please. We could live in a little cottage somewhere on a hill and never mind what the rest of the world thinks.'

He laughed at me, I remember, but it was the sort of laughter one makes when one is uncertain that one is listening to a joke. He twisted around to look at me, and I kissed his lips, and we kissed for a long while and got lost in it.

Later, as we trooped back to the dorms with our jars full of twigs and our notebooks filled with drawings of bugs that would have astonished even Darwin, Phelps said, 'You know, I love you. I know that sounds odd, but it's true. I do.'

We were fourteen.

In Kingham, the housemaid opens the door, and recognises my arrival as her marching orders. By the time she's gathered up her things and gone out the back way, my eyes have got accustomed to the gloom. The door slams behind her.

'Why don't you put any bally lights in this place?' I shout upstairs, pulling off first my boots, and then my coat.

'I'm a sculptor. I haven't any money.'

'Ridiculous.'

'What's ridiculous?' he calls.

'Sculpture. Create something that will earn you a living.' I remove my tie and undo my shirt, and take my collar off. 'Do you know what my lot publish? Romantic novels, for women. You might write something like that. Call yourself Flora something-or-other.'

'And whore myself for the sake of an electric light?'

'Absolutely, yes.'

He is propped up in bed, inevitably, bare-chested, pretending to read a book. On his head is an absurd tasselled cap that did not put in an appearance on my last visit. I remove it by pulling the tassel, releasing his unruly tangle of ash-blond curls, and I kiss him. The sheet slips lower on his body, revealing his eagerness. The book falls aside and is forgotten.

Later, when we are tangled together in the bedsheets, clammy and sated, he says, 'Hello, Rutherford.'

'Hello, Phelps, old thing,' I say.

He rolls over so that I can stroke his back. 'Father's going on about my joining the army, again,' he says.

'How tiresome for you.'

'Says a bit of military discipline would do me the world of good.'

'Perhaps it would; although I couldn't bear being away from you.'

His shoulders are strong; the muscles of his neck defined, like a David. Much too beautiful for coarse army clothes. I mentally fit him for an officer's uniform. It is no good – his nakedness overpowers the image. 'I shouldn't worry,' I tell him. 'Practically every boy at Walsingham went to OTC – the army is bound to prefer them over a flower like you.'

'I think I should object to the principle of it, even if it didn't.' He lights two cigarettes, and puts one between my lips. 'We can't all run around shooting one another.'

'Quite; and what do you propose we do when someone demands we hand over bits of the empire, my darling? Ask them to bugger off?'

'It's the inclination towards the martial that offends me.' He had been lying against me, but now removes himself.

'You're in earnest?'

'Yes, I am. Don't tell me you haven't noticed how eager everyone seems to be to prepare for war, as though war were a fait accompli? They talk of it in the same breath as the Glorious Twelfth.'

I do not want to argue. He is wrong, of course, to suppose that it is possible to maintain the integrity of one's borders without a little sabre-rattling, and sometimes more than that. No gain is made but at a cost of blood; no claim is defended but by means of the ultimate sanction: war. Civilisation, one sometimes suspects, is but a thin veneer concealing impulses to destruction that have raged unabated in our species since our cave-dwelling days.

'If the trouble is about borders, remove the borders altogether,' he advises. 'Let us all live on one planet that has no countries, and go about our lives creating beautiful works of art and making better medicines.'

I kiss Phelps on the shoulder. He turns to examine my face, for a moment – looking for what, precisely, I do not know. I sometimes think that there is something very naive about this young man – a quality that makes me fearful for his survival. Yes: he exudes a species of vulnerability that might help him to flourish if life were some fantasia painted by Titian; however, it is not. This is the twentieth century, and the empires of Europe surely cannot continue on their trajectories without there being some great confrontation. How will Phelps hope to survive, in such a world? He strokes his sculptor's thumbs across my cheeks; and then I am lost in his kisses and his simple passion, and I let myself forget everything.

3 August 1914

Picked up an Evening Standard *on the walk home from West Kensington. A glorious summer's day – quite at odds with Lord Grey's pronouncement in Parliament that the country shall stand side by side with plucky Belgium against the Kaiser – in other words, that we are going to war.*

Suddenly, the streets seem alive with a sense of purpose. On my way through Lowndes Square, I overheard a draper saying to his lad, 'Don't worry, they'll shout if they need you.'

The preening Prussian militarism of the Germans is a perfectly bloody thing, chewing up everything that stands before it. It cannot be imagined but that they intend chewing up this country, too.

What is remarkable is the lack of interest hitherto shown by the majority of people towards this set of circumstances, which has been bubbling up for months. Hardly anyone one speaks to seems to have so much as heard of Serbia, let alone know that it is under bombardment – have they not read about the Austrian archduke? No, the average Englishman is at this moment rather more concerned with Ireland, and Johnny Douglas' picks for the Ashes. All of a sudden, the German menace appears to him as something wondrous, mystical and unforeseen, like an eclipse to a tribe in the Congo basin. I wonder at the expenditure of effort that goes into making the newspapers, when their intended readership seems to ignore them altogether, and the only people who get any use from them are charladies, when they clean the silver.

4 August 1914

The deadline for the Germans to respond was set for eleven o'clock tonight. There was a queer mood in London, like none I have ever felt. Iris wanted nothing to do with it (her new friend, a very brusque young woman called Davenport, has been calling rather a lot lately, and not always at a respectable hour), so I went out to see what was going on. There were far more people out at that late hour than usual, and I followed the general direction of the crowd down to Big Ben.

There was quite a crowd – thousands of people, I should say – a veritable sea of boaters. There was chanting, and a counting down to the strike of eleven. When it came, the crowd let up a great cheer and there was real elation – we were going to do the right thing. We sang 'Rule Britannia'. Then someone suggested we should go and call for the king, and I was swept along – not unwillingly – to Buckingham Palace, where the crowd seemed to fill the Mall, making it quite impossible for carriages and motor cars to get through. This was nearly midnight. Presently the king and queen came out on to the balcony overlooking us, and we cheered and sang. Oh, we were all sorts, there – actors, fresh from Drury Lane, make-up still behind their ears; medical students, smelling of alcohol of the non-medicinal sort; tradesmen and City gentlemen; coarse sorts from the docks, all muddled in together.

I think that this war may prove to be a very good thing for our country, which has seemed to struggle to acclimatise to the modern age. Football and the Boat Race are all very well, but to define oneself one must have more than mere distractions: one must have a higher purpose, a cause that is noble and offers a possibility to transcend concerns that are merely personal. Defending the institutions in which one believes is such a cause. As Thoreau put it, Live your beliefs and you can turn the world around. *Inelegantly phrased, as we can see, but then of course Thoreau was an American.*

13 August 1914

The government has put out a general appeal for men to join the army. Overnight, there are posters everywhere – Your King and Country Need You. *It goes without saying that I have never seen anything like it in my lifetime. One just about recollects the heroes of the South African war, parading in full uniform with bandages about their heads – an impressive image – but they were regular soldiers, not members of the general population.*

Now, and with the exception of Phelps (whose letters are grown uncharacteristically dry), every male I know has rushed to join up. One has only to poke one's nose through the front door of any civic building, bank, post office or police station to discover a recruitment operation in progress – not that one could easily poke one's nose, nor anything else for that matter, anywhere close to the building, owing to the mob of eager applicants outside every such venue. I visited Father, in Stoke Newington, yesterday, and there was a queue in Church Street that extended from the public lending library to the cemetery gates.

At its head was a most impressive figure, all got up in the dress uniform of a sergeant major. He and several other uniformed military types, none of them especially dashing, had set up a trestle table in the street, and were using it as their base of operations, filtering from the queue those who appeared to be too young or knock-kneed or whatever else might make them ineligible for service. As I passed, he noticed me and said, 'Why aren't you in the queue, laddie?' I felt the eyes of all those men who were in the queue fall upon me, judging me. I reassured him, 'Oh, I'll be in the queue all right. One has a family, though – it would be wrong not to inform them of my intention first.'

'It's your family you'll be defending,' he said. 'They won't mind.'

'All the same.'

'Well, when you come back, bring your friends,' he told me. 'You look like a sportsman. Bring the team along – we'll get you all signed up together.'

There seems something archetypally British in the notion of an army comprised of sports teams and works associations, clubs of hobbyists and bands of pals. Oh yes: we may be reasonable and softly spoken, as a people, but at this very moment, the quiet determination of the British is being roused and mobilised, and brought to bear upon the forces of Hun expansionism.

I have never felt very much like a man, but now it is possible for me to look like one and feel like one, and give an account of myself. That is the path to the glory of the name of God.

Father says he would rather I do what I 'consider, taking all into account, to be for the best'. He says that, as it is I who must live with the consequences of the decision, it should be I alone who takes it. I think it is jolly decent of him not to force his point of view. There is an obvious practical case for taking a commission and gaining a year's experience of active military duty: doubtless any prospective employer would value the experience of leadership, resourcefulness and so on, and who knows what future employer may not want to know why one did not take on such a role in the defence of one's country? And yet these are mere side benefits when one considers the main point, which is, with the threat offered, the opportunity to attain a state of purity and grace in the face of adversity.

What is it, to live a life in which one's ambition – indeed, one's hope, one's esprit de vivre – can be purchased for the price of the next Alpine skiing excursion, or a four-seater Crossley, or some other trifle? So much for fortis est veritas. It seems sometimes that I am surrounded by minds that believe in the principle that anything worth having can be bought and sold, which degree of materiality sends me scurrying for the nearest and highest ideal upon which I can lay my hands.

I did not go back to the recruiting sergeant. While I most certainly intend becoming a soldier, there are distinctions between serving with this regiment or that. Nor is it thinkable that someone of my class should join but as an officer. According to Wilkes' father, who is *a lieutenant colonel in the Coldstreams, there's no hope whatever of our getting commissions at present, owing to the number of applications for same. It is quite infuriating to have spent months at Officer Training during the long vac while our contemporaries were free to roam and have larks, only now to find that particular avenue closed down. Of course, one could simply enlist – the 'pals' in the rugger team have gone in together – but after all one has not learnt how to shoot, how to plot a course, how to skin a rabbit &c. for no reason. There are no places left at all in the Territorials, so we must wait for something to come up with the regulars. When will this be? Qui sait?*

The Germans are crossing Europe at a rate of speed. According to the report in today's Times, *they are bayoneting babies in Belgium as they advance.*

The recruiting sergeant was perfectly right. There comes a moment when, through duty or through passion, and whether inspired by God or by family or by home, or perhaps in order to shore up one's personal honour, one must will oneself to become deaf to the voices of doubt and sentimentality, and one must decide, once and for all, to be a man.

20 February 1915

After an interminable winter practising how to make bivouacs and fix bayonets and give map references, yesterday I had to go up from Pontefract to divisional headquarters to interview a major general who agreed I was ready to go out. It being the third such meeting (the preceding ones having resulted in disappointment), I did not go to it with high hopes.

The man in question was inscrutable. He kept me in suspense until the very last; then the fellow seemed to imply that my still being in Blighty had been the result of some administrative negligence, an over-subscription for commissions, or something of the sort. It was quite clear, he said, that I had acquired the requisite skills to command men in the field. He asked me what I had been before joining the army.

'Junior editor at a literary magazine, sir,' I told him.

'Literary man, eh? Written anything important?'

'A few bits and pieces, but nothing lasting, sir.'

'Well, why not?'

'Well, you see, I'm not actually a writer, sir. I edit other people's work. Spot talent, bring out its strengths, that sort of thing.'

'I see.' Finally, he stood and shook my hand. 'Well, let's see what strengths you can bring out of a platoon of men.'

So there it is. My commission has finally come through. I am now Captain *John Rutherford.*

My company, along with the rest of its battalion, is due to leave for France on Monday. At the present moment they are in Folkestone, while I am up here in the East Riding – I will command around two hundred men, and be responsible for their discipline and well-being. My chest inflates with pride (as does my head, evidently).

I have written to Father, asking him to forward the various items I know I will need. The army provides a few basic pieces of equipment, but if one is to be away for a long time it will not do to be underprepared. Besides my uniform (which I must buy myself – some flogging around the shops in St James' is in order) I will need a stout pair of boots – the field of war being a notorious mire – as well as a watch of an approved type. Something reinforced around the face is to be preferred. A few extra pairs of socks and gloves, a swish-stick and a revolver, and I'll do.

26 February 1915

I am growing, or attempting to grow, moustaches. It is rather a feeble effort at this stage, I must say. I suppose I had an idea that merely by willing it to be so, and by avoiding it with the razor, my upper lip would luxuriate at once in a full, thick bit of hair, along the lines of Arthur Balfour.

After months of letters, today I saw Phelps in person. I do not think I shall see him again for some time.

He was dressed when I arrived fully overcoated; scarcely had I removed my officer's cap than he was escorting me by the elbow out of the house and into the frigid February air, slamming the door behind us. He'd got quite the wind up, that much was obvious.

'What the deuce has got into you?' I demanded to know.

'I might ask you the same question,' he retorted. 'Have you worn this fancy-dress costume of yours to add insult to injury?'

So that was it. We set off up the Kingham Road with our ears being bitten off by the cold wind.

'Look, I'm going to do my bit, and that's an end to it,' I said. 'I must say, if you profess to care for someone you might show them a little more support than this.'

'Support? Support for what?'

'I don't know whether you've noticed, but there's a war on.'

Phelps was in no mood to hear that sort of statement, apparently. He said, 'So when precisely did you find that you wanted to kill people?'

I told him not to be ridiculous.

'Ridiculous? That is what you're going to do, isn't it?'

'If I have to.'

He scowled at my revolver, holstered at my hip.

'Look,' I said, 'it's naive to imagine I won't have to use this, I know

that. But there are larger things at stake, in this. There are things worth fighting for.'

'There is nothing to warrant all this death.'

His tone had begun to grate on me somewhat. I felt he wasn't being reasonable. I told him he was not seeing the full picture.

He scoffed, 'All I see is a lot of idiots who want a licence to shoot each other.'

'Oh? And am I an idiot?'

'I thought you weren't,' he said. 'I really believed you weren't. And yet you want to go and murder your fellow man – for what? For some bloody silly idea. That's all nationhood is. A climate, and a lot of bluster. Don't you see? – It doesn't matter whether we have a king or a kaiser.'

He was serious, I could see. I thought that perhaps living out in the countryside, alone, had sent him barmy.

'I understand,' he went on. 'I do. I'm a pansy if I don't care to fight. And yet it's still the better choice.'

I said, slowly, 'If I don't stand up to be counted when my country looks to me, then I'm nothing but a hypocrite.'

'A living one.'

'And yet perhaps there are bigger things, things to which one must be prepared to sacrifice oneself.'

'Such as love,' he suggested. 'Give this up. Make me your wife – at least a de facto one. Come and make a home with me. I want us to get old together. A little place in the country, just we two, with no one to bother us… Wouldn't you like that? Wouldn't you?'

'Of course I would.'

'Well, then.' He snatched my hand. 'Do you love me?'

This stopped me in my tracks. We found ourselves standing together by a low wall that separated the winding road from the fields. The undulations of Oxfordshire stretched in every direction.

I said, 'Please, don't put me in an impossible—'

'Do you love me?' he said again.

I thought, for a moment, that perhaps I should pretend that I did not love him, or that my feelings had weakened so that he might take the separation more easily.

And then he walked away. Without any word, without so much

as an alteration in his expression, Phelps turned on his heel, and left me standing there.

I called his name – once; twice. I ordered him to come back. He merely kept walking, the hem of his overcoat wrapping itself around his thin ankles.

In a few days' time I will be in France. It hurts to think of not being with him – even, if he will write, to think of him saying nothing for fear of the censor. He is a sunbeam. I shall grow cold without him.

1 March 1915 – France

We heard the guns for the first time, today, as we marched along the road from Amiens towards the lines. The company came to a halt and listened. They sound like an engine – a monstrous one, ineluctable, unavoidable. Death itself, made of machinery.

We look at photographs in the penny papers, and talk of home.

3 March 1915

The farmhouse to which my company has been billeted is a typical French place, set in acres of flowing farmland; it is rustic and red-roofed and surrounded by giant outbuildings and heady meadow flowers – the bucolic idyll. The farmer himself is a well-fed fellow. As he trots up the dirt track to greet you, to a Greek chorus of young pigs becoming excitable in their sties at the approach of a stranger, it is with his rotten teeth on display, and with a handshake of the Continental sort – both hands clasped around one's own – and many slaps on one's back. Nothing could please him more, it seems, than to see les Anglais.

The wife is a different matter. While her husband carefully escorts us around the pits in the track and points out bits of handiwork of his with the split-rail fencing, all the while insisting we call him by his first name, she, the wife, is a flickering figure half concealed in the doorway, her face shrewish, her eyes clear and sharp, who, upon being observed for longer than a moment, withdraws into the depths of the blank-faced farmhouse.

Pierre goes on talking. He tells us that they have been lucky, so far, he and his wife. As he fills his pipe and explains why this should be so, the men loiter about and light cigarettes, and try to coax chickens to come to them. The shelling was bad, he says. It had been worse for his neighbour. When the front line had been formed, the neighbour happened to be on the Central side of it, not far from Serre. Pierre gestures with the stem of his pipe at the dark circles of earth that pock the ground all about us, like a cancer. One cannot help but be reminded of graves, recently filled. But these are circular. These are where shells have hit. 'I had horses,' he says.

I ask him where the line is now, and with his pipe he describes a line along a low ridge about a mile east, dotted with naked trees. It's the sort of feature of the landscape one might notice and suggest striking out for on an afternoon's walk in Cambridgeshire, hoping for what passes for a view in that part of the world. Detachments from the Ninth and the Welsh Fusiliers were responsible for driving the Germans back, apparently. I happen to know several of my year at Balliol were posted to the Ninth – they may have stood on this very spot, in fact. Pierre is reticent about events, and I find it almost impossible to imagine the sort of confrontation between armies that could have gone on in this world of green wheat and birds and capricious butterflies. It was all over in a day, he says – and then the farm was on the Allied side of the line, and the shelling had stopped. Pierre indicates a crop of crosses by the coppice to the north. The sunlight is harsh.

'Why did the German guns fire on you here?' I ask.

He shrugs, and gestures about him. 'I don't know who fired, he says. But now the Germans are farther back. We are out of range.'

I look for the neighbour's farm. When I cannot see it, I ask Pierre where it is.

Pierre licks his lips and attempts a smile. He wants me to understand him.

Pierre's farm is in good shape, all things considered. The white-walled farmhouse, with its two shuttered window sockets and the door lolling open, betrays no secrets. The corpse of a plough has been abandoned to rust; the barns and sheds, solid and patient as statuary, merely wait.

I say, 'What's happened here? Did our boys fire on you?'

Shouts go up from the men. They have spotted a reconnaissance aeroplane, French, by the look of it, fluttering high over the German lines. The conversation is suspended as we stop to will it on, using our hats to shield our eyes from the sun. The heat is baking the grasses. One is reminded by that perfume, as the ack-ack blossoms around our little plane, of childhood holidays: of beaches and bathing huts and the coarseness of salt, and ladies sitting pristine beneath parasols watching the tide roll away down Devonish sands. For a moment, the blue sky is a blue Atlantic, and I an infant, marvelling at the bigness of it all.

'I propose this barn for you and your men,' Pierre tells me, as he leads us towards the cluster of buildings. His gait is awkward. 'The *senior officers may stay in the house, with me and my wife. We have space for three.'*

'Thank you,' I say.

'They are coming later, I presume, the senior men?'

We pause in the clearing. There are bullet-holes in the side of the barn.

'We're it, actually,' I tell him.

Pierre casts his eye over we three officers, and over the men, his tufty brow cocked like that of an old family dog. His gaze falls on one or two in particular – the bantam O'Mally, little Anderson – before returning to me, or more exactly to my chest, from where it does not rise.

'There is hay in the barn,' he says. 'Tell your soldiers to make themselves comfortable.'

I ask him what's in the other barn, the one farthest west.

'Nothing,' he says. 'It is empty.'

The vacant barn is partly shielded from the view of the lines. A door high up in the gable end commands a view down across the vale and over the farmyard itself. A man positioned up by the pulley there would have no trouble spotting any advancing enemy, who would be forced to come one way or the other around the other buildings, and in doing so would make an easy target.

'Well, if it's all the same I'd prefer we take that one, instead,' I tell him. 'We can move the hay ourselves.'

'I say, you two seem to be hitting it off,' says Captain van Leys. 'What's he saying?'

'He says we're welcome,' I tell him.

4 March 1915

Today we came for the first time into the trenches. We are to stay here for four days and nights, replacing a company from the same battalion, who will relieve us when our shift is completed.

One approaches the trenches along duckboard, which, I have been informed by both my servant and a corporal who seems most eager to assist his new officer (even though I am a 'Saturday' – well, so is he!), is designed for the winter months, when the tranquil fields are transformed into a quagmire. The number of simple graves one espies as one approaches our lines do nothing to reassure one. Every few hundred yards one comes across short stakes poking out of the ground, sometimes with a name scratched into the wood; most without.

I begin to see that my efficacy shall be measured, not in medals, but in wooden stakes.

I had not foreseen the complexity of the earthworks here. At first there are sandbagged slits cut into the soil – one enters the rear (supply) trench via these. At once, signs of habitation are visible – coats hanging on hooks, ledges where men are clearly in the custom of sleeping – that sort of thing. The trench is far deeper than one might expect, and large wooden cross-supports can be seen every so often, keeping the trench walls up. From the supply trench, one must pass through even deeper communication trenches, wide enough only for one man at a time to pass through, which take one to the firing trench – the last 'safe' place before no man's land. The trenches are dug in sections that zigzag in order to avoid enfilade fire.

Danger is all around. The trenches receive the constant attention of the snipers and mortar crews in the German front line, who take potshots whenever they fancy there's something to be bagged. For this reason, 'keep your head down' is the order of the day, particularly for a six-footer like me.

Westerley (the corporal I mentioned above) seemed at first to know all the vulnerable points in the trench, having been here since January, during which time the company has had five different officers. As he showed me where everything was – the latrine; the place where digging for an observation post has been started – he would every so often advise 'I shouldn't stand there if I were you, sir', or 'You'll want to duck your head down a bit further there, sir'. Only at the sixth repetition of this play, and from the tittering of some of the men, did I understand that I was being baited.

'I should put you on latrine duty,' I told him.

'Thank you, sir,' he said.

'Do you want latrine duty?'

'Yes, sir. Man on latrine duty doesn't have to do no other duties, sir.'

'So all this "duck down", "don't stand there" – all a lot of eyewash.'

'No, sir,' he said. 'Captain Adams got hit through the head a week ago, sir. Stone dead, sir. Sniper.'

Westerley finished his tour by pulling aside a sort of canvas curtain that opened into a dugout in the trench wall about five feet tall, and with enough room for two beds and a writing table. 'This is where officers sleep, sir,' he said.

So this is the defence of one's country! – this is being a man. Cooking up precious potatoes, shaving in cold tea and drinking water flavoured with petrol from the dixies. In all of it, one tries one's best to keep one's eye on the noble reason for this squalor.

It is not easy. Try as one might, in the dugout one cannot help thinking of poor old Adams – one minute ducking in here to catch a bit of rest, the next standing in the wrong spot and – blam.

20 March 1915

I thought I would feel afraid. I thought too that some thought of Phelps would pass through my mind at just such a moment as this, and I might start to doubt my purpose. Not a bit of it. The reverse, in fact: I have sacrificed too much to be uncertain.

When I think that I was once able to love that man, who now, when the higher call comes, slopes off with his tail between his legs, I find the thought disgusts me.

We are a proud army of professionals and volunteers. We do not need his sort, nor do we seek his approval. When this score between nations is settled, as I believe it soon enough will be, and each man is held to account for what he did or did not do, let us see where he and I stand, in comparison to one another. Let us see which of us can walk the streets with his head held high, and which cannot.

I have a company of armed men, a revolver full of hollow-point bullets.

I and thousands like me are forsaking everything for what we believe. Our drive and motivation do not come from tangible commodities that this world has to offer. We are at war and I am a soldier.

THREE

014

'War,' says Marianne.

'Equality,' says Aiden.

'Crossrail,' says Amal.

'Immigrants,' says Tony.

The voices keep talking in my earbuds as I walk the streets. I don't need to speak to any of them. They keep on talking whether I answer them or keep my mouth shut and listen, so I keep my mouth shut and listen.

'We're involved in an illegal war and we should get out.'

'What's being done about ordinary people?'

'Outrageous. And for him to claim to represent the people...'

It is raining. The rain pours off billboard ads for *Big Brother* and *Green Wing* and Marks and Spencer. The grey buildings look like they've been left over from the time of the War of Independence.

'Just get in there, blow up Saddam Hussein and all his cronies, and get out again,' says Mike in Sydenham, wherever that is.

'I'm a Muslim, and I think what's going on in Afghanistan is terrible,' says Anwar in Beckton Heath.

'We got to stand up to Bush, show him we ain't just going to do what he tells us to do,' says Chris in Pimlico.

I say nothing.

The presenter is an Australian called Jono. 'You're listening to London's Biggest Conversation, 97.3,' he says, before handing over to the newsroom. It's syndicated news – they're using different mics than Jono in the studio.

Cities never look like the picture postcards. You don't know what they smell like until you get a faceful of the damp of wet passengers sitting on wet seats on the inside of a long, articulated city bus. I switch over from Jono and try to get into a play on some other station. Plummy types say things like 'Come through into the drawing room' and 'Honestly, darling, you know that's quite impossible.' When I switch back over to Jono, he is saying, 'What do you think the three best curries are? Have you ever tried to make a curry? How did it turn out? I want to hear from you.' I turn off.

A caller to my show once told me that the distances on the Tube map are different than they look, and so always to take the bus in London. Don't ask me why I remember that.

The bus takes a long time. A good long time.

013

'By refusing to speak its name, society tries to will a distasteful idea out of existence. It becomes taboo.

'As we know, this *doesn't* fix the problem. More often, the result of inhibiting dialogue is to polarise discourse. Take paedophilia, for instance. Many people limit themselves to a binary response – act / don't act. Any subtler debate has been prevented. That's the power inherent in the act of speaking or of staying silent.

'The word we are going to consider today is suicide.'

The professor pauses for dramatic effect; he unscrews the cap from a bottle of water, and swigs, reading his notes. I'd imagined he'd be a fire-and-brimstone preacher, but his manner is almost effeminate. His dark brown skin shines under the spot. When he talks, he seems like he's seeking out the faces of the hundred students in the lecture theatre, but he can't see out of the light; his gaze would have lingered on my face, like everybody's does, if he'd seen me. He doesn't know I'm here.

'Some of you will know me as a controversialist – I am not. I am an anthropologist and a sociologist, and suicide is a significant and under-examined part of both subjects. Today I'm going to talk about why suicide is not a binary, but a spectrum. There are *degrees* of death – for instance, a person can be classified brain-dead, yet able to respire and respond to stimuli; or they might have a heartbeat, but only with the help of a machine. Some functions of the body – hair growth, for example – continue. There is plenty of evidence that people have lived in comatose states that presented as brain death, and yet came out of those states and returned to something like normal health. Think of those from excavated Victorian graveyards with scratch marks inside the coffins, indicating a *misdiagnosis of death*. If it can be misdiagnosed, perhaps death isn't as simple as a yes or a no.

'With suicide, similarly, we are faced with a spectrum of pos-sibilities. If we take as our starting definition that suicide is the act whereby a person kills him or herself, we start running into problems almost immediately. Sure, deliberately drinking poison is suicide. What about smoking cigarettes, which we know to cause fatal illnesses? Those of you who smoke, are you in the process of committing suicide? Is there a difference between the two examples? What about if something is being done to you that will destroy you, and you fail to act to stop it from happening – is that failure to act also an act of suicide? And therefore, can suicide, which we started out calling an act, also consist within inactivity? When a soldier commits an act of bravery to save his colleagues, an act that he believes at the time, rightly or wrongly, is likely to result in his own death, is that suicide? If it is, why don't we call it suicide? To what extent is intentionality a part of suicide – if you do something so extremely dangerous that most people would consider that you are likely to die, and you don't believe you will, but you do die, have you committed suicide, or not?'

Outside the lecture theatre, it's still raining, and I tilt my head Godwards and let the rain wash my face. Is this what he fed you? This asshole makes suicide sound like a fucking pair of carpet slip-pers. He didn't have people paint over the stain of his partner's brains on the wall. He never watched a child turn into a zombie. I walk around the quad for a while in the rain, and students in twos and threes hugging books to their chest look at me in interest or disgust or open fear. How long before they call security and get me thrown out?

At the reception desk, a middle-aged guy in a blue jersey looks at me like he wants to punch me out. 'Dr McAllistair's office was on floor three, room 315,' he says. 'But she left, the end of last aca-demic year, according to this.' 'This' is some rat-ass papers, clipped to a board. 'What is it you need?'

'I don't fucking know. What about the suicide guy? What's his room?'

'Are you with the college?' he says.

'You know what? Fuck you.' And I'm out of there, out of the

building that was your workplace for a year, and I never saw it. How'd you make it in a dump like this? All this shitty weather and all the people looking like they're ready to give up on life, as they walk through more trash than you ever saw your whole life, big wet heaps of it on every sidewalk. Maybe that was part of why you did it. Maybe England fucking killed you.

No, I don't believe that. It was him. It was him, with his voice like ice cream. Professor Michael D. Butler. An innocuous, ordinary name for a guy who puts a book on suicide into the hand of a self-harmer. Where does that fit on the 'spectrum of death'? Is that the same as pulling the trigger?

Did he see your fucking scars?

I wonder whose face you thought of last, before you fired the gun.

012

Before long, I'm a Londoner. I hate the place, but I know it. Never make eye contact on public transport; don't give money to bums; don't expect shop assistants to give a shit. I've gotten a room at a hotel in the east of town, where the sink doesn't work and the window doesn't shut. At night, thoughts of my distant son keep me awake, plus the traffic noise and the shouting of drunks. I could have gotten somewhere better. I don't want to get comfortable.

In one of his journal entries, John Bertrand Rutherford mentions Hyde Park. I want to see it, but I don't know how to get there, so I buy an A–Z in a little bookstore from a looming shop clerk who looks at me like he knows me. In the back of the book are all the street names, and then I realise I don't just know where Rutherford liked to go for walks; I actually know where he lived. Mavering Gardens. And like magic, there it is in the book.

You can tell Mavering Gardens is where rich people live. There are no useful things anywhere around. No mailboxes, no pay-phones, no trashcans. No Starbucks, for crying out loud. In the journal, he talks about turning the corner on to the Gardens in the cab, and then walking up the steps and standing outside the front door. He doesn't mention which one. There are about twenty front doors on each side of the street. I look around for anything I could that might tell me which door was the one the Rutherfords lived behind.

Then I remember:

In order to make life difficult for the Zeppelin squadrons, the municipal council doesn't light the street lamp outside our window, which is a blessing. It means one can sleep.

The lamp-posts are old, and there's only one that ain't on a corner.

The African girl who opens the door looks at me at first with confusion, and then I turn my head and she gasps, touching her heart.
She wears jeans and a roll-neck, and a dainty gold crucifix.

'I'm sorry, little English,' she says. Her accent is French.

I think, *Christ on the cross: suicide.*

I say, '*Parlez-vous Français?*' It's French in the Canadian style,
but the words are the same.

'*Oui.*'

'*Moi, un peu. Je voudrais regarder l'intérieur de la maison, s'il
vous plaît.*'

She looks at me doubtfully. '*Pourquoi?*'

'*C'est difficile à expliquer. Mon ami il a habité ici.*'

'*La famille Wilson? Ils sont en vacances.*'

'*Non, pas les Wilsons. Un vieux ami. Années devant. Il est mort,
maintenant. Je voudrais seulement regarder et resouvenir.*'

Fuck, I wouldn't have bought it. I show her the journal, in the
hope it'll sway her. I flip through the pages. '*Regardez ici* – Mavering Gardens.'

She says, 'Oh…' and kneads her hands. '*Vous êtes americain?*'

'Canadian. *Puis-je entrer?*'

She looks behind her, into the long entry hall. It's the nave of a
domestic cathedral: waxed floors and white walls that go up, and
up. She steps back, holding the door open.

'*Merci,*' I tell her.

So here you are, Rutherford, old man. I'm in your home. Here's
the spot where the maid fell down, eighty-eight years ago. There's
the front sitting room where you rested your head on your wife's
lap – it has a big-ass plasma-screen TV in it, now, and a DVD collection containing every film ever made, from *Birth of a Nation* to
The Day after Tomorrow.

The hallway seems to go on for ever. There's a staircase from beside
the front door that disappears up out of view; underneath it, a kind
of blocked-off doorway shape that has been painted over fits with
my imagination of where the stairs down to the kitchen might have
been. I guess there isn't a downstairs any more. So the place where he
used to sit and stay warm is gone. How would he feel about that?

And then there's the study. The maid lets me go in alone. There's nothing in there but a ladder, a chair, some bedsheets and two buckets of paint. No carpet, even. Outside the window, I can see the side of the house continuing, and the little herb garden under the window, and there's some wrought-iron garden furniture there, and big plastic toys in yellows and reds.

I put the chair in the centre of the room, and sit there like the pilot of my own vessel. To my right is the fireplace. Gotta crane round to see it. It's been boarded up. To my left, the place where he must have sat writing this book. It's his view, out of his window, the one the snail crawled up. I put my radio on to a music station. A girl has started to sing a ballad. Aw, she's full of pain: her voice cracks as she sings, and Rutherford is right here with me.

What the fuck am I gonna do? What can I do that isn't the wrong fucking thing?

I will not tell you I'm okay, the girl sings
Wanted to be good, but it didn't work out that way

A log pops in the grate, bringing me out of my reverie. The journal lies open on my lap. The pen has dripped, leaving a patch of blue ink. That will teach me to drift off. I put the lid back on.

I do not know what compulsion this is, to confess every thought in ink. When I commit these thoughts to paper, do I write to be found out? Perhaps that is the reason behind every utterance, every word: not to record, not to communicate in banalities, but to be discovered.

Placing the journal in the drawer of the bureau, strapping the band over the blotting paper and locking the whole thing shut, is rather like closing my heart. The private man is gone; now the public man steps into the world.

'Have you been watching me for very long?' I ask.

I pause sufficiently long for Mary-Louisa – for it is she whose face I expect to see when I turn around – to respond – but when I look to the doorway there is no one there.

The letter is stamped and addressed. I shall post it myself, after dark. It will do me good to take a turn. I hope that at some point it will occur to the post office to install a pillar box on our road. It would be awfully convenient.

In the broadest terms, I have accepted Sedgwick's offer. I do not know how to accomplish what he asks of me without losing my sanity entirely; nevertheless, it is a living, and the only one I seem likely to be able to make in view of the war and the strikes, and my appearance and ill health. He feels that the combination of my 'unusual' appearance and the profundity of Lyons' poetry will prove irresistible in literary circles. The poet's words, read by his commanding officer. Of course, the whole enterprise is crass. I am to sit before an audience, exploiting my injuries for novelty and reading out his poems, poems such as 'Coming Home', written from the perspective of one who has returned from France – which, of course, he never shall. What will the listeners be thinking, I wonder. Merely that I failed, as his captain? Or will they hurl accusations?

'The lowest hell' is right.

The thought of how I have betrayed this man brings the acid up my throat and to the back of my mouth. I do not deserve to be alive in London, ready to see in the 1920s, and he does not deserve to be out there, rotting in the soil of France.

What was done on the Western Front was easy. It was too easy. I did what I was told to do, because I believed in it – any fool can do that.

011

There's a pub called the Earl of Lansbury, down the street from the college, and there's another one, the Elm, farther up the hill. Far as I can tell, if you're a sociable type, you like a little loud music and you don't mind hanging with the undergrads after hours, you go to the Earl, a fleapit where they don't understand the term 'tomato juice'. At the Elm, they play music from back in the day and over-charge on drinks, so the only people who use it are profession-als. That's where Butler drinks. He drinks an ale called Doombar, smokes two Marlboro Lights per pint, and reads the *Independent*. The landlord, Terry, knows him by name. They always talk a little about each other's day. Butler talks loudly, and keeps looking around at the other drinkers like he's telling them, too, without ever talking to them. I keep back around the corner.

Through this steady exchange of bullshit, I've learned that Butler is married and has two grown-up kids, one of whom is away studying and the other just back from overseas. He lives in Clapham. He's getting ready to give a series of lectures in the US starting September. He drives a Volvo S40, and regrets not having bought diesel, on account of the fuel consumption. He needs root canal work, but is afraid of the dentist. That last detail nearly killed me when I heard him say it. You never knew what it would look like, but the image of you slumped on the couch with your mouth hanging open never leaves me – and here was this guy, bitching about his toothache.

I wonder where you drank.

Pretty early on I figured how it had to be. The mechanics of it are simple, and once that's worked out, it's all about materials.

I spent a lot of time walking around town, learning where the bad parts are. Southwark looks bad, a lot of the north-west of town, plus most everywhere east of the financial district – Bethnal

Green, Bow, where there are streets lined with old concrete housing blocks that look hurricane-damaged, and all the shops are boarded up. In some of those places, rich arty types are moving in, but one block away are kids playing on mattresses with springs sticking out, and teenagers hang on street corners. I been to LA; I seen it before.

I buy a hoodie and some sneakers. I put a baseball cap on, then I pull the hood up. I go up to one of the kids.

'How's it going?' I say.

He raises his chin at me, but he doesn't say anything. He's an Asian kid with a fat gold chain under his baseball shirt. Fourteen, maybe.

I tell him, 'I'm looking to score.'

'Yeah, was' that, blood?'

My heart's going like a locomotive. 'I'm in the market for a piece.' I can't believe I've just said that.

Kid starts tutting at me. 'Piece of what?' he says.

'Not a piece *of* anything. A piece. Chrome.'

'What?'

I say, 'A fucking gun, numb-nuts.'

'Come again?'

'You heard me. I need two handguns. Can you or can you not put me in touch with someone?'

The kid seems to have forgotten the insult. It doesn't look like anyone's asked him that before.

He starts looking at the streets and buildings around us. I pull the hood a little to the side so he can see the part you decorated. 'Payback,' I say.

After that, he takes me seriously.

'What's it worth, bro?'

I say, a little too fast, 'Ten per cent if you hook me up.'

'Twenty.'

'Fine. Twenty.'

He keeps on rubbing his mouth.

'Gimme your number,' he says.

'No, I don't have a cell,' I lie. 'Do I sound like I'm from around here? 'Kay, look, I'll be back at this spot same time tomorrow. You got something for me then, we do business. If not, don't sweat it.' I raise my knuckles, the way I saw black dealers do it on TV.

He looks at my hand, cocks an eyebrow and says, 'A'ight. Same time.'

Walking away from that guy is one of the longest walks I ever took. I get around the corner and my legs dissolve under me.

010

Terry likes to talk. He remembered me, of course, when I started coming back to the Elm to nurse my Virgin Mary up in the nook by the dartboard, and from the off he made a point of keeping up a kind of ongoing conversation, which we dip into every new time I appear. Amazing how friendship comes off as interrogation in the ear of the guilty man.

I'm from Arkansas, apparently. It was the first place I could think of. The minute I said it, I realised I didn't know the first thing about Arkansas except for Little Rock being the state capital, or a major town at least. By astonishing coincidence, I happen to be from Little Rock. I'm visiting with family. It's been a month, almost, and I'm now (thanks to the local library) a leading expert on Arkansas (pop. 3,244,000, main industry agriculture).

'Terry,' I say, 'you ever see a woman with long black hair in here? This height?'

'What, today?'

'Say in the last year?'

Terry's eyes boggle. I guess he's thinking he's seen plenty of women come into the pub in the last year – too many to recollect one specific one. My tally is that generally there's about one woman to every thirty men in this place; but over a year, that's still a lot of women. 'She shaved her head, 'bout Christmas time.'

He snaps his fingers and says he knows who I mean. 'Colleague of Michael's, you mean.'

I say, 'Yeah?'

'I say colleague. Why, how'd you know her?'

'I might have the wrong person,' I say. 'She hung out with the professor who comes in here?'

'They had a little thing going on, that's right.' He nods over at the vacant table where Michael Butler always sits.

'What do you mean?'

'You know,' he says.

And he's right. I do know. The thought of it makes me want to puke.

I say, 'That can't be the right person, then. She was Chinese, right?'

'No, white.'

'Aw, there we are. I got the wrong person completely.'

Terry says, 'There we go. I thought that was funny, that you'd know Michael's bird.' Then he says, 'Same again?'

'No, I don't think I'm gonna stay, tonight.'

'You do look a bit green around the gills.'

'Yeah,' I say.

09

You're still alive. You're with me every step I take.

Nights I dream about you, and we talk about what's going on. And sometimes it's not you at all. Coupla times now I've woken up mid-sentence, and I find that I'm talking to no one. I do that a lot, now – waking, sleeping – it doesn't matter.

On the way to meet the numb-nuts kid the second time, I walk the long street where I bought the *A–Z*, and it's market day. Boho twenty-somethings with shades tend ragged blankets covered in junk from some Lagos trash heap; the blankets cover the pavement and the sidewalk as far up into the distance as I can see. I can't put my foot on to the ground without standing on some stained teddy bear or dented toast rack or pair of patched jeans; the central walkthrough, meanwhile, is thronging with people who've clearly taken the time to come from someplace else to look, and they walk along eating noodles or smoking weed, or taking photographs of all this shit. All the people selling from the blankets drink from the same brand of tin cans as the vagrants and dope fiends around by the ATMs. Hot spring sunshine beats down. No one pays me any attention – we're packed in too tight. You can't see jack if you get too close.

The way I've got it figured, even if the kid hasn't grassed me to the police, and actually knows someone who could sell me a handgun, and if that person is willing to sell that kind of stuff to someone he's never met before, the situation remains parlous. Anyone selling guns is, by definition, a gun-toting felon, and I'm planning to walk right up to them with a stack of money and no back-up and have it all work out. That's fucking stupid.

First I think, maybe I'll pretend to have a crew just around the corner. Then I think of all the no-name musicians I interviewed back in the day who were big in Germany or Japan: the fact of them making that claim made them look dumber than if they'd just let it be. Then I think maybe I could just play it like Obi-Wan Kenobi, and use being twice the kid's age to come off as wise and not to be fucked with. But I don't know who's showing up for this part of the deal.

I think maybe we could do it half-half: one of the guns today; then, if that's all right, another gun tomorrow. That way, the potential for making money tomorrow will be an incentive for them not to rip me off today. And tomorrow, I'll be carrying a gun. It seems like about the best way I can think of. I try to imagine walking around with a gun in the belt of my pants. They don't even have gun stores in this country. I wonder how they stop a crime if the perp has a gun. Tell him a joke, maybe, make him drop it because he's laughing too hard?

I'm nearly out of the crowds when a guy dressed like an Arab jumps out at me. 'How are you today, sir?' When I try to push past he says, 'Are you scarred on the inside, or just the outside?'

I stop so fast someone walks into the back of me.

Aw, I'm a hard-man right now, channelling Stallone or something. 'Say that again,' I tell him. I don't know what I think I'm gonna do to the guy, but I'm on my way to an arms deal. Scratch me, and I'll bleed adrenalin.

He's in his twenties, wears a long black beard, and looks like a strong breeze would blow him away.

'That's OK, we are all imperfect,' he says. 'None of us can look our creator in the eye and say we have matched his perfect intentions. Some of us carry our imperfections on the outside as well as inside ourselves. How did you get your scars?'

It seems I'm still standing here, even though I know his deal and I know mine. There are people packed around us so close we practically have to stand chest to chest to stay in contact. I look all around me: people.

'My girlfriend beat the shit out of me,' I tell him.

No one so much as glances my way.

'She poured boiling oil on me, and then she beat me with the pan.'

I wipe the corner of my mouth. I guess I'm expecting the

world to fall apart, but somehow the conversation seems to be continuing.

'I can see you're a man of experience – what you just referred to was God's will—'

'Asshole. It's the will of God I got fucked up like this?'

'God tests us,' he says. 'We know the best way to live our lives, and God tests us, to see how we measure up. You ever hear a voice inside you, telling you the right thing to do?'

'Oh, you could say that.'

'That's our connection to Allah. We ignore that voice at our peril,' he says. A copy of the Koran has appeared in his hands. 'When we are shown the path ahead, and we refuse to take it, we are thumbing our noses at God…'

I'm trembling. I say, 'I know what the path ahead is.'

'Be strong, brother. Have courage. If it is God's will, it will come to pass.'

'You think?'

'Mos' definitely.'

He has a trestle table set up near by, laden with flyers and CDs in cases, and there are some other young Muslim men around it, fishing passers-by out of the stream flowing through the Lane. One of them is shouting, 'Step forward, ladies and gentlemen. This is the good stuff, over here.'

My guy says, 'You like to read?'

'Depends what it is.'

'This might give you a whole new perspective.'

'Yeah, that's the type of thing I've been reading.' I take the leaflet, and then reach for his Koran. 'You say that's the most beautiful book?'

'Yes, but you're not going to understand it. It's in a kind of Arabic. Look.' He flicks through some pages, backwards. They're written in slanted script that looks like it's made out of banners, blowing in the wind.

'So how can I know what it says, if I don't read Arabic?'

'Through an imam. Through scholars, who can help you to understand.'

'And you said we're all imperfect.'

'That's right, we're flawed. Only Allah and Muhammad are perfect.'

'So the imam could screw up. They might tell me it says one thing, when actually it says something else.'

'No imam would ever lie.'

'But he might make a mistake.'

'If that is God's will,' says the young man, 'then so be it.'

'You know something, I used to hear this kind of bull all the time, in another life. Every religion, every magic book: "If it's God's will". I used to think God willed some pretty terrible shit, given he's supposed to be such a nice guy.'

'You think differently now?'

'Oh, I'll take God's will,' I say.

'You've found the path towards enlightenment.'

'No,' I say, 'you just offered me a rubber stamp, is all.'

And I smile at him, but it comes out broken, like it always does, and I leave the street preacher and his colleagues and his god, and I push into the crowd of souls, and I think of all the things that can leave a hole in a person's core; and I think how I failed you, the first time around.

08

The first phone call comes through to my cell when it's off. He leaves a message, in some kind of accent from Up North, as they call it – Manchester or Birmingham or something. Farther north the accent is, harder it is to understand. I met a guy from Newcastle, one time, and in the whole conversation the only word I understood was Newcastle. The guy on the phone has a softer accent, but that might be because of his age. Fifties, at a guess.

'I need to speak to you, Mr Knox,' he says. 'It's quite urgent. I hope you'll forgive my calling you on your mobile phone. I got your number from one of the staff at Bryde's Crossing School. Please could you give me a call? My name is Buster Lyons.'

The second call comes a day later. The phone is on the bed next to me when it rings. The same number. I think about the possibility of Buster Lyons working for some police department specialising in firearms offences. But then again, there is the name. I press the green button.

'Hello, Buster Lyons,' I say. 'Fuck, who'd have thought there were people called Buster Lyons?'

'Hello, is that Mr Knox?'

'Yeah. Do I know you?'

It sounds like there's relief in his voice. 'No, you don't, I'm sorry. But I knew Dr McAllistair. I'm terribly sorry for your loss.'

I pick a bullet out of the pile on the bed, and rub it between thumb and forefinger, feeling the smoothness. 'Knew her how?' I say.

'It's a bit complicated,' he says.

'Try me, Buster Lyons.'

He takes a deep breath. 'Well, I'll try to put this as briefly as I can. Dr McAllistair wrote an article about propaganda photographs taken of soldiers before a particular battle in the First World War.

It was very good, extremely detailed. Now, my family was very interested in that because my uncle, on my mother's side, was in that battle – in fact, he died there. My mother was just a little girl but she loved her brother. His name was James Lyons. You may have heard of him; he was a well-known poet. They never found his body. Well, the impression we got from the piece was that Dr McAllistair had read some personal papers connected to the commanding officer of James Lyons' battalion, a Captain Rutherford. He was the one who had Uncle James' poetry, and published the poems. He never liked to talk about what had happened – people didn't, back then. He died without saying what happened, exactly, to Uncle James. So I contacted Dr McAllistair. We thought, well, if we could possibly have a look at those papers, they might tell us what happened.'

I look at the journal, on the bedside table. 'So you spoke to Rachel about this?'

'I did, yes. She said she'd found fourteen diaries.'

'Fourteen?'

'That's what she told us. If I can be frank with you, I got the impression she didn't want to make them public. I thought that was very strange, for someone in her job. She stalled a bit, and then we never heard back from her.'

The sound of traffic outside my room is like a steady stream of air.

He says, 'Mother's been diagnosed with bowel cancer. She's ninety-eight. I wouldn't trouble you when you're suffering so much, but we may never get another chance.'

'I get it.'

'It's very difficult to mourn someone when they just vanish.'

'Yes it is.'

'Mother kept the family name when she married, and she often used to go on the trips to France, but what else could she do? Could you find it in your heart to let us have a look at them, just once? I'm willing to come over to you in Canada, that's no problem.'

I realise that I don't want to hand Buster Lyons the diaries at all. Giving away Captain John Rutherford would be like giving away a part of me.

Since when'd I get so damned selfish like that?

'Here's the thing,' I say. 'I'm not in Canada. I'm in London.'

'Oh.'

'I'll tell you the truth: I got two of the diaries.'

'Really?'

'He talks about promoting the kid's poetry, that's all. You know about that already, right? The other twelve – I don't know. She didn't have them when she died, I can tell you that. I went through everything of hers.'

'Oh my gosh,' he says. 'Oh dear.'

I tell him I don't understand why she wouldn't have given them to a museum or something. That's what historians do, isn't it?

'Well,' he says, 'I think she knew they'd make a splash. She seemed a very private person.'

Yeah, and you'd found out what it was like to be the centre of attention. Finding out something about a famous poet would put you right where you didn't want to be. I find myself thinking about your weird moods, in the last year – the way the temperature had suddenly changed. Maybe it hadn't been my perception, after all.

I feel for Buster Lyons. I really do. 'He never forgave himself for screwing up. Rutherford, I'm talking about. He carried a picture of James Lyons' house around with him. Even went to try and find it.'

There's a long silence.

'You still there, pal?'

'Yes. But that's very important, then. I was thinking maybe Uncle James got blown up and that's why they couldn't find him, but... well, if Rutherford took something off him after he died, then he must have been there in plain sight, at least for a while... Is there any way you could find out what Rachel did with those journals, please, Mr Knox? Please don't give up on this.'

'Man, I never gave up on anyone. Never.'

'Well... perhaps there's a friend she might have trusted, and said something to? Or what about someone she worked with?'

I put the phone in my lap and hold the side of my head, which is throbbing. Times like this, the eyeball that I no longer have feels like it's good to burst.

'There is someone,' I say. 'This is like a really sick joke. There is someone I got in mind. You wouldn't believe me if I told you.'

'I'm very grateful to you, Mr Knox.'

'My name's John,' I say.

After I put the phone down and he is gone, I try not to think about what a selfish thing that is to do: to promise resolution to someone and then disappear, taking all the answers with you.

And then I remember Mikey Lang, and the pastor, and my son, and I want to die.

07

The Elm is quietest between half past two and four o'clock. Terry is restocking after the lunch rush, so he doesn't talk too much. I buy my juice and I sit, and I wait.

Guns are much heavier than I thought. I tried tucking both of them in my belt, but one is much bigger and makes the belt stick out so the other one falls down. I tried one in the back of my belt and one in the front, but that made it impossible to move around without one or other of them falling out. So I have a knapsack with me.

The truth is, I had a whole bunch of pompous-ass speeches figured out. There was one that echoed the lecture I heard him give: *If I make you put the gun in your mouth and pull the trigger, is that suicide? Let's give that a try.* There was one that ranted about you and the fury of a bereaved man, but it sounded too much like the hitman in *Pulp Fiction*, quoting out of Ezekiel, and you deserve better than that. So I've more or less made up my mind that what I'm gonna do is hold one gun against his head, make him hold the other one in his mouth, and then ask him if he understands why this is happening. If he doesn't, I'll tell him. But he'll know. And then, one way or another, that motherfucker is gonna shoot himself. *That's* suicide.

One of the two guns is bright yellow. It's an athletics starting pistol that's been converted to fire live rounds, or so the friendly local small-arms dealer told me. The other one is a .38 special that looks like a truncated version of the kind of revolver they slung in the Wild West. I'll give him the yellow one; make him suck on that and look like a prick doing it. Even I don't take it seriously. That's the one in the bag.

Ordinarily, Michael Butler comes in a little after five. On Wednesdays, earlier. By four-thirty, it's hard to stay on my barstool, so I wander around a bit; reread Rutherford's journal; put some songs on the jukebox. I choose 'Lithium' and 'Californication' and 'Mrs Robinson'. After a while, I tell Terry to set me up a Jack, and I knock it back and tell him to hit me again.

'Hit you? Blimey, where d'you think this is, Dodge City?' he says.

'Just gimme a drink, willya?'

'Let me buy that,' says a voice over my shoulder. When I turn around, he says, 'Ah – a bourbon man.' Yeah, it's him. He greets Terry, who is already drawing his pint, and he sits on one of the tall stools next to me. He is the black of deepest, central Africa. He smells of day-old aftershave.

I try to speak but no words come out of my mouth. After a while, I manage a 'Thanks', like I've had to strike rock apart to find it.

'Michael Butler.' He offers me his hand. I don't take it. 'What's your name?' he says.

'Kurt,' I say.

'Kurt. Well, hello, Kurt. And what sort of day have you had?'

'OK,' I say.

'Kurt's from Arkansas,' says Terry.

That interests Michael Butler a whole lot. He wants to know all about Arkansas, and what I think of London by comparison.

I got plenty to say about Arkansas.

All the time I'm talking ('J.B. Hunt, Tyson Foods and Wal-Mart are all headquartered in the north-west part of the state') my mind's trying to put this together. All the scenarios I'd gotten worked out don't work like this. I was supposed to go over to him. I haven't decided yet whether to corner him when he goes to the restroom or follow him to his car and do it there, but the point remains that I was meant to be instigating this. What's made him come to me? And why now? Months, I've been coming in here, and today he makes a move? I tell him about the breakdown of beliefs in the Natural State ('Mostly Protestant, with about a third Baptist') and none of it makes any sense at all.

I say, 'So it's great to talk to you, but I notice we didn't ever talk before.'

'That is true.' Butler's suit is the colour of charcoal. Looks expensive. 'It's good to get to know one's brother man, though, isn't it? Talking and understanding have never been more important, especially now we find ourselves living in such troubled times.' He says, 'The truth is, sometimes I get bored with my own company. You ever feel that way?'

'I guess.'

'I spend most of my time fighting to keep my job – I'm regarded as something of a loose cannon, professionally. It's exhausting. Sometimes one needs distraction, not introversion... What about you?'

'What about me?'

'Why are you here at the Elm?'

I say, 'Same as everyone else, I guess. Get a little drunk...'

Butler smiles. He offers me a cigarette from a soft pack, and I say no. After he's lit his, and shaken out the match, he says, 'You're being self-effacing, of course. I've never seen you with anything stronger than a tomato juice. I always have a drink when I'm here – it's my Achilles heel. I have to be switched on to teach and lecture during the day, so it's like an off-switch for me. That's why I come here. And I'm sure some of the people who drink here come to delay going home to their families, and I'm not one of them, and some of them come because Terry looks after them – isn't that right, Terry?'

Terry says that's right.

'And then there are other people who come here because it's less noisy than the other pubs and they can hear themselves think, meaning presumably that elsewhere they don't find an environment to think in.

'I'm sorry if I'm boring you,' he adds, tapping ash. 'My subjects are anthropology and psychology, so this is how I think. Always trying to understand why everyone does everything, from the meta-group to the individual.'

'Right.'

'If I look at someone behaving in a way that seems out of keeping with the social norm, I always want to know why. Why are they behaving like that? What's driving them?'

'And you thought I was behaving strangely.'

'No, no,' says Butler. 'I meant it as a general observation, not a pointed remark.' He smiles, and I see how white his teeth are. For a smoker. For a Brit.

'What do you think about when you're watching other people?' he asks.

Fuck it. I tell Terry to set me up another Jack, and down my throat it goes, burning the whole way. 'All right,' I say. 'All right. What do I think about when I'm looking at someone else? I'm thinking, what does this person think of me? They can see my face is like this, and they can see it goes down my neck and therefore I might be scarred all over my body. What do they think caused that? You can tell it's not a birth defect, so something major happened to me. You can see them look suspicious. They're thinking, should I be scared of this guy? Is he a hero? Is he evil? And I can't bring up that conversation with every person who sees me in the street, so I just look at them, knowing that even before I've said a word to them they're deeply suspicious of me, and there's nothing I can do about that.'

Butler says, 'How does that make you feel?'

'What do you mean?'

'Does it make you angry?'

'You try having mothers pulling their kids away from you, or women in the street acting like you're going to rape them or something. I'm not that sort of person.'

'Of course you're not.'

He seems sincere. I say, 'If I were to get angry... well, there's a lot of anger there.'

Terry puts another one in front of me. You have to pay for each drink individually, in London. When I go for my pocket change, Terry tells me it's on the house.

'Thanks, old boy,' I say. I raise the glass to Terry, and to Michael motherfucking Butler. 'Your good health,' I say.

2 December 1940

Once, James Lyons was a young man who wrote poetry and worked on a farm. He would be forty-five years of age, had he lived, and, had I died, I would not be fifty. Sometimes it occurs to me that he is, through his talent and through my promotion of him these past twenty-five years, among the first rank of poets associated with the First World War, and I feel great pride. I have, I think, kept him alive. His quiet voice speaks to us from that time of tarnished gold, and sunsets, and mud. Sometimes, in the years when we have been ready to hear it, it has spoken of the many horrors of war, and we have listened sagaciously and agreed that war is the farthest point from civilisation; that it must never happen again. Other times – such as now, when they are tearing up the railings around Hyde Park to turn into ammunition – his words become a rallying cry, a distillation of the bulldog spirit – and, I fear, a lie.

The poet had two voices. He was two men: one pre and one post. Between these two men was a gulf of profound pain, so wide that these two separate entities never met, nor shared their different wisdom. There was no time when the dual identities were overlaid; rather, each one speaks out, making its unique pronouncements into a void, hoping that someone else is listening.

They listen. The general public, I mean. I might never have published the other ones, the young novelists, the social critics, the wry humorists, and yet financially my circumstances would remain assured. Oh yes, Private James Lyons has looked after me very nicely, thank you very much.

In Boston, in the United States, to hear a British 'veteran' with a skull for a face and a glass eye read out some of Lyons' prized pre-war works, the going rate is one dollar. In Bloomsbury, seats sell for 2s 6d. Some people come for the freak-show, I'm quite sure. (The irony is not lost on me. In the early days after being invalided out of the war, if you had told me that people would soon be willing to pay to look at my face, I think I should have done myself a mischief laughing.) Others, doubtless, come to drink a draught of the myth of James Lyons. He represents, to some of those people, the failure of the bond of trust between individual and state. For others, he is an heroic figure, sacrificing everything for lofty ideals. For others still, Lyons is the voice of a generation lost to time: he becomes their dead brother, their missing sweetheart, the son whose body was never found, and I am the conduit by which he reaches them, speaking, as it were, from beyond the grave.

'I gotta tell you, you are an inspiration to me, sir,' one young sailor told me, after a reading at a town hall in Norfolk, Virginia. He and two friends, all in sailor whites, had been in the front row for the recital – one could not fail to notice them against the sea of dark clothing. Now, they were at the front of the queue to my trestle table, where copies of Lyons' England *were stacked, waiting to be dedicated. 'It must be hard with your injury an' all, but you keep going non-stop to make sure we hear the poetry of this guy you commanded...'*

I believe I nodded at him non-committally, hoping he would go away, but he was not finished, not by a long chalk. He kept on telling me how he wasn't certain he'd made the right choice when he'd joined the US Navy – his parents were against it. 'But you have to stand up for what's right, don't you, sir? That's what you believe in, isn't it?'

It took an effort to force out the word 'yes'. I was aware how strangulated I must have sounded.

'That's right, sir. That's what separates real men from the rest.'

The bile was rising – I could feel the back of my neck growing hotter. 'Would you excuse me?' I asked him, offering a hand to shake. 'I need to...'

He shook it warmly. 'Absolutely, sir. I'll guard your books there until you get back.'

'Thank you...'

'Ensign Newton, sir. Friends call me Archie.'

I'm afraid I rather elbowed my way through the crowd to reach the toilet, and had barely enough time to lock myself in the cubicle before the vomit came, in a burning torrent, filling the pan with a sort of greenish soup, while outside American voices asked, 'Are you OK in there?'

'Yes, I'm fine,' I called out, as soon as I was able. 'I'm fine, really.'

This new war has a different character to the last – of that there is no doubt. The ardour for battle exhibited by young men in 1914 is reduced, twenty-six years on, but is not fully gone. All the good men went west in the last lot. They are replaced by another wave of firm-bodied, bright-eyed young men who are ready to fight; to die.

True, we have short memories, but they are short because we will not remember generationally. The first impulse, the youthful, uncon-sidered drive, is to destruction. Without absorbing the lessons of the past, every generation of young men that will ever live is doomed to leave bloody footsteps as it dances this same miserable dance.

In London, the bombs rain down on us nightly, now, and the city burns. Neither the Observer Corps nor the Auxiliary Fire Service want a man with one eye and only one functioning hand, nor the Home Guard – in fact, I seem to have become reduced to a single function: that is, speech. It is my lot to read aloud poems written by somebody else. A fellow at the Home Service wrote to me, asking whether I would consider appearing as part of the BBC's programme – I told him I would think about it. The wireless does offer the pos-sibility of reaching that audience that might not naturally take up a book.

But the truth is that I am no longer sure that what I am doing is by any means honourable. When reading his poems acted as an affir-mation of our mistakes, and the preference among readers was for those poems that decried the loss of life and innocence, one felt sure one was doing good. But this? Recreating those falsehoods? Persuad-ing young minds of the nobility of sacrifice? I am reminded, some-times, of a recruiting sergeant I saw many years ago, who looked me in the eye and told me that I ought to be on the front, fighting.

He was wrong. The exact opposite was correct: no one should have been there.

10 December 1940

Mavering Gardens received direct hits from several German incendiary bombs during the night. We all rushed around with buckets of water, but there was little to be done: the house at the end of the terrace was well up, and we had to wait for an appliance to come and put it out. By the time it got here, the next house along had caught fire too. There was nothing for the poor inhabitants to do but watch their place go up in flames that licked out of the windows and sent up a thick black cloud against the searchlights. Dreadful – truly dreadful. Explosions around us reminded us that we were far from being the only street in London to be suffering. What remained of the buildings in the morning was an unsteady shell, with walls that will have to be pulled down before they fall down on someone's head. What a pitiful sight, to see people picking through the ashes for anything they might salvage. There were three of them – the owner, his wife and her mother. I lent a hand – there wasn't much left.

'You can have this,' said the fellow whose house it had been – he'd been a linen merchant, I think, and was too old and too fat to be rummaging about in the ruins of his home. The poor bugger was covered in soot, and had only the clothes he stood up in. He stooped down to pull something out from among the masonry, and offered me a statue of a dancing ballerina, carved out of wood. 'We'll have to carry our things about with us – we'll have no place for trinkets.'

'But why don't you move in here?' I suggested.

'What – into your house?'

'Yes, why not? There's only me here. My wife's in Cambridge,' I explained, seeing his confusion. 'She's a director with the ATS. I'm sure she'd be glad to think that someone was making use of the room.'

He didn't take long to make up his mind. He put his arms around me in a most un-British gesture, transferring a great deal of soot in the process, and seemed about to kiss me when the sight of what he was about to kiss made him think better of it.

'I'll take that as a yes,' I remarked.

While the three of them found their way into their new home, ten doors along from their old one, I breathed in the London air. In the thin daylight, one could see plumes from fires still burning, and barrage balloons like great grey fish on cords, and below them, the buildings of Belgravia, with crosses taped across the windows in a ghastly recreation of the flight of the angel of death, and the French windows blocked up with sandbags.

And there he was, on the other side of the street, watching me. Not him – he is always with me. I mean the young man with the ash-blond shock of hair, and the piercing blue eyes. Age had refined him. Even from across the street, I could see his skin had been aged naturally by the years, not by the grime of cities, or toxic habits, or bitterness. He stayed planted there, his hands deep in his pockets.

'Is it really you?' I whispered.

He was wearing the same old overcoat. He still looked as though he'd recently scrambled out of bed. I wondered how I must look to him. Yes, I had changed. I'd grown old, I was sure of it.

'Hello, Rutherford,' he said. That voice made me suddenly very, very sad.

I tried to call back to him. At first my voice wouldn't come. Then I managed, 'Phelps, how...?'

'I've come to collect you,' he declared.

'What do you mean?'

'We're leaving.'

'What do you mean, leaving?'

'Do stop talking like some blessed parrot,' he told me, crossing the road. 'You and I are going away from all this.'

'To where?'

'No idea. I thought you might be able to help on that one. Where would you like to go?'

'Just hold on a moment,' I insisted. 'You can't just turn up here out of the blue and expect me to come running.'

'Why not? Aren't you pleased to see me?'

I looked up and down the street. There was no one to see.
I kissed him.

Oh, it was just a peck on the lips, but in that moment two and a half decades of lies evaporated, and I was whole again. He was real – a tangible, living thing. He was my beautiful man.

'I've missed you so frightfully,' I told him – his strong hands steadied me. 'I've done my best...'

And he said nothing, but held me as my protestations turned to sobs, as the weight of years and lies came crashing down upon me, knocking the air out of my lungs, making my legs fail, and my hands shake as they had not shaken in so very long. As my body was racked with this outpouring, this dam-burst, of self-pitying grief, I held on to him so very tightly.

I would never have cried, never again, had he not returned. I would never have allowed myself.

'Do you think your new house guest might be willing to tell a little lie?' asked Phelps, turning the ballerina over in his hands. 'To return the favour, as it were?'

'What are you talking about?'

'What if you'd been standing there?' He nodded towards a bomb crater.

'Then I'd be—'

'Gone. People go missing in war all the time.'

I know we were being watched. Those eyes that never blink: they were on us. But I did not care. Really, I did not care a jot.

06

The room smells of oranges, not damp. That's how I know something isn't right, even before I've woken up. It should smell of damp and bad carpets and the fabric conditioner smell venting from the laundromat two floors below. As I come to realise that I'm awake and that the pain I can feel in my head is real, I'm smelling oranges and wood polish.

I don't open my eye right away. The pain keeps it tight shut. I'm working through some half-conscious fantasy that I've gone backwards in time and am on the kitchen floor with boiling oil burning into my head. I sit bolt upright, and the light hits me. I'm in some guy's room.

There's no guy. I try to tell whether there ever was someone else – it was a double divan – but all there is is me, buck naked. The room seems outsized and expensive. There's a picture of Tupac on the wall. Then the pain gets to me, and I throw myself back into the bed feeling I need sleep more than anything in the world and that I'll never sleep again, that I'm famished and that the sight of actual food would make me puke right away, and that my mouth is so dry it's glued shut. Mother of God, it's some hangover.

Lying there clutching the sides of the bed to stop myself spinning, I try to recollect how I got here, and where here is.

I remember the Jack Daniel's.

Faster than you can say, I'm out of that bed. Faster than my ability to balance can deal with. Where the fuck is the bag? My feet are tangled up in the bedsheet and as the room tilts at forty-five degrees I take two hops sideways, uphill, and collide with a desk and a chest of drawers coming the other way. We all land together on the cold wood floor. Books and ornaments rain down on me. I'm thinking, *I sat on the stool where Butler came and joined me.*

Did I have it then? Yes – I tied the strap round the stool. What about when I left? When did I leave? I've got pictures and some oddments of conversation up until about the tenth glass of whisky, but after that I don't recall much. There was a car, at some point. At least I think there was. I think I remember some kid… I don't know. That bag might be anywhere right now.

Panting, I force myself on to my feet, using the walls for support. The bag is right there by the side of the bed, along with all my clothes. I drop on the bed and actually forget to have the hangover for the moment it takes to rummage through and find the two similar objects: the metallic lumps with the indented barrels and the tex-tured grips. I put my finger around a trigger. The thing fits in my hand like I was born with it there. The hangover comes surging back.

I pass out.

When I come round – and I have to presume it's a long time later, because I'm clear headed – I'm lying on the bed with my ass in the air and my hand in the bag, holding the gun. Something smells different in the room. A cup of tea is on the dresser. Steam's rising off it. There are voices outside the window. A lot of 'em.

I rub my face. Stubble looks ridiculous on me, as well you know. The right half of my jaw is like a peach; the left side like a GI's buzz-cut. My clothes stink of public house: smoke and what I got drunk on. There's no money left in my wallet. I've basically mugged myself.

The bed I slept in is the most comfortable one since I've been in England, like a one-night stand without the sex. I guess that's the first time I thought of sex in a long time. I don't plan on thinking about it again for a while more.

The window is covered with slatted blinds made out of some kind of dark wood. The window looks down on to a garden. I'm one floor up, and there are like seventy people down there having some kind of party. Men in jackets and women in hats. All the people are one type of black or another. I try to see if I know any faces. There's a two-man barbecue operation going on, both mid-dle-aged men drinking beer and soaking up the sun and turning pieces of meat over on the metal mesh. A big crowd of people are fussing over a table laden with bottles and surrounded by buckets, and at another table, still more people line up to fill their plates. Conversations are going on in twos and threes. Farther back in the garden, where there are trees, black kids in black swimsuits play in a big circular splashpool.

This is where I'm gonna find out what it feels like to kill somebody.

The door out of the bedroom leads on to a sort of landing. From downstairs flow voices and laughter and the sound of wine glasses. I try to find the bathroom. I'm shown the right door because a toilet flushes and a mother and a little baby, maybe a year old, come out of the bathroom. I manage to turn my head before she registers I'm there. When she sees me, I tell her, 'Hi, I'm Michael's friend,' and she says hi back and tells me her name is Deborah, and the baby is Theo. 'I'm Michael's sister,' she says. 'So you're one of his waifs and strays from the uni, are you? Why don't you come and get some chicken? Must be mad, hiding yourself away on a gorgeous day like this.'

'Hiding is right,' I say.

So far, I've kept the pretty side of my face covered. Now I warn Deborah to prepare to see something nasty. Then, slowly, I draw my hand away from my face.

Deborah looks totally unimpressed. She pulls up the leg of her pants. Where there should be ankle, there's a vertical metal bar.

'Car crash,' she says.

'Fuck.'

'Language!' she scolds, directing her scowl at the baby.

I say, 'Yeah. Sorry. How far..?'

Deborah puts her finger on the middle of her thigh.

'Christ. I'm sorry.'

'It was years ago,' she says. 'When we was kids. Michael probably told you. My dad lost his job, and decided to drive us off the side of the Hammersmith flyover. Five of us in the car. Only me and Michael survived. Which is why...' she grabs me by the wrist '...you don't waste sunshine and good food. Come on.'

And I get dragged down into the melee: the only face that doesn't fit. I'm used to that.

It's been a long time since I was in someone else's house. It's a parallel universe. *Here are the choices these folk made.* Michael Butler's choice seems to have been to surround himself with people, or stay surrounded. On the wall of the staircase there are portraits of his whole clan: smiling school students; three generations of Butlers wearing mortar boards and holding scrolls; hokey studio shots of the family en masse. And now me and Deborah are meeting people, and I'm getting introduced as Michael's friend, and I'm shaking hands with people of all shapes and sizes, most of 'em seeming actually pleased to meet me there. They react to my face – of course they do. Some of them ask me if I'm OK, like the injury only just happened. Deborah leads me out of the French windows into an explosion of sunlight that brings the hangover rushing back, and it warms my skin. I want to lie down in the thick grass at the sides of the lawn, where it meets the tall fences, and sleep in the sun.

'And this,' Michael Butler is saying, a little before I've even registered him being there, 'is my friend Kurt. Kurt is over from Little Rock, in Arkansas.'

There comes a chorus of 'Hello, Kurt's from a circle of people who are drinking white wine from glasses.

'I got a cousin in Jackson,' says a shaven-headed man in glasses and a church suit. I can't remember where Jackson is. Shit, I thought I'd gotten it down, but I don't even remember seeing a Jackson on the map. He says, 'That's right next door to you, isn't it – Mississippi?'

'Yup,' I say, hoping to hell it is. It's South, at least. I say, 'Very good of you to have me here.'

A beer finds its way to my hand.

'Take water with it, darling,' a tiny shrivelled old lady says. I reckon she could take her own advice. Maybe with a little water she'd rehydrate back up to full size.

Butler says, 'Kurt, this is my son Issy – come here, Is.' He opens a hug-arm to a tall youth dressed in a black robe. The kid is deep in conversation with some other young men. Issy's heard his dad all right, but he pays him no notice. 'Come on,' says Michael. His smile's stretched about as far as it'll go. Issy seems to tell the others he'll be right back, and over to our group he comes. Those robes look the same as the ones I saw the street preacher wear. He doesn't smile when we shake hands.

'Kurt is from Arkansas,' says Michael.

'Peace be on you,' says Issy. I don't see a lot of peace coming out of his eyes. He's grown a bit of beard, but he's too young for it to grow right, so it looks like a coupla black stumps on his chin.

'Issy's just come back to us from overseas,' says Michael.

I take the cue and say, 'Where you been?'

'To the Middle East. Pakistan, Iraq, Afghanistan. To witness what is really happening there.'

'Issy's reading Middle Eastern studies at SOAS,' Michael says. 'He's a talented poet, as well.'

It would piss me off if my dad kept making announcements about me like that, but then my dad never would have done – he'd have sat doing a jigsaw and let me speak for myself. Anyway, Issy isn't me. He's unafraid of silence.

I say, 'I used to know a soldier who served in Iraq...' and then I realise who I'm talking about, and how long that's been. He's been dead ten years. I could have changed the world, there, and I didn't.

Issy says, 'We are all soldiers, when our time comes.'

'Yeah.' Man, I feel shitty. Sweat, and shivers. 'Gotta man up some time.'

'Belief is nothing, if you do not act upon it.'

I tell him, 'Someone I loved called that type'a thinking a "ballet of revenges."'

'And what do you think?'

I look him in the eye. I tell him, 'I'm ready to dance.'

Issy looks me up and down, and returns to his friends without another word.

I say nothing, for a long time. I breathe in, and I breathe out.

The poison in my kidneys must be turning me green or something, because Michael tells me, 'Why don't you go sit in the shade; take a load off? I've got that book we were talking about.'

It's hard to remember the hatred I felt for this man, until I focus on remembering you. Last night I was fired up on liquor, and I'd have taken on the world and won. Today – oh, man. Rachel, can you forgive me? Even the recollection of the corpse that had once been you – it makes me miss you, so much, so much; but it doesn't make me hate him more. Oh, I'm gonna do it, just the same. That's what I came to do, and that's what I'm gonna do. It's the *right* thing to do. It's an act of love.

I don't know what book he's talking about. Someone gives me a plate of ribs, which I can't eat and hold a bottle, and I'm busy tryin' to juggle those when Michael comes back from the house with something in his hand. It's bound in brown leather.

'I asked you for that?' I say.

'Don't you remember?'

'Not entirely.'

'I told you about my specialist area of interest; I told you about this book, which a colleague lent me.'

'Ex-colleague.'

'That's right. You do remember.'

I say, 'Bits and pieces, you know.'

Michael licks his lips. 'Would you like to have a look?'

'Yeah.'

He puts it under my arm, and I hold it there. 'Be careful,' he tells me. 'It's eighty or ninety years old, and I have to give it back. It's written by a World War One veteran called—'

'John Rutherford. I remember.'

Michael hasn't let go of the book yet. Now he seems to search my face for something. 'Did I tell you that?' he says.

'How else would I know?' I try to sound light, rather than defensive, but I'm not sure I pull it off.

'Yeah,' he says. 'I don't remember telling you. Just take care of it, please – it can't be replaced.'

They've run an extension cord into the garden and a sound system is playing, now. I recognise Alicia Keys and Aretha. The shrieks of the kids jumping about in the water cut right through me, but the dappled shade of the apple trees, which are leafy and appleless, is exactly what I need, and it's good just to sit here, close enough to smell the smoke from the barbecue, and hear the bonhomie.

Before I open the book I glance up the garden. Michael Butler is talking to some other people, but he sees me look his way. I turn my attention back to the book, and don't dare look up a second time.

He knows. I don't know what he knows, but he knows something ain't right.

I try to focus on the handwriting in front of me, and Elvis starts singing 'Always On My Mind'.

I never felt more alone.

Whoever you figured would read your diary, John Rutherford, I can't believe you thought it would be someone so far removed from the world you knew. A Canadian, whose career didn't even exist when you were signing up to fight. Talk host? What the fuck was that, in 1915? Or radio, or TV? You lived half a world away, in a time of invitations and the season and going up to Oxford, while me, I'm in the backyard of a house owned by a black-skinned professor of suicide. The only thing you might recognise is the beer bottle. Brewed in Belgium, it says. They've left me to my own devices, which means they've left me to make trips to the drinks table and are mighty polite to me when I'm there: other people's civility is the load you must bear when you look broken – that, or invisibility.

I think we're all happier that I should be invisible, so I sit in the shadows of a low tree and put Nirvana on at a blistering volume in my ears, and watch the kids caper and scamper and I read about you.

TWO

25 September 1915

*When we went over the top we didn't really know what to expect.
We'd hardly glimpsed no man's land in daylight with our own eyes –
we'd always been told to keep our heads down because of the snipers,
you see. The colonel blew the whistle and he said, 'Up you go, lads.'
Most of the men were tight. They'd passed round this dixie of rum
while we were waiting – unrestricted. Some of them were so blotto
they didn't know where they were. I felt heroic – foolish, but there
it was.*

*Our objective was to get across no man's land, which was over-
looked by German-held colliery towers and slagheaps, and capture
the town beyond. Most of my men were Northerners, from places
like Accrington and Leeds (we were a Northern regiment, after all).
They didn't take kindly to my London accent. I believe there was
also a lot of resentment towards me because I'd got my promotion
in Blighty. Some of the men had been regular army since long before
the war, and they hated taking orders from an upstart officer, especially one so young and inexperienced. I was telling men thirty years
my senior what to do, even some old soldiers who'd fought in the
Africa campaigns, whole wars; meanwhile I had missed both of the
big shows, Ypres, and Festubert, merely by happening, each time, to
be deployed elsewhere. I'd lost very few men, until that point. Our
part of the lne had never made a name for itself. I had two sergeants:
Sergeant Davis and Sergeant Yeoman. Davis was a wet blanket –
I don't know how he got his stripes. He was a dentist in real life.
Yeoman had been a track inspector for the railways – he didn't take
any nonsense.*

*The first time we went over the top, we were scared, but we pre-
tended that it was the cold making our teeth chatter. It was autumn
in the Pas-de-Calais, and a mist hung over everything. It was six-
thirty in the morning, and we'd fashioned ladders out of old bits of*

wood, and stood them against the parapet, and the low trench was chock-full of men waiting to go up. One of the men had had an accident, and while one or two crude comments were made about the smell, the others and the officers pretended not to notice.

Overhead, our lot kept up the artillery barrage. It was utterly impressive – as though the sky were made of steel. So much for the shell shortage! Silver ribbons opening out across the sky, going from our guns to the German front lines. The noise was fearsome, and the ground constantly shook. Then the time came, and the barrage stopped completely, and we heard whistles blowing; I blew my whistle, and pulled my revolver and climbed up the ladder.

Captain Neames led the first wave over and Captain Chinnery led the second. By the time Chinnery's lot were going over, the Bosch had realised what was up. Chinnery was standing at the top of the ladders, helping a man up, when a shell went up next to him. It killed the soldier, and we all got covered in his blood. It made the air taste of iron. Chinnery looked rattled and stood there with his face dripping red, and then a gunshot got him through the side of his head – thwack – and down he went, dead. His arm was sticking out over the ledge by the ladder. Sergeant Yeoman saw that he'd better take over, and as he went up the ladder, he shook poor Chinnery's hand, by way of taking the sting out of the moment. Every man behind Yeoman shook Chinnery's hand as they went over.

I led the third wave.

In the interval of three years, the atrocities of war have become clichés; one does not speak of them in polite society for fear of being dull.

Before war broke out, no one discussed what a soldier actually did, other than in flighty heroic passages with rhyming line-endings; or else, castrato, with schoolboy magniloquence. He smote a legion of the enemy. His plucky comrades fell. It was considered bad form to talk about it all – and never in front of the fairer sex. Well, now the horror is out, and we're drowning in poetry. One is faced with the evidence of war every day, in bath chairs in the park, in convalescence, their stumps dressed in white and blankets over their laps, their useless laps. We reach for high language with which to mourn.

Well, I'll sell it on. I've nothing else to peddle except the myth of the ordinary hero, the poetry of Private James Lyons, the Voice of a Generation. Epitome of doomed youth. A typical tragedy.

What I fear is that war will never be understood, and soldiers especially, not by the public at large, not by the women whose photographs men carry, when at some point soldiering boils down to putting all one's feelings away, erasing the self, being so much meat and bone, a number, a tin hat. You mustn't have a personality when you go over the top. That's the moment it all drives towards: that is the You that your country needs. And yet, how is the public to make a connection with these non-people? The only soldier most people recognise is a passionate soldier, who expresses noble ideals and virtue, and who has some purpose in his warcraft, some sense of agency. The women understand Rupert Brooke's patriotism (Brooke, who never fought) better than they understand a thousand husbands who got called up, did their duty, hid their fear and whose corpses are out there now, half lost in the mud. Are only the poets and the scoundrels to be heard? Is every other version of that misery to be dismissed as cliché, because it does not entertain? What I have come to understand is that the ordinary man has neither the facility for relating his experience nor the desire to try. No: for most men, sharing how they happen to feel seems a mortal breach, a failure of some sort; talking about war merely infects the mental wounds. Have you never wondered why images of war seem hackneyed? It is because they must be given, if they are to be given truthfully, without feeling. One could not do what one must do if one felt too much. Feelings come much later, and in truth one hopes never to feel. Consequently, if they talk, soldiers talk of trenches and bombs and no man's land the way they talk of factories and teapots and soccer, with a certain glib familiarity, making the machinery of war sound workaday; failing to excite their listeners' sensations for fear of exciting their own. Meanwhile, the experience of walking into the mouth of the machine is annexed by those who transform it into what it is not: a species of poetical experience, rather than an experience for which there are no words.

When anyone reads an account of war, given by men, they will know its veracity by its reserved tone, its inability to make horrors come to life, its refusal to dwell on things, its readiness to look away. A true account will make the extreme seem prosaic, for that is what war does to you. It is not a failure of the material, nor some short-coming in men's descriptive powers.

Perhaps it is a problem of bridging the gulf between the ordinary and the martial. To someone who could not, from accounts given, feel the horror of an advance, I should offer the following challenge:

First, imagine yourself obliged to walk from one end of a soccer pitch to the other. Picture yourself doing so. The weather is fine; you are alone. Count the seconds as they pass, as you cover the ground.

All done? Very well. Next, imagine that same trip, but this time with a heavy rain having turned the ground to mud – the sort one's feet sink into, up to the ankle. Hike up your skirts, roll up your trousers, and off you go once more – the full length of the pitch. Feel the cold rains soaking you through. Imagine what a bally time you'll be having of it – lucky if you don't fall flat on your face, at some point. You slip and slide up the pitch, and lose a shoe, perhaps.

Now, let's try it once again, but this time with some blighter sitting in the stands, taking potshots at you with a rifle. Yes, a real rifle, with bullets that will kill you if you're hit. Once again, I want you to make your way the whole extent of that football pitch, through the sucking mud, whilst our friend tries to shoot you. It's an awful trek, suddenly, isn't it?

Next, I'll make you do all that again, and for good measure, this time you must carry a heavy pack on your back (making it much harder to get up if you should fall down), and a machine gunner will be positioned in the goalmouth towards which you are walking – his job is to kill you. There is nothing for you to hide behind, and you are not allowed to run, even if you could, through all that mud. The chap with the rifle will keep at you, too.

If you survive that – and very probably you will not survive – you'll be made to do it again, but this time with several further additions strewn in your way: vast loops of barbed wire, snagging you, perhaps even stopping you altogether, making you an easy target; explosive mines under the mud that might go off if you step on them, blowing your legs off; and the mutilated bodies of some of the friends you grew up with, with whom you were sharing cocoa only last night. Amidst all of that, and with Chummy firing his rifle (he's been joined by twenty of his mates, now, and they are all firing their rifles at you, too), you must walk through the mud into the machine-gun fire. Artillery shells are blowing up all around you, making screaming noises as they come in. Smoke flares mean you can only see ten feet ahead. And if by some miracle you get through that lot, you'll arrive in a trench full of men, real, living men, in all their variety, speaking a foreign language, and you'll be obliged to shove your bayonet into as many of them as you possibly can – you, who has never wanted anything but a quiet life with your wife and your child. No one is made for that experience – not men, whatever the women like to believe; not anyone.

And what words can ever communicate the interior life of a man at such a moment – or afterwards, when he wakes in the night, believing that he is still there?

Instead, we describe the objects, the images, the murk – and hope, somehow, that our listener can supply the feelings. But they cannot, for it is an experience beyond all of that.

That is why men cannot speak of war, and that is why, I am afraid, that the profoundest depths of Hell all too quickly seem tired and familiar, while the poets extemporise and emote, and the soldiers sit at home by their fires, and shake.

8 August 1916

I met him in the same way that one met all the new men: taking care not to acknowledge them too much.

Before the summer of 1916, I thought I had been part of a big show, and then I was flung into the biggest of all (for we British, at least; ask any Frenchman, and he would say Verdun). After the Somme offensive began, so disastrously and at such cost of life, things got far worse. It was a miracle that I was somehow physically unharmed, but our numbers were down: on 30 June, we had been 833 men strong. Three days later, ninety-two men were left. I was the only officer, and my survival was acknowledged only grudgingly; better officers had perished. And we were an army of amateurs. Most of our regular army soldiers were dead or wounded out of action, and of those who remained, none wanted to see any further action.

We got our new recruits on a splendid August day in 1916. We'd advanced a bit, and Fritz had taken to chucking over minenwerfers, which would land hissing at your feet – you had about five seconds to get out of the way before they went up. On this particular day, Fritz had obviously spotted where our latrine was, and had dropped one over, and it had killed the man on latrine detail. As a consequence, the smell was rather worse than usual, and the man's body was being carried, in several instalments, past the new lot as they arrived. They watched as the stretcher-bearers dumped him in the area at the back of the farm where various bayonets and bits of wood stood out of the ground at intervals.

We'd been given another captain, a lieutenant, and a couple of NCOs, along with a ragtag collection of men, mostly conscripts. Some of the 'men' didn't look old enough to grow a moustache, let alone carry a gun. They wore the new sort of tin hat. Most were older, and used to doing a day's work. Until that point, they'd been turning up in friendship or society groups – most of the 12th, for *example, were members of the same football team in Sheffield – but that practice seemed to have stopped. I thought: perhaps they are running out of sports teams.*

The new officers were the same age as I was – twenty-two – and yet I felt immeasurably older and more experienced. They had come directly from Officer Training and were rather easily excited. The captain was a music student called Burn-Jones, and he'd brought his fiddle with him, and the lieutenant's name was McMurray. We were expecting a new colonel at some point too, but for now we were to make do with what we had. When we'd first come out, our rotation had been four days in the line, four days out, but, with the pressure of undermanning, the length of time spent in the trenches was creeping up. By August it was seven days at a stretch, after which you were damned pleased to be able to go and wash yourself properly. That's when I first saw him: on a golden day, outside the farmhouse. He had stripped down to wash in a tin basin that had been set on a table there, and when I saw him my heart fell over itself. I think my mouth may have hung open. He was not beautiful in any conventional sense, but his chest, far from being concave like that of so many of the slum-dwellers who were getting drafted, was manly and defined, his young stomach muscles discernible, with a trail of soft chestnut down suggesting a course below, under the waistband of his trousers – from which I had to tear my eyes. His hair was a shade of brown that captured something of the amber of the afternoon sun.

He saw me looking at him. Panicked, I tried to think of some punctilio of army procedure I could bring him up on. One could face court martial for that sort of thing. But he smiled at me. Yes, he smiled at me, with his head dipped slightly, as though we were both in on some joke that had to do with his nakedness, and the fringe of his hair was wet and hung down in his eyes, and my heart was beating so fast that I thought that if I did not immediately find somewhere to sit down I would pass out on the spot. I did not go, however. I said, 'Name and rank?' and my voice cracked when I said it.

He said his name was James Lyons, and that he was a private.

'Where are you from, Private Lyons?'

'Cheshire, sir.'

I said, 'Cheshire? That's a beautiful place.'

'It is that, sir, yes, sir.'

'What do you do there?'

'Work on the land, sir. Ploughing, harvesting, sometimes help out with the horses.'

'That sounds like a wholesome life,' I said.

He looked at me askance.

'No?'

'It's all right,' he said, 'It's not easy finding people you can talk to. I mean properly debate and what have you. They're all farmers or farm-workers; all they've got to talk about is farming.'

'Oh yes? And what would you prefer to be talking about?'

He laughed, and put his vest back on, and I succeeded in keeping my eyes on his throughout. He watched me, watching him. They were hazel eyes. I wondered what he was laughing at.

I said, 'Did I say something funny?'

'No, sir. Sorry, sir.'

I had the distinct impression I was being made a fool of. He must have realised that my anger was rising, for he said, 'I'm laughing at myself, sir. Haven't I got a high opinion of myself? Such a delicate flower, and nobody understands me,' he said, falsetto. Then he dropped to a baritone: 'Hark at Lord Byron, here. Pick up your shovel and dig, lad.'

'What's Byron to do with it?'

'I write poems, sir. Always have.'

'Good for you… What do you write about?'

The boy – he was nineteen, or twenty at most, and not a boy at all – scratched his eyebrow. 'Well, about all sorts of things. You're not interested in poems, though, are you, sir?'

'Who do you like?'

'John Keats. Wordsworth. Housman.'

'Natural beauty.'

'Aye. Beauty of words, first.'

'What about Coleridge?'

'Off his head, sir. Like having a nightmare.'

'The nightmare of facing oneself, in isolation.'

'Yes,' said Private James Lyons, 'seeing yourself can be very hard.'

He looked as though he meant it.

'*So how does an agricultural labourer come to be familiar with the Romantics?*'

'*Well, number one, sir, I'll take the Imagists over the Romantics any day – much cleaner, much more concern for images. But number two... well, we do have books in Cheshire. Sir.*' *He waited to see whether I would find that comment amusing or insolent.*

'*You're a cheeky bugger, aren't you, Lyons?*'

'*I am exactly that, sir, yes, sir.*'

His expression was quite unreadable, making it impossible to work out whether I was receiving coded messages, or imagining them. No other troops were close by; just a few anxious chickens, patrolling and pecking in a corner of the yard. It occurred to me that someone so interested in words would have some care for the ones they chose to speak.

'*You didn't answer my question.*'

'*What do I write about?*' *He smiled, and by way of an answer gestured around us, his arm taking in the sweep of fallow fields and flattened coppices, that vista that seemed to stretch away in a process of infinite reduction until at the flat horizon it was folded into the barren sky.* '*This slattern land, and our fight to the death to have it.*'

The evening was coming on, and a cold breeze got under my clothes. I told him: '*You should wait until you've done some fighting before you play with big ideas like those.*'

He thrust his hands in his pockets, and nodded. '*But what if it's too late, by then?*'

A gramophone had been wound up in the barn, and the weedy strains of the only record anyone in our battalion seemed to possess began:

Up to mighty London came
An Irishman one day,
As the streets were paved with gold
Sure everyone was gay

I told Lyons to excuse me, marched around the barn, and stuck my head through the doors. Half a dozen of them were lying about in there, smoking cigarettes and hiding their playing cards.

'Turn that fucking racket off,' I said.

Their eyes bulged. When they'd collected themselves, one man ventured, 'It's patriotic, sir.'

'It is, if you're Irish,' I said. 'Tipperary is in Ireland. How many Irishmen are billeted here?'

'My grandmother was Irish.'

'My arse is Irish,' I said. 'We're a Yorkshire regiment. Why don't you go and play that rot to Fritz, all day long, see how he likes it?'

'Yes, sir.'

'There's nothing wrong with improving yourself, you know. You could read a book.'

'He can't read nothing, sir,' said another man.

I already felt rather dim.

'We heard you was having a nice talk about poems and that, so we thought we'd put on a record, mind our own business, like.'

'Play your damned record.'

'Yes, sir.'

'And put a sock in it. I've heard it quite enough.'

As I left the barn, I tried to guess exactly what had been implicit in the word 'nice'.

8 September 1916

By September, the temperature had dipped prematurely, and the rains had begun. The trenches were starting to fill with water. One recalled the horrors of the previous winter: cave-ins of trench walls; trench foot, leading to amputations; infection from the rats, which thrived in the conditions (and they could swim, the little swine) and the frosts, which would become more pronounced as the year wore on and crust the top of the two feet of water and freeze every one of us who stood out there, soaked to the skin, in a downpour that never seemed to stop. One man in our unit had died of pneumonia, last winter; we had slept (whether in the day or at night) on the ledges cut into the side of the trench, which sometimes were themselves inundated. Sickness from the conditions dragged one down, but did not excuse one from duty. Now, on the Somme, one sensed conditions beginning a reversal to such awfulness.

On top of this misery, there was the war to end war.

We'd taken Guillemont, at great cost. Ginchy was proving harder to capture. Their artillery was relentless. Come rain or shine, German snipers kept up with us, taking a daily break just after lunchtime. Of course, that meant that we kept well beneath the line of the parapet, and consequently the snipers, having no actual target, resorted to testing our defences at random, firing off rounds through the sandbags that made up the upper portion of the trench wall, on the off-chance that some wretched soldier would happen to be behind it at that moment. Two of our men got potted in this way, one week: one killed, and one shot in the hand – a Blighty wound, over which he did not bother to contain his delight. The trench water rose inch by inch.

This is not war. This is hiding like rats in a drainpipe, or rather in some mud-filled drainage ditch, wallowing, waiting to see what the Bosch are going to send up next. The snipers are a byword for all *that is detestable. The chief effect of their patient war – they fire one round per minute, and no more – is to grind one down.*

And then came the news that we were going to make a really big push. We had smelt it coming for some time – several of our senior officers had pressing matters to attend to at HQ, far behind the lines, or got promoted out of the line, or happened to be sick.

General Rawlinson came on horseback to address us, and we stood in square formation to pretend to listen to him. It was the usual bluster. The general – an old patrician and a Victorian through and through – explained that what was being asked of us was to create the conditions by which the war could at last be won, and peace secured, and the fighting stopped. The newer soldiers took these words very seriously. The men who'd been over the top before showed little restraint, and muttered insults loudly enough for everyone, including, possibly, the general, to hear. I was not minded to prevent the men from expressing their views. He was an old sod, and he was getting his feet massaged at HQ while we swam around in mud that contained parts of our comrades' bodies. We knew it, and he knew it. Yet is it not the compact into which one enters as a man, to take the brunt of whatever violence is on offer, and never complain? It goes without saying that women by no means escape the misery of war, and the raids on England, and London in particular, have seen to that, and poor Edith Cavell, but one begins to tire of the enthusiasm with which the women send their men over La Manche, the zeal with which they distribute the white feathers. Women suffer, and men suffer, but men are sent to die, and I no longer understand why that should be so. Will the world only be happy when all the men are dead?

We were sent back into the trenches three days before the assault began. The lot who were coming out had lost four men in their week of duty.

I asked a second lieutenant to brief me.

'They're keen on the wiring parties,' he said. 'We've been having a bally time of it. This lot we've been sending over seems to have given them the heebie-jeebies...' He meant the artillery bombardment of

the German positions. 'It has me, too. I'm happy to be out of it.' As he passed by me, he said in a low voice, 'Word of advice: rumour's doing the rounds you're a pansy, old man. I should put paid to that, if I were you. No one wants one of those next to him when he goes over.' As he passed, he allowed his shoulder to thump into mine.

On the day before we went over, we knew the time was at hand. I took James Lyons into the dugout and bolted the door from inside, and we kissed and held each other's heads. The feeling of his tongue against mine, the breaking dam of my emotions – I shall never forget it.

The sexual intention was without doubt, but to imagine that any sort of sexual act could take place between us was an absurdity – the prospect of the firing squad might have proved an effective deterrent had not the appalling conditions, lice, itching and poor hygiene not amply sufficed. We were wretched creatures, snatching what little there was of joy. I was twenty-two years old, and he nineteen. We were at the height of our powers as lovers; as men. We sat on duck-board in that dugout, dressed in our uniforms, listening to the shells pummelling the German side; holding hands.

'Are you scared?' he asked me.

'What – of that?' I thumbed outside. 'What is there to fear? Being shot for treason? Or cowardice, perhaps? If not that, then I shall be shot for what we've just done. Failing that, we'll let Jerry have a pop, eh? Seems reasonable, don't you think, since everyone else gets a go?'

'Your hand's shaking.'

I looked at my hand. He was right. I tried to pull it away, but Lyons wouldn't let it go, even when it twitched. He held it in both of his, and massaged it with his thumbs, and made it feel better.

'These bloody guns, all the time,' I said.

'Aye, those bloody guns. And us: "butterflies, opening and closing our wings on the muzzles of cannon".'

'What's that?' I asked.

'A poem,' Lyons said.

I squeezed his hand back. 'We'll be all right.'

15 September 1916

In the night before the big push, I went out with four men, as far as our wire. It was about two, long before the first light of dawn had started to appear. The mud was as ubiquitous on top as it was in the trench; where earlier in the year we'd been able to use shell-holes for cover, now they were beginning to fill with water and offer little safety. We slithered along in silence, checking for damage. The rain started up. It started as a smattering and quickly turned into a downpour. The air felt oppressive. Then came the first rumble of thunder. I whispered, 'Back to the trench! Move!'

'They'll not hear us in this lot, sir,' one of the men insisted. 'We could stay out all night.'

'No, they won't hear us,' I agreed. 'But what goes with thunder?'

– and back he went.

Colonel Mellor called the officers back to the reserve trench at about 3 a.m. Burn-Jones, willowish and gaunt, smoked cigarettes one after the other. He'd been at Ypres, I'd found out, and seldom spoke to anybody. McMurray was new to all of this, but a fortnight of being shelled had knocked the dust off him. We all accepted cocoa from the colonel's adjutant, and we sat in wet clothes in the dugout there, the only heat coming from the candle on the table.

'We're going over at seven-thirty,' Mellor said. 'We have a series of objectives, culminating in capturing the village of Lesboeufs' – he showed us on the map – 'which is fortified. We're to hold that so that the cavalry can get through. The Canadians are to take Courcelette, and the Londoners will be pushing through High Wood, and routing the German machine guns there.'

Burn-Jones exhaled. 'I rather thought the Thirty-third had given that a shot.'

'The general's learned his lessons. Anyway, we have land-ships, this time.'

This was meant to give us steel, but only McMurray looked pleased. We others had heard about the arrival of the land-ships – fewer than expected, because so many had broken down on the way.

'You'll capture the redoubt to the north-west of Flers and then join with the rest of the division as it advances. And one more thing,' the colonel said, 'I saw men running, last time.' He tutted. 'We are the British Expeditionary Force. We are not animals, scurrying about. We stay in formation, and we walk across no man's land, towards the German lines, like men.'

Burn-Jones looked at us one by one, and put his cigarette out.

There is nothing that can prepare one for the fear of going to one's death. One must embrace it, celebrate it, or else one's capacities will be overloaded and one shall founder.

I saw a poor devil shot. He had been a serial deserter. He said he couldn't face the fear of being asked to climb the ladder. There were several young officers sitting in on proceedings, to understand what was meant by the threat of a court martial, and after the presiding officer had passed sentence of death, the man looked over at us and said, 'Cheer up, lads. This is much better, putting an end to it. I wasn't built for this lark.' What else could we do but recoil from this acceptance of death? And yet, I could not help feeling that this fellow had really made good his final escape.

They put him in front of the squad – six soldiers, each armed with a rifle, who kept their backs to him until the final moment – and the sergeant pinned a bit of flannel on to his lapel: a target. The man stood with his head high throughout. His legs did not knock, nor his teeth chatter, both of which things really do happen when the fear grows great enough – I have seen it. When the soldiers turned to face him, I believe I saw him smile. The sergeant shouted, 'Take aim.' 'Go on!' cried the man. The squad fired, and the man fell on the floor, mortally wounded but writhing around all the same, as corpses do. The sergeant came over with a revolver and shot him through the head, and then the poor soul was still.

I should have felt appalled by this man's death, brutal and pathetic *as it was. Instead, the sensation was of having witnessed a beloved friend depart on an ocean liner for some distant home.*

I could see that the other young officers did not recognise that the dead soldier had triumphed.

As we trooped out of the courtyard, I looked back over my shoulder, and saw a butterfly fly up from the tall surrounding fence. For a moment I allowed myself to believe in the transmigration of the soul; that this haphazard fluttering creature, red and black, was the man's spirit ascending to the next world, seeking a new body within which to reside, or some such tripe, but it was nothing so far-fetched. He had got out, that was all. For us, the trial had just begun.

We didn't sleep – not a chance. Well before dawn, McMurray and Sergeant Carpenter took two waves over the top. McMurray's lot crept about a hundred yards out into no man's land and lay there, in the mud. Carpenter's lot stopped about thirty yards farther back, and they lay down too. No alarum was raised, and no Very lights happened to go up, so the Germans had no notion that an advance was under way. We'd been dropping shells on them for days, so in all likelihood Fritz was down in his deep front-line dugouts, sipping cocoa and deciding what he'd do when he got back to Bohemia or the Black Forest. He'd get the wind up that a show was on when we changed the pattern of our artillery. We'd given up on box-shelling – their bunkers were too deep. Now the bright idea was for our artillery to shell just ahead of the infantry as it advanced towards the German wire – a 'creeping barrage'. The tanks were to be allowed corridors through. It seemed a flawed plan, to me – the leaving of gaps – but everything about the war was wrong, by then. One felt one's life-force being choked out of one by the death-grip of a global mania: everybody was in uniform, and nobody was in charge.

The first sick fingers of dawn were beginning to poke through the clouds that morning as I stood in the front line on the Somme, and I was scared. I had been scared before, but not in the way I now felt. 'Pull yourself together,' I muttered under my breath, so indiscreetly that the man standing next to me asked me to repeat myself.

A runner came splashing up, pushing between the throng of men standing in the mud. He bore the transcription of a wire from Major

Tockridge. O.T.T. 0730, it said. That was all. In the dark, the men's eyes were the brightest thing.

'Half past seven,' I said.

There was a barely concealed groan. They'd been hoping for a postponement. So had I.

In the last hour before sunrise, it started to rain heavily, so that we stood shaking violently in sodden clothes, keeping our rifles dry as best we could. Where there was shelter, men took it, but there wasn't much: the water poured down all angles of the trench, bringing parts of the trench wall with it. Word came up after a while that there had been a cave-in farther along. Two soldiers from the Scots regiment had been pulled out dead. Those men who weren't already shuddering violently grew restive at this news.

I looked from face to face. I looked at him, and he at me, and I felt a fissure rising from the very pit of my stomach. 'In half an hour, we are going over the top,' I said, 'and we are to start by capturing the German trenches and the redoubt behind them.' A few months previously, this instruction would have been received with agreement. Now, there was no reaction. 'Did you hear me?' I asked. 'If so, say yes, sir.'

One or two voices muttered something in the affirmative.

'Didn't you hear the captain?' said the sergeant. 'He just gave you an order.'

One man started crying.

Another, barely able to talk, said, 'Dunno what a redoubt is, sir.'

I said, 'It's the German fortifications on that rise, overlooking the village. Sergeant, let's get the rum round.'

'Sir.'

'Let me make myself clear,' I said, addressing the dozens of men in our section of the trench. Burn-Jones looked up with interest. 'Some of us standing here now will not make it back from this show. Fritz wants to put a bullet in you, and he's quite a good shot. But we are better than he is, we are more determined than he is, and we have God on our side —'

'Bollocks,' said someone.

'— but we must support each other. Failure on your part to act decisively could be the death of the man standing next to you.' I had

rather hoped that these words would stir up some esprit de corps; but I was wrong. They just stood there in the gloaming, trying to keep the pouring rain off their faces, each man muttering things to his god or his girlfriend. Some waited blank-eyed, like stone angels, watching over the tombs of the dead. Still others stared at the watch in my hand as if it and it alone contained the remainder of their time on Earth. They were the ones I had to inspire: each man who had been unable to resist looking into his future, and had seen the truth.

The silver-rimmed watch on my wrist said a quarter past seven. I ordered the men to stand ready.

The artillery fire overhead, to the thunder of which we were by now very used, stopped. In its place came a desperate silence, as though the world had stopped too. It was terrible. Burn-Jones looked my way, and we checked our watches – no, they had not stopped. The artillery was switching patterns fifteen minutes early. Presently, at a distance of miles, a big gun fired, then five, then twenty, and now the heart of the world was beating again, and the scream of shells as they passed overhead was choral. The earth trembled once more.

They knew we were coming, now. The two squads, prostrate in the French mud, and the sluggish land-ships, already in the field – all were hopelessly vulnerable.

A Very light went up from their side, and the half-light became full light. No, no, no. All bloody wrong, I thought.

The men had started to jostle one another like a truckload of pigs, arrived at the abattoir gate.

Farther along, a man started climbing a ladder. 'Wait for it!' shouted Burn-Jones, but the fellow was nimble and fast, and went over by himself.

That's the thing with shell-shock – it is impossible to say how and when it will affect one. Some extreme cases are taken to hospital, where they march up and down like drill sergeants, out of their minds. Others turn very quiet; others still appear perfectly normal until the strain becomes too much and they take matters into their own hands. Only so much weight can be placed upon a man before he buckles beneath the load.

No one had tried to stop him – to grab a leg, or something. He had flipped, and might shoot any challenger. Everyone looked after him, knowing exactly why he'd gone over like that, and half-wondering whether he might not survive. Then came the rat-tat-tat of the German guns. They had seen him, at the very least. Now they would be looking for him, and what would they notice? – aha, a lot of other soldiers, lying there in the mud, waiting to attack.

I shoved through the mass of bodies to confer with Burn-Jones. 'We've to go over now, surely?' I hissed. 'McMurray is nothing but a target.'

'We shall be walking into our own barrage.'

'If we don't, we shall be letting half our men die. Do you want to explain our actions to McMurray's wife?'

'Bit rich, what?' said Burn-Jones. 'This is no time for emotion.'

Another machine gun had started to fire.

I said, 'How long do you suppose before they shell this trench?'

Burn-Jones shook his head. 'If I was the Hun,' he said, 'I'd be letting us have it right away – flush us out.'

'So would I.' I swore with exasperation, making the men start. 'We have no choice.'

'Disobey orders?'

'No, of course not. We wait until the right time, and then we give it merry hell.' The minute hand on my watch, in the Very light, showed eleven minutes remaining. Eleven minutes was a long time to do nothing but wait for the end of one's life. I stood transfixed, watching the clock counting down.

'Where's that man… you!' I said, picking out the fellow I was after. 'Where's that bally gramophone of yours?'

It was in with the tins of bully beef and blankets that we wanted to keep out of the mud for as long as possible; and it was serviceable.

'Let's have some music,' I said.

We stood in the trench that morning, bathed in red and green lights, hundreds of men all up and down the front, and we listened to the scratchy sound of the singer, singing.

And the men chanted the chorus as though it meant something to them, and we tried to hold our weapons with the rain numbing our hands and numbing our faces, and I knew that I had to do what was right, I had to do what was expected of me, and I knew that I would never be able to look at myself in the mirror again without remembering this day and these men and what I had done to them.

The hands on the watch reached seven twenty-five.

The shelling started.

The whizz-bangs were the most unnerving of things, because one heard their shriek only a moment or two before the impact, so there was no time to get out. The first one to arrive landed squarely on the gramophone, thus achieving in a second what for weeks I had only dreamt of doing. The second, which came soon after, dropped into one of the communication trenches where our second wave was waiting, much as we were. We heard the screams all too clearly.

'Hold your positions!'

There was something close to panic, now. The Germans' range was uncanny.

Bullets were beginning to flick clods of dirt from the top of the parados. 'I've four guns, three ahead and one from somewhere on the right – can't see him,' shouted the periscope operator.

'Can you see any of ours?'

'There's nothing—' With a clang, the periscope was knocked out of the man's hands.

Then one of the second wave appeared on the parapet. He had had a close shave – once we had pulled him into the trench he showed us the graze on his throat where the bullet had passed. 'It's murder up there,' he said. 'They changed the artillery too soon.'

'Well, shape up and get ready, you're going back over with us in four minutes.'

'Not me, sir.'

I begged his pardon, and the fellow wiped a layer of mud from his boot, to show me the neat hole through it, from top to sole. The mud on the sole was red.

'Even luckier than the other one,' I said, bitterly. 'You had better hope the medic agrees the Germans did it to you.'

Someone had started to vomit.

'Get back to the dressing station.' The watch said two and a half minutes. I could feel the shakes settling in. 'Where's that rum?' The stuff tasted bloody awful.

'Men, we will be going over the top in two minutes' time. When I blow my whistle, get up the ladders as fast as you can. Keep low, go to the gap in the wire and get through. Stay in squad formation.'

There was a general fluttering of panic.

'We are under orders to walk across no man's land. Do not run. Walk.'

'Fuck off.'

'Who said that?' I drew my revolver. 'Who said that?'

Something fell into the trench at its farther end, and there was an almighty explosion. I saw the flash. Three or four men were vaporised, and other men either knocked dead by the blast or thrown into the mud. Those nearby tried to pull out the living men from beneath the dead ones.

Do not underestimate the weight of a dead human being.

Another man bolted, and was pulled back.

'Hold firm!' I yelled.

The watch counted down with terrible slowness. Time seemed to have forgotten about us. I allowed myself to look at James Lyons, and he looked at me. I know that other men saw that communication pass between us. I know they knew what it meant.

Another whizz-bang screamed. We all ducked down in our tin helmets. That one went off in front of the trench, somewhere close to the wire.

One minute.

'I'm not fucking going,' said one of the men.

'He'll get us killed,' said another, meaning me.

Some of the men ignored this, or did not hear, but the opinion seemed to rouse some support. The sergeant, this time, did not intercede.

'As you can see,' I said, 'the Bosch have realised that we're on the move. They will make it their business to drop everything they've got on our heads. That means anyone still in here after the show starts is a sitting duck. Captain Burn-Jones will be leading you. Follow him.' As I spoke, I forced myself to meet the eyes of every man, James Lyons included. 'I know the rumours that are going about,' I told them. 'You think me less of a man than you. Let us see about that. I will be the last man out of this trench. If any of you refuses to climb *the ladder, under section four of the rules of engagement I will shoot you on the spot for cowardice. Do I make myself clear?'*

Even in the cacophony, one could hear the silence.

'Captain Rutherford asked you a question,' shouted the sergeant. 'Did you hear him?'

And they mumbled that they had.

Thirty seconds. I placed the whistle between my teeth. I bit the whistle. It was a detestable tin thing, of the type one might use to summon one's dog.

Farther up, Burn-Jones did the same. The men who were to be first over the top took a half-step out of the mud on to the lowest rung, and waited.

The silver case of the wristwatch stood open in my gloved hand, and the minute hand, with its lime strip, pointed to the twenty-ninth minute.

We heard the whistles from all along the front line. Perhaps our watches were a few seconds slow. We heard the whistles: the sound of beat bobbies and station platforms and Saturday afternoon football, and it was chilling. I blew my whistle. I blew as hard as I could so that I did not sound afraid, and I found that I could not stop. The men on the ladders clambered up. All but one.

'Get up there,' I told him, and a moment later I realised who it was. 'That's a direct order. Get up the ladder, now!'

He was gripping the ladder with both hands, but he was not moving. His skin had turned snow white. Once again I told him to climb, and the men waiting to go up behind him shoved him, to no avail. They looked from me to him. I know what they were thinking. With every sinew in my body, I wanted Private James Lyons to climb that ladder.

The sergeant was almost out of the trench. I thought perhaps he could pull Lyons up, but the back of the sergeant's head blew out and his body toppled back down into the trench water. 'Climb!' I shouted at Lyons, pointing my revolver at him. 'Climb!'

I didn't think I could pull the trigger. The thought flashed through my mind to turn the gun on myself, but I couldn't do that either. I shoved the barrel of the gun into his head and said, 'James, climb the damned ladder!'

Until that point, I remember a great deal of the noise, but at that point the memory returns to me as curiously peaceful. The bursts of earth and the lights falling through the sky seem, in the memory, balletic; a silent celebration; natural, like flowers coming into bloom. There was Burn-Jones, rolling about at the top of the ladder, holding his legs; there was one of the tanks – hideous and determined, like an iron slug, crawling over our trenches farther down the line. England lay behind us and the German army lay before us. We stood at the place where awful forces met: at a fault-line in time itself, a crossing-over of histories, where white-hot gases from the centre of the Earth rose up and scalded mere men. I remember the twitches that I had fought to suppress making my body convulse. I remember the faces of the men around me. Finally I remember the poet James Lyons, shaking violently and holding the ladder for support, turn his head to me with an effort, his jaw trembling violently, so that he could see the gun aimed directly at his face.

I squeezed the trigger.

James Lyons' eye went dark instantly, and the face of the man standing behind him was crimson and wet. Lyons fell sideways, into the mud, and half-sank there, looking upward with his remaining eye as if appealing to a higher justice.

The men remaining in the trench – and there were precious few of us, now, because for some reason the reserve troops had not come – went very swiftly to the ladders.

I did not feel anything when I executed Private James Lyons. What I had done seemed measured and reasonable. He had been delaying the attack on the German line by blocking the ladder; he had represented a challenge to the chain of command. It had been necessary.

I stood there in the mud pretending to supervise the escalation of the ladder. A machine gun was ranged on the top of our trench, and each man who climbed up was butchered. I shepherded them up the ladder, and back down they came, without faces, without heads. The Lewis gunner was the last one to go up, and he waded to the other end of the empty trench and went up there, to outmanoeuvre the machine guns. I saw him run just beyond view, and then there was an explosion, and the Lewis gun came back into the trench, its barrel bent out of shape.

In the last moments of my war, I thought, I must take the redoubt, *and then another thought superseded it, and I pulled open Lyons' tunic. There was the tan, leather-bound notebook in which he wrote his poems. The splash next to me barely registered on my consciousness, and when I saw that it was a* minenwerfer *I felt no fear. I felt nothing.*

My shaking hands were transparent.

The bomb went off.

ONE

05

The kids in the garden have played too hard. One of them is yelling at another, when I look up. Another has fallen down, and is rolling around by the splashpool holding his legs, crying out for his mommy. I rip the music out of my ears and vomit hard on to the side of the fence. It comes out green. My eye streams and I'm shaking so hard I can barely stay upright, but the gag reflex keeps on heaving up more poison, like some kind of bust drain bringing up all the waste that never quite got washed away and was lurking there all this time.

Oh God, can you forgive me for this? Did I really think I could pull the trigger? But that's the thing: I *could* have done it. I *would* have done it.

There are strings of sputum hanging off my chin and I wipe them off with the corner of my shirt, the one that stinks of last night. The party is in full swing, and no one's paying me the least bit of attention. There's Butler, talking to a pregnant woman who's fanning herself. Eventually he feels me watching, and he looks up and sees me planted there at the end of his lawn like an old dead tree he can't bring himself to chop down. We look at each other a long time, while the pregnant woman keeps on talking. After a while, he returns his attention to her, and he doesn't look my way again.

Inside the house, downstairs, the throng has gotten thicker and people are drunker. That kid is in the kitchen, getting little white Band-Aids put on his knees by a cooing grandma.

Upstairs, the wood and the blinds make it cool. There is no one around. I sneak into the room where I slept the night, the one overlooking the backyard. My cell has some charge left.

'Hello?' His voice comes after a couple of rings.

'I need to speak to Josh,' I tell him.

'Sure,' said Maxwell. 'You OK?'

'Just put him on.'

In the quiet that follows, I can't hear quite enough to piece together how things are shaping up in Tennessee this morning – there's a cotton-candy thickness to the silence that I listen to from thousands of miles across the ocean. There is no footfall; no sounds of doors or running or people calling out for each other. For all I know, Josh might be standing by the phone right now, in that place I can't picture, looking at the receiver, afraid to pick it up. I check my watch, and a whole minute ticks by; then two.

There's a clatter, and then Josh's voice on the line, breathless. 'Dad?'

'Hey, kiddo.'

Josh says, 'I miss you, Dad.'

'I miss you too, son,' I say, and damn it, I knew I was gonna cry and I can't stop myself, and I say, 'Josh, I'm sorry, son, I'm so sorry.' The words are so hard I can't hardly put them together in my mouth. After we've both cried, and once I can breathe again, I say, 'I just went nuts. I wasn't me.'

'I know.' Josh says, 'I want to come home.'

'Me too, pal, me too. We're gonna do that,' I say, and the relief is like a punch in the gut. 'You and me, OK? We'll work it out. Start over.'

'I miss Mom.'

'I do too. For a long time, now.'

He goes quiet. I tell him, 'Whatever else you do, you just remember all the good times you had with your mom, all the jokes you guys had.'

'Where are you?'

I say, 'Don't worry about that. I'm gonna be home soon – all I gotta do is buy a flight.'

'OK.'

'OK. I love you, you hear me?'

After his voice is gone, I sit on the bed a long time, listening to the sound of each slow breath coming out of me. I'd like to tell you I'm thinking something profound, but I'm not, not at all. It's enough not to have my head full of violence. It's enough to be alive. Where else was it gonna go, after I was standing there with the body of Michael Butler lying on the floor, with half his head missing? You hear all the time about men who go on some kind of rampage and finish up by killing themselves. Sure, I think I might have painted myself into that corner. I'd have done it, and then I'd have realised how the rest of the world, having not yet stumbled upon my little crime, would just carry on doing what it was doing; how nothing much had changed. I'd have realised, not how terrified of punishment I was, but how insignificant was this accomplishment I'd paid for with my life.

I'd have realised there was no point to me. Worthless, in spite of my righteous anger and my high ideals. I would have realised I wasn't worth fighting for.

Maybe that's how it works, when you're prepared to die for something so much bigger than you.

Taking one last look around the room, I pick up the knapsack and throw in your journal and the cell phone.

Even with those items, the bag seems less heavy than it should. *No, there's no way.* Just to be sure, I pour the contents of the bag on to the bed. Something pinches a nerve in my belly.

Neither of the guns is there.

It's no use rummaging through what's there, because what's there is the T-shirts they were wrapped in, a copy of the *London Lite* newspaper, a candy bar, and what I just put in the bag ten seconds ago. I cover my face with my hands – it's the only way I can stop from hyperventilating. They were most certainly both in that bag – I remember waking up with one of them in my hand. I recall leaving it there when I left the room.

I think about the way Michael looked up the garden at me. Yeah, he might know. When he looked away like that: maybe that was confidence, knowing I'd been disarmed, or maybe it had been something else. But why not call the cops? Why am I not in cuffs already? Maybe the cops are already on their way. Within about a minute of discovering the guns were gone, the choice has become whether it's more dangerous to stay and try to get the guns back, or to take off and leave the evidence in Michael Butler's house.

In the street outside the house, the heat of the sun is rising up out of the pavement and pulsing from the brickwork of the ordinary houses. Every step I take, I feel more like a ghost walking away from the place of his own death. I play the limerick game to stop myself thinking about getting shot in the back.

There once was a fellow called John
Walking all by himself in the sun
He'd learned all kinds of dirt
Having called himself Kurt
And he thought, No, I don't have a gun.

I actually burst out laughing as I walked, making everyone at a bus stop react. It's the perfect limerick. I wish I could share it with you properly.

No one comes running out of the house after me. There's no rush of squad cars, and cops telling me to lie face down on the ground. The world continues to behave exactly as though nothing had happened.

If Michael Butler was the one who took the handguns, am I in more or less danger than if Issy took them?

I get on a bus that looks like it goes east, and swing into a back seat. What will Butler do? How long did he suspect me? Hell, I'd been so drunk I mighta just told him outright, last night, right there in the pub: *Hey, bro, I'm here to shoot you. Here's my gun, dude.* So maybe he's just pleased to be alive, right now.

Maybe that's enough. It's enough for me. I'm pleased my enemy is alive and I am pleased I'm alive. It means we all get another chance to do things better than we've done before. I think about reporting him, of course I do, but I don't want to blow my luck.

I know, now, that I'm going back to my boy. There's just one thing I gotta set straight first.

04

The ordinary carriages of the train are laid out like an airplane, with all the seats stacked up too close and the luggage overhead, and the colour scheme picked out to make you feel like travelling is no big deal. I've gotten a place in first class, which means I get a table, plus a white paper towel on the headrest of my chair. A guy comes around and sells me a Bud and nuts.

After Euston Station slides away, for a while I watch the passing of the outskirts of the city: all kinds of buildings, some made out of crumbling bricks, some made out of pipes and mirrors; high-rises full of storeys; streets of beat-down shops; football stadium lighting towers and retail parks and construction cranes and public houses, all paused in the act of tumbling over one another in the battle to survive.

They start to thin out, after a while. The buildings get lower, as the sun begins to set, and they come in towns instead of in one endless amorphous conurbation. Now there are fields – not expanses of land like in Canada, but neatly cultivated patches of green, bordered with hedgerow. There are jet planes cutting pink trail-lines into the reddening sky. The beer and the length of the day and all that has occurred make my thoughts swim.

Across from me, on the other side of the carriage, he sits against the window and watches the world go by. I watch him for a long time. He wears a hat and a high-collared coat and keeps his head turned away, so that all I have to go on is the strip of reflection in the window that flashes when something outside catches the sunlight.

It is two in the afternoon by the time the train gets to Crewe, and I've slept at least half the way here. A woman in uniform comes and wakes me up. She shudders when I turn my head to tell her thanks. It was a sleep like none I'd ever had: an embrace; an abyss. Afterwards, I think maybe that's what it feels like to be dead.

The local train to Penbury takes a half-hour, and now I'm step-ping into his life.

Yeah, he came to this part of the world. John Rutherford. He walked on these same roads. In some places you can see where the municipal authorities have laid a new road over an old one, and the cobbles are only visible as a strip at each side of the street, where the drains are. A fracture in time: where you look through the present to see the past.

His figure walks ahead of me, the whole way, after we get off the train in Penbury town. He's taller than I thought he'd be. When he walks, his trenchcoat flaps around behind him like a cloak, and he keeps his collar turned up as we pass through the main street, past stores called Boots the Chemist and WHSmith and Superdrug, past a building that once was a pub but is now boarded up and offered to let. He turns a certain number of corners, and I have to trot along to keep up. I guess no one ever records how fast a walker they are, when they're writing their diary. Dude has long legs.

People react more, out here in the small towns. My face, I'm talking about. It's more like home. When I check myself in the shop window to see what they see, I'm looking at a middle-aged man wearing one half of a Halloween mask under a baseball cap. I stick out for two reasons, then, because people avoid baseball caps in this country like they passed a law against them.

Eventually you turn a final corner, on to a big side-street lined with buildings, which leads on up a low hill and away out of sight.

By the time I round the corner, he's gone. For a minute I stop there. He went away too quickly to have carried on along the road; he must have gone into one of the buildings; but these look like mostly domestic places, maybe Victorian, with low front doors and front windows that have been converted out of retail use. One or two couples around with waterproof jackets on and cameras slung around their necks stop to look at the flowers in window boxes or point at the steeple of the church, and there are tearooms where people are re-enacting the fifties. Cars pull off the main drag and drive up the hill. Mothers with baby-walkers and little kids on reins come by. One kid sees me. I like how his eyes get big and he's so astonished he doesn't think to tell his mommy – he just keeps staring and walking, staring and walking. One day, in twenty or thirty years, he'll remember this face out of context and he'll try to work out what it was that he saw. The best-kept place on this side of the street has a notice in the window saying VACANCIES. Above the front door, there's a black rectangular notice, detailing the hotelier's right to sell liquor. The hotelier is called Mrs E.W. Castle.

The name jumps out at me. Takes a minute to place it, but then I do: the biplane; the picture from the *English Post*. The landlady called Castle. Then I work out the math: assuming Mrs Castle was, say, thirty years old when you stayed here in the twenties, she'd now be about one hundred and ten years old. That's some old hotelier. Practically biblical. So maybe she's really long gone, and it's just the sign that's still here.

I knock on the door, and pain shoots through my hand. It's summer, but the arthritis in my bad hand has stopped restricting itself to cold seasons. And there's a bell, and I ring that too, and assume the front-door pose: head turned to show my good side.

Whatever kind of thin white curtain is up against the window is disturbed. Then someone tries to work the latch from the inside – it clicks and bolts are pulled, but the door won't open. Finally they get it right. Two Japanese women are laughing and saying thank you over and over again, and bowing, and talking Japanese, and they come past me without looking up, toting one massive pink plastic suitcase between them. They leave the door open.

After they've gone, I see who they were saying thank you to.

There's an old woman in the hallway, standing in the new calm. She's dressed in a blouse with a brooch at the throat, and wears a pinafore over her skirt. She holds her heart. She's standing there looking at me like I was the first human being she ever saw. My own silhouette, framed in the oblong of light from the doorway, is reflected, twice, in her spectacles.

'You came back,' she says.

For a long minute I stand there in the place he once stood and I'm him, too. Both of us. Put us together and you've got one whole pretty face and one from hell; one that's seen plenty, and one that can't see an inch.

'You're Mrs Castle?'

'I am.' Her attitude has changed now she's heard my voice. 'Beg pardon, I thought you were someone else.' She primps a bunch of tourist leaflets in a display case. 'How can I help you?'

'You knew John Rutherford.'

The primping stops. I have her undivided attention, once again. She says, 'How—'

'Can I come in?'

This thing has blindsided her. 'Yes. Yes, of course,' she says, remembering herself. 'Yes, come into the dining room. They've all finished; it's just the girl who does the rooms...'

The building is small, even for a British building. Everything is painted in light colours, but there's still the feeling of twilight about it. She shows me through into a brighter room, whose windows look out on the street. He'd have sat there, by the window, his good right side toward the room, sipping his tea.

I sit down at a linen-clothed table covered in breakfast crumbs. Mrs Castle takes off her apron and joins me. She summons a Polish girl to come get us drinks. Man, this whole country seems to run on Polish people.

'How do you take your tea, Mr...?'

'Knox. I'll take coffee if you've got it – without milk, cold water to cool it down, and a straw.'

After the drinks have arrived – Mrs Castle gets her tea in a pot, which she pours with solemn ceremony – she waits for me to explain myself.

I say, 'I'm chasing a ghost. More than one, tell you the truth. I came to this country for reasons I don't even want to talk about, and I'm connected with this guy Rutherford somehow, and I don't get it. I mean, it's like looking in a mirror – exactly like it.'

'Are you from Canada?' says Mrs Castle.

Now I know something's up. 'OK, that's out of sight. No one ever says that. Everyone always assumes I'm American.'

'But you're not.'

'No, you're right: I'm from near a little town called Clinton, Ontario.'

She shakes her head dismissively.

I say, 'This is the place he came, right? This is the guesthouse he kept coming to?'

Mrs Castle sits back in her chair. She looks tired. She says, 'I was just a little girl when he used to stay here. Every year, he came back, sure as the seasons. Always used to take the same room, up at the top, and he used to shout out in his sleep. He was a very troubled man, was the captain. You couldn't make a loud noise near him, or he'd go into a fit. Shock, it was, from the war. I remember Mother dropped a tray of cutlery, once – we thought he was going to die. Lying on the floor, shaking like a fish on land, he was.' Her gaze is falling on a particular bit of carpet, like Rutherford's shape might still be there. 'He were always very good to me and my mother, though. Very gentlemanly. They don't make men like that any more.'

'Why? What'd he do?'

'He cared about this place. Penbury, I mean, and this guest-house. Used to give his money to the working men's club and the church fund and so forth, all without leaving his name, but of course we all knew. We didn't get many visitors from London back in those days. And he was very... well, you wouldn't forget him if you saw him.'

'He looked like me.'

'You look like him. Yes. His injury was quite shocking. Used to make other children cry. I were never scared of him, though. You could tell he were the last person in the world who'd ever hurt you.'

We sit together without words for some time. We let the street noise wash in.

'Now,' she says, 'may I ask your connection to the captain?'

I say, 'The truth is, I don't know. My girlfriend had some of his journals, but they come and go – I think she was interested in him because of his connection with the poet James Lyons.'

'James Lyons? Really?'

'You know him?'

'He was a local lad, wasn't he? Before my time, of course.'

'Rutherford got Lyons' work published.'

'Oh, I see. Of course, he never used to talk about his work.'

'When did you last see him?'

'During the war. The second one. I'd have been seventeen, eighteen. Truth be told, I had a bit of a crush on the captain. He was much older than I was, and he had his injury, but he was very attractive, for all that. But he was homosexual, of course, or gay, they call it now, so there was no chance of anything coming of it.'

'You knew that?'

'Of course we did.' She chuckles. 'You've obviously never worked in a guesthouse.'

'I thought that being gay was, like, a crime here? Oscar Wilde and all that.'

She pours another cup from the teapot. 'They stayed here, the two of them, for about four months, when they were waiting to go. I dare say we've still got the chest of things they left behind.'

I tell her, 'Go where? You've lost me.'

'Just a minute, I'll ask Iryna to have a look.' And she shouts out the Polish girl's name, and, when she comes, gives precise instructions: a green trunk with brass fittings, in the attic space, somewhere on the left. Under the Christmas lights, most likely. I get the feeling Lil Castle has looked in that case once or twice. Iryna's built for shot-put, so I don't doubt we're gonna see the case pretty soon.

'I thought they lived separate lives,' I say. 'In his journal, the two of them just lived a kind of façade – she saw who she wanted to see, he—'

'She?' says Mrs Castle. 'There wasn't any woman involved, I told you. I'm talking about his gentleman friend. His lover, I suppose you'd have to say.'

Iryna's gotten the trunk. 'I always thought he might come back for it,' says Mrs Castle, as it is set before us. 'You give up hope, eventually, of course, don't you? I got to my sixties and I thought, if he was ever coming, he'd have come by now.' She springs the big central catch, which snaps open. 'I'm eighty-two, you know,' she says.

'And looking very good on it, ma'am.'

'Well, the captain's long dead, I'm afraid.'

I feel bad for her. All the years she waited around, thinking he might come back. 1940, according to the internet page. Killed by the Germans after all, but not on the Somme – in London, his home town. That was a lot of wasted hope.

The chest is stuffed full. There's a hat, of the kind they wore back in World War Two; it's grey with a dark band. I know zero about hats, but even I can tell right away the hat is made out of quality materials. Mrs Castle puts it on my head, and straightens the brim. I think I even see a little glint of admiration. 'You'll do,' she says. I look at myself in the mirror.

The man in the mirror looks a little different from me, although the hat is the same, and the fucked-up face is the same. It's him, just like it's always him. He's standing in the reflection of the dining room, with one side of his face wrecked and mangled, and he doesn't care who sees. There are people in the mirror with him, eating their bacon-and-egg breakfasts, reading black-and-white newspapers. He has his coat over his arm. I guess he's leaving soon. At a table behind him, where his half-eaten breakfast waits for his return, sits a young man with hair the colour of chalk-dust. He reminds me a little of Barney. He looks at me, and smiles, too.

'Are you all right?' says Mrs Castle.

He looks proud of being who he is. He doesn't skulk, the way I do. He's able to stand like that because he's come to terms with what he's done.

'I'm fine. I'm good,' I say.

'It suits you,' she says.

I guess I must've blinked or something, because now the mirror reflects the present, not the past, and my reflection is my own again.

The box isn't done giving up treasures yet. There's a discharge certificate, dated January 1919, from Dartmoor Work Camp. It refers to a commuted sentence having been served by someone called Oliver Riordan Phelps. There's a typewritten sheet of questions, dated 1916.

Why can't you arrange military service with your conscience?
What do you do to further peace, or is your attitude the only peaceful thing about you?
Would you rather experience losses than have to use force?

What is violence, exactly?
What do your beliefs say?

There's what's left of a white feather, and a sepia photograph, blurred at the edges and shaped to fit the oval window of a cardboard frame. It depicts a bride and groom. Neither is smiling.

There's a map of the world, folded up. At first sight, it seems to be clean. Out of habit, I look at the place where I grew up, the featureless bit of red between Toronto and Ottawa. I feel my heartbeat accelerate like crazy. There's a faint pencil mark exactly where Clinton would be.

I think I may have said *what the fuck* and I don't know if that was in my head or not.

'That's where I live,' I say, like a kid in kindergarten. Mrs Castle looks weirded out, too. 'That's my home.'

There are no other marks on the map, and nothing on the back. But there it is, over my home: a mark... showing what?

'How long has this been in the box?' I ask.

'Like I said, since he was here in 1941.'

'So why is there a mark there?'

The rest of the stuff in the box is ornamental, or fragile, or both – a glass paperweight with a drop-shaped bubble in it; a wooden statue of a dancer. At the bottom of the chest, there's a piece of writing paper. The text starts mid-sentence. It says,

there now – just a clearing. It's your affair what you put there – building materials, certainly, are not in short supply, and there's a daily bus to Clinton, where one can buy nails, tools &c.

One final thing: I should be grateful if you do not bring this letter with you. We do what we can, but as Oliver knows only too well from the last lot, anyone unwilling to murder his fellow man is perceived as a national menace. Also, leave behind anything a deckhand could not justify having about his person. The port authorities are fond of running spot-checks on the merchant vessels when they've nothing better to do.

The very best of luck to you both. Don't ever let anyone persuade you that refusing to be drawn into the madness, when 'those about you are losing their heads' or however it was that your countryman

*Kipling put it, is anything but an act of great bravery. Remember
how he lost his son.*
    Disappear well, my very great friends.
    Your humble and obedient servant, and brother in peace,
    Reginald H. Feldman Jr.
    Cobb Creek, 1941

'Disappear well,' I repeat... and then something comes into focus
in my mind. 'You said 1941 as well, didn't you?'
    'Yes. What about it?'
    'Wikipedia said 1940.'
    'Well, no, Coventry was 1940, he arrived Christmas time 1940
and left in 1941. Definitely '41.'
    'He was dead in 1941.'
    'He certainly wasn't.'
    'So he didn't die in the Blitz?'
    Mrs Castle laughs. 'I should hope not,' she says. 'Otherwise we'd
have been talking to a ghost. He put in a call to us after the war,
you see.'
    'He was alive *after* the war? So why...?' My mind's racing, but
nothing clever's coming out. I have the feeling I heard the name
Cobb Creek someplace before, a bunch of times, but I can't say
where. 'So he didn't die; instead he came up here from London
and then... ran away?'
    'There were places you could go, if you could get there,' said
Mrs Castle. 'Peace camps, they were called. Everybody knew, but
nobody said anything, of course. We were all supposed to join in
here. First few years, we were all scared stiff Hitler was coming to
invade us. We even got bombed here in Penbury.'
    You fucking ran away. You, the British war hero: when war
came around, you ran away.
    The smell of bread is drifting to us from the bakery across the
street. I say, 'So we're saying what? That he went to Canada? – I
don't understand. Mrs Castle, you got a computer?'
    Mrs Castle has a computer. It's on her reception desk, and it's an
old one, but it connects to the net. I type 'Cobb Creek' into Google
with shaking fingers. I know I know that name.

The search results appear. Wikipedia's the first one, of course. I click on it.

The article that appears is headed 'Bryde's Crossing'.

Bryde's Crossing is a rural residential area on the outskirts of Clinton, Falkirk County, Ontario, Canada. Population as of 2004 approx 220.

Established in 1827 at a turn in the River Cobb, a tributary of the Tay River, the cluster of houses, many now demolished, originally provided homes for workers constructing the Rideau Canal. The area was called Cobb Creek until 1950, when it was renamed in honour of Major Stewart Bryde, who lived there between 1923 and 1935 and served with distinction in the Battle of the Scheldt in World War Two.

Famous ex-residents of Bryde's Crossing include singer Martha Kaye and radio presenter John Knox.

'My home,' I heard myself say. 'He lived where I lived.'

My head's gotten light. Everything's closing in on me.

Rutherford, how can it be that you lived there? I never saw you, and surely, surely I'd have remembered your face. I knew most of the families around our way. None of them had a grandpa with half his face missing. And apart from those families, there was no one else: just me and my parents, and of course the two old brothers, the ones who we never saw, who lived on the other side of the lagoon, in the old wood cabin...

Oh God.

I remember the day we walked across the frozen lagoon, you and I, and the butterfly Josh saw, as we drove to you that final night. I remember how it lit up red in the beams of the headlights.

03

The day is getting old, in Cheshire, England. In Ontario, it'll still be the middle of the day.

'Steinwitz,' he says, when he picks up.

'Hey, Doc.'

'Johnny, that you? We're worried stupid. Where the hell are you?'

'I'm in England.'

'You just disappeared, you never told anybody.'

I say, 'Yeah, well, I just needed to… you know.'

The silence tells me he doesn't know.

'I got a favour to ask,' I tell him.

When the train arrives back in Crewe, the coffee place is still open – a little mom-and-pop stand, dwarfed by the structure of the station itself, which is all black-painted girders keeping a dirty glass roof up. The place looks like it's claimed a lot of souls in its time. Everyone has grey faces. A group of girls in short pink skirts and sashes and light-up devil ears are squealing at one another. A kid dragging his teddy bear along the floor holds his mommy's hand. Man, I can't wait to get out of this place.

In back of Crewe Station, the cab rank is thin compared to London, but there are cars. I tell the driver where I want to go.

'Not from round here?' he says, looking at me in the rear-view.

I say, 'Oh yeah, you could stiff me on the fare.'

We don't talk much after that.

While we drive, I realise you might never have come to this part of Britain, Rachel, but he was here, he was definitely here, and now I'm here too. In the dark, we drive mostly on overlit highways with articulated trucks pounding up and down; later, we turn off and the streets sometimes aren't lit. I think of the night I found you dead – when we drove home through the dark, and I was too late. Always too fucking late, every time.

And finally, we drive on unmarked, grass-verged roads, bordered with guilty-seeming trees that shift in the cab's headlights, and we stop at what seems to be a gap in a hedge.

'This it?' I say.

'It's what you asked for.'

I hand him the money and tell him to stick around.

'I'll be on waiting time,' he says.

'We're all on waiting time,' I tell him, which is almost enough to make him drive away. I give him a bunch more money and, getting out, say, 'Stay.'

Looking through the gap in the hedge, I can make out a car track leading down a valley. As my eye gets used to the dark, I begin to see that the valley is wide and that there is a stone cottage in it. There are lights on in a coupla windows, but faint, like they're behind thick curtains. Behind me, the insect noise of the cab's radio is buzzing around the corpse of an Elton John number.

For a long time, I lean against a rotted gatepost, thinking about what I'm gonna say. I try to imagine if I'd never known about how you'd died, in our home in Bryde's Crossing. What about if you'd just gone, one day, vanished into thin air, like you did to Maxwell – how would I feel, then? How do you mourn someone whose life never properly stops? I don't think you'll ever die, my darling, and that's wonderful, because I get to go on being with you, but it hurts. It hurts because I don't ever get to be me again. I don't get to walk away. And maybe that's the whole point: that people are sticky, and they get stuck together, and there's no saying what parts will break off when they try to get unstuck.

I walk down into the valley, and it feels like Ontario. For the first time since I've been in England, I can see stars.

The front door of the place is at the top of three tall steps. A wide concrete ramp has been added to the side of them. I ring the doorbell.

'Is there anybody there?' I yell.

In the door's glass panel, a moonlit face looks back at me. He looks a lot like me, but the devastation of his face is on the opposite side. He holds my gaze while someone in the house calls out I should wait a moment and while, in my peripheral vision, some light falls on to the scrub, out of one of the windows. There's a shuffling behind the front door, then the curtain opens behind the glass, and a man peers out. He looks so much like my dad that I forget to turn my head in time. I guess what he sees is Freddie Krueger standing in the night outside his house, and he does what any human being would do under those circumstances.

I guess I've had my fill of that, now.

'I'm John Knox,' I say, and behind it are the phantom words that I don't have to say, any more. 'You called me about your uncle James?'

His eyes turn into big circles. He scrabbles at some kind of security chain, and then he's out on the step, unsure whether to take my hand. Maybe he thinks it might hurt me. I take his, instead. 'You're Buster Lyons, right?'

He says he is, he is, like he's realising it for the first time himself. Turns out he's older than I'd imagined him, dressed like someone who reads books and keeps a cat. He smells of malt whisky; his face is growing pink with excitement and bad veins. 'Come in, come in,' he says.

'I can't stop for long. Got a cab waiting, and the guy hates me,' I say.

'Oh dear, right, I see. You're welcome to stop, of course.'

Inside, the decor is simple, and light on ornament. Lyons leads me from an entry vestibule dotted with rubber boots and walking sticks into a snugger room with a fireplace. This is where all the warmth of the house is concentrated. An artificial fire flickers merrily, and in front of it, on a couch in a prim style, sits a pinched old lady, sleeping. Her hair is all gone. The skin seems loose on her skull. By her side are reading glasses and a word-search book.

'I'll just wake her,' he says, unnecessarily. 'Mother! Visitor here to see us.'

It produces no response.

'Sorry,' he tells me. 'She's not long taken her tablets. I'll just be a moment...'

While he tries again to rouse her, I back off and thrust my hands in my pockets; check out the room. Looks like these guys live an austere type of existence. Out of the window I can see the cab driver, smoking a cigarette. In here, there's a shelf full of photographs. People at a lot of ages, in a lot of times, each one in a frame of its own. It all says: *people matter.* There's one in a silver frame of a kid in a military uniform. I'd guess he's about nineteen. The picture is sepia, artfully faded at the edges.He has one of those weak-ass moustaches and his hair is oiled into a parting.

I think, so you're the mighty poet, are you? You're what all this has been about.

I look into the boy's eyes, and try to imagine being in love with him. I close my eyes, and kid myself that I can feel his lips kiss mine, but it isn't true. He looks so damned serious. The British flag is hung on the wall behind him, and I guess someone's told him not to blink. I thought of the photograph Mikey Lang had of himself in uniform in front of Old Glory, on the day he passed out of basic at Fort Leonard Wood. Man, nothing changes. Everywhere in this world, everywhere in time, we pump 'em up with ideas that are too big for them, make 'em feel like kings, and then we let 'em go rip each other to shreds, these serious young men, while back home we raise glasses of their blood to the lofty, bullshit ideas they're rolling about in mud for. And the worst part is if they come back – because there are no ideas for that.

Worst of all, we keep on making the weapons better and better. The machine gun, the tank, the Bomb. What can possibly happen but that one day the serious young men take everyone else with them?

Yeah: if I contribute to a world where that's allowed to happen, is *that* suicide?

'Have you seen his picture?' says a woman's voice, guttural with age. It takes me by surprise.

I say, 'Yes, ma'am, I'm looking at it now.'

'He was a beauty of a lad, wasn't he?'

I turn the heavy frame over. On the back it says, James Frederick Lyons, Altrincham, 1916.

'Not my type, ma'am, but he was a looker all right.'

'You've come all this way,' she says. 'Come and sit with me on the settee, won't you?'

She hasn't moved from where I first saw her. She pats the couch, and I put James Lyons back on the shelf.

'Mother's losing her sight,' Buster confides, loud enough for her to hear. I already know that, from the way she doesn't turn her head when she speaks. Her eyes roll back a little too far. I frown at the word-search book and he says, 'That's mine.' I realise he is giving me permission to present myself to her – he is saying, she can't see your face, so it's OK. I sit down beside her. The couch just about swallows me.

Buster brings tea and cake. They taste good. He gets me a towel when he sees I can't drink without dribbling; meanwhile he pours a little of his own tea into the saucer, and slurps it out of that.

I apologise for turning up so late.

'That's all right,' says Mrs Lyons. 'Thank you for making such a long journey.'

'I'm from a country seven thousand miles coast to coast. Cheshire ain't far to come.' I like how she doesn't know to draw away when I put my hand on her hand. 'Buster told me you're sick. I'm sorry.'

'I'm not sorry. Ninety-eight is quite old enough. None of this works properly, any more...' She takes my hand, suddenly, and her hand is strong and hard, like Mom's when she was old. 'Thank you for doing this, Mr Knox. I know you've been through so much to be worrying about my family. Buster told me your poor partner got taken. I'm very sorry to hear about that. Very sorry. Was she ill?'

It's tough to bullshit someone while you're holding their hand. I hold her hand right back. 'Yeah, I guess she was ill,' I say.

'She mustn't have been very old.'

Aw, that one hits home. 'You're gonna make me cry, Mrs Lyons.'

She squeezes my hand harder, and says, 'I lost my husband twenty-four years ago. I still say good morning to him.'

For a while, we sit there in shared communion with our lost partners.

After a bit of time has passed, Buster finishes his tea.

'Well,' says Mrs Lyons. 'So you've found something out about Jimmy.'

I say, 'Yeah, I did.'

Yeah, I found out your big brother froze up and never even made it out the trench.

I take a deep breath. They are rapt, the pair of them. I say, 'There are fourteen diaries in total, right? I don't have a clue where most of them are – at least... well, I've got an idea, I guess. Anyway, I approached someone who used to know Rachel. I guess you might call him a colleague. She'd given him another one of the diaries – it contained stuff pertinent to his field. So I asked to have a look at it, and, uh – so, Mrs Lyons, that one gives an account of what happened to your brother.'

Buster buries his head in his hands, silently. His mother's eyes keep searching around for something in the air above her. I catch myself contemplating her; weighing the power I have over her.

The last thing he saw was the one man he trusted putting a gun in his face.

I take Rutherford's journal out of my bag, and place it in her hands. Buster wipes his eyes and puts his glasses on, and I let her feel it, turning it over in those incredible hands, talons draped with chicken-skin. She strokes the cover, and traces the outline of the pages.

'I'm all at sixes and sevens,' she says. 'After all this time of trying to find out, now it's here I'm not sure if I should know.'

I think about the twenty-minute gap; how I could have called you, how you might have lived.

'Lemme read it for you,' I say. Mrs Lyons relinquishes the book like someone setting a bird free.

I leaf through to the page headed 6 October 1916, the date and the words beneath it written in by John Rutherford, describing the agonising wait as the watches count down; the men going over; the death of the poet. I hold the book open in front of Mrs Lyons, where Buster can read from it too.

I meet Buster's eye.

'I blew the whistle,' I say. 'All along the line, one could hear the whistles blowing – the sound of Saturday morning football and bobbies and railway porters, and I blew my whistle too, as hard as I could. Once I had started, I found I could not stop. Some of the men were frightened – dash it, *I* was frightened, I own it – but they pushed forward in the mire of that trench, and jostled one another around the foot of the ladders.'

Buster has gotten increasingly confused about why I'm not looking down at the page as I speak these words; why I'm keeping my eye steady on him. He peers through his glasses at the text, and then back at me.

'The shelling was quite awful, already, and we were taking losses in the support trenches. One could hear the cries of the men there. This seemed to spur on the lads in the firing trench. Private James Lyons forced his way past another man, who was dithering, and climbed up the ladder. His hands were steady as he pulled himself up. The men around him saw this, and the boost to their morale was obvious, and up they went, one after the next, ready to take on the German army.'

Mrs Lyons gives a little moan. Buster is craning over her to read the words on the page.

'By the time I finally got up the ladder myself,' I say, trying to resist imitating all those dumb British accents out of comedy shows, 'the battlefield was carnage. The machine guns' bullets swept across the battlefield like cobras dancing in their baskets. Man after man was felled by their bite. And in the midst of it all, there he was,' I say, running my finger along a line of different words, 'James Lyons, pausing to help another man, who had been cut down; even among the explosions and with the air alive with bullets, checking to see whether he might assist his fellow man. The other fellow must have been dead, for Lyons stood up, and no sooner had he done so, his legs seemed to give out beneath him, he clutched at his chest, and fell on to his back in the mud.'

Mrs Lyons' eyes are fixed on some point on the ceiling. I'd expected her to cry, but she doesn't, she just keeps on staring blindly; inhaling; exhaling. Buster has gotten to the end of the page, to the part where Rutherford shot the kid. I turn the page.

'By the time I reached him, he was quite dead,' I say. 'I tore open his uniform – a bullet had gone through his heart. It is some slight consolation that his death should have been instantaneous, and he should not have suffered. I took his personal effects from his body, and rejoined the battle. That is the last time I saw James Lyons. No man's land took a great many lives in that battle, and many of the bodies, of soldiers of both sides, are gone for ever – lost in the "Flanders mire", as Lyons himself put it – he used poetic licence, of course – he died in France. It is dreadful that we should have lost so great a poet and so great a man, before he had the opportunity to live out his very considerable promise, and the bitterest irony that the subject of his best-loved poem, "Coming Home", should have been the very thing denied him.' I draw breath, and watch Buster finish reading. When he's done, he takes off his glasses, and looks at me, and nods. I said, 'That's all there is, Mrs Lyons.'

'I knew it,' she whispers. 'I always knew it.'

02

On the train back to London, I'm alone.

At stations we pass through, I look out for him, for his tall frame waiting on a platform, but he isn't there. I pull the hat down over my eyes and doze, and dream. My dreams are of me and you, kissing under the street lights of the wharf in San Francisco, and it feels electric. There is a lot of life to be lived.

I try to reach Josh from a callbox at Crewe, and again in Euston, but the line is busy. I try him again after I've arrived back in the bed and breakfast, that same unlovely room. The same beep. When I put the phone down I lie on the bed wondering how in hell I got to be here, what stupid impulse had pulled me across an ocean and dumped me in this godforsaken box, where the only window looks out on to the brick wall of the building next door, and it all drips with city grease, and city noise.

I seek an internet café. There's a sketchy one off the main street, run by Kenyans; the whole time I'm there, the Kenyans keep up an argument about some kind of soap opera that's showing on a TV in the corner.

They're all on Wikipedia, these days. All of 'em. There's Pastor Lang, older than I remember, addressing a congregation in South Africa, next to Archbishop Tutu. There's Millicent Davenport, in a picture from the sixties, campaigning for equal pay for women at some auto plant, and Iris Rutherford, who got a hospital named after her. Seems like everyone I ever knew is on there, except you. I'm on there, still, in a station publicity photo from 1992. The internet never forgets. *John Knox*, it says, *was a radio talk host and domestic abuser.*

I check my Hotmail. The email from Steinwitz is in my inbox.

Hey John,

I did as you asked. We found the place all right. I never would have guessed it was there behind all those bushes. Judith's husband David helped me break in the door. He's a big guy. We saved the hinges but you're going to want a new door.

I'd prefer to be telling you some of this in person, not like this. She was certainly here – it's like a second home – a bed and everything. Also a desk and stacks of letters – I'll show you those. From England, mostly. Also, letters for you, in a box. Someone called Fiona, hoping you're OK – they go back around nine years.

We didn't find the diaries at first but there's a bit of an attic space so we looked there – et voilà. A box with a lot of old stuff in it, including diaries, just like you said. John Rutherford, right? They go from I think 1919 up to 1970. I scanned the last couple of pages for you – attached.

John, we also found a gun holster. Looks old – David says maybe military – it would be right for the gun Rachel used.

There's no way you could have known about this, John. She hid it all the way back here – there was no way you could ever have known.

Johnny, get yourself back here, will you? You got to start putting things back together some time, right? You're a father. If not for you, do it for your boy.

All right, lecture over.

I download the attachment. Reading it sends shivers through me. It starts with chest pains, and ends within touching distance.

When I'm done reading, I print it, and turn my attention to getting the fuck out of London.

The earliest flight to Ottawa isn't for three days, but there's a seat on one to Toronto leaving tomorrow at noon. It costs a fortune, but what the hell – I book it. That final click of the mouse – confirm – feels like the end of the story.

Afterwards, I try to interest myself in news on the BBC site, but the soap opera row is boiling over, so I go for a walk and buy fish and chips from a place on the Holloway Road, or try to, anyway – the owner pulls up the back of his shirt to show me a marbled pink mess of wrecked skin. 'Bloke who used to work here,' he says. 'Second day on, he's changing the oil, doesn't know how long it takes to cool down. Lifts it out, realises it's burning his hands, drops it – wallop.'

'Before you know it.'

'I knew it all right.' He winces, knowing I know. 'How'd you get yours?'

'I got attacked.'

'They done that on purpose?'

I let out a long, deep breath. 'Yeah. Yeah, I guess they did.'

He makes the food into a white paper loaf, warm and smelling good. He won't take my money.

'Be lucky, eh?' he says.

There's been some kind of celebration going on in the centre of London town, and people are drifting back drunk. They point at me and gasp and make puke-mimes, but I don't care. Londoners are like New Yorkers – they don't care how much they might offend a person, because there are always more people. I sit out on a bench and watch the world go by: cars and bodies and trash breezing through a concrete canyon in waning light. The fish supper tastes great. I think about how I've managed to get through this unscathed – how I got to have the second chance that James Lyons never did.

From inside the trashcan, the headline of the *Metro* newspaper reads *Bush: God Told Me To Invade Iraq*. I dump the remains of my meal on top of it.

27 July 1970

Woken by the chest pains, once again. It is like being sat on – one cannot breathe at all, nor does the sensation dissipate upon waking. No, it is assuredly not a dream. I gasp, striving not to panic, until the worst of it is over. Then I glance at the straggle-haired head on the pillow beside mine. No: his sleep has not been disturbed. When he sleeps, he looks like a boy again.

Dear, dear Phelps. Oh, I know I must seem irresponsible. I am of course afraid that one day he shall awake to find me lifeless, and yet I would sooner wish this grizzly episode upon him than oblige us to live under the shadow of a condition that may kill me outright at any moment or darken our lives for much, much longer. People live with this sort of thing for years, don't they? We already have to contend with his asthma and his forgetfulness – it is a burden I bear gladly, but I would not add to it.

It is after dark – the time when I can move around freely. I think I must only have slept for four hours, today. Day or night, really, I believe I have not slept a decent sleep in fifty years. Perhaps it has something to do with the encroaching awareness that one may not have very many hours left, and that one does not want to squander them. No: far more often it has been because of him *– my Banquo, my albatross. Once, I believed that time might heal that festering wound. It seems to me now that time has no such power.*

I rise, and shave the half of my face that still needs it. The other half, of course, has not aged – not a bit. It is the same half-mask I wore in London, as a young man. I no longer bother with the eye. It sits in its box, staring.

They are coming again, just as we came. One sees them on the farms, everywhere, toiling away with axes or rakes, shirts stripped down, anxious to see whether the figure who's stopped to observe them over the barbed-wire fence is a scout from the US Draft Board.

Sometimes they see my face, and their eyes linger. They are not appalled by the little old man with the mangled face. No: they recognise fraternity. Sometimes I wave at them, and they at me, like old friends, and I thank God that these strong young men have not been hoovered up and sent to be butchered in the swamps of Asia.

The night air is cold, but not too cold. Only around November does my face start to ache; only then must the balaclava be worn. I pull on my boots. It gets harder, as age twists up these fingers. Soon even my ability to work with a chisel will be lost to arthritis. We shall have to fall back upon our savings then, I suppose. But the truth is, we are neither one in good health, and would neither one care to live without the other. I have lived fifty-five years longer than I deserved to, already.

He's there, in the forest, when I find my way along the track between the trees that leads to the turn of the Bryde Road. Sometimes he'll be sitting on a tree stump, smoking a cigarette, his rifle upright between his legs, propped into the nook of his shoulder. Sometimes he'll be standing far along the road, where the road dips out of sight, his back to me, watching the stars.

He never speaks to me, nor I to him. I suppose I am comfortable in his presence, after a peculiar fashion. He goes about his business, and I go about mine. Phelps knows, I believe, who it is that catches my eye out of the window over the sink, from time to time – but he says nothing about it; just squeezes my shoulder.

Oh, what a thing it is to have the perspective age brings; the assurance; the skill of not caring quite so much – but to know it too late. What is life for, when it is possible to learn so much, and at such cost, only to discover that the best answer is a surrender to wilful ignorance? Eventus stultorum magister, and every new age brings a new foolishness. Truly, no generation aged quite so far as my own.

A man's voice is calling. It is indistinct, and distant. As I emerge on to the starlit road, I see a figure far along its rugged surface. I recognise his thin frame – he is often to be seen running, for sport, in all but the harshest weather. He is our landlord, the paterfamilias from the big place a mile farther along the valley. It must be close to midnight, and he is walking and hunting about, away through the valley, and calling. I wonder what it is that he has lost. Something sentient, one supposes.

I withdraw back to the treeline, and pick my way through the shadows at the edge of the forest, keeping him just within sight. They are a small family, in the big house, and are respectful of their neighbours on the farthest reaches of their land. Although their young boy has once or twice ventured on to the lagoon with his friends in makeshift watercraft, we have not suffered at their hands – not a bit of it. Other than cards at Christmas, I think they barely remember we are there.

The entrance to the land upon which the Knox family's home stands is ungated – merely an opening in the row of bushes that happens to line the road. I pass through.

Unusually, he has not accompanied me, I notice. It is rare to have walked so far, so slowly, without seeing him pass between the trees, or hearing his footfall near by. The lights of the house are all out. I hum a song to keep myself from being unnerved by the silence. I suppose that one can become habituated to anything, and anyone. It just requires all the patience in the world. I have become so used to his presence that I get lonely when he is not there.

The dark spaces between the dark trees yawn like mouths that have lost the power to scream.

There is a shed by the driveway to the house. In the darkness, I'm sure I hear a little sniffle, like a child's tears. I stop to listen.

01

Rachel?

I wake up with the first police siren of the day, and am in the dining room the minute it opens, thoroughly pissing off the Polish girl, whose job it seems to be to cremate the breakfast. I feel reborn. Outside, the sky's as big as it gets. There are planes up there already. They are making white scars, the type that fade with time and disappear.

The girl slams a clean cup in front of me after I tell her the coffee milk is curdled; it makes a sound like a gun report. I don't know whether she knows she's scaring me. Probably I'm scaring her; and besides, disfigured people are always the bad guys, right?

The thing is, men are *meant* to be wounded. That's how the world sees its menfolk: as so much meat for the mincing machine. A man who doesn't want to be destroyed is a failed man. Screw that. I say the man who wants to be destroyed is the failure. Like Rutherford said, fucking yourself up is a cinch. It can be done in a moment, and there's no shortage of things you can get wrecked by. Well, I don't want to be that man any more. I want to live.

When she smashes out through the kitchen door to get fresh coffee, I get up and leave.

Prokofiev's on the radio in the room. I think Rutherford would have liked that. Maybe you would too. I'm not sure, any more. With my one change of clothes already packed, along with the journals and your photograph, I shave with a disposable razor, taking the clean half of my jaw first and then turning to deal with the few coarse tufts that have sprouted out of the other. I'm finished by the time the 8 a.m. news comes on. 'The prime minister, Tony Blair, has congratulated London mayor Ken Livingstone on

London's successful bid to stage the 2012 Olympic Games. Celebrations were held yesterday in Trafalgar Square...'

And then I'm out, out of that rathole hotel, with John Rutherford's hat on my head, into a beautiful big sky-blue London day full of butterflies and freedom.

I get it, now. I get why you didn't tell James Lyons' sister what happened to her hero brother. We need all the heroes we can get, even the ones who aren't so heroic after all.

The Tube's already stuffed with people getting to work. The crowds leave passages only barely wide enough for one person at a time to get through, and when the first train comes there's only just room to get through the doors. I let a couple of trains go by in the hope of an emptier one, but they're all about the same; in the end, I just have to plunge in there. Can't wait all day. The trip's an hour long but simple – one train, all the way to Heathrow. My face makes people make space for me. I even get a seat. I'm wedged against the glass partition looking at a carriage full of miserable-looking people, but I feel too good to let them get me down.

Maybe I'll become a historian myself. What do you think of that? Like you said, history isn't yesterday – it's all around us, all the time. It's now. Or maybe an artist, or something. Maybe I'll write a book. I spent the last ten years doing nothing, and I'm hungry to get some dirt under my nails. Who cares what you do, so long as you do something, and you believe in it, right?

And I remember your smile, and making love to you, and for a moment feel self-conscious, in case any of these British drones is able to read my mind – but they can't. They don't get to know about you. All that you were – all that we were, together – all the storms – it's in me. I understand how Rutherford must have felt, carrying James Lyons around in his heart, all those years. I guess Rutherford's in me, too. We're like a set of Russian dolls, all of us, with those who've gone before us stacked up inside. You're the second-biggest doll; and then there's me, the biggest doll, the biggest empty shell.

We've paused at King's Cross St Pancras for people to pour out of the carriage and others to pour on. I remember how you came into the studio that first time, and it makes me sad. It never made me feel that before.

In curved glass on the opposite of the carriage, I catch a glimpse between the people of a man I think I recognise – but it's just me. Behind the reflection, on a poster, a twice-life-size ballerina gazes in on us with sad eyes.

The train is filling up, now. The platform attendant wants to get things moving faster: he blows his whistle. The sound reverberates right through the station. Above him, the minutes on the LED information board count down.

I'm sorry I didn't do what I should have, Rachel. I never knew what to do. All I knew was what I wanted, what I believed in, and that was you.

And now the last people have squeezed on to the train. One of them, up close to the glass, looks at me, at my face. He's a black kid, maybe nineteen years old, with one of those weak-ass moustaches. He has a rucksack in his hand.

Oh God, Rachel, I've been missing you for such a very long time, my darling. Every day since we met, you've been my first thought, and my last. I close my eye – and there you are.

I'm full of butterflies, Rachel.

I'm coming home.